George W. Hill

Tables of Venus

prepared for the use of the American ephemeris and nautical almanac

George W. Hill

Tables of Venus
prepared for the use of the American ephemeris and nautical almanac

ISBN/EAN: 9783337332426

Printed in Europe, USA, Canada, Australia, Japan

Cover: Foto ©Andreas Hilbeck / pixelio.de

More available books at **www.hansebooks.com**

OF

VENUS,

PREPARED FOR THE USE OF

THE AMERICAN EPHEMERIS AND NAUTICAL ALMANAC.

BY

GEORGE W. HILL.

PUBLISHED BY AUTHORITY OF THE SECRETARY OF THE NAVY.

BUREAU OF NAVIGATION,
WASHINGTON.
1872.

PREFACE.

The following tables of Venus have been prepared to take the place of the unsatisfactory elements and tables heretofore used in the preparation of the *American Ephemeris and Nautical Almanac.*

The elements given in Le Verrier's *Annales de l'Observatoire Imperial de Paris*, Tome VI., have been corrected by the discussion of an extended series of observations; Le Verrier's expressions for the perturbations have been modified by changes in the adopted values of the planetary masses; and the tables have been carefully arranged so as to facilitate the computation either of particular places, or of an Ephemeris, of the planet.

The work has been performed by Mr. George W. Hill, who has long been one of the most efficient Assistants in the preparation of the works published by this office.

J. H. C. COFFIN,
Prof. Math. U. S. N.,
Superintendent of Nautical Almanac.

Washington, *May*, 1872.

CONTENTS.

INTRODUCTION.

CONSTRUCTION AND USE OF THE TABLES.

THE Tables are based on the following elements:—

Epoch, 1850, Jan. 0.0, Washington Mean Time.

$$
\begin{aligned}
L' &= 244^\circ\ 18'\ 18''.32 \\
\pi' &= 129\ 27\ 42.86 \\
\Omega' &= 75\ 19\ 53.10 \\
i' &= 3\ 23\ 35.01 \\
e' &= 0.006843113 \\
n' &= 2106641''.35447
\end{aligned}
$$

These elements have been derived from a discussion of the data furnished by the transits of Venus in 1761 and 1769, and by observations made at Greenwich in the interval 1836–1870, at Paris in the interval 1838–1866, and at Washington in the interval 1863–1867. In this discussion the Solar Theory of HANSEN and OLUFSEN was used.* Consequently these Tables should be used in conjunction with the *Tables du Soleil* of these authors.†

The value of the Precession of the Equinoxes, according to PETERS,‡ is

$$50''.2411\, t + 0''.0001134\, t^2,$$

where the unit of t is the tropical year, and it is counted from 1800. If we make the unit the Julian year, and count t from 1850, the formula will be

$$50''.25351\, t + 0''.0001134\, t^2.$$

The formulæ which define the motion of the plane of the ecliptic are, according to HANSEN and OLUFSEN,§

$$
\begin{aligned}
\sin i'' \sin \Omega'' &= +\ 0''.053916\, t + 0''.00001887\, t^2, \\
\sin i'' \cos \Omega'' &= -\ 0''.467839\, t + 0''.00000562\, t^2.
\end{aligned}
$$

In order to obtain the tropical motion of the planet, it is necessary to add, to the sidereal motion, the precession, and the small term,

$$-\ \tfrac{1}{2} \sin i' \sin i'' \sin (\Omega' - \Omega''),$$

the numerical value of which is $+\ 0''.01382\, t$. This it is also necessary to add to the longitude of the perihelion.

* *Tables du Soleil, exécutées d'après les ordres de la Société Royale des Sciences de Copenhague, par MM. P. A. Hansen et C. F. R. Olufsen.* *Copenhague.* 1853.

† The Pulkowa constant of aberration 20''.4451 should however be employed instead of 20''.255.

‡ *Peters' Numerus Constans Nutationis*, p. 71. § *Tables du Soleil*, p. 21.

INTRODUCTION.

The values of the planetary masses, adopted, are

Mercury	$m = \frac{1}{4865751}$,	Mars	$m''' = \frac{1}{3200900}$,
Venus	$m' = \frac{1}{408134}$,	Jupiter	$m^{\text{iv}} = \frac{1}{1050}$,
The Earth and Moon	$m'' = \frac{1}{322800}$,	Saturn	$m^{\text{v}} = \frac{1}{3560}$.

The mass of Mercury is that of ENCKE,* the mass of the Earth and Moon is that found by Prof. S. NEWCOMB,† and which corresponds to the value 8″.848 of the mean horizontal parallax of the Sun; the values of the other masses are those adopted by HANSEN and OLUFSEN. On these values of the disturbing masses depend the expressions of the secular and periodic perturbations used, with the single exception, that, since the discussion of the observations indicated 32″.515 as the value of the annual tropical motion of the node, this value has been preferred to the value 32″.2931, given by theory. If we suppose that the modification of the values of the masses, necessary to produce the first number, should be applied to Venus alone, the mass of this planet would be reduced to $\frac{1}{427240}$.

Thus the following are the expressions of the varying elements, the longitudes being referred to the mean equinox and ecliptic of date, and t reckoned from 1850, Jan. 0.0, Washington Mean Time:—

$$
\begin{aligned}
L' &= 244^\circ\ 18'\ 18''.32 + 2106691''.62180\,t + 0''.0001134\,t^2,\\
\pi' &= 129\ 27\ 42.86 + 50.0494\,t - 0.000592\,t^2,\\
\Omega' &= 75\ 19\ 53.10 + 32.5150\,t + 0.000151\,t^2,\\
i' &= 3\ 23\ 35.01 + 0.03814\,t - 0.0000016\,t^2,\\
e' &= 0.006843113 - 0.00000050009\,t + 0.0000000000128\,t^2,\\
&= 1411''.494 - 0''.10315\,t + 0''.00000265\,t^2.
\end{aligned}
$$

The value of the semi-axis major of the planet's orbit is given by the equation

$$a' = \left[\frac{1 + m'}{1 + m''} \cdot \frac{n''^2}{n'^2}\right]^{\frac{1}{3}} a''.$$

To be consistent, we must employ the same linear unit for the radius vector of Venus as that which HANSEN and OLUFSEN have used for the radius vector of the Earth. From an examination of their formulæ, it appears that they have taken as unity, not a'', but, in the notation of LAPLACE, the quantity

$$a'' + \tfrac{1}{6}\,\Sigma\, m\, a''^2 \frac{d\,A^{(0)}}{d\,a''},$$

Σ denoting summation with respect to all the masses which produce sensible perturbations in the motion of the Earth. Hence their value of a'' is

$$1 - \tfrac{1}{6}\,\Sigma\, m\, a''^2 \frac{d\,A^{(0)}}{d\,a''},$$

And, the numerical values being substituted, we obtain

$$\log a'' = 9.9999998786.$$

The tropical motion of the Sun, in a Julian year, is, according to the *Tables du Soleil*, equal to

$$360^\circ - 22''.56009 - 0''.380853 \times 0.01677 + 50''.23414.$$

If from this is subtracted 50″.25351, our value of the precession, the value of n'', we adopt, is obtained,

$$n'' = 1295977''.41415.$$

And consequently,

$$\log a' = 9.8593376699.$$

* *Astronomische Nachrichten, No.* 443.

† *Astronomical and Meteorological Observations made at the United States Naval Observatory during the year* 1865. *Appendix II., p.* 29.

INTRODUCTION.

The expression of the equation of the centre, for the epoch 1850.0, is

$$+ 2822''.971 \sin M + 12''.074 \sin 2M + 0''.072 \sin 3M.$$

The expression of the logarithm of the elliptic radius vector for the same time is

$$9.859342748 - 0.002971874 \cos M - 0.000015253 \cos 2M - 0.000000099 \cos 3M.$$

The elliptic heliocentric latitude referred to the ecliptic of date may be found from the formula

$$\log \sin \text{lat.} = 8.7722149 + 13.54\, t + \log \sin [\text{orb. long.} + (360^\circ - \Omega')].$$

The secular perturbation of the orbit longitude is given by the formula,

$$(-0''.12691 \sin M - 0''.00108 \sin 2M)\, \mathbf{m}.$$

m denoting the number of anomalistic revolutions of the planet from the epoch.

The secular perturbation of the logarithm of the radius vector is given by the formula, (in units of the eighth decimal),

$$(-0.046 + 13.360 \cos M + 0.137 \cos 2M)\, \mathbf{m}.$$

The following are the expressions for the periodic perturbations of Venus; l, l' &c. denoting the mean longitudes of the several planets in their order, referred to the mean equinox of 1850.0. They have been obtained by multiplying the expressions given in LE VERRIER'S "*Annales de l' Observatoire Imperial de Paris*," Tome VI, by the proper factors.

Perturbations of the Orbit Longitude.

ACTION OF MERCURY.

$$
\begin{aligned}
&+ 0''.014 \sin (l - l') \\
&- 0.010 \sin 2 (l - l') \\
&- 0.005 \sin 3 (l - l') \\
&+ 0.021 \sin (2l - l' + 284^\circ) \\
&+ 0''.328 \sin (l - 2l' + 254^\circ.8) \\
&+ 0.015 \sin (2l - 3l' + 74^\circ) \\
&+ 0.047 \sin (3l' - l + 35^\circ) \\
&+ 0.139 \sin (2l - 4l' + 328^\circ.3) \\
&+ 0.453 \sin (2l - 5l' + 35^\circ.1).
\end{aligned}
$$

ACTION OF THE EARTH.

$$
\begin{aligned}
&- 4''.984 \sin (l' - l'') \\
&- 11.489 \sin 2 (l' - l'') \\
&+ 7.260 \sin (3l' - 3l'' + 0^\circ\ 7'.6) \\
&+ 1.050 \sin (4l' - 4l'' + 0^\circ\ 10') \\
&+ 0.335 \sin (5l' - 5l'' + 1^\circ.5) \\
&+ 0.143 \sin 6 (l' - l'') \\
&+ 0.067 \sin 7 (l' - l'') \\
&+ 0.035 \sin 8 (l' - l'') \\
&+ 0.019 \sin 9 (l' - l'') \\
&+ 0.013 \sin 10 (l' - l'') \\
&+ 0.007 \sin 11 (l' - l'') \\
&+ 0.004 \sin 12 (l' - l'') \\
&+ 0.003 \sin 13 (l' - l'') \\
&+ 0.059 \sin (4l' - 3l'' + 227^\circ.7) \\
&+ 0.099 \sin (3l' - 2l'' + 53^\circ.2) \\
&+ 0.049 \sin (2l' - l'' + 51^\circ) \\
&+ 0.070 \sin (l'' + 109^\circ.2) \\
&+ 0.093 \sin (2l'' - l' + 18^\circ.2) \\
&+ 3.515 \sin (2l' - 3l'' + 268^\circ\ 7'.5) \\
&+ 0''.687 \sin (3l' - 4l'' + 268^\circ.1) \\
&+ 1.620 \sin (4l' - 5l'' + 268^\circ\ 24'.5) \\
&+ 0.210 \sin (5l' - 6l'' + 89^\circ.5) \\
&+ 0.055 \sin (6l' - 7l'' + 89^\circ) \\
&+ 0.024 \sin (7l' - 8l'' + 88^\circ) \\
&+ 0.013 \sin (8l' - 9l'' + 90^\circ) \\
&+ 0.022 \sin (2l'' + 210^\circ) \\
&+ 0.044 \sin (3l'' - l' + 53^\circ) \\
&+ 1.495 \sin (5l'' - 3l' + 198^\circ\ 24') \\
&+ 0.188 \sin (4l' - 6l'' + 340^\circ.7) \\
&+ 0.096 \sin (5l' - 7l'' + 337^\circ.5) \\
&+ 0.155 \sin (6l' - 8l'' + 163^\circ.1) \\
&+ 0.015 \sin (7l' - 9l'' + 160^\circ) \\
&+ 0.013 \sin (5l'' - 2l' + 77^\circ) \\
&+ 0.218 \sin (5l' - 8l'' + 66^\circ.5) \\
&+ 0.013 \sin (7l' - 10l'' + 67^\circ) \\
&+ 0.067 \sin (9l' - 13l'' + 346^\circ.2) \\
&+ 2.820 \sin (8l' - 13l'' + 227^\circ\ 58') \\
&+ 0.026 \sin (13l'' - 7l' + 198^\circ).
\end{aligned}
$$

Action of Mars.

$- 0''.048 \sin (l' - l''')$

$+ 0.059 \sin 2 (l' - l''')$

$+ 0.019 \sin (l' - 2\, l''' + 155^\circ)$

$+ 0.657 \sin (2\, l' - 3\, l''' + 332^\circ\, 44')$

$+ 0''.009 \sin (3\, l' - 4\, l''' + 333^\circ)$

$+ 1.168 \sin (l' - 3\, l''' + 117^\circ\, 56')$

$+ 0.019 \sin (2\, l' - 4\, l''' + 126^\circ)$

$+ 0.021 \sin (3\, l' - 6\, l''' + 281^\circ)$

$+ 0.082 \sin (2\, l' - 6\, l''' + 74^\circ.8)$.

Action of Jupiter.

$- 2''.959 \sin (l' - l^{iv} + 0^\circ\, 31')$

$+ 0.880 \sin 2 (l' - l^{iv})$

$+ 0.041 \sin 3 (l' - l^{iv})$

$+ 0.007 \sin 4 (l' - l^{iv})$

$+ 0.026 \sin (2\, l' - l^{iv} + 113^\circ)$

$+ 1.557 \sin (l^{iv} + 169^\circ\, 50')$

$+ 0''.477 \sin (l' - 2\, l^{iv} + 155^\circ.6)$

$+ 0.167 \sin (2\, l' - 3\, l^{iv} + 12^\circ.1)$

$+ 0.019 \sin (3\, l' - 4\, l^{iv} + 12^\circ)$

$+ 0.094 \sin (l' + l^{iv} + 2^\circ.3)$

$+ 0.055 \sin (2\, l^{iv} + 143^\circ)$

$+ 0.046 \sin (l' - 3\, l^{iv} + 164^\circ)$

$+ 0.027 \sin (2\, l' - 4\, l^{iv} + 24^\circ)$.

Action of Saturn.

$- 0''.178 \sin (l' - l^{v})$

$+ 0.050 \sin 2 (l' - l^{v})$

$+ 0''.205 \sin (l^{v} + 190^\circ)$

$+ 0.025 \sin (l' - 2\, l^{v} + 151^\circ)$

$+ 0.010 \sin (2\, l' - 3\, l^{v} + 90^\circ)$.

Perturbation of the second order, depending on the product of the masses of the Earth and Mars.

$$+ 0''.282 \sin (4\, l''' + 3\, l' - 7\, l'' + 147^\circ.1).$$

Perturbations of the Common Logarithm of the Radius Vector, in units of the eighth decimal.

Action of Mercury.

$+ 4.3$

$+ 8.1 \cos (l - l')$

$+ 1.1 \cos 2 (l - l')$

$+ 6.1 \cos (2l - l' + 285^\circ)$

$+ 4.3 \cos (l' + 105^\circ)$

$+ 15.3 \cos (2\, l - 4\, l' + 150^\circ.7)$

$+ 22.2 \cos (l - 2\, l' + 75^\circ.1)$

$+ 1.9 \cos (2\, l - 3\, l' + 75^\circ)$

$+ 3.5 \cos (3\, l' - l + 207^\circ)$

$+ 7.5 \cos (2\, l - 5\, l' + 226^\circ)$.

Action of the Earth.

$- 18.6$

$+ 228.2 \cos (l' - l'')$

$+ 998.6 \cos 2 (l' - l'')$

$- 841.8 \cos (3\, l' - 3\, l'' + 0^\circ\, 8')$

$- 145.2 \cos 4 (l' - l'')$

$- 52.2 \cos (5\, l' - 5\, l'' + 0^\circ\, 20')$

$- 23.0 \cos 6 (l' - l'')$

$- 11.5 \cos 7 (l' - l'')$

$- 6.4 \cos 8 (l' - l'')$

$- 3.5 \cos 9 (l' - l'')$

$- 2.6 \cos 10 (l' - l'')$

$+ 7.2 \cos (4\, l' - 3\, l'' + 45^\circ)$

$+ 11.7 \cos (3\, l' - 2\, l'' + 230^\circ.5)$

$+ 6.6 \cos (2\, l' - l'' + 230^\circ)$

$+ 3.1 \cos (l' + 105^\circ)$

$+ 4.7 \cos (l'' + 286^\circ)$

$+ 3.2 \cos (2\, l'' - l' + 114^\circ)$

$+ 76.8 \cos (2\, l' - 3\, l'' + 89^\circ.8)$

$+ 46.1 \cos (3\, l' - 4\, l'' + 88^\circ.9)$

$+ 162.2 \cos (4\, l' - 5\, l'' + 88^\circ\, 52')$

$+ 25.6 \cos (5\, l' - 6\, l'' + 268^\circ.7)$

$+ 7.7 \cos (6\, l' - 7\, l'' + 268^\circ)$

$+ 4.2 \cos (7\, l' - 8\, l'' + 270^\circ)$

$+ 3.7 \cos (2\, l'' + 30^\circ)$

$+ 4.5 \cos (3\, l'' - l' + 249^\circ)$

$+ 17.2 \cos (5\, l'' - 3\, l' + 21^\circ.8)$

$+ 7.2 \cos (4\, l' - 6\, l'' + 159^\circ)$

$+ 7.1 \cos (5\, l' - 7\, l'' + 172^\circ)$

$+ 17.2 \cos (6\, l' - 8\, l'' + 338^\circ.2)$

$+ 6.9 \cos (9\, l' - 13\, l'' + 158^\circ)$

$+ 2.4 \cos (13\, l'' - 7\, l' + 25^\circ)$.

Action of Mars.

$+ 3.5 \cos (l' - l''')$

$- 7.9 \cos 2 (l' - l''')$

$+ 68.1 \cos (2 l' - 3 l''' + 152°.6).$

Action of Jupiter.

$- \quad 19.2$

$+ 290.2 \cos (l' - l^{iv} + 0° \, 20')$

$- 133.0 \cos 2 (l' - l^{iv})$

$- \quad 7.0 \cos 3 (l' - l^{iv})$

$+ \quad 1.1 \cos (2 l' - l^{iv} + 237°)$

$+ \quad 8.8 \cos (l^{iv} + 352°)$

$+ 46.9 \cos (l' - 2 l^{iv} + 335°.0)$

$+ 24.8 \cos (2 l' - 3 l^{iv} + 192°.1)$

$+ \quad 9.6 \cos (l' + l^{iv} + 182°)$

$+ \quad 4.4 \cos (l' - 3 l^{iv} + 340°)$

Action of Saturn.

$+ 18.7 \cos (l' - l^{v})$

$- 4.3 \cos 2 (l' - l^{v})$

$+ 2.5 \cos (l' - 2 l^{v} + 334°).$

Perturbations of the Latitude.

Action of the Earth.

$+ 0''.012 \sin (2 l' - 2 l'' + 175°)$

$+ 0.016 \sin (3 l' - 3 l'' + 356°)$

$+ 0.013 \sin (4 l' - 3 l'' + 284°)$

$+ 0.026 \sin (3 l' - 2 l'' + 286°)$

$+ 0.078 \sin (2 l' - l'' + 285°)$

$+ 0.124 \sin (l' + 104°.5)$

$+ 0.092 \sin (2 l'' - l' + 104°.5)$

$+ 0''.075 \sin (2 l' - 3 l'' + 75°.5)$

$+ 0.081 \sin (3 l' - 4 l'' + 75°.5)$

$+ 0.308 \sin (4 l' - 5 l'' + 75°.3)$

$+ 0.050 \sin (5 l' - 6 l'' + 256°)$

$+ 0.014 \sin (6 l' - 7 l'' + 258°)$

$+ 0.020 \sin (3 l'' - l' + 20°)$

$+ 0.028 \sin (6 l' - 8 l'' + 343°)$

$+ 0.015 \sin (9 l' - 13 l'' + 143°).$

Action of Jupiter.

$+ 0''.020 \sin l' - l^{iv} + 153°)$

$+ 0.159 \sin (l' - 2 l^{iv} + 61°.8)$

$+ 0''.023 \sin (l' + l^{iv} + 284°)$

$+ 0.018 \sin (l' - 3 l^{iv} + 74°).$

Action of Saturn.

$$+ 0''.017 \sin (l' - 2 l^{v} + 28°).$$

The tropical motion of Venus in different intervals of time, for the epoch 1850.0, is,

	°	′	″
in one mean solar day	1	36	7.807315,
in 365 " " days	224	47	29.669971,
in 366 " " days	226	23	37.477286,
in 100 Julian years	199	12	42.180000,
in 100 Julian years less one day	197	36	34.372685.

Denoting by d the number of days elapsed from the epoch (1850, Jan. 0.0, Washington mean time), the values of l, l', &c., are—

$$
\begin{aligned}
l &= 324°.0656 + 4°.0923387467 \, d, \\
l' &= 244.3050 + 1.6021304695 \, d, \\
l'' &= 100.0159 + 0.9856091228 \, d, \\
l''' &= 83.2669 + 0.5240328545 \, d, \\
l^{iv} &= 159.9594 + 0.0830912762 \, d, \\
l^{v} &= 14.8203 + 0.0334596753 \, d.
\end{aligned}
$$

INTRODUCTION.

The Arguments employed in these tables have severally the following meanings:—

The Argument $\mathbf{m}$ is an integer, which denotes the number of times Venus has passed through its perihelion since the beginning of 1850; it is negative before this epoch, and remains constant during an anomalistic revolution of the planet.

Argument I is the number of mean solar days since $M = 0°$.
" II is the number of Julian years since $8\,l' - 13\,l'' + 318° \, 47' = 0°$.
" III is the number of mean solar days since $l' - 3\,l''' = 0°$.
" IV is the number of mean solar days since $5\,l'' - 3\,l' + 288° \, 27' = 0°$.
" V is the number of mean solar days since $2\,l' - 3\,l'' = 0°$.
" VI is the number of mean solar days since $l' - l'' = 0°$.
" VII is the number of mean solar days since $4\,l' - 5\,l'' + 1° \, 59' = 0°$.
" VIII is the number of mean solar days since $2\,l' - 3\,l''' + 65° \, 32' = 0°$.
" IX is the number of mean solar days since $l' - l^{iv} = 0°$.

" X is the value of l, when last $l' = 129° \, 27' \, 14''.5$,* in parts of 60 to a circumference.
" XI is the value of l'', when last $l' = 129° \, 27' \, 14''.5$, in parts of 240 to a circumference.
" XII is the value of l''' when last $l' = 129° \, 27' \, 14''.5$, in parts of 60 to a circumference.
" XIII is the value of l^{iv}, when last $l' = 129° \, 27' \, 14''.5$, in parts of 60 to a circumference.
" XIV is the value of l^{v}, when last $l' = 129° \, 27' \, 14''.5$, in parts of 36 to a circumference.

" XV is Arg. XI + Arg. XIII + 0.22 + day of the year, of Hansen and Olufsen.
" XVI is Arg. I + 0.22052 + 0.01791 + day of the year, of Hansen and Olufsen.

Arguments X—XIV remain constant during a period of Argument I, and are augmented, in each case, by a certain fixed quantity, when Venus passes through its perihelion and $\mathbf{m}$ is increased by a unit.

From the data previously given, are readily obtained the following expressions for the value of the different arguments; i denoting an integer, in general so taken that the Argument may be less than its period:

$$\begin{aligned}
\mathrm{I} &= 71^{d}.681535 + d + 0^{d}.0000001224\, t^2 - 224^{d}.700777861\, \mathbf{m},^{\dagger} \\
\mathrm{II} &= 167^{y}.9 + t - 238^{y}.92\, i, \\
\mathrm{III} &= 11801^{d}.26 + d - 11987^{d}.25\, i, \\
\mathrm{IV} &= 457^{d}.137 + d - 2050^{d}.209\, i, \\
\mathrm{V} &= 762^{d}.072 + d - 1454^{d}.9358\, i, \\
\mathrm{VI} &= 231^{d}.0375 + d - 583^{d}.92137\, i, \\
\mathrm{VII} &= 80^{d}.466 + d - 243^{d}.16187\, i, \\
\mathrm{VIII} &= 186^{d}.467 + d - 220^{d}.56628\, i, \\
\mathrm{IX} &= 55^{d}.526 + d - 236^{d}.99191\, i, \\
\mathrm{X} &= 5.1167 + 33.25863\, \mathbf{m} - 60\, i, \\
\mathrm{XI} &= 19.5741 + 147.64477\, \mathbf{m} - 240\, i \\
\mathrm{XII} &= 7.6168 + 19.62509\, \mathbf{m} - 60\, i, \\
\mathrm{XIII} &= 25.6671 + 3.11178\, \mathbf{m} - 60\, i, \\
\mathrm{XIV} &= 1.2422 + 0.75181\, \mathbf{m} - 36\, i, \\
\mathrm{XV} &= 4037^{d}.4 + d - 6798^{d}.262\, i, \\
\mathrm{XVI} &= 1^{d}.64 + d - 365^{d}.24219\, i.
\end{aligned}$$

The values of the obliquity of the ecliptic and of the nutation, employed in these Tables, are those given in the *Tables du Soleil*,

$$\epsilon = 23° \, 27' \, 31''.42 - 0''.46784\, t - 0''.000001405\, t^2,$$

$$\Delta\psi = -17''.332 \sin \Omega_{☾} + 0''.208 \sin 2\,\Omega_{☾} - 1''.254 \sin 2\,\odot,$$

$$\Delta\epsilon = +9''.271 \cos \Omega_{☾} - 0''.089 \cos 2\,\Omega_{☾} + 0''.551 \cos 2\,\odot,$$

$\Omega_{☾}$ being the longitude of the Moon's ascending node, and $\odot$ the Sun's true longitude.

* This is the value of the longitude of the perihelion at the epoch 1850.0, which was employed in computing the tables of the perturbations to double entry.

† Rigorously, the Argument which should be employed as the horizontal Argument of the tables of perturbations to double entry, has this expression,

$$71^{d}.68641 + d - 224^{d}.700801109\, \mathbf{m},$$

But Argument I may safely be used in its stead, as the error, in the interval from 850 A. D. to 2850 A. D. cannot exceed 0''.005.

INTRODUCTION.

The rectangular coördinates of a planet, referred to the equinox and equator, are most readily computed by means of the formulæ—

$$x = k_x\, r \sin(\lambda + K_x) + p_x\, \delta\beta,$$
$$y = k_y\, r \sin(\lambda + K_y) + p_y\, \delta\beta,$$
$$z = k_z\, r \sin(\lambda + K_z) + p_z\, \delta\beta,$$

where λ is the orbit longitude, and $\delta\beta$ the perturbation of the latitude, expressed in parts of the radius

The quantities k_x, K_x, &c., are obtained from the following formulæ:—

Find h, H, g, G from the equations

$$h \sin H = \sin^2 \frac{i}{2} \sin 2\,\Omega, \qquad g \sin G = \sin i \cos \Omega,$$
$$h \cos H = \sin i \sin \Omega, \qquad g \cos G = 1 - 2 \sin^2 \frac{i}{2} \cos^2 \Omega,$$

then

$$k_x \sin K_x = 1 - 2 \sin^2 \frac{i}{2} \sin^2 \Omega, \qquad k_y \sin K_y = h \sin(H + \epsilon),$$
$$k_x \cos K_x = h \sin H, \qquad k_y \cos K_y = g \cos(G + \epsilon),$$
$$k_z \sin K_z = -h \cos(H + \epsilon),$$
$$k_z \cos K_z = g \sin(G + \epsilon).$$

The values of p_x, p_y and p_z are, λ' denoting the longitude reduced to the ecliptic,

$$p_x = -r \sin\beta \cos\lambda',$$
$$p_y = -r \sin\beta \cos\epsilon \sin\lambda' - r \cos\beta \sin\epsilon,$$
$$p_z = -r \sin\beta \sin\epsilon \sin\lambda' + r \cos\beta \cos\epsilon.$$

These formulæ avail for obtaining x, y, and z referred to any equinox and equator, provided that the longitudes λ, Ω are referred to the same equinox, and the proper values are assigned to the inclinations i and ϵ.

But when the values of k_x, K_x, &c., have been computed for mean equinox of date, the effect of nutation on these quantities will be most easily computed by the aid of these differential coefficients,

$$\frac{d.\log k_x}{d\epsilon} = 0, \qquad \frac{dK_x}{d\epsilon} = 0,$$

$$\frac{d.\log k_y}{d\epsilon} = -\frac{M k_z}{k_y} \cos(K_y - K_z), \qquad \frac{dK_y}{d\epsilon} = \frac{k_z}{k_y} \sin(K_y - K_z),$$

$$\frac{d.\log k_z}{d\epsilon} = \frac{M k_y}{k_z} \cos(K_y - K_z), \qquad \frac{dK_z}{d\epsilon} = \frac{k_y}{k_z} \sin(K_y - K_z),$$

$$\frac{d.\log k_x}{d\Omega} = \frac{2M}{k_x} \sin^2 \frac{i}{2} \cos(K_x + 2\,\Omega),$$

$$\frac{dK_x}{d\Omega} = -\frac{2}{k_x} \sin^2 \frac{i}{2} \sin(K_x + 2\,\Omega),$$

$$\frac{d.\log k_y}{d\Omega} = \frac{M}{k_y}\left[2 \sin^2 \frac{i}{2} \cos\epsilon \sin(K_y + 2\,\Omega) + \sin i \sin\epsilon \sin(K_y + \Omega)\right],$$

$$\frac{dK_y}{d\Omega} = \frac{1}{k_y}\left[2 \sin^2 \frac{i}{2} \cos\epsilon \cos(K_y + 2\,\Omega) + \sin i \sin\epsilon \cos(K_y + \Omega)\right],$$

$$\frac{d.\log k_z}{d\Omega} = \frac{M}{k_z}\left[2 \sin^2 \frac{i}{2} \sin\epsilon \sin(K_z + 2\,\Omega) - \sin i \cos\epsilon \sin(K_z + \Omega)\right],$$

$$\frac{dK_z}{d\Omega} = \frac{1}{k_z}\left[2 \sin^2 \frac{i}{2} \sin\epsilon \cos(K_z + 2\,\Omega) - \sin i \cos\epsilon \cos(K_z + \Omega)\right],$$

where M denotes the modulus of common logarithms. In computing the variations of $\log k_x$, $\log k_y$, and $\log k_z$, $\Delta\epsilon$ and $\Delta\Omega$ or $\Delta\psi$ must be expressed in parts of the radius.

In computing the aberration, the constant of Struve should be used. The aberration time is then given by the formula, Δ being the distance of the planet from the Earth.

$$\log.\ \text{aberration time in days} = 7.76052 + \log.\ \Delta.$$

The parallax is given by the formula

$$\text{parallax} = \frac{8''.848}{\Delta},$$

and the semi-diameter by the formula

$$\text{semi-diameter} = \frac{8''.546}{\Delta}.$$

In the computation of the perturbations produced by Venus on other planetary bodies, the values of the inclination of the orbit and the longitude of the ascending node referred to the ecliptic and equinox of some fixed date are needed; also the reduction of the longitude to this ecliptic and equinox is wanted. If the current time be $1850 + t$, and the fixed date $1850 + t_0$, and ψ denote the general precession from 1850 to $1850 + t$, and λ denote the orbit longitude, and ψ_0 denote the general precession from 1850 to $1850 + t_0$, the formulæ, we are in quest of, are

$$\begin{aligned} i_0 &= i - 0''.06634\,(t - t_0), \\ \Omega_0 &= \Omega - (\psi - \psi_0) + 7''.8616\,(t - t_0), \\ \lambda_0 &= \lambda - (\psi - \psi_0) - 0''.01382\,(t - t_0). \end{aligned}$$

Or, with sufficient accuracy for our purpose,

$$\begin{aligned} i_0 &= 3^\circ\ 23'\ 35'' + 0''.03814\,t_0 - 0''.02820\,(t - t_0), \\ \Omega_0 &= 75^\circ\ 19'\ 53'' + 32''.515\,t_0 - 9''.882\,(t - t_0), \\ \lambda_0 &= \lambda - 50''.273\,(t - t_0). \end{aligned}$$

In the American Ephemeris the heliocentric coördinates of the planets are given, for the purpose of the computation of special perturbations, referred to the ecliptic and equinox of the 2400000th day of the Julian period, and of every 5000th day thereafter. If d denote the number of days between the epoch and the current time, (it will be negative when the current time is before the epoch,) the formulæ for the computation of these coördinates, for Venus, are;—

Epoch = 2400000th day of the Julian Period = 1858, Nov. 16.

$$\begin{aligned} \lambda_0 &= \lambda - 0''.13763\,d, \\ x_0 &= [9.99929]\,r\sin(\lambda_0 + 89^\circ\ 58'\ 32''), \\ y_0 &= [9.99995]\,r\sin(\lambda_0 + 0^\circ\ 1'\ 29'') \\ z_0 &= [8.7722]\,r\sin(\lambda_0 + 284^\circ\ 35'\ 18'' + 0''.027\,d). \end{aligned}$$

Epoch = 2405000th day of the Julian Period = 1872, July 25.

$$\begin{aligned} \lambda_0 &= \lambda - 0''.13764\,d, \\ x_0 &= [9.99929]\,r\sin(\lambda_0 + 89^\circ\ 58'\ 32''), \\ y_0 &= [9.99995]\,r\sin(\lambda_0 + 0^\circ\ 1'\ 28''), \\ z_0 &= [8.7722]\,r\sin(\lambda_0 + 284^\circ\ 27'\ 53'' + 0''.027\,d). \end{aligned}$$

Epoch = 2410000th day of the Julian Period = 1886, Apr. 3.

$$\begin{aligned} \lambda_0 &= \lambda - 0''.13765\,d, \\ x_0 &= [9.99928]\,r\sin(\lambda_0 + 89^\circ\ 58'\ 33''), \\ y_0 &= [9.99995]\,r\sin(\lambda_0 + 0^\circ\ 1'\ 27'') \\ z_0 &= [8.7723]\,r\sin(\lambda_0 + 284^\circ\ 20'\ 28'' + 0''.027\,d). \end{aligned}$$

Epoch = 2415000th day of the Julian Period = 1899, Dec. 11.

$$\begin{aligned} \lambda_0 &= \lambda - 0''.13766\,d, \\ x_0 &= [9.99928]\,r\sin(\lambda_0 + 89^\circ\ 58'\ 34''), \\ y_0 &= [9.99995]\,r\sin(\lambda_0 + 0^\circ\ 1'\ 26'') \\ z_0 &= [8.7723]\,r\sin(\lambda_0 + 284^\circ\ 13'\ 3'' + 0''.027\,d). \end{aligned}$$

Epoch = 2420000th day of the Julian Period = 1913, Aug. 20.

$$\begin{aligned} \lambda_0 &= \lambda - 0''.13766\,d, \\ x_0 &= [9.99928]\,r\sin(\lambda_0 + 89^\circ\ 58'\ 34''), \\ y_0 &= [9.99995]\,r\sin(\lambda_0 + 0^\circ\ 1'\ 24''), \\ z_0 &= [8.7723]\,r\sin(\lambda^\circ + 284^\circ\ 5'\ 37'' + 0''.027\,d). \end{aligned}$$

In the above expressions of the rectangular coordinates, the logarithms of the constant factors, inclosed in [ ], have been given, instead of the constants themselves; and the perturbations of the latitude have been neglected.

Table I. contains the longitudes of the principal Observatories from Washington, as given by Dr. GOULD in the American Ephemeris for 1870. West longitudes are considered as positive.

Tables II., III., and IV. are tables of Astronomical Dates in mean solar days, from which any date, given in the usual form of reference to the Christian era, may be reduced to its value in days and decimals of a day of the Julian period. They are taken from PEIRCE'S Lunar Tables. By adding the days given for the current century to the days of the previous centennial date, we obtain the number of days elapsed of the Julian Period for Jan. 0^d Mean Noon in common years and for Jan. 1^d in bissextile years. To this should be added the days and decimals of a day for fractional parts of a year given in Tables III. and IV.

Table V. contains the periods of the various arguments, and multiplies of them, which it is sometimes necessary to subtract, to render the arguments less than their periods.

Table VI. contains for Washington Mean Noon of Jan. 0^d in common years, Jan. 1^d in bissextile years, of each year from 1750 to 1950, the following quantities:

$$L = 244^\circ\ 18'\ 18''.32 - 0^\circ\ 47'\ 40''.00 + 2106691''.6218\ t$$
$$+ 0''.0001131\ t^2 + 0''.282 \sin(4\ l''' + 3\ l' - 7\ l'' + 147^\circ.1),$$

the integer **m**, the Arguments I.—XIV., the logarithm of the sine of the inclination, and the supplement to 360° of the mean longitude of the ascending node. The term 0° 47′ 40″.00 in L is equivalent to the sum of all the constants which have been added to the quantities in the tables of the equation of the centre, and of the periodic perturbations of the orbit longitude, in order to render them always positive.

Table VII. contains for every day of the year, the motion of the mean longitude, and the motion of the supplement of the node, and the fraction of the year from the beginning of the year.

Table VIII. contains the motion of L for hours, minutes and seconds; also for tenths, hundredths and thousandths of a day.

Table IX. contains the factor of a small correction to be applied to L, on account of the inequality of its motion. The quantity taken from this table must be multiplied by the fraction of the year obtained from the preceding table, and the product added to L.

Table X. contains the Equation of the Centre for every tenth of a day of Argument I. Its secular variation, corresponding to the fractional part of the anomalistic period, is included in the numbers of the table. The constant added, to render all the numbers positive, is 47′ 3″.50.

Tables XI.—XXV. contain the perturbations of the Orbit Longitude. They are given in units of hundredths of a second of arc.

And particularly,—Table XI. contains the factor of the secular perturbation for each day of Argument I. The quantity taken from this table must be multiplied by the integer **m**. The logarithm of the factor is also given, as some may prefer making the multiplication by the aid of logarithms.

Table XII. contains the factor of that part of the secular perturbation which varies as the square of the time. It is given at intervals of 4 days of the Argument I. The quantity taken from this table, must be multiplied by $\left(\frac{\mathbf{m}}{100}\right)^2$. The logarithm of the factor is also given. The formula for the numbers of this table is

$$+ 2.01 \sin M.$$

Table XIII. contains the long period term, due to the action of the Earth,

$$+ 2''.820 \sin(8\ l' - 13\ l'' + 227^\circ\ 58').$$

It is given at intervals of 2 years of the Argument II. The constant added to render all the numbers positive is 2″.82.

Table XIV. contains the terms

$$+ 1''.168 \sin(l' - 3\ l''' + 117^\circ\ 56')$$
$$+ 0''.082 \sin(2\ l' - 6\ l''' + 74^\circ.8)$$

due to the action of Mars. They are given at intervals of 200 days of the Argument III. The constant added is 1″.15.

Table XV. contains the term

$$+ 1''.495 \sin(5\ l'' - 3\ l' + 198^\circ\ 24'),$$

due to the action of the Earth. It is given at intervals of 40 days of the Argument IV. The constant added is 1″.50

INTRODUCTION.

Table XVI. contains the terms

$$+ 3''.515 \sin (2\, l' - 3\, l'' + 268^\circ\ 7'.5)$$
$$+ 0''.188 \sin (4\, l' - 6\, l'' + 340^\circ.7),$$

due to the action of the Earth. They are given at intervals of 16 days in the Argument V. The constant added is 3″.60.

Table XVII. contains the terms

$$- \overset{''}{4}.984 \sin (l' - l'')$$
$$- 11.489 \sin (2\, l' - 2\, l'')$$
$$+ 7.260 \sin (3\, l' - 3\, l'' + 0^\circ\ 7'.6)$$
$$+ 1.050 \sin (4\, l' - 4\, l'' + 0^\circ.10')$$
$$+ 0.335 \sin (5\, l' - 5\, l'' + 1^\circ.5)$$
$$+ 0.143 \sin (6\, l' - 6\, l'')$$
$$+ \overset{''}{0}.067 \sin (7\, l' - 7\, l'')$$
$$+ 0.035 \sin (8\, l' - 8\, l'')$$
$$+ 0.019 \sin (9\, l' - 9\, l'')$$
$$+ 0.013 \sin (10\, l' - 10\, l'')$$
$$+ 0.007 \sin (11\, l' - 11\, l'')$$
$$+ 0.004 \sin (12\, l' - 12\, l'')$$
$$+ 0.003 \sin (13\, l' - 13\, l''),$$

due to the action of the Earth. They are given at intervals of 2 days in the Argument VI. The constant added is 16″.65.

Table XVIII contains the term

$$+ 1''.620 \sin (4\, l' - 5\, l'' + 268^\circ\ 24'.5),$$

due to the action of the Earth. It is given at intervals of 4 days in the Argument VII. The constant added is 1″.62.

Table XIX. contains the term

$$+ 0''.657 \sin (2\, l' - 3\, l''' + 332^\circ\ 44'),$$

due to the action of Mars. It is given at intervals of 4 days in the Argument VIII. The constant added is 0″.66.

Table XX. contains the terms

$$- 2''.959 \sin (l' - l^{\mathrm{iv}} + 0^\circ\ 31')$$
$$+ 0''.880 \sin (2\, l' - 2\, l^{\mathrm{iv}})$$
$$+ 0''.041 \sin (3\, l' - 3\, l^{\mathrm{iv}})$$
$$+ 0''.007 \sin (4\, l' - 4\, l^{\mathrm{iv}}),$$

due to the action of Jupiter. They are given at intervals of 2 days in the Argument IX. The constant added is 3″.35.

Table XXI. contains the perturbations due to the action of Mercury. The formula has already been given at page 3. The tabulation is to double entry, the horizontal argument being I., and the vertical argument X., which remains constant during a period of Argument I. When Argument I. surpasses the limit of the table, 224^{d}.7 should be subtracted from it, and 33.26 should be added to Argument X.; and if this last surpasses 60, 60 may be subtracted from it. The constant added to the numbers, to render them positive, is 0″.85.

Table XXII. contains the residual perturbations due to the action of the Earth. The analytical expression is that given on page 3 with the omission of the terms which have been tabulated in Tables XIII., XV., XVI., XVII., and XVIII. The tabulation is to double entry, the horizontal argument being I., and the vertical argument XI., which remains constant during a period of Argument I. When 224^{d}.7 is subtracted from Argument I., 147.64 should be added to Argument XI.; and if this last exceeds 240, 240 may be subtracted from it. The constant added to the numbers of this table is 1″.40.

Table XXIII. contains the residual perturbations due to the action of Mars. The analytical expression is that given at page 4, with the omission of the terms which have been tabulated in Tables XIV. and XIX. The tabulation is to double entry, the horizontal argument being I., and the vertical argument XII., which remains constant during a period of Argument I. When 224^{d}.7 is subtracted from Argument I., 19.6 must be added to Argument XII.; and if this last exceeds 60, 60 may be subtracted from it. The constant added to the numbers of this table is 0″.15.

Table XXIV. contains the residual perturbations due to the action of Jupiter. The analytical expression is that given at page 4, with the omission of the terms which have been tabulated in Table XX. The tabulation is to double entry, the horizontal argument being I., and the vertical argument XIII., which remains constant during a period of Argument I. When 224^{d}.7 is subtracted from Argument I., 3.11 must be added to Argument XIII.; and if this last exceeds 60, 60 may be subtracted from it. The constant added to the numbers of this table is 2″.35.

Table XXV. contains the perturbations due to the action of Saturn. The analytical expression is given on page 4. The tabulation is to double entry, the horizontal argument being I., and the vertical argument XIV., which remains constant during a period of Argument I. When $224^d.7$ is subtracted from Argument I., 0.8 must be added to Argument XIV., and if this last exceeds 36, 36 may be subtracted from it. The constant added to the numbers of this table is $0''.40$.

The preceding tables give the Orbit Longitude of Venus referred to the mean equinox of date.

Table XXVI. contains the common logarithm of the Elliptic Radius Vector, for every tenth of a day of Argument I. Its secular variation, corresponding to the fractional part of the anomalistic period is included. The formula tabulated is

$$9.85934275 - 0.0000257 - 0.00297187 \cos M$$
$$- 0.00001525 \cos 2M - 0.00000010 \cos 3M$$
$$+ \frac{\text{Arg. I} - 71^d.7}{224^d.7} \text{(quantity from Tab. XXVII)}.$$

The term 0.0000257 is equivalent to the sum of all the constants, which have been added in the tables of the periodic perturbations, in order to render the numbers always positive.

Tables XXVII.—XXXV. contain the perturbations of log. r; they are given uniformly in units of the eighth decimal; and specially :—

Table XXVII. contains the factor of the secular perturbations for each day of Argument I. The quantity taken from this table must be multiplied by the integer $\mathfrak{m}$. The logarithm of the factor is also given.

Table XXVIII contains the factor of that part of the secular perturbation which varies as the square of the time. It is given for intervals of 4 days in the Argument I. The quantity taken from this table must be multiplied by $\left(\frac{\mathfrak{m}}{100}\right)^2$. The formula for the numbers of this table is $- 2.1 \cos M$.

Table XXIX. contains the terms

$$\begin{array}{ll}
- \ \ 18.6 & - 23.0 \cos (6l' - 6l'') \\
+ 228.2 \cos (l' - l'') & - 11.5 \cos (7l' - 7l'') \\
+ 998.6 \cos (2l' - 2l'') & - \ \ 6.4 \cos (8l' - 8l'') \\
- 841.8 \cos (3l' - 3l'' + 0^\circ 8') & - \ \ 3.5 \cos (9l' - 9l'') \\
- 145.2 \cos (4l' - 4l'') & - \ \ 2.6 \cos (10l' - 10l''), \\
- \ \ 52.2 \cos (5l' - 5l'' + 0^\circ 20') &
\end{array}$$

due to the action of the Earth. The constant added is 1594.

Table XXX. contains the term

$$+ 162.2 \cos (4l' - 5l'' + 88^\circ 52'),$$

due to the action of the Earth. The constant added is 162.

Table XXXI. contains the terms

$$\begin{array}{ll}
- \ \ 19.2 & - 133.0 \cos (2l' - 2l^{\text{iv}}) \\
+ 299.2 \cos (l' - l^{\text{iv}} + 0^\circ 20') & - \ \ \ 7.0 \cos (3l' - 3l^{\text{iv}}),
\end{array}$$

due to the action of Jupiter. The constant added is 445.

Table XXXII. contains the perturbations due to the action of Mercury. The formula has already been given on page 4. The constant added is 34. The tabulation is to double entry, and the remarks which have been made with regard to Table XXI. also apply here.

Table XXXIII. contains the residual perturbations due to the action of the Earth. The formula is that given at page 4 with the omission of the terms which have been tabulated in Tables XXIX. and XXX. The constant added is 150. The tabulation is to double entry, and the remarks made with regard to Table XXII. apply here.

Table XXXIV. contains the perturbations due to the action of Mars. The formula has been given at page 5. The constant added is 80. The tabulation is to double entry, and the remarks made with regard to Table XXIII apply here.

Table XXXV. contains the residual perturbations due to the action of Jupiter. The formula is that given on page 5, when the terms tabulated in Table XXXI. are omitted. The constant added is 60. The tabulation is to double entry, and the remarks made with regard to Table XXIV. apply here.

Table XXXVI. contains the perturbations due to the action of Saturn. The formula has been given at page 5.

The constant added is 25. The tabulation is to double entry, and the remarks made with regard to Table XXV apply here.

These tables (XXVI.—XXXVI.) suffice for finding the logarithm of the radius vector.

Tables XXXVII. and XXXVIII. contain the perturbations of the latitude expressed in units of hundredths of a second of arc.

Table XXXVII. contains the perturbations due to the action of the Earth. The formula has been given at page 5. The constant added is 0″.62. The tabulation is to double entry, and the remarks made with regard to Table XXII. apply here.

Table XXXVIII. contains the perturbations due to the action of Jupiter. The formula has been given at page 5. The constant added is 0″.21. The tabulation is to double entry, and the remarks made with regard to Table XXIV. apply here.

The latitude of Venus is then obtained in the following way. The elliptic latitude is obtained from the formula

$$\log \sin (\text{elliptic lat.}) = \log \sin i + \log \sin [\text{orbit long.} + (360^\circ - \Omega)],$$

in which the orbit longitude is corrected for perturbations. Then the true latitude is given by the formula

True Latitude = Elliptic Latitude + the sum of the quantities derived from Tables XXXVII. and XXXVIII. — 0″83.*

Table XXXIX. contains, for the beginning of each year between 1750—1950, the values of the quantities K_x, K_y, K_z, $\log k_x$, $\log k_y$, $\log k_z$ and the Arguments XV. and XVI. on which depend respectively the lunar and solar nutation.

The beginning of the year for Arguments XV. and XVI. must be understood as being the Washington mean noon of Jan. 0, (Jan. 1 in bissextile years,). But the other six quantities of this Table are given for this time of the beginning of the year only for 1850, and backwards and forwards from this epoch they proceed by intervals of a tropical year. This modification has been made, in order that the motion of these quantities for the fractional part of the year might be included in Table XLI. From each of the quantities K_x, K_y, and K_z, there has been subtracted the constant 20″.00, and from $\log k_y$ the constant 0.0000089, and from $\log k_z$ the constant 0.0000560. These constants are equivalent, in each case, to the sum of the constants which have been added to the quantities in Tables XL. and XLI. to render them positive. Moreover to K_x has been added the small correction, due to lunar nutation, over and above the lunar nutation itself; and to $\log k_x$ has been added the small correction due to lunar nutation.

Table XL. contains the variations of the quantities K_x, K_y, K_z, $\log k_y$, and $\log k_z$ which are produced by lunar nutation. The two last are expressed in units of the seventh decimal place. These quantities have all been computed for the epoch 1850, and are subject to small secular changes, which, except in the case of the correction of K_z, are barely sensible in the course of a century. The variation of ΔK_z in a century has therefore been given in the adjacent column.

The constants which have been added to render the numbers positive, are 18″.00 to ΔK_x, 18″.00 to ΔK_y, 17″.00 to ΔK_z, 88 units to $\Delta \log k_y$, 430 units to $\Delta \log k_z$. The lunar nutation of the equinox can be obtained from the value of ΔK_x by subtracting 18″.00. The formulæ for the quantities tabulated are

$$\begin{aligned}
\Delta K_x &= 18''.00 + \Delta \psi,\\
\Delta K_y &= 18''.00 + 1.0044\, \Delta \psi + 0.0690\, \Delta \varepsilon,\\
\Delta K_z &= 17''.00 + 0.9198\, \Delta \psi + 0.3323\, \Delta \varepsilon,\\
\text{sec. var. of } \Delta K_z &= + 0.0030\, \Delta \varepsilon,\\
\Delta \log k_y &= 88 + 0.5469\, \Delta \psi - 9.480\, \Delta \varepsilon,\\
\Delta \log k_z &= 430 - 2.531\, \Delta \psi + 45.71\, \Delta \varepsilon,
\end{aligned}$$

when for $\Delta \psi$ and $\Delta \varepsilon$ are substituted those parts of the values of these quantities given on page 6 which depend on Ω ☾. The part of ΔK_x which has been applied to K_x in Table XXXIX is

$$+ 0.0015\, \Delta \psi,$$

and the value of $\Delta \log k_x$ which has been added to k_x in the same Table is

$$- 0.0181\, \Delta \psi.$$

*The single term in the perturbations of the latitude, due to the action of Saturn, has not been tabulated. It seemed superfluous to take account of it, when the corresponding term in the latitude of the Earth, producing, at maximum, an effect in the geocentric position of Venus, nearly three times greater, is neglected by Hansen and Olufsen in their "*Tables du Soleil.*"

INTRODUCTION.

Table XLI. contains the variations of the quantities K_x, K_y, K_z, $\log k_y$, and $\log k_z$ which are produced by solar nutation, augmented by the motion of the quantities in the fractional part of the tropical year. $\Delta \log k_y$, and $\Delta \log k_z$ are expressed in units of the seventh decimal place. The quantities have been computed for the epoch 1850. The secular variation ΔK_z, becoming sensible in the course of a century, is given in the adjacent column. The last column contains the solar nutation of the equinox. The constants which have been added are 2″.00 to ΔK_x, 2″.00 to ΔK_y, 3″.00 to ΔK_z, 1 unit to $\Delta \log k_y$, and 130 units to $\Delta \log k_z$. The formulæ for the quantities tabulated are,

$$\Delta K_x = 2''.00 + 0''.05 \ \tau + \Delta \psi,$$
$$\Delta K_y = 2''.00 + 0''.126 \ \tau + \Delta \psi + 0''.038 \sin (2 \odot + 98^\circ.2),$$
$$\Delta K_z = 3''.00 - 1''.861 \ \tau + \Delta \psi + 0''.194 \sin (2 \odot + 71^\circ.0),$$
$$\text{sec. var. } \Delta K_z = + 0''.049 \ \tau,$$
$$\Delta \log k_y = 1 + 22.145 \ \tau + 5.3 \sin (2 \odot + 263^\circ.5),$$
$$\Delta \log k_z = 130 - 103.110 \ \tau + 25.4 \sin (2 \odot + 83^\circ.8),$$

τ denoting the fraction of the year, and the value of $\Delta \psi$ being

$$- 1''.254 \sin 2 \odot.$$

The proper values of K_x, K_y &c., needed for computing the values of x, y, and z referred to the true equinox and equator of date, are therefore obtained, by adding the quantities obtained from Tables XL. and XLI. to the quantities given in Table XXXIX. *for the beginning of the year.* And there is no need of interpolation in this last Table, except for log. k_z, which however is nearly constant.

Table XLII. contains the values of the factors by which the perturbation of the latitude, obtained from Tables XXXVII. and XXXVIII. by subtracting 0″.83, and expressed in hundredths of a second of arc, must be multiplied, in order to obtain the corresponding corrections of the coördinates x, y, and z expressed in units of the seventh decimal place. The Argument is the Orbit Longitude.

Table XLIII. contains the Parallax and Semidiameter. The Argument is the logarithm of the planet's distance from the Earth. The formulæ have already been given at page 8. The value of the semidiameter here given has still need to be increased by a constant quantity for the effect of irradiation, but varying for different observers and instruments, when the reduction of observations is in question.

Tables XLIV. and XLV. give the means of obtaining the mean longitude and arguments for a time not contained between the limits 1750—1950.

Table XLIV. contains the quantities which must be added to the quantities of the 19th century contained in Tables VI. and XXXIX., to obtain the mean longitude and arguments for the beginning of the corresponding year of any other century between 300 B. C. and 2300 A. D. The numbers in the columns headed $t' - 50$, must be multiplied by $(t' - 50)$, t' denoting the number of years from the beginning of the century, and the products added to the numbers of the preceding column. In the case of $\log \sin i$, the numbers of the column headed $t' - 50$ must be understood as being in units of the last decimal place of $\log \sin i$. In using this Table for dates which are B. C. the given year must be conceived as increased algebraically by a unit. It will be noticed that two lines occur for the argument 1500: the first is for dates which are according to the Julian calendar (Old Style), and the second for those which are according to the Gregorian calendar (New Style). The Julian calendar ends with Oct. 4, 1582; and the Gregorian begins with Oct. 15, 1582.

Table XLV. contains the values of the inequality of the longitude to long period,

$$+ 0''.282 \sin (4\, l''' - 7\, l'' + 3\, l' + 147^\circ.1),$$

and of certain multiples of the period of the argument in years. As this inequality has been added to the numbers of the column headed L in Table VI., we must enter the Table first with the argument equal to the corresponding year of the 19th century and take the equation with the opposite sign; and next with the argument equal to the year of the given date, and take the corresponding equation: then both these quantities must be added to the L resulting from the previous Tables. If the year of the given date is not found in the limits of this Table, that multiple of the period of the argument, which is requisite, must be added to it or subtracted from it.

Table XLVI. contains the Reduction of the Orbit Longitude to the ecliptic. The Argument is the "Orbit Longitude + 360° — ☊", or this angle diminished by 180° when it exceeds 180°. It is given for every 10′ of the

Argument. The arrangement of the Table will be easily understood. The Table is constructed for the epoch 1850.0, and the variation in a century, of the numbers tabulated, is given in the last column but one, for every degree. The formula for the reduction to the ecliptic is

$$-180''.914 \sin 2 (\lambda + 360^\circ - \Omega) + 0''.079 \sin 4 (\lambda + 360^\circ - \Omega),$$

and for its secular variation

$$-0''.113 \sin 2 (\lambda + 360^\circ - \Omega).$$

DIRECTIONS FOR THE USE OF THE TABLES.

The given time must be reduced to Washington Mean Time by the aid of Table I. The hours, minutes and seconds can then be reduced to the equivalent decimal part of a day by Table IV.; and the whole number of days which have elapsed since the beginning of the year can be found from Table III.

The values of the mean longitude L, **m** and the fourteen arguments of the perturbations are taken from Table VI. for the given year, if it lies between 1750 and 1949. If we do not want the heliocentric longitude and latitude of the planet, but intend to compute the geocentric coördinates by the Gaussian process, the quantities, in the columns of this Table, headed Log. sin i and $360^\circ - \Omega$, will not be needed.

From Table VII. will be obtained the motion of L from the beginning of the year to the given day; and also the fraction of the year; from Table IX. the factor which must be multiplied by the fraction of the year and the product added to L; and from Table VIII. the motion of L for hours, minutes and seconds, or for decimal parts of a day. The quantities obtained from Tables VII.—IX. being added to the L from Table VI., we obtain the tabular mean longitude of the planet for the given date.

To Arguments I.—IX., II. excepted, we add the number of days and decimal part of a day which have elapsed since the beginning of the year; to Argument II. we add the fractional part of the year. If any argument thus obtained, exceed its period given in Table V., we subtract as many multiples of the period as may be necessary to reduce it below its period. To the Argument **m**, we add as many units, as we have subtracted multiples of its period from Argument I., and to Arguments X.—XIV. we add severally the same number of multiples of the numbers 33.26, 147.64, 19.6, 3.11, and 0.8. The values of these multiples are given in Table V. If any Argument X.—XIV. exceed its period given in Table V., we may subtract from it the largest contained multiple of its period.

The Equation of the Centre is obtained from Table X. with the Argument I. The perturbations of the longitude in hundredths of a second of arc will be obtained with the proper arguments from Tables XI.—XXV. The number obtained from Table XI. must be multiplied by the integer **m**, and the number from Table XII. by the factor $\left(\frac{\mathbf{m}}{100}\right)^2$; the logarithms of the numbers in these two tables have also been given in the adjacent column, in order that, if preferred, the multiplication may be performed by their aid. The Equation of the Centre and these perturbations being added to the mean longitude, we obtain the orbit longitude referred to the mean equinox of date.

The Logarithm of the Elliptic Radius Vector is obtained from Table XXVI. with the Argument I; and its perturbations, in units of the eighth decimal, with the proper arguments from Tables XXVII.—XXXVI. The number obtained from Table XXVII. must be multiplied by the integer **m**, and the number from Table XXVIII. by the factor $\left(\frac{\mathbf{m}}{100}\right)^2$; the logarithm of the number is also given in Table XXVII., in order that, if preferred, the multiplication may be performed by its aid. If the sum of the numbers thus obtained from Tables XXVII.-XXXVI. be divided by 10, and the quotient be added to the last figures of the quantity obtained from Table XXVI., we shall have the common logarithm of the radius vector of the planet.

If we diminish by 83 the sum of the numbers, obtained from Tables XXXVII. and XXXVIII. with the proper arguments, we shall have, in hundredths of a second of arc, the perturbations of the latitude.

The values of K_x, K_y, &c., and Arguments XV. and XVI. are to be taken from Table XXXIX. for the given year. And to Arguments XV. and XVI. should be added the number of days and the decimal part of a day elapsed since the beginning of the year; and if Argument XV. exceed its period, given in Table V., the period should be subtracted from it. The corrections of K_x, K_y, &c., are obtained from Tables XL. and XLI., with the respective Arguments XV. and XVI. In the case of K_z in each Table, the variation in 100 years, given in the adjacent column, must be taken into account; we multiply it by the fractional part of the century elapsed since 1850, and add the product to the quantity obtained from the preceding column. These corrections being added to the values of K_x, K_y, &c., obtained *without interpolation* from Table XXXIX., we have the proper values of these quantities for computing the rectangular coördinates of the planet referred to the true equinox and equator of date.

If r denote the radius vector, and λ the orbit longitude of the planet, these coördinates are obtained by the formulæ

$$x = k_x\, r \sin(\lambda + K_x),$$
$$y = k_y\, r \sin(\lambda + K_y),$$
$$z = k_z\, r \sin(\lambda + K_z).$$

The values of the coördinates thus found need correction for the effect of perturbations in latitude. To obtain these corrections we multiply the perturbations of the latitude, expressed in hundredths of a second of arc, respectively by the three factors obtained from Table XLII. with the argument λ, and the products are the respective corrections of the coördinates expressed in units of the seventh decimal.

If X, Y and Z denote the coördinates of the Sun referred to the same system of planes as x, y and z, the geocentric right ascension α, declination δ, and distance from the Earth Δ, of the planet, are obtained from the equations,

$$\Delta \cos\alpha \cos\delta = x + X,$$
$$\Delta \sin\alpha \cos\delta = y + Y,$$
$$\Delta \sin\delta \quad = z + Z.$$

The α and δ thus obtained have still to be corrected for aberration, if we desire the apparent position of the planet. The aberration time T in days is given by the equation

$$\log T = 7.76052 + \log \Delta\,; \text{ or, } T = .005761\, \Delta.$$

If $\frac{d\,\alpha}{d\,t}$ and $\frac{d\,\delta}{d\,t}$ denote the daily variation of α and δ at the given date, the corrections for aberration are

$$\Delta\,\alpha = -\,T\frac{d\,\alpha}{d\,t},$$

$$\Delta\,\delta = -\,T\frac{d\,\delta}{d\,t}.$$

Finally, from Table XLIII., we can obtain, with the argument $\log \Delta$, the parallax and semidiameter of the planet.

If we desire to have the heliocentric longitude and latitude, we take from Table VI. the values of $\log. \sin i$ and $360° - \Omega$ for the given year. The motion of $360° - \Omega$ for the fraction of the year is given in Table VII.; that of $\log \sin i$ can readily be inferred from Table VI. Then if the latitude be computed from the equation,

$$\log \sin \text{lat.} = \log \sin i + \log \sin (\lambda + 360° - \Omega),$$

and the perturbations of the latitude, which have already been obtained, be added to it, we shall have the heliocentric latitude required. The ecliptic heliocentric longitude, referred to the mean equinox of date, will be got by adding to λ the reduction to the ecliptic, from Table XLVI. As the value of the reduction, given in the body of the Table, is for the epoch 1850, we must apply to it the variation in 100 years multiplied by the fraction of a century elapsed since 1850. The heliocentric longitude referred to the true equinox of date will be found by adding the nutation of the equinoxes in longitude. The lunar nutation will be obtained by subtracting 18″ from ΔK_x in Table XL.; the solar nutation is given in the last column of Table XLI.

x, y, and z may then be obtained by the formulæ

$$x = r \cos l \cos \lambda'$$
$$y = r \cos l \sin \lambda' \cos \epsilon' - r \sin l \sin \epsilon'$$
$$z = r \cos l \sin \lambda' \sin \epsilon' + r \sin l \cos \epsilon'$$

in which λ' and l are the heliocentric longitude and latitude, and $\epsilon' = \epsilon + \Delta\,\epsilon$, the apparent obliquity of the ecliptic.

If the given year is not between the limits 1750—1949, we take from Tables VI. and XXXIX, the values of L, **m**, the Arguments I.—XVI., log sin i and 360° − ☊, for the corresponding year of the 19th century, (remembering to add algebraically a unit to the year if the given date is before the Christian era.)

We add to these the quantities obtained from Table XLIV., with the given century as the Argument. Moreover we add to L, I, log sin i and 360° − ☊ respectively the quantities given in the adjacent columns, headed $t' - 50$, multiplied by this factor, (t' denoting the number of years of the given century,) noticing that in the case of log sin i, the quantities in the column headed $t' - 50$ are in units of the last decimal of this quantity. It will be observed that the argument 1500 occurs twice in Table XLIV.; the first line is to be employed for dates in old style, the second for dates in new style.

After this, we proceed precisely as before, except that Table VIII. not being available, we employ in its stead Table XLV., which we enter twice, first with the corresponding year of the 19th century as the argument, and subtracting from L the equation obtained; next with the given year, as the argument, or this augmented or diminished by the requisite number of multiples of the period, which will be found at the bottom of the Table; and adding to L the equation thus obtained.

In this case, we must necessarily deduce the heliocentric longitude and latitude of the planet, since the tables for finding K_x, K_y, &c., are restricted to the years 1750—1949. The method of computing by rectangular coördinates is only to be preferred when we have the coördinates of the sun ready at hand.

In computing an ephemeris we shall avoid the horizontal interpolation in the tables to double entry, if, instead of computing the perturbations, for the Washington Mean Noon of some particular day, and for equal intervals thereafter, we compute the value of the perturbations, for the times, when Arg. I. is an exact multiple of 8 days, and then the interpolation, with reference to Arg. I., can be performed on the sums. It will be found that the interval of 8 days is not too long for the secure interpolation of intermediate values. However, if **m** should be quite large, that is, if the given time is quite distant from 1850, the terms of the perturbations, which involve this factor, may be computed separately, for the times, for which, the ephemeris is wanted. In all cases, the interpolation of the sums of the perturbations, to the times of the ephemeris, will be easier, if these sums are first interpolated into the middle, that is, for every 4 days. In the computation of an isolated position even, this method of obtaining the perturbations, first for the times when Arg. I. is a multiple of 8 days, can be followed with advantage, at least as far as regards the tables to double entry.

The following examples will sufficiently illustrate the foregoing precepts:—

1. Required an ephemeris of the heliocentric position of Venus, for Washington Mean Noon, at intervals of 2 days, and covering the time of the Transit on Dec. 8th, 1874.

We will commence the calculation of the perturbations at $310^d.3195$ from the beginning of the year = Nov. $6^d.3195$, when the value of Argument I. is 160^d.

Preparation of the Arguments.

	m	I.	II.	III.	IV.	V.	VI.	VII.	VIII.	IX.
Table VI., 1874,	39	$74^d.3513$	$191^y.9$	8583^d	346^d	$798^d.5$	$241^d.22$	$92^d.5$	$129^d.8$	$52^d.83$
Day of Year,		310.3195	0.8	310	310	310.3	310.35	310.3	310.3	310.35
Table V., Periods,	1	−224.7008						−243.2	−220.6	−236.90
Arguments for Date,	40	160.0000	192.7	8893	656	1108.8	551.57	159.6	219.5	126.19
No. of days to end of period							40.00		8.0	
Table V., Periods,							−583.92		−220.6	
							7.65		6.9	

	X.	XI.	XII.	XIII	XIV.	XV.	XVI.
Table VI., 1874,	42.20	17.72	53.0	27.03	30.6	$6005^{d}.2$	$1^{d}.8$
Table V., Incr. of m = 1,	33.26	147.64	19.6	3.11	0.7	310.0	310.0
Periods,	−60.00		−60.0				
Arguments for Date,	15.46	165.36	12.6	301.4	31.3	6315.2	311.8

Perturbations of the Longitude, in hundredths of a second.

Arg. I.	160	168	176	184	192	200	208	216	224
Table XI	+491	+507	+498	+464	+406	+328	+232	+124	+10
Table XIII	188	187	187	187	187	187	187	187	186
Table XIV	157	157	157	158	158	159	159	159	160
Table XV	123	126	128	131	134	136	139	141	144
Table XVI	347	334	321	308	294	281	268	255	242
Table XVII	1793	1708	1665	1656	1667	1679	1672	1631	1548
Table XVIII . . .	260	231	200	167	134	101	72	46	25
Table XIX	0	1	5	12	22	34	48	62	77
Table XX	431	519	591	642	668	670	650	612	563
Table XXI	22	23	25	27	29	31	34	39	44
Table XXII	139	138	139	141	143	145	145	141	135
Table XXIII . . .	24	23	22	20	18	16	13	12	10
Table XXIV . . .	254	244	234	225	219	216	216	218	222
Table XXV	36	33	32	32	34	36	40	45	51
Sums	4265	4231	4204	4170	4113	4019	3875	3672	3417

NOTE.—The inequality from Table XII. is insensible at this epoch, as is also the corresponding one of Log. r in Table XXVIII.

Perturbations of Log r, in units of the eighth decimal.

Arg. I.	160	168	176	184	192	200	208	216	224
Table XXVII . . .	−133	−15	+104	+219	+323	+411	+478	+522	+538
Table XXIX . . .	2146	1989	1850	1753	1716	1748	1841	1978	2136
Table XXX . . .	292	309	320	324	321	311	295	274	248
Table XXXI . . .	17	66	141	236	339	440	528	594	636
Table XXXII . . .	50	46	36	24	13	9	9	12	11
Table XXXIII . .	231	221	214	210	211	216	224	235	245
Table XXXIV . .	85	70	57	46	36	29	23	20	19
Table XXXV . . .	140	134	125	112	99	85	73	65	60
Table XXXVI . .	36	32	27	22	17	11	6	3	0
Sums	2864	2852	2874	2946	3075	3260	3477	3703	3893

Perturbations of the Latitude, in hundredths of a second.

Arg. I.	160	168	176	184	192	200	208	216	224
Table XXXVII . .	39	43	46	53	59	65	71	76	80
Table XXXVIII . .	34	35	36	36	35	34	32	30	27
Constant	−83	−83	−83	−83	−83	−83	−83	−83	−83
Sums	−10	−5	−1	+6	+11	+16	+20	+23	+24

Interpolating the perturbations of the longitude and log r to intervals of 4 days, we have,

Arg. I.	Pert. of the Long.	Diff.	Pert. of Log r.	Diff.	Arg.	Pert. of the Long.	Diff.	Pert. of Log r.	Diff.
d 160	″ 42.65		2864		d 192	″ 41.13		3075	
164	42.47	− 18	2855	− 9	196	40.72	− 41	3162	+ 87
168	42.31	16	2852	− 3	200	40.19	53	3260	98
172	42.18	13	2858	+ 6	204	39.54	65	3365	105
176	42.04	14	2874	16	208	38.75	79	3477	112
180	41.89	15	2903	29	212	37.80	95	3592	115
184	41.70	19	2946	43	216	36.72	108	3703	111
188	41.45	25	3003	57	220	35.50	122	3804	101
192	41.13	− 32	3075	+ 72	224	34.17	− 133	3893	+ 89

The Orbit Longitude and Log. r. Washington Mean Noon.

Date. 1874.	Day of Year.	Arg. I.	Mean Longitude from Tables VI.–VIII.	Equa. of the Centre from Table X.	Pert. of the Long.	Orbit Long.	Log. Elliptic r from Table XXVI.	Pert. of Log. r.	Log. r.
Dec. 3	d 337	d 186.6505	68° 3′ 8″.37	5′ 45″.20	41″.54	68° 9′ 35″.11	9.8578827	298	9.8579125
5	339	188.6505	71 15 23.98	7 5.00	41.40	71 23 10.38	9.8577382	301	9.8577683
7	341	190.6505	74 27 39.59	8 32.38	41.24	74 36 53.21	9.8575986	305	9.8576291
9	343	192.6505	77 39 55.21	10 7.11	41.07	77 50 43.39	9.8574644	309	9.8574953
11	345	194.6505	80 52 10.82	11 48.87	40.87	81 4 40.56	9.8573358	313	9.8573671
13	347	196.6505	84 4 26.44	13 37.36	40.64	84 18 44.44	9.8572135	318	9.8572453

Inequalities of K_x, K_y, &c.

Day of Year.	ΔK_x.			ΔK_y.			ΔK_z.			$\Delta \log k_y$.		
	Table XL.	Table XLI.	Sum.	Table XL.	Table XLI.	Sum.	Table XL.	Table XLI.	Sum.	Table XL.	Table XLI.	Sum.
d 310	″ 10.68	″ 0.78	″ 11.46	″ 11.23	″ 0.83	″ 12.06	″ 12.81	″ 0.24	″ 13.05	5	19	24
320	10.82	0.85	11.67	11.37	0.90	12.27	12.96	0.19	13.15	5	21	26
330	10.96	1.07	12.03	11.52	1.11	12.63	13.11	0.28	13.39	5	23	28
340	11.11	1.39	12.50	11.66	1.42	13.08	13.26	0.49	13.75	4	25	29
350	11.25	1.80	13.05	11.81	1.83	13.64	13.40	0.80	14.20	4	27	31
360	11.40	2.26	13.66	11.95	2.30	14.25	13.55	1.19	14.74	4	28	32
370	11.54	2.68	14.22	12.10	2.72	14.82	13.70	1.57	15.27	3	28	31

Day of Year	$\Delta \log k_z$.			K_x.	K_y.	K_z.	Log k_x.	Log k_y.	Log k_z.
	Table XL.	Table XLI.	Sum.						
d 310	828	46	874	89° 58′ 23″.90	1° 27′ 22″.22	352° 44′ 25″.01	9.9992854	9.9598380	9.6179135
320	829	34	863	24.11	22.43	25.11	4	82	424
330	830	23	853	24.47	22.79	25.35	4	84	414
340	831	14	845	24.94	23.24	25.71	4	85	406
350	833	7	840	25.49	23.80	26.16	4	87	401
360	834	3	837	26.10	24.41	26.70	4	88	398
370	835	2	837	26.66	24.98	27.23	4	87	398

Computation of the Rectangular Coördinates.

Date, 1874.	$\lambda + K_x$.	$\lambda + K_y$.	$\lambda + K_z$.	log k_x sin ($\lambda + K_x$).	log k_y sin ($\lambda + K_y$).	log k_z sin ($\lambda + K_z$).
Dec. 3	158° 7′ 59″.90	69° 36′ 58″.20	60° 54′ 0″.70	9.5703515	9.9317544	9.5593398
5	161 21 35.27	72 50 33.57	64 7 36.05	9.5039252	9.9400684	9.5720679
7	164 35 18.20	76 4 16.50	67 21 18.96	9.4237611	9.9468769	9.5830998
9	167 49 8.49	79 18 6.79	70 35 9.22	9.3235684	9.9522237	9.5925170
11	171 3 5.76	82 32 4.07	73 49 6.48	9.1911412	9.9561415	9.6003850
13	174 17 9.75	85 46 8.06	77 3 10.45	8.9973798	9.9586533	9.6067565

Date, 1874.	log x.	log y.	log z.	x.	y.	z
Dec. 3	9.4282640	9.7896669	9.4172523	+0.2680798	+0.6161223	+0.2613680
5	9.3616935	9.7978367	9.4298362	0.2299818	0.6278223	0.2690520
7	9.2813902	9.8045060	9.4407289	0.1911570	0.6375379	0.2758855
9	9.1810637	9.8097190	9.4500123	0.1517273	0.6452366	0.2818463
11	9.0485083	9.8135086	9.4577521	0.1118171	0.6508915	0.2869142
13	8.8546251	9.8158986	9.4640018	+0.0715525	+0.6544833	+0.2910729

TABLE XLII.

Date, 1874.	Factors for			Pert. of the Lat.	Δx.	Δy.	Δz.
	Δx.	Δy.	Δz.				
Dec. 3	+0.001	−0.147	+0.323	+ 7	0	−1	+2
13	0.000	−0.141	+0.321	+14	0	−2	+4

Date, 1874.	x.	y.	z.	Date, 1874.	x.	y.	z.
Dec. 3	+0.2680798	+0.6161222	+0.2613682	Dec. 9	+0.1517273	+0.6452364	+0.2818467
5	0.2299818	0.6278222	0.2690523	11	0.1118171	0.6508913	0.2869146
7	+0.1911570	+0.6375377	+0.2758858	13	+0.0715525	+0.6544831	+0.2910733

2. Required the heliocentric longitude and latitude and the logarithm of the radius vector of Venus for 1769, June 3^d 10^h 10^m Paris mean time.

This is equivalent to June 3^d 4^h 52^m $26^s.98$ Washington mean time = $154^d.20309$ from the beginning of the year.

Preparation of the Arguments.

	m	I.	II.	III.	IV.	V.	VI.	VII.	VIII.	IX.
Table VI., 1769	−132	$148^d.1850$	$86^y.9$	6195^d	465^d	$276^d.8$	$430^d.03$	$162^d.6$	$158^d.4$	$95^d.51$
Day of Year		154.2031	0.4	154	154	154.2	154.20	154.2	154.2	154.20
Table V., Periods	1	−224.7008					−583.92	−243.2	−220.6	−236.99
Arguments for date	−131	77.6873	87.3	6349	619	431.0	0.31	73.6	92.0	12.72

	X.	XI.	XII.	XIII.	XIV.	log sin i.	360° − ☊.	XV.	XVI.
Tables VI., XXXIX, 1769	54.98	210.46	57.1	34.91	10.0	8.7721047	285° 23′ 59″.5	$1646^d.5$	$2^d.3$
Tables V., VII.	33.26	147.64	19.6	3.11	0.8	5	−13.7	154.2	154.2
Periods	−60.00	−240.00	−60.0						
Args., &c., for date	28.24	118.10	16.7	38.02	10.8	8.7721052	285 23 45.8	1800.7	156.5

Mean Longitude.

	L.
	° ′ ″
Table VI., 1769	4 57 7.69
Table VII., June 3	246 44 2.33
Table IX. 4^h	16 1.301
" " 52^m	3 28.282
" " $26^s.98$	1.801
Table VIII., 1769, $(-0''.015 \times 0.4) =$	−0.006
Mean Longitude,	252 0 41.40

Longitude.

Mean Longitude			252° 0′ 41″.40
Equation of the Centre			1 25 39.70
Table XI., $-10.363 \times (-131)$			+13.57
Table XII., $+1.66 \times (-1.31)^2$			+ 0.03
Table XIII.,			4.66
Table XIV.,			0.32
Table XV.,			1.12
Table XVI.,			4.45
Table XVII.,			16.68
Table XVIII.,			2.05
Table XIX.,			1.21
Table XX.,			2.93
Arg. I.,	72	80	
Table XXI.,	82	80	
Table XXII.,	145	150	
Table XXIII.,	10	8	
Table XXIV.,	310	308	
Table XXV.,	15	17	
Sums	562	563	
Interpolated,			5.63
Orbit Longitude,			253 27 13.75
Red. to Ecliptic, Table XLVI.,			+7.26
Lunar Nutation, Table XL.,			+17.29
Solar Nutation, Table XLI.,			− 0.68
Heliocentric Longitude,			253 27 37.62

Logarithm Radius Vector.

Log. Elliptic r, Table XXVI.,			9.8610042
Table XXVII., $-7.66 \times (-131)$			+1003
Table XXVIII., $+1.2 \times (-.1.31)^2$			+ 2
Table XXIX.,			1716
Table XXX.,			6
Table XXXI.,			600
Arg. I.	72	80	
Table XXXII.,	48	49	
Table XXXIII.,	39	36	
Table XXXIV.,	40	51	
Table XXXV.,	82	77	
Table XXXVI.,	14	10	
Sums,	223	223	
Interpolated,			223
Log. r,			9.8610377

Latitude.

Orbit Longitude,			253° 27′ 13″.75
$360° - ☊$,			285 23 45.8
Arg. of Latitude,			178 50 59.5
Log sin Arg. of Latitude,			8.3025984
Log sin i			8.7721052
Log sin Latitude			7.0747036
Elliptic Latitude			+0° 4′ 4″.98
Arg. I.	72	80	
Table XXXVII.,	65	57	
Table XXXVIII.,	17	15	
Sums	82	72	
Interpolated			0.75
Constant			− 0.83
Latitude			+0 4 4.90

Encke's reduction of the observations of the Transit of Venus in 1769 gives 253° 27′ 13″.17 and +0° 4′ 4″.56 as the orbit longitude and latitude.* But according to the *Tables du Soleil* of Hansen and Olufsen, the longitude and latitude of the Sun, adopted by Encke, must be corrected, respectively, by + 0″.64 and +0″.04. Thus we may adopt 253° 27′ 13″.81 and +0° 4′ 4″.52 as the values given by observation, and the residuals, Obs. — Cal., are respectively + 0″.06 and — 0″.38.

If Encke's reduction of the Transit of 1761 is compared with the Tables, in the same way, the residuals will be found to be — 0″.33 and + 0″.40.

3. Required the heliocentric position of Venus for 1639, Dec. 4^d 3^h 44^m 55^s Paris mean time.

This time is equivalent to Dec. 3^d 22^h 27^m $21^s.98$ Washington mean time = $337^d.93567$ from the beginning of the year.

Preparation of the Arguments.

	m	I.	II.	III.	IV.	V.	VI.	VII.	VIII.	IX.
		d	y	d	d	d	d	d	d	d
Table VI., 1839 .	— 18	98.2956	156.9	7786	2358	1108.9	303.49	196.3	138.7	66.39
Table XLIV, 1600 .	—326	204.4585	38.9	10863	932	1153.7	526.09	144.6	180.0	182.50
Terms × (t' — 50),		+0.0005								
Day of Year, . .		337.9357	0.9	338	338	337.9	337.94	337.9	337.9	337.94
Periods, ...	+ 2	—449.4016		-11987	-2959	-1454.9	—583.92	—486.3	—440.1	-473.98
Arguments for date,	—342	191.2887	196.7	7000	669	1145.6	583.60	192.5	216.5	112.85

	X.	XI.	XII.	XIII.	XIV.	log sin i.	360° — ☊.	XV.	XVI.
							° ′ ″	d	d
Tables VI., XXXIX, 1839	6.46	1.97	14.4	29.66	23.7	8.7721999	284 46 4.6	19.4	1.3
Table XLIV., 1600 .	17.69	107.80	22.2	5.56	6.9	-0.0002732	+1 48 17.0	1732.9	+0.4
Terms × (t' — 50), .						—24	— 0.6		
Day of Year, or Periods	6.52	55.29	39.3	6.22	1.5	+12	— 30.1	337.9	337.9
Periods			—60.0						
Arguments for date, .	30.67	165.06	15.9	41.44	32.1	8.7719255	286 33 50.9	2090.2	339.6

Mean Longitude.

	L.
	° ′ ″
Table VI., 1839	285 59 48.72
Table XLIV., 1600,	324 46 55.79
Term × (t' — 50),	+ 0.458
Table VII., Dec. 3,	179 55 51.07
Table IX., 22^h,	1 28 7.157
" " 27^m,	1 48.146
" " $21^s.98$,	1.466
Table XLV., 1839.9 with opp. sign,	—0.176
" " 1942.3 = 1639.9 + 302.4,	—0.279
Mean Longitude,	72 12 32.35

* Der Venus-durchgang von 1769, p. 107.

Longitude.

	° ′ ″
Mean Longitude,	72 12 32.35
Equation of the Centre,	9 1.83
Table XI., + 10.309 × (− 342),	−35.26
Table XII., − 1.61 × (3.42)²,	−0.19
Table XIII.,	1.60
Table XIV.,	0.59
Table XV..	1.27
Table XVI.,	2.87
Table XVII.,	16.67
Table XVIII.,	1.30
Table XIX.,	0.01
Table XX.,	2.69

Arg. I.	184	192	
Table XXI.,	107	109	
Table XXII.,	140	142	
Table XXIII,	25	25	
Table XXIV.,	428	436	
Table XXV.,	35	34	
Sums	735	746	
Interpolated			7.45

Orbit Longitude,	72 21 33.18
Red. to Ecliptic, Table XLVI.,	+6.79
Lunar Nutation, Table XL.,	+16.34
Solar Nutation, XLI.,	− 0.73
Heliocentric Longitude,	72 21 55.58

Logarithm Radius Vector.

Log. Elliptic r, Table XXVI,	9.8575552
Table XXVII., + 7.86 × (− 342),	−2687
Table XXVIII.,	− 15
Table XXIX.,	1716
Table XXX.,	321
Table XXXI.,	9

Arg. I.	184	192	
Table XXXII.,	24	28	
Table XXXIII.,	210	212	
Table XXXIV.,	108	96	
Table XXXV.,	35	52	
Table XXXVI.,	26	20	
Sums	403	408	
Interpolated			408
Log. r,			9.8575527

Latitude.

	° ′ ″
Orbit Longitude,	72 21 33.18
360° − ☊,	286 33 50.9
Arg. of Latitude,	358 55 24.1
Log sin Arg. of Lat.	n 8.2739219
Log sin i,	8.7719255
Log sin Latitude,	n 7.0458474
Elliptic Latitude,	−0 3 49.23

Arg. I.	184	192	
Table XXXVII.,	54	61	
Table XXXVIII.,	9	12	
Sums	63	73	
Interpolated,			0.72
Constant			−0.83
Latitude,			−0 3 49.34

If Encke's reduction of Horrox's observations of the Transit at this time be corrected to conform with the position of the Sun as derived from Hansen and Olufsen's Tables, the residuals of the orbit longitude and heliocentric latitude are found to be respectively + 11″.4 and − 18″.9.

CORRECTION OF THE ELEMENTS OF THE ORBIT OF VENUS.

The Elements, adopted for comparison with observation, are, in the main, those on which LEVERRIER has based his Tables.

They are—

Epoch, 1850, Jan. 1.0, Paris Mean Time.

	°	′	″
L' =	245	33	14.70
π' =	129	27	14.5
☊′ =	75	19	52.3
i' =	3	23	34.83
e' =	0.00684331		
n' =	2106641″.3831		

The value of n' has been changed in order to make the adopted tropical motion coincide with LEVERRIER's value. The values of the disturbing masses, and, in fact, of all the constants needed in the theory, are, with two exceptions, those given in the Introduction. But the annual tropical motion of the node at the epoch 1850 employed is 32″.2931 as it results from the adopted values of the planetry masses: and the true longitude of the Sun is derived from the apparent longitude of HANSEN's and OLUFSEN's *Tables du Soleil* by subtracting the effect of aberration corresponding to the constant 20″.255.

All the elements, except the mean motion, are determined, with nearly all the precision possible by the modern observations; that is to say, those comprehended in the interval from 1836 up to the present time. The addition of the observations made previously to 1836 to the discussion, would scarcely increase this precision. For the mean motion we must employ ancient observations; and for this purpose it seems better to depend on the data furnished by the Transits of 1761 and 1769, than on the somewhat uncertain observations of Bradley.

Encke's reduction of these Transits, corrected to conform with the positions of the Sun derived from the *Tables du Soleil*, will be adopted. All the longitudes mentioned here are referred to the mean equinox of date.

For the Transit of 1761 Encke gives

Paris Mean Time = 1761, June 5ᵈ 17ʰ 30ᵐ.

		°	′	″
True Longitude of the Sun	=	75	35	49.6,
Latitude of the Sun	=		+	0.6,
Orbit Longitude of Venus	=	255	35	34.45,
Heliocentric Latitude of Venus	=	−	3	45.91,

But the *Tables du Soleil* give 75° 35′ 52″.05 and + 0″.53 as the longitude and latitude of the Sun. Consequently the adopted position of Venus is

		°	′	″
Orbit Longitude	=	255	35	36.90,
Heliocentric Latitude	=	−	3	45.84.

For the Transit of 1769, Encke gives

Paris Mean Time = 1769, June 3ᵈ 10ʰ 10ᵐ.

		°	′	″
True Longitude of the Sun	=	73	27	13.8,
Latitude of the Sun	=			0.0,
Orbit Longitude of Venus	=	253	27	13.17,
Heliocentric Latitude of Venus	=	+	4	4.56.

The *Tables du Soleil* give 73° 27′ 14″.25 and +0″.04 as the longitude and latitude of the Sun. Consequently the adopted position of Venus is

		°	′	″
Orbit Longitude of Venus	=	253	27	13.62,
Heliocentric Latitude of Venus	=	+	4	4.52.

The meridian observations have been corrected to conform with the constant 8″.848 of solar parallax, and to the following expression for the semi-diameter:

$$\frac{8''.316}{\Delta} + 0''.57.$$

In other respects Leverrier's reduction has been adopted. With regard to the Greenwich and Paris observations which have accumulated since Leverrier made his investigation, that is, from 1858 forward, as, on comparing the places, given in the several annual volumes, for the fundamental time-stars, with Dr. GOULD's *Standard Places, &c.*, no sensible *average* difference in the right ascensions could be discovered, no correction for difference of equinoxes has been applied to them. To the Washington observations in declination in the years 1866, 1867, has been applied the correction +0″.75. (See *Washington Observations for* 1867, Appendix III., pp. 20, 21.)

In forming the following normals, Paris observations have been combined with Greenwich; but Washington observations have been kept separate. The normals, formed from them, are those given for Washington Mean Noon. The Paris Observations used are not in great number, and belong to the years 1838 and 1856—1866. The comparisons are Obs. — Cal.

Normals in the inferior part of the Orbit.

No.	Greenwich M. T.	App. R. A.	App. Dec.	No. Obs.	Δα	Δδ
	d	h m s	° ′ ″		s	″
1	1836, June 9.0	8 16 6.380	+21 53 40.12	4	+0.082	+0.62
2	July 2.0	8 52 43.140	+16 16 11.35	5	−0.057	+0.63
3	July 13.0	8 43 59.799	+14 17 35.12	4	−0.054	−0.32
4	Aug. 7.0	7 47 48.091	+13 41 44.35	3	+0.228	−0.60
5	Aug. 30.0	7 56 5.580	+15 11 1.98	4	+0.083	−1.71
6	1838, Jan. 12.0	22 36 4.483	− 8 23 42.65	7	+0.079	+0.18
7	Feb. 2.0	23 19 4.936	− 0 5 1.83	5	−0.163	+5.07
8	Feb. 22.0	23 11 48.498	+ 3 26 16.93	3	+0.050	+2.00
9	March 12.0	22 33 39.400	− 0 1 38.66	3	+0.178	+1.75
10	March 24.0	22 23 12.226	− 3 12 55.39	10	+0.111	−1.18
11	April 7.0	22 37 31.008	− 4 49 5.56	13	+0.096	−1.02
12	1839, Sept. 21.0	12 58 21.552	−14 51 58.87	4	−0.147	−0.66
13	Oct. 12.0	12 19 41.626	− 9 44 43.41	9	+0.017	+0.82
14	1841, May 1.0	3 50 40.861	+25 34 41.55	6	+0.009	+0.39
15	May 27.0	2 59 23.728	+17 18 40.10	5	+0.251	+1.95
16	June 12.0	2 59 45.783	+14 23 34.07	4	−0.021	−0.92
17	1842, Dec. 15.0	17 56 8.706	−22 32 23.92	5	−0.140	+2.31
18	1843, Jan. 10.0	17 15 35.705	−17 35 57.26	2	−0.042	+0.29
19	1844, May 31.0	7 46 25.585	+23 55 35.09	6	−0.047	+1.23
20	July 30.0	7 49 49.182	+13 59 37.31	6	−0.046	−0.68
21	1846, Jan. 16.0	22 44 36.217	− 6 45 4.41	3	−0.074	+0.13
22	Feb. 8.0	23 14 37.585	+ 1 8 50.95	4	−0.092	+0.20
23	March 18.0	22 15 8.390	− 3 5 52.55	2	+0.210	−3.17
24	1847, Aug. 15.0	12 16 12.840	− 4 47 4.42	4	+0.052	+0.69
25	Sept. 23.0	12 43 32.402	−13 41 51.42	4	−0.203	+0.61
26	Nov. 15.0	12 36 33.246	− 3 37 36.16	5	+0.206	−0.82
27	1849, May 2.0	3 36 3.678	+21 41 22.91	5	+0.187	+0.09
28	June 8.0	2 49 10.035	+14 4 37.76	10	−0.087	+3.60
29	1850, Nov. 23.0	18 8 47.037	−26 55 13.20	3	−0.159	−2.65
30	Dec. 17.0	17 33 52.085	−21 38 46.95	2	−0.033	−0.47
31	1851, Jan. 20.0	17 20 48.740	−17 41 28.31	4	+0.296	−0.76
32	1852, July 10.0	8 24 23.066	+15 40 33.60	9	+0.010	+0.41
33	Aug. 16.0	7 25 42.850	+15 24 38.50	4	+0.182	−0.78
34	Sept. 5.0	8 4 29.218	+15 58 35.33	4	+0.126	−1.14
35	1854, Jan. 20.0	22 50 6.361	− 5 16 4.06	6	+0.061	−0.04
36	Feb. 3.0	23 6 4.528	− 0 31 39.68	3	+0.012	+1.67
37	Feb. 20.0	22 49 33.074	+ 1 19 46.87	5	+0.221	+0.45
38	1855, Aug. 18.0	12 20 36.824	− 5 57 52.34	7	+9.007	+0.32
39	Sept. 20.0	12 35 48.073	−12 52 25.49	5	+0.120	+2.32
40	Oct. 12.0	11 55 6.943	− 6 28 37.38	4	+0.076	−1.62
41	Nov. 16.0	12 36 57.050	− 3 23 38.41	5	+0.148	−0.90
42	1857, Feb. 16.0	0 49 21.025	+ 6 27 10.65	13	+0.063	+0.46
43	March 18.0	2 36 3.575	+19 31 12.35	5	−0.058	−0.37
44	April 16.0	3 35 55.521	+25 33 57.52	7	+0.027	−0.85
45	May 21.0	2 42 50.763	+16 59 35.65	8	+0.118	+0.56
46	June 13.0	2 50 26.725	+13 31 18.27	13	+0.020	+0.81

No.	Greenwich M. T.	App. R. A.	App. Dec.	No. Obs.	Δα	Δδ
	d	h m s	° ′ ″		s	″
47	1857, June 26.0	3 20 19.536	+ 11 46 46.18	12	+ 0.081	+ 1.07
48	1858, Aug. 17.0	12 21 4.321	− 2 10 32.51	9	− 0.139	+ 1.03
49	Sept. 18.0	11 31 57.511	− 17 21 17.46	4	− 0.058	− 1.56
50	Oct. 10.0	16 2 1.666	− 21 42 17.26	10	− 0.086	− 0.62
51	Nov. 7.0	17 37 19.017	− 28 1 51.96	11	+ 0.050	− 3.24
52	Nov. 29.0	17 55 9.651	− 25 51 31.11	9	+ 0.311	− 4.70
53	Dec. 21.0	17 7 52.455	− 20 4 43.46	4	+ 0.203	− 2.23
54	1859, Jan. 10.0	16 58 27.618	− 17 21 53.14	7	+ 0.051	+ 3.60
55	Jan. 29.0	17 40 25.353	− 18 26 8.21	8	+ 0.138	+ 0.17
56	1860, May 3.0	5 53 18.564	+ 26 36 37.27	4	+ 0.031	+ 1.43
57	May 23.0	7 16 2.843	+ 25 23 36.95	5	+ 0.012	+ 1.53
58	June 19.0	8 23 55.823	+ 19 58 30.44	5	+ 0.103	+ 2.43
59	July 10.0	8 11 15.899	+ 16 8 22.57	6	+ 0.103	+ 2.50
60	Aug. 31.0	7 48 10.699	+ 16 21 14.53	7	+ 0.203	+ 0.18
61	Sept. 22.0	9 1 57.720	+ 14 41 24.01	11	+ 0.174	− 0.67
62	1861, Dec. 10.0	20 31 32.810	− 21 9 42.34	4	− 0.020	− 1.44
63	Dec. 26.0	21 37 51.853	− 15 29 11.52	7	+ 0.036	− 1.41
64	1862, Jan. 16.0	22 38 24.381	− 6 59 2.66	9	+ 0.063	− 0.43
65	Feb. 12.0	22 50 59.987	+ 0 17 57.58	2	+ 0.201	− 2.41
66	March 11.0	21 58 59.897	− 3 59 31.67	5	+ 0.211	+ 3.72
67	April 23.0	23 14 6.685	− 4 20 27.06	9	+ 0.061	+ 0.09
68	May 13.0	0 26 3.479	+ 1 19 59.00	4	− 0.069	+ 2.83
69	1863, July 11.0	10 21 37.937	+ 10 53 34.89	7	− 0.014	+ 0.74
70	Aug. 1.0	11 35 5.496	+ 1 22 1.05	6	− 0.004	− 2.34
71	Aug. 12.0	12 4 25.882	− 3 26 49.57	7	+ 0.106	− 4.25
72	Sept. 1.0	12 35 55.785	− 10 23 46.78	6	− 0.108	+ 0.38
73	Sept. 19.0	12 24 54.206	− 11 49 46.67	6	+ 0.117	+ 1.85
74	Oct. 28.0	11 50 36.106	− 1 43 20.76	2	+ 0.117	− 3.63
75	Nov. 20.0	12 47 33.271	− 3 53 37.08	5	+ 0.202	− 2.15
76	1865, Feb. 13.0	0 38 41.720	+ 5 8 4.61	4	− 0.042	− 1.17
77	March 25.0	2 51 9.362	+ 21 44 33.17	7	− 0.008	+ 0.69
78	April 9.0	3 23 1.559	+ 24 46 29.99	10	+ 0.057	+ 0.96
79	April 25.0	3 20 45.253	+ 24 31 33.59	11	+ 0.102	− 0.08
80	May 7.0	2 56 28.204	+ 21 8 3.49	7	+ 0.201	+ 1.48
81	May 24.0	2 28 59.092	+ 14 58 17.96	9	+ 0.233	+ 1.59
82	June 11.0	2 42 18.347	+ 13 4 19.61	8	+ 0.208	+ 0.26
83	June 22.0	3 7 28.235	+ 14 5 20.47	7	+ 0.139	− 0.07
84	July 11.0	4 9 16.618	+ 17 22 1.01	9	+ 0.106	+ 0.31
85	1866, Sept. 25.0	15 1 14.407	− 20 15 30.52	3	+ 0.066	+ 0.55
86	Oct. 16.0	16 21 17.041	− 26 5 30.30	7	+ 0.017	− 1.53
87	Oct. 27.0	17 2 22.875	− 27 36 58.50	3	− 0.002	+ 0.46
88	Nov. 15.0	17 44 28.581	− 27 42 20.26	9	+ 0.208	− 0.31
89	Nov. 30.0	17 39 2.404	− 25 25 42.81	4	+ 0.417	+ 0.05
90	Dec. 28.0	16 41 36.668	− 18 5 53.53	2	+ 0.359	+ 0.19
91	1867, Feb. 7.0	18 9 47.537	− 19 2 58.09	6	+ 0.174	+ 1.04
92	March 30.0	21 52 48.772	− 12 51 21.47	2	+ 0.015	− 0.29
93	1868, May 6.0	6 7 11.831	+ 26 42 54.56	6	− 0.111	+ 0.76
94	May 19.0	7 0 21.501	+ 25 57 6.61	3	+ 0.051	+ 0.95
95	May 29.0	7 34 52.419	+ 24 29 40.91	4	+ 0.103	+ 0.74
96	June 12.0	8 8 50.822	+ 21 41 50.55	9	+ 0.059	+ 0.79
97	June 29.0	8 16 30.999	+ 18 13 10.72	7	+ 0.203	− 0.09
98	July 14.0	7 47 9.381	+ 16 9 52.23	6	+ 0.177	+ 1.23
99	July 28.0	7 14 21.065	+ 15 34 15.57	4	+ 0.173	− 1.35
100	Aug. 15.0	7 11 41.426	+ 16 13 52.99	1	+ 0.050	− 0.96
101	Aug. 26.0	7 32 23.633	+ 16 38 18.77	4	+ 0.104	+ 0.03
102	Sept. 4.0	7 57 43.509	+ 16 35 5.21	4	− 0.069	− 0.37
103	Sept. 18.0	8 46 43.419	+ 15 25 27.66	6	+ 0.001	− 0.63
104	1869, Dec. 1.0	19 55 0.743	− 23 33 19.35	2	+ 0.033	+ 0.09
105	Dec. 23.0	21 26 28.614	− 16 37 52.39	1	+ 0.038	+ 0.94
106	1870, Jan. 3.0	22 2 46.594	− 12 18 0.76	1	+ 0.092	+ 1.72
107	Jan. 27.0	22 48 13.855	− 3 24 26.46	4	+ 0.339	+ 2.61
108	Feb. 21.0	22 19 12.992	− 1 11 10.51	3	+ 0.257	+ 2.49
109	March 19.0	21 49 6.160	− 6 42 37.21	2	+ 0.195	+ 1.21
110	April 5.0	22 18 31.856	− 7 18 36.33	2	+ 0.087	+ 2.55
111	April 12.0	22 37 59.072	− 6 36 2.61	3	+ 0.266	+ 2.67
112	April 22.0	23 10 0.139	− 4 46 21.21	3	+ 0.060	+ 2.31

No.	Greenwich M. T.	App. R. A.	App. Dec.	No. Obs.	Δα	Δδ
	d	h m s	° ′ ″		s	″
113	1870, May 23.0	1 5 55.518	+ 4 51 43.03	7	+ 0.036	+ 0.63
114	June 13.0	2 33 32.558	+ 12 31 56.06	4	+ 0.118	— 0.12
115	July 13.0	4 53 4.820	+ 20 50 51.48	5	+ 0.017	+ 1.00
116	Aug. 8.0	7 5 26.170	+ 22 6 39.93	3	— 0.032	+ 1.00
117	Aug. 25.0	8 32 16.460	+ 19 12 2.24	5	— 0.107	+ 0.34
118	Sept. 15.0	10 11 53.930	+ 12 4 3.63	2	— 0.060	+ 0.89
119	Sept. 26.0	11 6 21.896	+ 7 13 14.51	5	— 0.026	+ 0.78
120	Oct. 12.0	12 19 50.532	— 0 31 51.43	5	— 0.170	+ 1.03
121	Nov. 1.0	13 52 35.280	— 10 11 46.16	4	— 0.157	— 0.24
122	Nov. 18.0	15 15 37.167	— 17 20 12.09	3	— 0.012	+ 1.06
123	Dec. 24.0	18 28 7.770	— 23 56 17.07	1	— 0.033	— 1.33
124	1871, Jan. 4.0	19 28 19.110	— 22 55 7.73	1	— 0.029	+ 1.12

No.	Washington M. T.	App. R. A.	App. Dec.	No. Obs.	Δα	Δδ
	d	h m s	° ′ ″		s	″
125	1863, Aug. 19.0	12 19 46.295	— 6 19 30.41	13	+ 0.078	+ 1.33
126	Sept. 12.0	12 31 6.510	— 12 5 21.23	9	+ 0.071	+ 1.08
127	Oct. 19.0	11 42 32.127	— 2 57 57.34	10	+ 0.236	— 0.91
128	Nov. 15.0	12 32 43.563	— 2 56 9.17	11	+ 0.071	+ 0.35
129	1865, Feb. 7.0	0 16 19.073	+ 2 10 43.90	6	+ 0.034	+ 0.11
130	Feb. 23.0	1 16 59.279	+ 10 9 15.81	4	— 0.039	+ 0.14
131	March 11.0	2 13 1.700	+ 17 6 32.28	8	+ 0.037	+ 1.02
132	March 28.0	3 2 8.034	+ 22 35 31.27	3	— 0.113	+ 1.20
133	April 18.0	3 26 40.672	+ 25 11 16.40	6	+ 0.010	+ 1.84
134	May 2.0	3 7 27.361	+ 22 47 40.20	4	+ 0.210	+ 0.61
135	May 18.0	2 31 22.761	+ 16 46 48.36	7	+ 0.091	+ 1.46
136	June 4.0	2 32 28.520	+ 13 9 9.64	8	+ 0.095	+ 0.42
137	June 26.0	3 19 28.164	+ 14 43 23.83	9	+ 0.079	0.00
138	July 20.0	4 45 13.373	+ 18 57 33.95	8	+ 0.080	+ 1.11
139	1866, Sept. 12.0	14 9 6.234	— 15 7 32.81	5	— 0.062	— 0.62
140	Oct. 6.0	15 46 27.321	— 23 49 35.82	4	— 0.031	— 0.75
141	Oct. 19.0	16 36 2.952	— 26 39 2.71	8	+ 0.061	— 2.11
142	Nov. 9.0	17 36 3.668	— 28 1 18.33	7	+ 0.134	— 1.56
143	Nov. 28.0	17 42 2.599	— 25 52 0.26	6	+ 0.385	— 1.88
144	Dec. 19.0	16 55 50.052	— 20 0 53.68	2	+ 0.570	+ 2.20
145	1867, Jan. 22.0	17 17 25.170	— 17 59 43.41	10	+ 0.222	— 0.14

Normals in the superior part of the Orbit.

No.	Greenwich M. T.	App. R. A.	App. Dec.	No. Obs.	Δα	Δδ
	d	h m s	° ′ ″		s	″
146	1858, Jan. 23.0	19 46 16.637	— 21 53 48.46	3	+ 0.022	— 2.26
147	April 23.0	2 56 59.252	+ 16 35 27.79	5	— 0.005	— 0.10
148	June 14.0	7 27 55.977	+ 23 33 18.26	13	+ 0.078	— 0.13
149	July 19.0	10 17 52.789	+ 12 10 47.22	5	— 0.035	+ 0.11
150	1859, Feb. 23.0	19 14 56.589	— 19 15 37.66	7	+ 0.022	— 0.82
151	March 18.0	20 57 4.220	— 16 11 30.29	6	+ 0.188	+ 2.39
152	June 17.0	3 46 35.988	+ 18 29 1.65	4	+ 0.033	— 0.40
153	July 19.0	6 31 41.515	+ 23 6 57.50	11	— 0.021	— 0.31
154	Aug. 23.0	9 32 0.652	+ 15 49 11.42	8	— 0.016	— 0.44
155	Nov. 13.0	16 1 34.918	— 20 45 38.42	5	+ 0.014	— 1.75
156	Dec. 17.0	19 5 56.987	— 23 55 27.75	4	+ 0.013	— 3.39
157	1860, Jan. 17.0	21 46 14.280	— 15 10 47.89	5	+ 0.016	— 2.66
158	Feb. 29.0	1 0 24.170	+ 6 15 55.78	3	— 0.062	— 0.77
159	April 19.0	4 48 31.013	+ 25 10 19.92	4	— 0.014	— 0.01
160	Oct. 21.0	11 13 17.826	+ 5 51 46.41	5	+ 0.086	— 0.82
161	Dec. 10.0	14 42 35.914	— 13 40 52.46	5	— 0.060	— 0.81
162	1867, May 14.0	1 11 9.973	+ 5 31 41.60	6	+ 0.113	+ 0.44
163	June 17.0	3 49 8.762	+ 18 38 58.87	5	+ 0.050	+ 1.11
164	Aug. 18.0	9 10 1.066	+ 17 23 44.04	6	— 0.059	+ 0.60
165	Oct. 15.0	13 41 6.075	— 9 28 37.18	4	+ 0.009	— 1.01

Normals in the superior part of the Orbit.

No.	Greenwich M. T.	App. R. A.	App. Dec.	No. Obs.	$\Delta\alpha$	$\Delta\delta$
	d	h m s	° ′ ″		s	″
166	1867, Nov. 19.0	16 36 3.118	−22 25 31.51	5	−0.007	−0.51
167	1868, Oct. 16.0	10 10 43.471	+8 38 39.82	9	+0.100	+0.01
168	Dec. 17.0	15 18 16.956	−16 23 36.95	6	+0.083	+0.83
169	1869, Jan. 12.0	17 32 57.506	−22 22 25.57	5	+0.050	−1.48
170	April 20.0	1 36 7.195	+8 43 59.95	6	−0.070	+0.55
171	June 17.0	6 29 55.781	+24 7 55.16	5	−0.020	+0.32
172	July 16.0	9 1 6.090	+18 33 2.87	4	−0.208	+0.78
173	Aug. 26.0	12 10 0.084	−0 7 34.79	5	−0.010	+0.29
174	Sept. 24.0	11 5 26.833	−13 7 17.72	4	−0.183	+1.02
175	Oct. 13.0	15 49 46.368	−21 42 44.87	5	−0.026	+1.43

In order to have as few unknown quantities, in the equations of condition, as possible, the differences $\Delta\alpha$ and $\Delta\delta$ have been changed into $\cos\eta . \Delta\theta$ and $\Delta\eta$; θ denoting the geocentric longitude of Venus referred to a plane drawn through the centre of the Earth parallel to the plane of the orbit of Venus, and η denoting the corresponding latitude. The formulæ used are given in WATSON's *Theoretical Astronomy*, pp. 153—159.

In the following equations, we have put

$$x = \Delta L'_0 - 2\sin^2\frac{i'}{2}\Delta\Omega', \qquad y = 100\,\Delta n', \qquad z = \Delta e', \qquad u = e'(\Delta\pi' - 2\sin^2\frac{i'}{2}\Delta\Omega'),$$

all expressed in seconds of arc; and x', y', z' and u' denote the similar quantities in reference to the solar elements. In the computation of the coefficients of the last, roughly approximate formulæ have been used.

A mean of the Transits of 1761 and 1769 gives

$$+0.992\,x - 0.839\,y + 1.61\,z + 1.17\,u + 1.00\,x' - 0.84\,y' + 0.83\,z' - 1.82\,u' = +1''.745.$$

The indeterminate correction of the Sun's semi-diameter nearly disappears from this mean.

The following equations of condition are numbered with the same number as the normals, from which they are derived. The last column contains the residuals which remain after the elements have been corrected as shown in the sequel.

Equations of condition.

No.	x	y	z	u	x'	y'	z'	u'			Residuals.
1	−0.40x	+0.05y	−0.36z	−1.44u	+1.43x'	−0.19y'	−0.21z'	−3.06u'	=	+1″.01	+0″.97
2	−1.37	+0.18	−0.87	−2.97	+2.41	−0.32	−1.45	−4.69	=	−0.95	−1.02
3	−2.05	+0.28	−0.87	−4.16	+3.08	−0.41	−2.17	−5.74	=	−0.69	−0.71
4	−2.07	+0.28	−0.02	−4.28	+3.11	−0.41	−2.65	−5.57	=	+3.37	+3.37
5	−0.80	+0.11	+0.31	−2.15	+1.80	−0.24	−2.22	−3.16	=	+1.41	+1.43
6	−0.31	+0.04	−0.42	+1.41	+1.30	−0.16	+1.86	+2.32	=	+1.27	+0.08
7	−0.98	+0.12	−0.93	+2.31	+1.98	−0.24	+3.56	+2.59	=	−0.23	−1.25
8	−2.27	+0.27	−2.31	+4.06	+3.27	−0.39	+5.84	+3.12	=	+1.48	−0.38
9	−2.44	+0.29	−3.04	+3.85	+3.40	−0.40	+6.26	+2.85	=	+3.13	+1.22
10	−1.70	+0.20	−2.53	+2.69	+2.70	−0.32	+5.18	+2.00	=	+1.13	−0.27
11	−0.90	+0.11	−1.76	+1.56	+1.91	−0.22	+3.05	+1.01	=	+0.96	+0.08
12	−2.06	+0.21	+3.53	−2.38	+3.08	−0.32	−6.12	−0.14	=	−1.66	−2.07
13	−2.51	+0.26	+4.64	−2.02	+3.51	−0.36	−7.01	+0.39	=	+0.29	−0.34
14	−2.00	+0.17	−4.12	−0.54	+3.00	−0.26	+4.57	−3.99	=	+0.22	−0.91
15	−2.09	+0.18	−4.05	−1.48	+3.10	−0.27	+4.28	−4.47	=	+4.08	+3.09
16	−1.12	+0.10	−2.39	−1.18	+2.12	−0.14	+2.72	−3.49	=	−0.59	−1.14
17	−2.69	+0.19	+3.71	+3.87	+3.69	−0.26	−1.82	+7.26	=	−2.09	−1.20
18	−1.58	+0.11	+1.80	+2.98	+2.58	−0.18	−0.65	+5.38	=	−0.63	−2.10
19	−0.27	+0.01	−0.63	−1.18	+1.27	−0.07	+0.21	−2.76	=	−0.81	−0.95
20	−2.40	+0.13	−0.41	−4.82	+3.40	−0.18	−2.47	+6.18	=	−0.57	−1.14

Equations of condition.

No.											Residuals.
										″	″
21	$-0.47x$	$+0.02y$	$-0.47z$	$+1.64u$	$+1.47x'$	$-0.06y'$	$+2.19z'$	$+2.48u'$	=	−0.98	−1.79
22	−1.54	+0.06	−1.31	+3.16	+2.54	−0.10	+1.37	+3.00	=	−1.19	−2.93
23	−1.95	+0.07	−2.61	+3.15	+2.95	−0.11	+5.79	+2.51	=	+1.84	−0.20
24	−0.40	+0.01	+1.03	−1.15	+1.40	−0.03	−2.79	−1.18	=	+0.42	+0.24
25	−2.29	+0.05	+3.87	−2.60	+3.28	−0.07	−6.58	−0.29	=	−2.95	−3.92
26	−0.55	+0.01	+1.78	−0.38	+1.55	−0.03	−3.33	+1.04	=	+3.15	+2.75
27	−2.22	+0.02	−4.51	−0.53	+3.22	−0.02	+4.94	−4.09	=	+2.47	+0.72
28	−1.22	+0.01	−2.59	−1.14	+2.22	−0.01	+3.02	−3.46	=	+0.04	−0.85
29	−1.55	−0.01	+2.84	+1.97	+2.55	+0.02	−2.07	+4.94	=	−2.24	−3.81
30	−2.73	−0.03	+3.75	+3.93	+3.72	+0.04	−2.06	+7.28	=	−0.41	−3.18
31	−0.88	−0.01	+1.17	+2.02	+1.88	+0.02	−1.96	+4.10	=	+4.28	+3.11
32	−2.18	−0.05	−1.24	−4.31	+3.18	+0.08	−1.77	−6.06	=	−0.38	−1.64
33	−1.26	−0.03	+0.04	−2.92	+2.26	+0.06	−2.00	−4.22	=	+2.07	+1.48
34	−0.44	−0.01	+0.19	−1.60	+1.44	+0.04	−1.92	−2.50	=	+1.59	+1.39
35	−0.68	−0.03	−0.51	+1.96	+1.68	+0.07	+2.58	+2.70	=	+0.46	−0.68
36	−1.37	−0.06	−1.02	+2.96	+2.37	+0.10	+3.95	+3.09	=	+0.71	−1.20
37	−2.43	−0.10	−2.15	+4.44	+3.42	+0.14	+5.83	+3.70	=	+2.52	−0.59
38	−0.54	−0.03	+1.14	−1.33	+1.54	+0.09	−3.10	−1.20	=	−0.19	−0.52
39	−2.27	−0.13	+3.71	−2.77	+3.27	+0.19	−6.49	−0.59	=	+0.25	−1.20
40	−2.32	−0.13	+4.26	−2.04	+3.27	+0.19	−6.59	−0.07	=	+1.34	−0.27
41	−0.46	−0.03	+1.64	−0.39	+1.46	+0.09	−3.12	+0.99	=	+2.17	+1.73
42	+0.13	+0.01	−0.89	+0.28	+0.87	+0.06	+1.91	+0.52	=	+1.01	+0.85
43	−0.25	−0.02	−1.34	+0.16	+1.24	+0.09	+2.71	−0.68	=	−0.68	−1.18
44	−1.37	−0.10	−3.10	+0.07	+2.37	+0.17	+4.12	−2.66	=	+0.01	−1.57
45	−2.17	−0.16	−4.30	−1.15	+3.17	+0.23	+4.76	−4.18	=	+1.79	−0.31
46	−0.86	−0.06	−2.06	−0.91	+1.86	+0.14	+2.50	−3.03	=	+0.55	−0.31
47	−0.41	−0.03	−1.38	−0.72	+1.41	+0.11	+1.57	−2.63	=	+1.49	+1.01
48	+0.28	+0.02	+0.81	−0.23	+0.72	+0.06	−1.45	−0.59	=	−2.32	−2,18
49	+0.13	+0.01	+0.92	+0.17	+0.87	+0.08	−1.91	+0.43	=	−0.21	−0.26
50	−0.05	0.00	+1.06	+0.48	+1.04	+0.09	−1.96	+1.41	=	−0.98	−1.26
51	−0.80	−0.07	+1.95	+1.04	+1.79	+0.16	−2.15	+3.30	=	+0.98	−0.08
52	−2.13	−0.19	+3.57	+2.60	+3.10	+0.28	−2.37	+5.96	=	+4.52	+1.97
53	−2.58	−0.23	+3.49	+3.83	+3.51	+0.32	−2.09	+6.93	=	+3.16	−0.06
54	−1.28	−0.12	+1.70	+2.46	+2.26	+0.20	−0.80	+4.79	=	+0.13	−1.67
55	−0.48	−0.04	+0.81	+1.49	+1.47	+0.13	+0.19	+3.29	=	+1.94	+1.03
56	+0.09	+0.01	−0.55	−0.78	+0.92	+0.09	+1.02	−1.78	=	+0.55	+0.58
57	−0.17	−0.02	−0.62	−1.07	+1.18	+0.12	+0.55	−2.81	=	+0.44	+0.27
58	−1.03	−0.11	−1.08	−2.31	+2.05	+0.21	−0.57	−4.25	=	+0.95	+0.14
59	−2.27	−0.24	−1.37	−4.41	+3.29	+0.35	−1.62	−6.32	=	+1.02	−0.62
60	−0.52	−0.05	+0.10	−1.72	+1.52	+0.16	−1.83	−2.76	=	+2.87	+2.49
61	−0.06	−0.01	+0.16	−1.09	+1.07	+0.11	−1.89	−1.47	=	+2.61	+2.58
62	+0.07	+0.01	−0.02	+1.02	+0.92	+0.11	+0.26	+2.12	=	−0.58	−0.88
63	−0.12	−0.01	−0.16	+1.21	+1.11	+0.13	+1.00	+2.37	=	+0.07	−0.48
64	−0.62	−0.07	−0.36	+1.89	+1.61	+0.19	+2.35	+2.74	=	+0.72	−0.48
65	−2.12	−0.26	−1.60	+4.07	+3.07	+0.37	+5.13	+3.73	=	+1.87	−1.35

Equations of condition.

No.										Residuals.
									″	″
66	−2.11x	−0.26y	−2.45z	+3.60u	+3.07x′	+0.37y′	+5.41z′	+3.15u′	= +4.21	+1.01
67	−0.23	−0.03	−0.97	+0.86	+1.22	+0.15	+2.71	+0.18	= +0.87	+0.23
68	+0.03	0.00	−0.80	+0.55	+0.96	+0.12	+2.05	−0.56	= +0.23	−0.06
69	+0.09	+0.01	+0.17	−0.82	+0.92	+0.12	−1.17	−1.65	= −0.45	−0.54
70	−0.17	−0.02	+0.73	−1.00	+1.18	+0.16	−2.14	−1.49	= +0.89	+0.73
71	−0.41	−0.05	+0.98	−1.22	+1.41	+0.19	−2.79	−1.31	= +3.22	+2.87
72	−1.19	−0.16	+1.98	−2.02	+2.20	+0.30	−4.49	−1.05	= −1.61	−2.63
73	−2.29	−0.31	+3.67	−2.89	+3.29	+0.45	−6.57	−0.78	= +0.77	−1.19
74	−1.43	−0.16	+2.56	−0.97	+2.14	+0.29	−4.55	+0.41	= +3.09	+1.95
75	−0.31	−0.04	+1.41	−0.36	+1.31	+0.18	−2.77	+1.06	= +3.64	+3.24
76	+0.13	+0.02	−0.88	+0.33	+0.97	+0.15	+1.93	+0.85	= −1.03	−1.21
77	−0.48	−0.07	−1.66	+0.23	+1.64	+0.25	+3.39	−0.81	= +0.13	−0.74
78	−1.09	−0.17	−2.64	+0.21	+2.25	+0.31	+4.25	−1.90	= +1.03	−0.58
79	−2.05	−0.32	−4.24	−0.17	+3.16	+0.18	+5.41	−3.27	= +1.30	−1.37
80	−2.51	−0.39	−4.99	−0.61	+3.50	+0.54	+5.80	−3.80	= +3.15	+0.05
81	−1.84	−0.28	−3.75	−1.02	+2.67	+0.41	+4.41	−3.24	= +3.72	+1.53
82	−0.78	−0.12	−2.03	−0.71	+1.64	+0.25	+2.66	−2.17	= +2.94	+1.95
83	−0.45	−0.07	−1.47	−0.65	+1.27	+0.20	+1.89	−2.22	= +1.89	+1.30
84	−0.07	−0.01	−0.98	−0.51	+0.94	+0.15	+0.91	−2.01	= +1.51	+1.32
85	+0.04	+0.01	+1.03	+0.20	+1.08	+0.18	−2.25	+0.55	= +0.69	+0.53
86	−0.24	−0.04	+1.28	+0.45	+1.39	+0.23	−2.49	+1.68	= +0.95	+0.41
87	−0.51	−0.09	+1.62	+0.66	+1.67	+0.28	−2.61	+2.47	= −0.10	−1.00
88	−1.36	−0.23	+2.76	+1.48	+2.52	+0.43	−2.92	+4.38	= +2.78	+0.78
89	−2.36	−0.40	+3.97	+2.75	+3.45	+0.58	−3.24	+6.23	= +5.62	+2.27
90	−1.95	−0.33	+2.75	+3.06	+2.73	+0.46	−2.12	+5.43	= +4.99	+2.07
91	−0.20	−0.03	+0.64	+1.14	+1.02	+0.17	+0.16	+2.49	= +2.58	+2.00
92	+0.24	+0.01	−0.01	+0.86	+0.66	+0.11	+1.23	+0.92	= +0.53	+0.47
93	+0.04	+0.01	−0.58	−0.82	+0.97	+0.18	+0.98	−1.93	= −1.45	−1.45
94	−0.14	−0.02	−0.64	−1.01	+1.15	+0.21	+0.65	−2.46	= +0.68	+0.49
95	−0.35	−0.06	−0.76	−1.27	+1.36	+0.25	+0.34	−2.95	= +1.31	+0.90
96	−0.81	−0.15	−1.05	−1.93	+1.83	+0.34	−0.20	−3.87	= +0.68	−0.18
97	−1.75	−0.32	−1.47	−3.45	+2.78	+0.51	−1.00	−5.52	= +2.86	+1.13
98	−2.47	−0.46	−1.39	−4.75	+3.49	+0.65	−1.61	−6.68	= +2.36	+0.02
99	−2.10	−0.39	−0.73	−4.28	+3.12	+0.58	−1.72	−5.98	= +2.60	+0.64
100	−1.05	−0.20	−0.11	−2.57	+2.06	+0.38	−1.67	−3.99	= +0.79	−0.19
101	−0.60	−0.11	+0.02	−1.85	+1.61	+0.30	−1.70	−3.02	= +1.48	+0.92
102	−0.35	−0.06	+0.06	−1.47	+1.35	+0.25	−1.75	−2.40	= −0.92	−1.26
103	−0.09	−0.02	+0.11	−1.13	+1.09	+0.20	−1.82	−1.62	= +0.20	+0.12
104	+0.12	+0.02	+0.09	+0.96	+0.87	+0.17	−0.09	+2.01	= +0.46	+0.23
105	−0.09	−0.02	−0.10	+1.21	+1.10	+0.22	+0.87	+2.40	= +0.79	+0.26
106	−0.32	−0.06	−0.20	+1.48	+1.31	+0.26	+1.49	+2.60	= +1.84	+0.95
107	−1.21	−0.25	−0.70	+2.81	+2.22	+0.44	+3.45	+3.30	= +5.70	+3.37
108	−2.63	−0.53	−2.15	+4.76	+3.58	+0.72	+5.86	+4.25	= +4.49	−0.01
109	−1.44	−0.29	−1.91	+2.58	+2.42	+0.49	+4.41	+2.42	= +3.11	+0.51
110	−0.63	−0.13	−1.27	+1.40	+1.62	+0.33	+3.31	+1.13	= +2.10	+0.78

Equations of condition.

No											Residuals.
										″	″
111	− 0.42x	− 0.09y	− 1.09z	+ 1.13u	+ 1.41x'	+ 0.29y'	+ 3.02z'	+ 0.72u'	=	+ 4.67	+ 3.68
112	− 0.20	− 0.01	− 0.92	+ 0.87	+ 1.20	+ 0.21	+ 2.65	+ 0.23	=	+ 1.74	+ 1.08
113	+ 0.11	+ 0.03	− 0.76	+ 0.16	+ 0.86	+ 0.17	+ 1.70	− 0.82	=	+ 0.76	+ 0.63
114	+ 0.24	+ 0.05	− 0.80	+ 0.21	+ 0.75	+ 0.15	+ 1.09	− 1.20	=	+ 1.98	+ 2.03
115	+ 0.39	+ 0.08	− 0.49	− 0.22	+ 0.68	+ 0.14	+ 0.24	− 1.39	=	+ 0.96	+ 1.27
116	+ 0.37	+ 0.08	− 0.55	− 0.61	+ 0.64	+ 0.13	− 0.42	− 1.24	=	− 0.50	− 0.12
117	+ 0.38	+ 0.08	− 0.29	− 0.77	+ 0.62	+ 0.13	− 0.77	− 1.00	=	− 1.55	− 1.11
118	+ 0.40	+ 0.08	+ 0.15	− 0.82	+ 0.60	+ 0.12	− 1.07	− 0.59	=	− 1.13	− 0.63
119	+ 0.41	+ 0.08	+ 0.33	− 0.77	+ 0.60	+ 0.12	− 1.16	− 0.31	=	− 0.66	− 0.17
120	+ 0.41	+ 0.09	+ 0.60	− 0.59	+ 0.59	+ 0.12	− 1.19	+ 0.28	=	− 2.75	− 2.27
121	+ 0.42	+ 0.09	+ 0.81	− 0.23	+ 0.58	+ 0.12	− 1.08	+ 0.48	=	− 2.23	− 1.81
122	+ 0.42	+ 0.09	+ 0.81	+ 0.12	+ 0.58	+ 0.12	− 0.85	+ 0.80	=	− 0.45	− 0.09
123	+ 0.42	+ 0.09	+ 0.43	+ 0.73	+ 0.57	+ 0.12	− 0.12	+ 1.16	=	− 0.14	− 0.21
124	+ 0.42	+ 0.09	+ 0.22	+ 0.82	+ 0.57	+ 0.12	+ 0.14	+ 1.16	=	− 0.25	− 0.05
125	− 0.62	− 0.08	+ 1.24	− 1.44	+ 1.63	+ 0.22	− 3.30	− 1.23	=	+ 0.50	− 0.03
126	− 1.88	− 0.26	+ 2.98	− 3.12	+ 2.88	+ 0.39	− 5.80	− 0.87	=	+ 0.49	− 1.02
127	− 1.65	− 0.21	+ 3.29	− 1.47	+ 2.65	+ 0.37	− 5.52	+ 0.04	=	+ 3.61	+ 2.02
128	− 0.43	− 0.06	+ 1.57	− 0.43	+ 1.43	+ 0.20	− 3.07	+ 0.93	=	+ 0.82	+ 0.31
129	+ 0.18	+ 0.03	− 0.85	+ 0.36	+ 0.81	+ 0.12	+ 1.70	+ 0.76	=	+ 0.51	+ 0.43
130	+ 0.06	+ 0.01	− 1.00	+ 0.24	+ 0.96	+ 0.14	+ 2.18	+ 0.27	=	− 0.35	− 0.56
131	− 0.15	− 0.02	− 1.22	+ 0.19	+ 1.15	+ 0.17	+ 2.58	− 0.38	=	+ 0.88	+ 0.42
132	− 0.57	− 0.09	− 1.81	+ 0.19	+ 1.56	+ 0.24	+ 3.19	− 1.29	=	− 1.10	− 2.05
133	− 1.62	− 0.25	− 3.52	+ 0.03	+ 2.67	+ 0.41	+ 4.51	− 2.92	=	+ 0.68	− 1.50
134	− 2.41	− 0.37	− 4.84	− 0.46	+ 3.57	+ 0.55	+ 5.16	− 4.03	=	+ 3.34	+ 0.29
135	− 2.21	− 0.34	− 4.40	− 1.02	+ 3.22	+ 0.49	+ 4.97	− 4.07	=	+ 1.74	− 0.93
136	− 1.18	− 0.18	− 2.60	− 0.95	+ 2.18	+ 0.34	+ 3.20	− 3.21	=	+ 1.44	0.00
137	− 0.35	− 0.05	− 1.32	− 0.63	+ 1.36	+ 0.21	+ 1.51	− 2.54	=	+ 1.09	+ 0.56
138	+ 0.02	0.00	− 0.83	+ 0.52	+ 0.97	+ 0.15	+ 0.35	− 2.12	=	+ 1.32	+ 1.23
139	+ 0.15	+ 0.03	+ 0.92	+ 0.09	+ 0.84	+ 0.14	− 1.89	+ 0.22	=	− 0.60	− 0.59
140	− 0.07	− 0.01	+ 1.10	+ 0.35	+ 1.07	+ 0.18	− 2.09	+ 1.26	=	− 0.20	− 0.50
141	− 0.30	− 0.05	+ 1.35	+ 0.52	+ 1.29	+ 0.22	− 2.13	+ 1.99	=	+ 1.23	+ 0.64
142	− 1.01	− 0.17	+ 2.28	+ 1.15	+ 2.00	+ 0.31	− 2.30	+ 3.70	=	+ 2.00	+ 0.49
143	− 2.22	− 0.38	+ 3.80	+ 2.57	+ 3.21	+ 0.51	− 2.63	+ 6.05	=	+ 5.49	+ 2.34
144	− 2.54	− 0.43	+ 3.66	+ 3.57	+ 3.51	+ 0.60	− 2.36	+ 6.78	=	+ 7.55	+ 3.84
145	− 0.61	− 0.10	+ 1.02	+ 1.61	+ 1.60	+ 0.27	− 1.65	+ 3.56	=	+ 3.16	+ 1.98
146	+ 0.42	+ 0.03	+ 0.30	+ 0.80	+ 0.58	+ 0.05	+ 0.38	+ 1.13	=	0.00	− 0.06
147	+ 0.41	+ 0.03	− 0.80	− 0.24	+ 0.59	+ 0.05	+ 1.02	− 0.58	=	− 0.11	+ 0.11
148	+ 0.39	+ 0.03	− 0.04	− 0.83	+ 0.62	+ 0.05	+ 0.06	− 1.26	=	+ 1.08	+ 1.40
149	+ 0.31	+ 0.03	+ 0.56	− 0.61	+ 0.66	+ 0.06	− 0.81	− 1.12	=	− 0.51	− 0.25
150	− 0.02	0.00	+ 0.38	+ 1.00	+ 1.04	+ 0.10	+ 1.03	+ 2.11	=	+ 0.79	+ 0.40
151	+ 0.16	+ 0.01	+ 0.12	+ 0.89	+ 0.83	+ 0.08	+ 1.43	+ 1.18	=	+ 3.21	+ 3.00
152	+ 0.38	+ 0.01	− 0.83	− 0.03	+ 0.62	+ 0.06	+ 0.61	− 1.11	=	+ 0.34	+ 0.49
153	+ 0.40	+ 0.01	− 0.58	− 0.59	+ 0.60	+ 0.06	− 0.13	− 1.19	=	− 0.29	0.00
154	+ 0.42	+ 0.01	+ 0.06	+ 0.83	+ 0.59	+ 0.06	− 0.83	− 0.83	=	− 0.08	− 0.03
155	+ 0.42	+ 0.01	+ 0.72	+ 0.43	+ 0.58	+ 0.06	− 0.81	+ 0.85	=	+ 1.01	+ 1.21

Equations of condition.

No.											Residuals
										″	″
156	$+0.41x$	$+0.01y$	$-0.25z$	$-0.81u$	$+0.59x'$	$+0.06y'$	$-0.10z'$	$+1.21u'$	=	+ 0.38	+ 0.75
157	+ 0.39	+ 0.01	− 0.41	+ 0.72	+ 0.60	+ 0.06	+ 0.65	+ 1.08	=	− 0.61	− 0.57
158	+ 0.35	+ 0.04	− 0.85	+ 0.04	+ 0.65	+ 0.07	+ 1.38	+ 0.24	=	− 1.16	− 1.04
159	+ 0.19	+ 0.02	− 0.61	− 0.65	+ 0.81	+ 0.08	+ 1.26	− 1.29	=	− 0.19	− 0.07
160	+ 0.21	+ 0.02	+ 0.35	− 0.80	+ 0.77	+ 0.08	− 1.76	− 0.15	=	+ 1.50	+ 1.69
161	+ 0.34	+ 0.04	+ 0.81	− 0.24	+ 0.66	+ 0.07	− 0.94	+ 1.06	=	− 0.53	− 0.30
162	+ 0.31	+ 0.06	− 0.63	+ 0.52	+ 0.66	+ 0.11	+ 1.25	− 0.55	=	+ 1.72	+ 1.80
163	+ 0.38	+ 0.07	− 0.82	− 0.05	+ 0.62	+ 0.11	+ 0.60	− 1.10	=	+ 0.98	+ 1.22
164	+ 0.42	+ 0.07	− 0.02	− 0.85	+ 0.59	+ 0.10	− 0.75	− 0.90	=	− 0.97	− 0.50
165	+ 0.42	+ 0.07	+ 0.83	− 0.13	+ 0.58	+ 0.10	− 1.13	+ 0.28	=	+ 0.52	+ 0.89
166	+ 0.41	+ 0.07	+ 0.64	+ 0.55	+ 0.58	+ 0.10	− 0.70	+ 0.95	=	+ 0.01	+ 0.24
167	+ 0.17	+ 0.03	+ 0.29	− 0.85	+ 0.83	+ 0.16	− 1.81	− 0.43	=	+ 1.38	+ 1.57
168	+ 0.35	+ 0.07	+ 0.82	− 0.10	+ 0.65	+ 0.12	− 1.16	+ 0.75	=	+ 0.61	+ 0.90
169	+ 0.38	+ 0.07	+ 0.75	+ 0.38	+ 0.61	+ 0.12	− 0.07	+ 1.29	=	+ 0.85	+ 1.09
170	+ 0.42	+ 0.08	− 0.79	+ 0.24	+ 0.58	+ 0.11	+ 1.10	− 0.35	=	− 0.73	− 0.48
171	+ 0.42	+ 0.08	− 0.35	− 0.76	+ 0.59	+ 0.11	+ 0.18	− 1.15	=	− 0.27	+ 0.20
172	+ 0.42	+ 0.08	+ 0.27	− 0.81	+ 0.58	+ 0.11	− 0.50	− 1.05	=	− 3.06	− 2.55
173	+ 0.38	+ 0.07	+ 0.79	− 0.27	+ 0.62	+ 0.12	− 1.27	− 0.50	=	− 0.26	+ 0.10
174	+ 0.31	+ 0.06	+ 0.81	+ 0.20	+ 0.64	+ 0.13	− 1.35	+ 0.18	=	− 2.86	− 2.65
175	+ 0.32	+ 0.06	+ 0.65	+ 0.55	+ 0.68	+ 0.13	− 1.25	+ 0.80	=	− 0.73	− 0.60

The equations derived from the latitudes η contain two more unknown quantities,

$$v = \Delta i' \quad , \quad w = \sin i' . \Delta \Omega',$$

but in them the variation of the solar elements will be neglected.

The mean of the Transits of 1761 and 1769 gives

$$-0.059\,x + 0.050\,y - 0.095\,z - 0.069\,u + 0.00\,v + 1.000\,w = -1''.165.$$

From this mean the indeterminate correction of the Sun's semi-diameter is nearly eliminated.

Equations of condition.

No.								
								″
1	$-0.01x$	$+0.00y$	$-0.01z$	$+0.00u$	$+0.61v$	$+1.24w$	=	+ 0.82
2	− 0.10	+ 0.01	− 0.21	− 0.08	− 0.36	+ 1.95	=	+ 0.41
3	− 0.12	+ 0.02	− 0.31	− 0.11	− 1.09	+ 2.04	=	− 0.49
4	+ 0.17	− 0.02	− 0.41	+ 0.25	− 2.13	+ 0.88	=	− 0.14
5	+ 0.20	− 0.03	− 0.37	+ 0.17	− 1.60	− 0.40	=	− 1.51
6	+ 0.09	− 0.01	− 0.14	− 0.10	+ 0.12	− 1.35	=	+ 0.02
7	+ 0.20	− 0.02	− 0.23	− 0.35	+ 1.17	− 1.42	=	+ 5.62
8	+ 0.19	− 0.02	− 0.30	− 0.49	+ 2.32	− 0.77	=	+ 1.54
9	− 0.14	+ 0.02	− 0.54	− 0.16	+ 2.42	+ 0.46	=	+ 0.64
10	− 0.23	+ 0.03	− 0.54	− 0.07	+ 1.88	+ 1.10	=	− 1.70
11	− 0.18	+ 0.02	− 0.36	− 0.10	+ 1.05	+ 1.38	=	− 1.48
12	− 0.22	+ 0.02	− 0.01	− 0.58	− 2.34	− 0.09	=	− 1.49
13	+ 0.11	− 0.01	− 0.33	− 0.36	− 2.06	− 1.55	=	+ 1.04
14	+ 0.12	− 0.01	+ 0.21	− 0.24	+ 1.57	+ 1.68	=	+ 0.34
15	+ 0.03	0.00	− 0.02	− 0.09	+ 0.06	+ 2.34	=	+ 0.63

Equations of condition.

No.								″
16	+ 0.02x	0.00y	+ 0.01z	+ 0.05u	− 0.75v	+ 1.69w	=	− 0.77
17	+ 0.01	0.00	− 0.07	+ 0.04	+ 0.27	− 2.68	=	+ 2.21
18	− 0.15	+ 0.01	− 0.12	+ 0.32	+ 1.60	− 1.45	=	+ 0.21
19	+ 0.01	0.00	+ 0.02	0.00	+ 0.78	+ 0.97	=	+ 1.13
20	+ 0.10	0.00	− 0.38	+ 0.18	− 2.05	+ 1.36	=	− 0.77
21	+ 0.11	0.00	− 0.17	− 0.11	+ 0.33	− 1.45	=	+ 0.53
22	+ 0.23	− 0.01	− 0.28	− 0.45	+ 1.63	− 1.35	=	+ 0.73
23	− 0.23	+ 0.01	− 0.57	− 0.06	+ 2.13	+ 0.86	=	− 4.07
24	− 0.13	0.00	− 0.12	− 0.25	− 0.86	+ 1.09	=	+ 0.95
25	− 0.17	0.00	− 0.07	− 0.56	− 2.43	− 0.35	=	− 0.67
26	+ 0.07	0.00	− 0.09	− 0.11	+ 0.09	− 1.54	=	+ 0.53
27	+ 0.10	0.00	+ 0.18	− 0.24	+ 1.52	+ 1.83	=	− 0.65
28	+ 0.01	0.00	0.00	+ 0.02	− 0.62	+ 1.79	=	+ 3.82
29	− 0.06	0.00	+ 0.14	− 0.05	− 1.03	− 1.91	=	− 2.56
30	0.00	0.00	− 0.07	+ 0.07	+ 0.49	− 2.67	=	− 0.52
31	− 0.15	0.00	− 0.15	+ 0.29	+ 1.60	− 0.73	=	− 0.13
32	− 0.10	0.00	− 0.30	− 0.06	− 1.04	+ 2.13	=	+ 0.55
33	+ 0.21	+ 0.01	− 0.38	+ 0.27	− 1.92	+ 0.18	=	− 0.52
34	+ 0.16	0.00	− 0.30	+ 0.10	− 1.27	− 0.63	=	− 0.79
35	+ 0.14	+ 0.01	− 0.21	− 0.20	+ 0.59	− 1.54	=	− 0.38
36	+ 0.22	+ 0.01	− 0.27	− 0.39	+ 1.41	− 1.47	=	+ 1.29
37	+ 0.16	+ 0.01	− 0.37	− 0.14	+ 2.39	− 0.81	=	− 0.72
38	− 0.16	− 0.01	− 0.12	− 0.30	− 0.98	+ 1.12	=	+ 0.33
39	− 0.18	− 0.01	− 0.09	− 0.56	− 2.43	− 0.21	=	+ 2.84
40	+ 0.17	+ 0.01	− 0.42	− 0.29	− 1.88	− 1.59	=	− 1.00
41	+ 0.06	0.00	− 0.08	− 0.10	+ 0.20	− 1.44	=	+ 0.10
42	+ 0.06	0.00	− 0.06	− 0.11	+ 0.31	− 0.86	=	+ 0.03
43	+ 0.13	+ 0.01	+ 0.04	− 0.25	+ 1.18	− 0.46	=	+ 0.64
44	+ 0.18	+ 0.01	+ 0.22	− 0.32	+ 1.78	+ 0.86	=	− 0.92
45	− 0.05	0.00	− 0.03	− 0.14	+ 0.33	+ 2.36	=	− 0.04
46	+ 0.02	0.00	+ 0.01	+ 0.05	− 0.80	+ 1.48	=	+ 0.66
47	+ 0.05	0.00	− 0.01	+ 0.10	− 1.04	+ 0.90	=	+ 0.64
48	− 0.03	0.00	− 0.05	− 0.05	+ 0.03	+ 0.70	=	+ 0.07
49	− 0.07	− 0.01	− 0.02	− 0.13	− 0.68	+ 0.61	=	− 1.75
50	− 0.09	− 0.01	+ 0.09	− 0.16	− 1.15	+ 0.14	=	− 0.90
51	− 0.11	− 0.01	+ 0.19	− 0.12	− 1.37	− 1.06	=	− 3.16
52	− 0.03	0.00	+ 0.09	− 0.03	− 0.71	− 2.35	=	− 4.41
53	− 0.03	0.00	− 0.07	+ 0.13	+ 0.84	− 2.49	=	− 1.78
54	− 0.14	− 0.01	− 0.10	+ 0.29	+ 1.54	− 1.26	=	+ 3.67
55	− 0.12	− 0.01	− 0.14	+ 0.19	+ 1.15	− 0.21	=	+ 0.35
56	+ 0.04	0.00	+ 0.06	− 0.05	+ 0.93	+ 0.14	=	+ 1.39
57	+ 0.03	0.00	+ 0.05	− 0.02	+ 0.90	+ 0.79	=	+ 1.57
58	− 0.05	0.00	− 0.10	− 0.02	+ 0.18	+ 1.80	=	+ 2.67
59	− 0.08	− 0.01	− 0.30	− 0.03	− 1.11	+ 2.13	=	+ 2.72
60	+ 0.16	+ 0.02	− 0.31	+ 0.13	− 1.37	− 0.50	=	+ 0.58

Equations of condition.

No.								″
61	+ 0.10x	+ 0.01y	− 0.19z	− 0.01u	− 0.63v	− 0.90w	=	− 0.01
62	0.00	0.00	− 0.01	0.00	− 0.70	− 0.73	=	− 1.35
63	+ 0.04	0.00	− 0.07	− 0.02	− 0.37	+ 1.15	=	− 1.50
64	+ 0.13	+ 0.01	− 0.20	− 0.17	+ 0.44	− 1.54	=	− 0.74
65	+ 0.22	+ 0.03	− 0.34	− 0.47	+ 2.04	− 1.19	=	− 3.38
66	− 0.21	− 0.03	− 0.59	− 0.02	+ 2.26	+ 0.54	=	+ 2.46
67	− 0.08	− 0.01	− 0.14	− 0.09	+ 0.16	+ 1.25	=	− 0.29
68	− 0.03	0.00	− 0.03	− 0.05	− 0.40	+ 0.89	=	+ 3.00
69	− 0.04	0.00	− 0.07	− 0.03	+ 0.26	+ 0.90	=	+ 0.62
70	− 0.07	− 0.01	− 0.09	− 0.11	− 0.36	+ 1.15	=	− 2.16
71	− 0.14	− 0.02	− 0.13	− 0.25	− 0.80	+ 1.15	=	− 3.21
72	− 0.23	− 0.03	− 0.07	− 0.49	− 1.74	+ 0.76	=	− 0.32
73	− 0.17	− 0.02	− 0.12	− 0.56	− 2.41	− 0.21	=	+ 2.40
74	+ 0.16	+ 0.02	− 0.28	− 0.18	− 0.74	− 1.75	=	− 2.59
75	+ 0.04	+ 0.01	− 0.05	− 0.07	+ 0.33	− 1.30	=	− 0.70
76	+ 0.06	+ 0.01	− 0.07	− 0.10	+ 0.26	− 0.86	=	− 0.80
77	+ 0.16	+ 0.02	+ 0.09	− 0.30	+ 1.43	− 0.21	=	+ 0.69
78	+ 0.19	+ 0.03	+ 0.21	− 0.34	+ 1.75	+ 0.50	=	+ 0.68
79	+ 0.18	+ 0.02	+ 0.20	− 0.30	+ 1.72	+ 1.54	=	− 0.50
80	+ 0.01	0.00	+ 0.03	− 0.17	+ 1.22	+ 2.20	=	+ 0.45
81	− 0.04	− 0.01	− 0.03	− 0.09	+ 0.07	+ 2.22	=	+ 0.26
82	+ 0.02	0.00	+ 0.01	+ 0.04	− 0.76	+ 1.50	=	− 0.82
83	+ 0.04	+ 0.01	0.00	+ 0.08	− 0.99	+ 1.02	=	− 0.72
84	+ 0.05	+ 0.01	− 0.04	+ 0.10	− 1.06	+ 0.30	=	− 0.07
85	− 0.08	− 0.01	+ 0.01	− 0.16	− 0.88	+ 0.49	=	+ 0.83
86	− 0.11	− 0.02	+ 0.12	− 0.17	− 1.29	− 0.09	=	− 1.35
87	− 0.12	− 0.02	+ 0.17	− 0.16	− 1.41	− 0.56	=	+ 0.45
88	− 0.10	− 0.02	+ 0.20	− 0.09	− 1.26	− 1.63	=	− 0.07
89	− 0.03	0.00	+ 0.07	− 0.01	− 0.61	− 2.49	=	+ 0.58
90	− 0.09	− 0.02	− 0.05	+ 0.23	+ 1.23	− 2.00	=	+ 1.14
91	− 0.11	− 0.02	− 0.17	+ 0.15	+ 1.24	+ 0.17	=	+ 0.70
92	− 0.04	− 0.01	− 0.07	− 0.03	+ 0.01	+ 0.75	=	− 0.49
93	+ 0.04	+ 0.01	+ 0.06	− 0.05	+ 0.96	+ 0.26	=	+ 0.83
94	+ 0.03	+ 0.01	+ 0.06	− 0.02	+ 0.95	+ 0.69	=	+ 0.99
95	+ 0.02	0.00	+ 0.04	− 0.01	+ 0.82	+ 1.06	=	+ 0.89
96	− 0.02	0.00	− 0.04	0.00	+ 0.44	+ 1.61	=	+ 0.92
97	− 0.09	− 0.02	− 0.21	− 0.05	− 0.41	+ 2.14	=	+ 0.44
98	− 0.03	0.00	− 0.31	+ 0.05	− 1.44	+ 2.02	=	+ 1.56
99	+ 0.14	+ 0.03	− 0.33	+ 0.27	− 1.96	+ 1.25	=	− 1.15
100	+ 0.20	+ 0.04	− 0.34	+ 0.26	− 1.79	+ 0.12	=	− 0.91
101	+ 0.17	+ 0.03	− 0.31	+ 0.17	− 1.48	− 0.35	=	+ 0.19
102	+ 0.14	+ 0.03	− 0.27	+ 0.09	− 1.18	− 0.62	=	− 0.52
103	+ 0.10	+ 0.02	− 0.20	0.00	− 0.72	− 0.86	=	− 0.60
104	− 0.01	0.00	+ 0.01	0.00	− 0.79	− 0.52	=	+ 0.02
105	+ 0.03	+ 0.01	− 0.06	− 0.01	− 0.43	− 1.12	=	+ 0.74

Equations of condition.

No.								″
106	+ 0.07x	+ 0.01y	− 0.13z	− 0.06u	− 0.08v	− 1.38w	=	+ 1.18
107	+ 0.20	+ 0.04	− 0.28	− 0.33	+ 1.14	− 1.61	=	+ 0.54
108	+ 0.05	+ 0.01	− 0.16	− 0.30	+ 2.17	− 0.62	=	+ 0.96
109	− 0.24	− 0.05	− 0.53	0.00	+ 1.77	+ 0.91	=	+ 0.22
110	− 0.16	− 0.03	− 0.31	− 0.07	+ 0.88	+ 1.27	=	+ 1.94
111	− 0.12	− 0.02	− 0.23	− 0.09	+ 0.56	+ 1.28	=	+ 1.03
112	− 0.08	− 0.02	− 0.14	− 0.09	+ 0.16	+ 1.20	=	+ 1.81
113	− 0.01	0.00	− 0.01	− 0.03	− 0.57	+ 0.65	=	+ 0.34
125	− 0.17	− 0.02	− 0.12	− 0.33	− 1.12	+ 1.08	=	+ 1.69
126	− 0.23	− 0.03	− 0.07	− 0.49	− 2.24	+ 0.23	=	+ 1.42
127	+ 0.19	+ 0.03	− 0.39	− 0.22	− 1.30	− 1.73	=	+ 0.59
128	+ 0.06	+ 0.01	− 0.08	− 0.10	+ 0.16	− 1.43	=	+ 0.76
129	+ 0.05	+ 0.01	− 0.07	− 0.08	+ 0.11	− 0.85	=	− 0.11
130	+ 0.08	+ 0.01	− 0.05	− 0.16	+ 0.56	− 0.85	=	+ 0.64
131	+ 0.12	+ 0.02	+ 0.01	− 0.24	+ 1.03	− 0.61	=	+ 0.74
132	+ 0.17	+ 0.02	+ 0.12	− 0.31	+ 1.51	− 0.08	=	+ 1.60
133	+ 0.18	+ 0.03	+ 0.24	− 0.33	+ 1.81	+ 1.08	=	+ 1.68
134	+ 0.07	+ 0.01	+ 0.13	− 0.29	+ 1.47	+ 1.98	=	− 0.50
135	− 0.06	− 0.01	− 0.05	− 0.18	+ 0.46	+ 2.31	=	+ 0.90
136	− 0.01	0.00	0.00	− 0.01	− 0.51	+ 1.80	=	− 0.11
137	+ 0.05	+ 0.01	− 0.01	+ 0.09	− 1.03	+ 0.84	=	− 0.35
138	+ 0.05	+ 0.01	− 0.06	+ 0.09	− 0.99	+ 0.03	=	+ 0.88
139	− 0.06	− 0.01	− 0.02	− 0.12	− 0.56	+ 0.66	=	− 0.91
140	− 0.09	− 0.02	+ 0.07	− 0.17	− 1.13	+ 0.23	=	− 0.84
141	− 0.11	− 0.02	+ 0.14	− 0.17	− 1.34	− 0.22	=	− 1.90
142	− 0.11	− 0.02	+ 0.21	− 0.11	− 1.37	− 1.26	=	− 1.37
143	− 0.04	− 0.01	+ 0.11	− 0.05	− 0.77	− 2.38	=	− 0.65
144	− 0.03	− 0.01	− 0.05	+ 0.12	+ 0.77	− 2.51	=	+ 3.52
145	− 0.14	− 0.02	− 0.14	+ 0.24	+ 1.48	− 0.50	=	+ 0.28

To apply to these equations the rigorous method of least squares would be very laborious: hence a method of "Equivalent Factors" has been used; the equations have been multiplied either by whole numbers or by fractions which are ready multipliers. In this way, the following *Normal Equations* were derived from the equations of condition which have $\cos\eta . \Delta\theta$ for their absolute terms,

								″
+195.84x	−44.809y	+127.71z	+ 73.19u	−251.90x′	+43.027y′	− 85.48z′	+119.25u′	= − 8.77
− 44.78	+47.099	− 83.68	− 62.84	+ 41.04	−48.460	+ 41.17	− 96.06	= −113.43
+120.94	−83.889	+427.28	+133.17	−136.59	+82.936	−410.76	+400·15	= +162.30
+ 70.03	−62.965	+135.64	+365.81	− 73.13	+63.350	+114.76	+508.04	= +197.06
−255.15	+42.172	−138.12	− 80.06	+425.61	−27.182	+ 91.22	−132.67	= + 92.63
+ 40.68	−48.373	+ 82.84	+ 61.99	− 26.27	+51.815	− 41.45	+ 94.13	= +121.18
− 83.42	+41.537	−422.53	+119.76	+102.83	−40.091	+644.06	−111.82	= − 23.87
+112.81	−95.792	+406.68	+505.65	−126.69	+94.621	−120.34	+902.21	= +264.18

If u is eliminated from these equations, the result is

+181.83x	−32.213y	+100.57z	−237.27x'	+30.352y'	−108.44z'	+ 17.60u'	= − 48″.20
− 32.75	+36.284	− 60.38	+ 28.48	−37.577	+ 60.88	− 8.78	= − 79.58
+ 95.45	−60.971	+377.90	−109.97	+59.874	−452.54	+215.20	= + 90.56
−239.82	+28.394	−108.43	+409.63	−13.317	+116.34	− 21.48	= +135.76
+ 28.81	−37.705	+ 59.85	− 13.88	+41.080	− 60.90	+ 8.04	= + 87.79
−106.35	+62.147	−466.94	+126.77	−60.831	+606.49	−278.15	= − 88.38
+ 16.01	− 8.770	+219.18	− 25.60	+ 7.053	−278.97	+199.94	= − 8.21

And if from these z is eliminated, the result is

+156.43x	−15.987y	−208.00x'	+14.418y'	+11.99z'	−39.67u'	= − 72″.30
− 17.50	+26.542	+ 10.91	−28.055	−11.42	+25.60	= − 65.11
−212.43	+10.900	+378.08	+ 3.863	−13.51	+40.27	= +161.74
+ 13.69	−28.049	+ 3.54	+31.598	+10.77	−26.04	= + 73.45
+ 11.59	−13.190	− 9.11	+13.151	+47.33	−12.25	= + 23.52
− 39.35	+26.593	+ 38.18	−27.674	−16.50	+75.13	= − 61.46

It is evident now, that since the principal co-efficients of z' and u' have fallen from 644.06 and 902.21 to 47.33 and 75.13, no very reliable values of these quantities can be obtained from these equations. The elimination of y gives

+145.89x	−201.43x'	− 2.480y'	+ 5.11z'	−24.25u'	= −111″.52
−205.24	+373.60	+15.384	− 8.82	+29.76	= +188.48
− 4.80	− 15.07	+ 1.950	− 1.30	− 1.01	= + 4.64
+ 2.89	− 3.69	− 0.791	+41.65	+ 0.47	= − 6.84
− 21.82	+ 27.25	+ 0.435	− 5.06	+49.48	= + 3.78

The elimination of x from these gives

+90.23x'	+11.895y'	− 1.63z'	− 4.35u'	= +31″.63
+ 8.44	+ 1.868	− 1.13	+ 0.21	= + 0.97
+ 0.30	− 0.742	+41.55	+ 0.95	= − 6.63
− 2.88	+ 0.064	− 4.30	+45.85	= −12.89

The elimination of x' from these gives

+0.755y'	− 0.98z'	+ 0.62u'	= − 1″.99
−0.782	+41.56	+ 0.96	= − 6.74
+0.444	− 4.35	+45.71	= −11.88

The only condition, relative to the solar elements, which can be obtained with any weight, from these equations, is

$$x' + 0.132\,y' = +\,0''.335.$$

That is, the mean longitude of the Sun of HANSEN and OLUFSEN's Tables ought to be increased by a third of a second at the epoch 1863. As, however, these Tables will, probably, be used, for a long time to come, in computing the solar coördinates of the *American Ephemeris*, y', z' and u' will be put severally equal to zero; and as it has been decided to use the Pulkova constant of aberration, x' will be put equal to $+\,0''.19$. With these assumptions, the values of x, y, z and u are

$$x = -\,0''.502,\quad y = -\,2''.863,\quad z = -\,0''.040,\quad u = +\,0''.195.$$

The equation of condition derived from the Transits of 1761 and 1769 being excluded, the normal equations, determining the corrections of the inclination and the longitude of the ascending node, are

+ 2.51 x	+ 0.390 y	+ 1.84 z	− 0.67 u	+ 163.26 v	− 0.42 w	= + 26″.02
− 4.46	− 0.105	− 0.29	− 1.06	− 5.86	+ 188.58	= + 24 .11

From these are obtained the following values of v and w.

$$v = +0''.18, \quad w = +0''.12 \text{ or } \Delta \Omega' = +2''.0.$$

But from the equation furnished by the Transits in 1761 and 1769,

$$\Delta \Omega' = -17''.84.$$

If the first result is supposed to belong to 1855.0, and the second to 1765.4, the proper value of the correction is

$$\Delta \Omega' = +0''.9 + 0''.222\, t.$$

The origin of the pretty large correction $-0''.02863$, of the mean motion of Venus, is easily shown. In his investigation, LEVERRIER (*Annales*, Vol. VI., p. 72) found the following value of $\Delta n'$,

$$\Delta n' = +0''.00035 + 0''.0689\, \nu + 0''.0959\, \nu' + 0''.1207\, \nu'';$$

but the value of this quantity used in forming his Tables is the first term only. If the values of ν, ν' and ν'' corresponding to the change from LEVERRIER's values of the masses to those here adopted, be substituted in this expression, the correction of LEVERRIER's mean motion, from this cause, is found to be

$$\Delta n' = -0''.01588.$$

Moreover, a comparison of the values of the Sun's mean longitude in the Tables of HANSEN and OLUFSEN and of LEVERRIER, gives

$$\text{Han.} - \text{Lev.} = -0''.93 - 0''.01074\, t.$$

From the way in which $\Delta n'$ and $\Delta n''$ are involved in the equations of condition, it may be concluded, that if $\Delta n''$ were left indeterminate in the solution, the value of $\Delta n'$, obtained, would be roughly,

$$\Delta n' = (\Delta n') + 1.2\, \Delta n'',$$

$(\Delta n')$ denoting the value of $\Delta n'$ on the supposition of $\Delta n'' = 0$. Thus on making $\Delta n'' = -0''.01074$, the correction of the mean motion of Venus, from this cause is

$$\Delta n' = -0''.01289.$$

The sum of these two corrections is

$$\Delta n' = -0''.02877$$

which is almost identical with that derived from the equations of condition.

The increment of the motion of the node, $0''.222$, requires that the mass of Venus should be reduced from $\frac{1}{408134}$ to $\frac{1}{427240}$. This agrees with LEVERRIER's result: setting out with the mass 0.0000024885, he found that it should be multipled by the factor 0.948, which would make the mass $\frac{1}{423900}$.

The corrections to be added to the elements, with which we set out, to obtain the elements, from which the Tables are constructed, are

$$\begin{aligned}
\Delta L' &= -\ 0''.502, \\
\Delta \pi' &= +\ 28''.46, \\
\Delta \Omega' &= +\ 0''.90 + 0''.222\, t, \\
\Delta i' &= +\ 0''.18, \\
\Delta e' &= -\ 0.000000196, \\
\Delta n' &= -\ 0''.02863.
\end{aligned}$$

The Tables have been compared with the occultation of Mercury by Venus, observed at Greenwich May 28, 1737. The observations made are

Greenwich M. T. h m s	
9 40 3.9.	Mercury distant from Venus not more than a tenth part of the diameter of Venus.
9 48 10.2.	Mercury wholly occulted by Venus.

INTRODUCTION.

The position of Mercury being derived from Prof. WINLOCK's Tables, the apparent position of the two planets, as seen from Greenwich, and in longitude and latitude, are

Greenwich M. T.	l.	b.	l'.	b'.	$l'-l$.	$b'-b'$
d h	° ′ ″	° ′ ″	° ′ ″	° ′ ″	″	″
May 28 8	89 24 23.05	+2 9 12.90	89 31 49.97	+2 10 9.98	+446.92	+57.08
9	89 27 56.68	+2 9 5.67	89 31 14.38	+2 9 42.02	+197.70	+36.35
10	89 31 30.35	+2 8 58.43	89 30 39.63	+2 9 14.28	− 50.72	+15.85

And interpolating

Greenwich M. T.	$l'-l$.	$b'-b$.	Dist. of Centres.
h m s	″	″	″
9 40 3.9	+31.73	+22.64	38.96
9 48 10.2	− 1.79	+19.87	19.95

With the addition of 0″.57 for irradiation, the semi-diameters of Mercury and Venus are respectively 3″.98 and 26″.97: hence at the first observation, the distance of the limbs of the planet is 8″.01, 2″.6 more than a tenth part of the diameter of Venus; at the second observation, the distance of the centres is less than the difference of semi-diameters; hence the Tables are verified by the statement of the observer. Venus being, at the time, a thin crescent, and about half of Mercury's disc being illuminated, it is plain that it would be difficult for the obsever to estimate the distance in fractional parts of the apparent diameter of Venus.

LEVERRIER's remarks on this occultation are impaired by a mistake made in the last line of his computation.

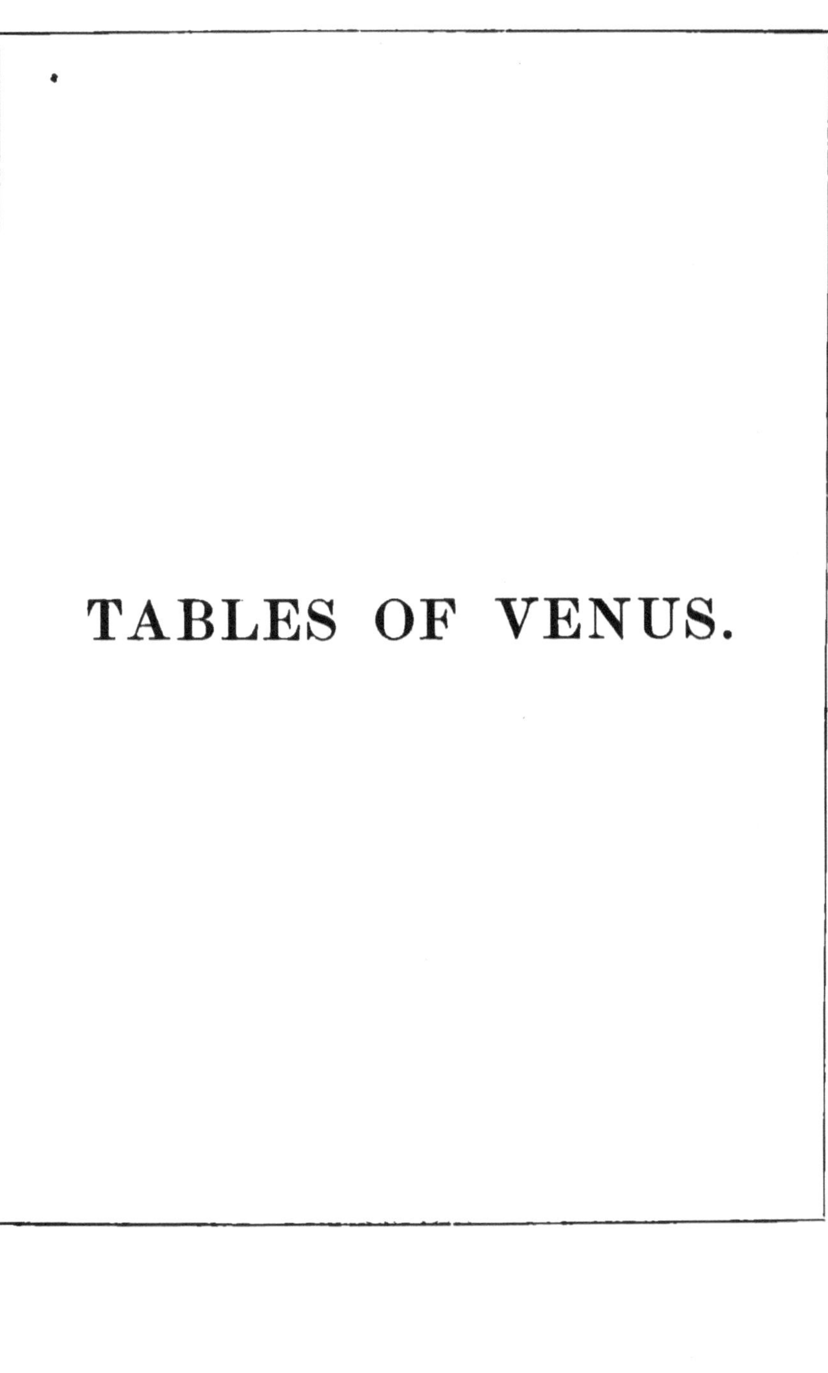

TABLES OF VENUS.

TABLE I.

LONGITUDE OF THE PRINCIPAL OBSERVATORIES FROM WASHINGTON.

West Longitudes are marked +

Place.	Longitude from Washington in Time.	In Decimals of a Day.	Place.	Longitude from Washington in Time.	In Decimals of a Day.
	h m s	d		h m s	d
Åbo,	—6 37 20.32	—0.2759296	Leipsic,	— 5 57 46.87	—0.2484592
Albany,*	—0 13 12.87	—0.0091767	Leyden,	— 5 26 8.57	—0.2264881
Allegheny,*	+0 11 50.20	+0.0082199	Liverpool,	— 4 56 12.34	—0.2056984
Altona,	—5 47 58.54	—0.2416498	Madras,	—10 29 9.67	—0.4369175
Ann Arbor,	+0 26 42.67	+0.0185494	Madrid,	— 4 53 27.00	—0.2037847
Armagh,	—4 41 36.92	—0.1955662	Mannheim,	— 5 42 3.06	—0.2375354
Athens,	—6 43 7.58	—0.2799488	Markree,	— 4 34 24.00	—0.1905556
Berlin,	—6 1 47.77	—0.2512473	Marseilles,	— 5 29 40.55	—0.2289415
Bilk,	—5 35 17.77	—0.2328445	Melbourne,	—14 48 7.17	—0.6167496
Bonn,	—5 36 36.02	—0.2337502	Milan,	— 5 44 58.20	—0.2395625
Breslau,	—6 16 22.19	—0.2613679	Modena,	— 5 51 55.53	—0.2443927
Brussels,	—5 25 41.29	—0.2261723	Moscow,	— 7 38 29.29	—0.3183946
Cambridge, (Eng.)	—5 8 35.08	—0.2142949	Munich,	— 5 54 38.00	—0.2462731
Cambridge, (Mass.)	—0 23 41.54	—0.0164530	Naples,	— 6 5 10.95	—0.2535990
Cape of Good Hope,	—6 22 8.09	—0.2653711	New York,*	— 0 12 15.47	—0.0085124
Chicago,	+0 42 14.26	+0.0293317	Nicolajew,	— 7 16 6.53	—0.3028534
Cincinnati,*	+0 29 46.94	+0.0206822	Olmütz,	— 6 17 15.43	—0.2619841
Christiania,	—5 51 6.69	—0.2438274	Oxford,	— 5 3 9.79	—0.2105300
Clinton,	—0 6 35.08	—0.0045727	Padua,	— 5 55 41.17	—0.2470043
Copenhagen,	—5 58 31.05	—0.2489703	Palermo,	— 6 1 37.00	—0.2511227
Cracow,	—6 28 2.80	—0.2694768	Paramatta,	—15 12 18.64	—0.6335491
Dorpat,	—6 55 6.02	—0.2882641	Paris,	— 5 17 33.02	—0.2205211
Dublin,	—4 42 50.39	—0.1964165	Philadelphia,*	— 0 7 33.64	—0.0052505
Durham,	—5 1 52.64	—0.2096370	Prague,	— 6 5 53.52	—0.2540917
Edinburgh,	—4 55 29.34	—0.2052007	Pulkowa,	— 7 9 31.06	—0.2982757
Florence,	—5 53 15.12	—0.2453139	Rome,	— 5 58 8.58	—0.2487098
Geneva,	—5 32 49.24	—0.2311344	San Fernando,	— 4 43 22.42	—0.1967873
Georgetown,*	+0 0 6.20	+0.0000718	Santiago,	— 0 25 30.00	—0.0177083
Göttingen,	—5 47 58.49	—0.2416192	Senftenberg,	— 6 14 3.00	—0.2597570
Gotha,	—5 51 3.39	—0.2437892	Speyer,	— 5 41 58.00	—0.2374769
Greenwich,	—5 8 12.39	—0.2140323	Stockholm,	— 6 20 26.35	—0.2641939
Hamburg,	—5 48 5.95	—0.2417355	St. Petersburg,	— 7 9 25.87	—0.2982161
Helsingfors,	—6 48 1.32	—0.2833486	Sydney,	—15 13 12.77	—0.6341756
Hudson,*	+0 17 32.06	+0.0121766	Upsala,	— 6 18 42.70	—0.2629942
Kasan,	—8 24 41.14	—0.3501761	Utrecht,	— 5 28 43.67	—0.2282832
Königsberg,	—6 30 11.87	—0.2709707	Vienna,	— 6 13 44.09	—0.2595381
Kremsmunster,	—6 4 45.03	—0.2532990	Wilna,	— 6 49 23.33	—0.2842978

NOTE.—These Longitudes, except of places marked with a *, are dependent on that of Cambridge, Mass., the latest correction of which is $+ 0^s.46 = 0^d.0000053$.

TABLE II.

Number of Days elapsed since the Beginning of the Julian Period, at the Date Jan. 0 in Common Years, and Jan. 1 in Bissextile Years.

Year.	Date in Mean Solar Days.	Year.	Date in Mean Solar Days.	Year in the Century.		Days from previous Centennial Date.	Year in the Century.		Days from previous Centennial Date.
				If Negative.	If Positive.		If Negative.	If Positive.	
—4713 *B.*	0	—1000	1356173	100	1	0	50	51	18262
—4712	365	— 900	1392698	99	2	365	49 *B.*	52 *B.*	18628
—4711	730	— 800	1429223	98	3	730	48	53	18993
—4710	1095	— 700	1465748	97 *B.*	4 *B.*	1096	47	54	19358
—4709 *B.*	1461	— 600	1502273	96	5	1461	46	55	19723
—4708	1826	— 500	1538798	95	6	1826	45 *B.*	56 *B.*	20089
—4707	2191	— 400	1575323	94	7	2191	44	57	20454
—4706	2556	— 300	1611848	93 *B.*	8 *B.*	2557	43	58	20819
—4705 *B.*	2922	— 200	1648373	92	9	2922	42	59	21184
—4704	3287	— 100	1684898	91	10	3287	41 *B.*	60 *B.*	21550
—4703	3652	1	1721423	90	11	3652	40	61	21915
—4702	4017	101	1757948	89 *B.*	12 *B.*	4018	39	62	22280
—4701 *B.*	4383	201	1794473	88	13	4383	38	63	22645
—4700	4748	301	1830998	87	14	4748	37 *B.*	64 *B.*	23011
—4600	41273	401	1867523	86	15	5113	36	65	23376
—4500	77798	501	1904048	85 *B.*	16 *B.*	5479	35	66	23741
—4400	114323	601	1940573	84	17	5844	34	67	24106
—4300	150848	701	1977098	83	18	6209	33 *B.*	68 *B.*	24472
—4200	187373	801	2013623	82	19	6574	32	69	24837
—4100	223898	901	2050148	81 *B.*	20 *B.*	6940	31	70	25202
—4000	260423	1001	2086673	80	21	7305	30	71	25567
—3900	296948	1101	2123198	79	22	7670	29 *B.*	72 *B.*	25933
—3800	333473	1201	2159723	78	23	8035	28	73	26298
—3700	369998	1301	2196248	77 *B.*	24 *B.*	8401	27	74	26663
—3600	406523	1401	2232773	76	25	8766	26	75	27028
—3500	443048	1501	2269298	75	26	9131	25 *B.*	76 *B.*	27394
—3400	479573	1583	2299238	74	27	9496	24	71	27759
—3300	516098	1584 *B.*	2299604	73 *B.*	28 *B.*	9862	23	78	28124
—3200	552623	1585	2299969	72	29	10227	22	79	28489
—3100	589148	1586	2300334	71	30	10592	21 *B.*	80 *B.*	28855
—3000	625673	1587	2300699	70	31	10957	20	81	29220
—2900	662198	1588 *B.*	2301065	69 *B.*	32 *B.*	11323	19	82	29585
—2800	698723	1589	2301430	68	33	11688	18	83	29950.
—2700	735248	1590	2301795	67	34	12053	17 *B.*	84 *B.*	30316
—2600	771773	1591	2302160	66	35	12418	16	85	30681
—2500	808298	1592 *B.*	2302526	65 *B.*	36 *B.*	12784	15	86	31046
—2400	844823	1593	2302891	64	37	13149	14	87	31411
—2300	881348	1594	2303256	63	38	13514	13 *B.*	88 *B.*	31777
—2200	917873	1595	2303621	62	39	13879	12	89	32142
—2100	954398	1596 *B.*	2303987	61 *B.*	40 *B.*	14245	11	90	32507
—2000	990923	1597	2304352	60	41	14610	10	91	32872
—1900	1027448	1598	2304717	59	42	14975	9 *B.*	92 *B.*	33238
—1800	1063973	1599	2305082	58	43	15340	8	93	33603
—1700	1100498	1600 *B.*	2305448	57 *B.*	44 *B.*	15706	7	94	33968
—1600	1137023	1601	2305813	56	45	16071	6	95	34333
—1500	1173548	1701	2342337	55	46	16436	5 *B.*	96 *B.*	34699
—1400	1210073	1801	2378861	54	47	16801	4	97	35064
—1300	1246598	1901	2415385	53 *B.*	48 *B.*	17167	3	98	35429
—1200	1283123	2001	2451910	52	49	17532	2	99	35794
—1100	1319648	2101	2488434	51	50	17897	1 *B.*	100 *B.*	36160
—1000	1356173	2201	2524958	50	51	18262		100	36159

TABLE III.

Number of Days from Jan. 0 in Common Years, and Jan. 1 in Bissextile Years.

Day of Month.	January. Common Year.	January. Bissextile Year.	February. Common Year.	February. Bissextile Year.	March.	April.	May.	June.	July.	August.	September.	October.	November.	December.	1582. October.	1582. November.	1582. December.
1	1	0	32	31	60	91	121	152	182	213	244	274	305	335	274	295	325
2	2	1	33	32	61	92	122	153	183	214	245	275	306	336	275	296	326
3	3	2	34	33	62	93	123	154	184	215	246	276	307	337	276	297	327
4	4	3	35	34	63	94	124	155	185	216	247	277	308	338	277	298	328
5	5	4	36	35	64	95	125	156	186	217	248	278	309	339		299	329
6	6	5	37	36	65	96	126	157	187	218	249	279	310	340		300	330
7	7	6	38	37	66	97	127	158	188	219	250	280	311	341		301	331
8	8	7	39	38	67	98	128	159	189	220	251	281	312	342		302	332
9	9	8	40	39	68	99	129	160	190	221	252	282	313	343		303	333
10	10	9	41	40	69	100	130	161	191	222	253	283	314	344		304	334
11	11	10	42	41	70	101	131	162	192	223	254	284	315	345		305	335
12	12	11	43	42	71	102	132	163	193	224	255	285	316	346		306	336
13	13	12	44	43	72	103	133	164	194	225	256	286	317	347		307	337
14	14	13	45	44	73	104	134	165	195	226	257	287	318	348		308	338
15	15	14	46	45	74	105	135	166	196	227	258	288	319	349	278	309	339
16	16	15	47	46	75	106	136	167	197	228	259	289	320	350	279	310	340
17	17	16	48	47	76	107	137	168	198	229	260	290	321	351	280	311	341
18	18	17	49	48	77	108	138	169	199	230	261	291	322	352	281	312	342
19	19	18	50	49	78	109	139	170	200	231	262	292	323	353	282	313	343
20	20	19	51	50	79	110	140	171	201	232	263	293	324	354	283	314	341
21	21	20	52	51	80	111	141	172	202	233	264	294	325	355	284	315	345
22	22	21	53	52	81	112	142	173	203	234	265	295	326	356	285	316	346
23	23	22	54	53	82	113	143	174	204	235	266	296	327	357	286	317	347
24	24	23	55	54	83	114	144	175	205	236	267	297	328	358	287	318	348
25	25	24	56	55	84	115	145	176	206	237	268	298	329	359	288	319	349
26	26	25	57	56	85	116	146	177	207	238	269	299	330	360	289	320	350
27	27	26	58	57	86	117	147	178	208	239	270	300	331	361	290	321	351
28	28	27	59	58	87	118	148	179	209	240	271	301	332	362	291	322	352
29	29	28		59	88	119	149	180	210	241	272	302	333	363	292	323	353
30	30	29			89	120	150	181	211	242	273	303	334	364	293	324	354
31	31	30			90		151		212	243		304		365	294		355

TABLE IV.

Reduction of Hours, Minutes, and Seconds of Time to Decimals of a Day.

Hours.	Decimal of a Day.	Min.	Decimal of a Day.	Min.	Decimal of a Day.	Sec.	Decimal of a Day.	Sec.	Decimal of a Day.
1	0.0416667	1	0.0006944	31	0.0215278	1	0.0000116	31	0.0003588
2	0.0833333	2	0.0013889	32	0.0222222	2	0.0000231	32	0.0003704
3	0.1250000	3	0.0020833	33	0.0229167	3	0.0000347	33	0.0003819
4	0.1666667	4	0.0027778	34	0.0236111	4	0.0000463	34	0.0003935
5	0.2083333	5	0.0034722	35	0.0243056	5	0.0000579	35	0.0004051
6	0.2500000	6	0.0041667	36	0.0250000	6	0.0000694	36	0.0004167
7	0.2916667	7	0.0048611	37	0.0256944	7	0.0000810	37	0.0004282
8	0.3333333	8	0.0055556	38	0.0263889	8	0.0000926	38	0.0004398
9	0.3750000	9	0.0062500	39	0.0270833	9	0.0001042	39	0.0004514
10	0.4166667	10	0.0069444	40	0.0277778	10	0.0001157	40	0.0004630
11	0.4583333	11	0.0076389	41	0.0284722	11	0.0001273	41	0.0004745
12	0.5000000	12	0.0083333	42	0.0291667	12	0.0001389	42	0.0004861
13	0.5416667	13	0.0090278	43	0.0298611	13	0.0001505	43	0.0004977
14	0.5833333	14	0.0097222	44	0.0305556	14	0.0001620	44	0.0005093
15	0.6250000	15	0.0104167	45	0.0312500	15	0.0001736	45	0.0005208
16	0.6666667	16	0.0111111	46	0.0319444	16	0.0001852	46	0.0005324
17	0.7083333	17	0.0118056	47	0.0326389	17	0.0001968	47	0.0005440
18	0.7500000	18	0.0125000	48	0.0333333	18	0.0002083	48	0.0005556
19	0.7916667	19	0.0131944	49	0.0340278	19	0.0002199	49	0.0005671
20	0.8333333	20	0.0138889	50	0.0347222	20	0.0002315	50	0.0005787
21	0.8750000	21	0.0145833	51	0.0354167	21	0.0002431	51	0.0005903
22	0.9166667	22	0.0152778	52	0.0361111	22	0.0002546	52	0.0006019
23	0.9583333	23	0.0159722	53	0.0368056	23	0.0002662	53	0.0006134
24	1.0000000	24	0.0166667	54	0.0375000	24	0.0002778	54	0.0006250
		25	0.0173611	55	0.0381944	25	0.0002894	55	0.0006366
		26	0.0180556	56	0.0388889	26	0.0003009	56	0.0006481
		27	0.0187500	57	0.0395833	27	0.0003125	57	0.0006597
		28	0.0194444	58	0.0402778	28	0.0003241	58	0.0006713
		29	0.0201389	59	0.0409722	29	0.0003356	59	0.0006829
		30	0.0208333	60	0.0416667	30	0.0003472	60	0.0006944

TABLE V.

Periods of the Arguments with their multiples.

	1 Period.	2 Periods.	3 Periods.
Argument I	$224^{d}.7008$	$449^{d}.4016$	$674^{d}.1023$
" II	$238^{y}.9$	$477^{y}.8$	$716^{y}.8$
" III	$11987^{d}.$	$23974^{d}.$	$35962^{d}.$
" IV	$2959^{d}.$	$5918^{d}.$	$8878^{d}.$
" V	$1454^{d}.9$	$2909^{d}.9$	$4364^{d}.8$
" VI	$583^{d}.92$	$1167^{d}.84$	$1751^{d}.76$
" VII	$243^{d}.16$	$486^{d}.33$	$729^{d}.49$
" VIII	$220^{d}.6$	$440^{d}.1$	$661^{d}.7$
" IX	$236^{d}.99$	$473^{d}.98$	$710^{d}.98$
" X	60 units	120 units	180 units
" XI	240 units	480 units	720 units
" XII	60 units	120 units	180 units
" XIII	60 units	120 units	180 units
" XIV	36 units	72 units	108 units
" XV	$6798^{d}.3$	$13596^{d}.5$	$20394^{d}.8$
" XVI	$365^{d}.2$	$730^{d}.5$	$1095^{d}.7$

Increments of Arguments X–XIV for an increase of 1, 2 and 3 in the integer **m**.

	Increment of **m** = 1.	Increment of **m** = 2.	Increment of **m** = 3.
Argument X	33.26	6.52	39.78
" XI	147.64	55.29	202.93
" XII	19.6	39.3	58.9
" XIII	3.11	6.22	9.31
" XIV	0.8	1.5	2.3

Mean Longitude, Arguments, &c., for Washington Mean Noon of Jan. 0 in common years, Jan. 1 in bissextile years.

Year.	L	m.	I.	II.	III.	IV.	V.	VI.	VII.
	° ′ ″		d	y	d	d	d	d	d
1750	45 54 5.24	−163	173.9096	67.9	11242	2403	611.5	497.08	31.2
1751	270 41 31.89	161	89.5080	68.9	11607	2768	976.5	278.16	153.0
1752*B.*	137 5 12.35	159	6.1061	69.9	11973	175	1342.5	60.24	32.7
1753	1 52 42.00	158	146.4056	70.9	351	540	252.5	425.24	154.5
1754	226 40 11.66	156	62.0040	71.9	716	905	617.5	206.32	33.2
1755	91 27 41.31	−155	202.3032	72.9	1081	1270	982.5	571.32	155.0
1756*B.*	317 51 18.77	153	118.9016	73.9	1447	1636	1348.5	353.40	34.7
1757	182 38 48.42	151	34.5000	74.9	1812	2001	258.6	134.48	156.5
1758	47 26 18.08	150	174.7993	75.9	2177	2366	623.6	499.48	35.2
1759	272 13 47.73	148	90.3977	76.9	2542	2731	988.6	280.56	157.1
1760*B.*	138 37 25.19	−146	6.9961	77.9	2908	137	1354.6	62.63	36.7
1761	3 24 54.84	145	147.2953	78.9	3273	502	264.7	427.63	158.6
1762	228 12 24.50	143	62.8937	79.9	3638	867	629.7	208.71	37.2
1763	92 59 54.15	142	203.1929	80.9	4003	1232	994.7	573.71	159.1
1764*B.*	319 23 31.61	140	119.7913	81.9	4369	1598	1360.7	355.79	38.7
1765	184 11 1.27	−138	35.3898	82.9	4734	1963	270.7	136.87	160.6
1766	48 58 30.92	137	175.6890	83.9	5099	2328	635.7	501.87	39.2
1767	273 46 0.58	135	91.2874	84.9	5464	2693	1000.7	282.95	161.1
1768*B.*	140 9 38.04	133	7.8858	85.9	5830	100	1366.7	65.03	40.7
1769	4 57 7.69	132	148.1850	86.9	6195	465	276.8	430.03	162.6
1770	229 44 37.35	−130	63.7834	87.9	6560	830	641.8	211.11	41.3
1771	94 32 7.00	129	204.0826	88.9	6925	1195	1006.8	576.11	163.1
1772*B.*	320 55 44.47	127	120.6811	89.9	7291	1561	1372.8	358.18	42.8
1773	185 43 14.12	125	36.2795	90.9	7656	1926	282.9	139.26	164.6
1774	50 30 43.78	124	176.5787	91.9	8021	2291	647.9	504.26	43.3
1775	275 18 13.43	−122	92.1771	92.9	8386	2656	1012.9	285.34	165.1
1776*B.*	141 41 50.89	120	8.7755	93.9	8752	63	1378.9	67.42	44.8
1777	6 29 20.55	119	149.0748	94.9	9117	428	288.9	432.42	166.6
1778	231 16 50.21	117	64.6732	95.9	9482	793	653.9	213.50	45.3
1779	96 4 19.86	116	204.9724	96.9	9847	1158	1018.9	578.50	167.1
1780*B.*	322 27 57.32	−114	121.5708	97.9	10213	1524	1384.9	360.58	46.8
1781	187 15 26.98	112	37.1692	98.9	10578	1889	295.0	141.66	168.6
1782	52 2 56.64	111	177.4684	99.9	10943	2254	660.0	506.66	47.3
1783	276 50 26.29	109	93.0669	100.9	11308	2619	1025.0	287.74	169.1
1784*B.*	143 14 3.76	107	9.6653	101.9	11674	26	1391.0	69.81	48.8
1785	8 1 33.41	−106	149.9645	102.9	52	391	301.0	434.81	170.6
1786	232 49 3.07	104	65.5629	103.9	417	756	666.0	215.89	49.3
1787	97 36 32.73	103	205.8621	104.9	782	1121	1031.0	580.89	171.1
1788*B.*	324 0 10.19	101	122.4605	105.9	1148	1487	1397.0	362.97	50.8
1789	188 47 39.85	99	38.0590	106.9	1513	1852	307.1	144.05	172.6
1790	53 35 9.51	− 98	178.3582	107.9	1878	2217	672.1	509.05	51.3
1791	278 22 39.16	96	93.9566	108.9	2243	2582	1037.1	290.13	173.1
1792*B.*	144 46 16.63	94	10.5551	109.9	2609	2948	1403.1	72.21	52.8
1793	9 33 46.28	93	150.8543	110.9	2974	354	313.2	437.21	174.6
1794	234 21 15.94	91	66.4527	111.9	3339	719	678.2	218.29	53.3
1795	99 8 45.60	− 90	206.7519	112.9	3704	1084	1043.2	583.29	175.2
1796*B.*	325 32 23.07	88	123.3503	113.9	4070	1450	1409.2	365.36	54.8
1797	190 19 52.72	86	38.9488	114.9	4435	1815	319.2	146.44	176.7
1798	55 7 22.38	85	179.2480	115.9	4800	2180	684.2	511.44	55.3
1799	279 54 52.04	− 83	94.8464	116.9	5165	2545	1049.2	292.52	177.2

Constant subtracted from *L* = 47′ 46″.

TABLE VI.

Mean Longitude, Arguments, &c., for Washington Mean Noon of Jan. 0 in common years, Jan. 1 in bissextile years.

Year.	VIII.	IX.	X.	XI.	XII.	XIII.	XIV.	Log. sin *i*.	360° — ☊.
	d	d							° ′ ″
1750	55.9	28.28	43.96	193.18	48.7	58.45	22.7	8.7720788	285 31 16.8
1751	200.3	156.29	50.48	8.77	28.0	4.67	24.2	0802	33 41.3
1752*B*.	125.2	48.30	56.99	64.06	7.2	10.89	25.7	0815	33 11.8
1753	49.1	176.31	30.25	211.70	26.9	11.01	26.5	0829	32 39.3
1754	193.5	67.33	36.77	26.99	6.1	20.23	28.0	0842	32 6.9
1755	117.4	195.34	10.03	174.63	25.7	23.34	28.7	8.7720856	285 31 34.4
1756*B*.	42.2	87.35	16.55	229.92	5.0	29.56	30.2	0870	31 1.8
1757	186.7	215.36	23.06	45.21	44.2	35.79	31.7	0883	30 29.4
1758	110.5	106.38	56.32	192.86	3.9	38.90	32.5	0897	29 56.9
1759	34.4	234.38	2.84	8.15	43.1	45.12	34.0	0911	29 24.4
1760*B*.	179.8	126.40	9.36	63.44	22.4	51.35	35.5	8.7720924	285 28 51.9
1761	103.7	17.42	42.62	211.08	42.0	54.46	0.2	0938	28 19.4
1762	27.6	145.43	49.13	26.37	21.2	0.68	1.7	0951	27 47.0
1763	172.0	36.44	22.39	174.02	40.9	3.79	2.5	0965	27 14.5
1764*B*.	96.9	165.45	28.91	229.31	20.1	10.02	4.0	0979	26 41.9
1765	20.7	56.47	35.43	44.60	59.4	16.24	5.5	8.7720992	285 26 9.5
1766	165.2	184.47	8.68	192.24	19.0	19.35	6.2	1006	25 37.0
1767	89.0	75.49	15.20	7.53	58.2	25.58	7.7	1020	25 4.5
1768*B*.	13.9	204.50	21.72	62.82	37.5	31.80	9.2	1033	24 32.0
1769	158.4	95.51	51.98	210.46	57.1	34.91	10.0	1047	23 59.5
1770	82.2	223.52	1.49	25.75	36.4	41.14	11.5	8.7721060	285 23 27.0
1771	6.1	114.51	34.75	173.40	56.0	44.25	12.3	1074	22 54.6
1772*B*.	151.5	6.55	41.27	228.69	35.2	50.47	13.8	1088	22 22.0
1773	75.4	134.56	47.79	43.98	14.5	56.69	15.3	1101	21 49.5
1774	219.8	25.58	21.05	191.62	34.1	59.81	16.0	1115	21 17.1
1775	143.7	153.59	27.56	6.91	13.4	6.03	17.5	8.7721128	285 20 44.6
1776*B*.	68.6	45.60	34.08	62.20	52.6	12.25	19.0	1142	20 12.1
1777	213.0	173.61	7.34	209.85	12.2	15.37	19.8	1156	19 39.6
1778	136.9	64.63	13.86	25.14	51.5	21.59	21.3	1169	19 7.1
1779	60.7	192.64	47.12	172.78	11.1	24.70	22.0	1183	18 34.6
1780*B*.	206.2	84.65	53.63	228.07	50.4	30.92	23.5	8.7721197	285 18 2.1
1781	130.0	212.66	0.15	43.26	29.6	37.15	25.0	1210	17 29.6
1782	53.9	103.68	33.41	191.00	49.2	40.26	25.8	1224	16 57.1
1783	198.3	231.68	39.93	6.29	28.5	46.48	27.3	1237	16 24.7
1784*B*.	123.2	123.70	46.44	61.58	7.7	52.71	28.8	1251	15 52.1
1785	47.1	14.72	19.70	209.23	27.4	55.82	29.5	8.7721265	285 15 19.6
1786	191.5	142.72	26.22	24.52	6.6	2.04	31.1	1278	14 47.1
1787	115.4	33.74	59.48	172.16	26.2	5.15	31.8	1292	14 14.7
1788*B*.	40.2	162.75	6.00	227.45	5.5	11.38	33.3	1306	13 42.1
1789	184.7	53.76	12.51	42.74	44.7	17.60	34.8	1319	13 9.6
1790	108.5	181.77	45.77	190.39	4.4	20.71	35.6	8.7721333	285 12 37.2
1791	32.4	72.79	52.29	5.68	43.6	26.94	1.1	1346	12 4.7
1792*B*.	177.8	201.80	58.81	60.97	22.9	33.16	2.6	1360	11 32.1
1793	101.7	92.81	32.06	208.61	42.5	36.27	3.3	1374	10 59.7
1794	25.6	220.82	38.58	23.90	21.7	42.50	4.8	1387	10 27.2
1795	170.0	111.84	11.84	171.54	41.4	45.61	5.6	8.7721401	285 9 54.7
1796*B*.	94.9	3.85	18.36	226.83	20.6	51.83	7.1	1415	9 22.1
1797	18.7	131.86	24.87	42.12	59.9	58.05	8.6	1428	8 49.7
1798	163.2	22.88	58.13	189.77	19.5	1.17	9.3	1442	8 17.2
1799	87.0	150.89	4.65	5.06	58.7	7.30	10.8	8.7721456	285 7 44.7

TABLE VI.

Mean Longitude, Arguments, &c., for Washington Mean Noon of Jan. 0 in common years, Jan. 1 in bissextile years.

Year.	L.	m.	I.	II.	III.	IV.	V.	VI.	VII.
	° ′ ″		d	y	d	d	d	d	d
1800	114 42 21.70	—81	10.4148	117.9	5530	2910	1414.2	73.60	55.8
1801	9 29 51.36	80	150.7141	118.9	5895	315	324.3	438.60	177.7
1802	231 17 21.02	78	66.3425	119.9	6260	680	689.3	219.68	56.3
1803	99 4 50.67	77	206.6417	120.9	6625	1045	1054.3	0.76	178.2
1804 B.	325 28 28.14	75	123.2401	121.9	6991	1411	1420.3	366.76	57.8
1805	190 15 57.80	—73	38.8386	122.9	7356	1776	330.4	147.84	179.7
1806	55 3 27.46	72	179.1378	123.9	7721	2141	695.4	512.84	58.3
1807	279 50 57.12	70	94.7362	124.9	8086	2506	1060.4	293.91	180.2
1808 B.	146 14 31.58	68	11.3346	125.9	8452	2872	1426.4	75.99	59.9
1809	11 2 4.24	67	151.6339	126.9	8817	278	336.4	440.99	181.7
1810	235 49 33.90	—65	67.2323	127.9	9182	643	701.4	222.07	60.4
1811	100 37 3.56	64	207.5315	128.9	9547	1008	1066.4	3.15	182.2
1812 B.	327 0 41.03	62	124.1299	129.9	9913	1374	1432.4	369.15	61.9
1813	191 48 10.69	60	39.7284	130.9	10278	1739	342.5	150.23	183.7
1814	56 35 40.35	59	180.0276	131.9	10643	2104	707.5	515.23	62.4
1815	281 23 10.01	—57	95.6260	132.9	11008	2469	1072.5	296.31	184.2
1816 B.	147 46 47.47	55	12.2245	133.9	11374	2835	1438.5	78.39	63.9
1817	12 31 17.13	54	152.5237	134.9	11739	241	348.6	443.39	185.7
1818	237 21 46.79	52	68.1221	135.9	116	606	713.6	224.46	64.4
1819	102 9 16.45	51	208.4213	136.9	481	971	1078.6	5.54	186.2
1820 B.	328 32 53.92	—49	125.0198	137.9	847	1337	1444.6	371.54	65.9
1821	193 20 23.58	47	40.6182	138.9	1212	1702	354.6	152.62	187.7
1822	58 7 53.24	46	180.9174	139.9	1577	2067	719.6	517.62	66.4
1823	282 55 22.90	44	96.5159	140.9	1942	2432	1084.6	298.70	188.2
1824 B.	149 19 0.37	42	13.1143	141.9	2308	2798	1450.6	80.78	67.9
1825	14 6 30.03	—41	153.4135	142.9	2673	204	360.7	445.78	189.7
1826	238 53 59.69	39	69.0119	143.9	3038	569	725.7	226.86	68.4
1827	103 41 29.36	38	209.3112	144.9	3403	934	1090.7	7.94	190.2
1828 B.	330 5 6.82	36	125.9096	145.9	3769	1300	1.8	373.94	69.9
1829	194 52 36.49	34	41.5080	146.9	4134	1665	366.8	155.02	191.7
1830	59 40 6.15	—33	181.8073	147.9	4499	2030	731.8	520.02	70.4
1831	284 27 35.81	31	97.4057	148.9	4864	2395	1096.8	301.09	192.2
1832 B.	150 51 13.28	29	14.0041	149.9	5230	2761	7.8	83.17	71.9
1833	15 38 42.94	28	154.3034	150.9	5595	167	372.8	448.17	193.8
1834	240 26 12.60	26	69.9018	151.9	5960	532	737.8	229.25	72.4
1835	105 13 42.27	—25	210.2010	152.9	6325	897	1102.8	10.33	194.3
1836 B.	331 37 19.73	23	126.7995	153.9	6691	1263	13.9	376.33	73.9
1837	196 24 49.40	21	42.3979	154.9	7056	1628	378.9	157.41	195.8
1838	61 12 19.06	20	182.6971	155.9	7421	1993	743.9	522.41	74.4
1839	285 59 48.72	18	98.2956	156.9	7786	2358	1108.9	303.49	196.3
1840 B.	152 23 26.19	—16	14.8940	157.9	8152	2724	19.9	85.57	75.9
1841	17 10 55.86	15	155.1932	158.9	8517	129	384.9	450.57	197.8
1842	241 58 25.52	13	70.7917	159.9	8882	494	749.9	231.64	76.4
1843	106 45 55.18	12	211.0909	160.9	9247	859	1114.9	12.72	198.3
1844 B.	333 9 32.65	10	127.6893	161.9	9613	1225	26.0	378.72	77.9
1845	197 57 2.32	— 8	43.2878	162.9	9978	1590	391.0	159.80	199.8
1846	62 41 31.98	7	183.5870	163.9	10343	1955	756.0	524.80	78.5
1847	287 32 1.65	5	99.1854	164.9	10708	2320	1121.0	305.88	200.3
1848 B.	153 55 39.12	3	15.7839	165.9	11074	2686	32.1	87.96	80.0
1849	18 43 8.78	— 2	156.0831	166.9	11439	92	397.1	452.96	201.8

Constant subtracted from $L = 47' 40''$.

Mean Longitude, Arguments, &c., for Washington Mean Noon of Jan. 0 in common years, Jan. 1 in bissextile years.

Year.	VIII.	IX.	X.	XI.	XII.	XIII.	XIV.	Log. sin *i*.	360° — ☊.
	d	d							° ′ ″
1800	10.9	41.90	11.17	60.35	38.0	13.61	12.3	8.7721469	285 7 12.2
1801	155.3	169.91	41.43	207.99	57.6	16.72	13.1	1483	6 39.8
1802	79.2	60.93	50.91	23.28	36.9	22.95	11.6	1496	6 7.3
1803	3.1	188.93	24.20	170.93	56.5	26.06	15.4	1510	5 34.8
1804 B.	148.5	80.95	30.72	226.22	35.7	32.28	16.9	1523	5 2.2
1805	72.4	208.96	37.24	41.51	15.0	38.51	18.4	8.7721537	285 4 29.8
1806	216.8	99.98	10.50	189.15	31.6	41.62	19.1	1550	3 57.3
1807	140.7	227.98	17.01	4.41	13.9	47.84	20.6	1564	3 24.8
1808 B.	65.5	120.00	23.53	59.73	53.1	51.07	22.1	1578	2 52.2
1809	210.0	11.02	56.79	207.37	12.7	57.18	22.9	1591	2 19.7
1810	133.8	139.02	3.31	22.66	52.0	3.40	24.4	8.7721605	285 1 47.3
1811	57.7	30.04	36.56	170.31	11.6	6.51	25.1	1618	1 14.8
1812 B.	203.1	159.05	43.08	225.60	50.9	12.74	26.6	1632	0 42.2
1813	127.0	50.06	49.60	40.89	30.1	18.96	28.1	1646	285 0 9.7
1814	50.9	178.07	22.86	188.53	49.7	22.07	28.9	1659	284 59 37.2
1815	195.3	69.09	29.37	3.82	29.0	28.30	30.4	8.7721673	284 59 4.8
1816 B.	120.2	198.10	35.89	59.11	8.2	31.52	31.9	1686	58 32.2
1817	44.0	89.11	9.15	206.76	27.9	37.63	32.6	1700	57 59.7
1818	188.5	217.12	15.66	22.05	7.1	43.85	34.1	1713	57 27.2
1819	112.3	108.14	48.93	169.69	26.7	46.97	34.9	1727	56 54.7
1820 B.	37.2	0.15	55.44	224.98	6.0	53.19	0.4	8.7721741	284 56 22.2
1821	181.6	128.16	1.96	40.27	45.2	59.41	1.9	1754	55 49.7
1822	105.5	19.18	35.22	187.91	4.9	2.53	2.7	1768	55 17.2
1823	29.4	147.19	41.71	3.20	44.1	8.75	4.2	1781	54 44.7
1824 B.	174.8	39.20	48.25	58.49	23.4	14.97	5.7	1795	54 12.2
1825	98.7	167.21	21.51	206.14	43.0	18.08	6.4	8.7721808	284 53 39.7
1826	24.6	58.23	28.03	21.43	22.2	24.31	7.9	1822	53 7.2
1827	167.0	186.23	1.29	169.07	41.9	27.42	8.7	1836	52 34.7
1828 B.	91.9	78.25	7.81	224.36	21.1	33.64	10.2	1849	52 2.1
1829	15.7	206.26	14.32	39.65	0.4	39.87	11.7	1863	51 29.6
1830	160.2	97.27	47.58	187.30	20.0	42.98	12.4	8.7721876	284 50 57.1
1831	84.0	225.28	54.10	2.59	59.2	49.20	13.9	1890	50 24.7
1832 B.	8.9	117.30	0.62	57.88	38.5	55.43	15.4	1904	49 52.1
1833	153.3	8.32	33.88	205.52	58.1	58.54	16.2	1917	49 19.6
1834	77.2	136.32	40.39	20.81	37.4	4.76	17.7	1931	48 47.1
1835	1.1	27.34	13.65	168.45	57.0	7.87	18.4	8.7721944	284 48 14.6
1836 B.	146.5	156.35	20.17	223.74	36.2	14.10	19.9	1958	47 42.0
1837	70.4	47.36	26.69	39.03	15.5	20.32	21.5	1971	47 9.6
1838	214.8	175.37	59.94	186.68	35.1	23.43	22.2	1985	46 37.1
1839	138.7	66.39	6.46	1.97	14.4	29.66	23.7	1999	46 4.6
1840 B.	63.5	195.40	12.98	57.26	53.6	35.88	25.2	8.7722012	284 45 32.0
1841	208.0	86.41	46.24	204.90	13.2	38.99	26.0	2026	44 59.5
1842	131.8	214.42	52.75	20.19	52.5	45.21	27.5	2039	44 27.0
1843	55.7	105.44	26.01	167.84	12.1	48.33	28.2	2053	43 54.5
1844 B.	201.1	234.44	32.53	223.13	51.4	51.55	29.7	2067	43 21.9
1845	125.0	125.46	39.05	38.42	30.6	0.77	31.2	8.7722080	284 42 49.5
1846	48.9	16.48	12.31	186.06	50.2	3.88	32.0	2094	42 17.0
1847	193.3	144.49	18.82	1.35	29.5	10.11	33.5	2107	41 44.5
1848 B.	118.2	36.50	25.34	56.64	8.7	16.33	35.0	2121	41 11.9
1849	42.0	164.51	58.60	201.28	28.4	19.41	35.7	8.7722134	284 40 39.4

TABLE VI.

Mean Longitude, Arguments, &c., for Washington Mean Noon of Jan. 0 in common years, Jan. 1 in bissextile years.

Year.	L	m.	I.	II.	III.	IV.	V.	VI.	VII.
	° ′ ″		d	y	d	d	d	d	d
1850	213 30 38.45	0	71.6815	167.9	11804	457	762.1	234.04	80.5
1851	108 18 8.11	1	211.9808	168.9	182	822	1127.1	15.12	202.3
1852*B*.	331 41 45.58	3	128.5792	169.9	548	1188	38.1	381.12	82.0
1853	199 29 15.25	5	44.1776	170.9	913	1553	403.1	162.19	202.8
1854	64 16 41.92	6	184.4769	171.9	1278	1918	768.1	527.19	82.5
1855	289 4 14.58	8	100.0753	172.9	1643	2283	1133.1	308.27	204.3
1856*B*.	155 27 52.05	10	16.6738	173.9	2009	2649	44.2	90.35	84.0
1857	20 15 21.72	11	156.9730	174.9	2374	55	409.2	455.35	205.8
1858	215 2 51.39	13	72.5715	175.9	2739	420	774.2	236.43	84.5
1859	109 50 21.05	14	212.8707	176.9	3104	785	1139.2	17.51	206.3
1860*B*.	336 13 58.53	16	129.4691	177.9	3470	1151	50.3	383.51	86.0
1861	201 1 28.19	18	45.0675	178.9	3835	1516	415.3	164.59	207.8
1862	65 48 57.86	19	185.3668	179.9	4200	1881	780.3	529.59	86.5
1863	290 36 27.53	21	100.9652	180.9	4565	2246	1145.3	310.67	208.3
1864*B*.	157 0 5.00	23	17.5637	181.9	4931	2612	56.3	92.75	88.0
1865	21 47 34.67	24	157.8629	182.9	5296	18	421.3	457.75	209.8
1866	246 35 4.34	26	73.4613	183.9	5661	383	786.3	238.82	88.5
1867	111 22 34.00	27	213.7606	184.9	6026	748	1151.3	19.90	210.3
1868*B*.	337 46 11.48	29	130.3590	185.9	6392	1114	62.4	385.90	90.0
1869	202 33 41.15	31	45.9575	186.9	6757	1479	427.4	166.98	211.8
1870	67 21 10.82	32	186.2567	187.9	7122	1844	792.4	531.98	90.5
1871	292 8 40.49	34	101.8551	188.9	7487	2209	1157.4	313.06	212.4
1872*B*.	158 32 17.96	36	18.4536	189.9	7853	2575	68.5	95.14	92.0
1873	23 19 47.63	37	158.7528	190.9	8218	2940	433.5	460.14	213.9
1874	248 7 17.30	39	74.3513	191.9	8583	346	798.5	241.22	92.5
1875	112 54 46.97	40	214.6505	192.9	8948	711	1163.5	22.30	214.4
1876*B*.	339 18 24.45	42	131.2489	193.9	9314	1077	74.5	388.30	94.0
1877	204 5 54.12	44	46.8474	194.9	9679	1442	439.5	169.37	215.9
1878	68 53 23.79	45	187.1466	195.9	10044	1807	804.5	534.37	94.5
1879	293 40 53.46	47	102.7451	196.9	10409	2172	1169.5	315.45	216.4
1880*B*.	160 4 30.94	49	19.3435	197.9	10775	2538	80.6	97.53	96.0
1881	24 52 0.61	50	159.6428	198.9	11140	2903	445.6	462.53	217.9
1882	249 39 30.28	52	75.2412	199.9	11505	308	810.6	243.61	96.6
1883	114 26 59.95	53	215.5404	200.9	11870	673	1175.6	24.69	218.4
1884*B*.	310 50 37.43	55	132.1389	201.9	249	1039	86.6	390.69	98.1
1885	205 38 7.10	57	47.7373	202.9	615	1404	451.6	171.77	219.9
1886	70 25 36.77	58	188.0366	203.9	980	1769	816.6	536.77	98.6
1887	295 13 6.45	60	103.6350	204.9	1345	2134	1181.6	317.85	220.4
1888*B*.	161 36 43.93	62	20.2335	205.9	1711	2500	92.7	99.92	100.1
1889	26 24 13.60	63	160.5327	206.9	2076	2865	457.7	464.92	221.9
1890	251 11 43.27	65	76.1312	207.9	2441	271	822.7	246.00	100.6
1891	115 59 12.95	66	216.4304	208.9	2806	636	1187.7	27.08	222.4
1892*B*.	342 22 50.43	68	133.0289	209.9	3172	1002	98.8	393.08	102.1
1893	207 10 20.10	70	48.6273	210.9	3537	1367	463.8	174.16	223.9
1894	71 57 49.78	71	188.9265	211.9	3902	1732	828.8	539.16	102.6
1895	296 45 19.45	73	104.5250	212.9	4267	2097	1193.8	320.24	224.4
1896*B*.	163 8 56.93	75	21.1235	213.9	4633	2463	104.8	102.32	104.1
1897	27 56 26.61	76	161.4227	214.9	4998	2828	469.8	467.32	225.9
1898	252 43 56.29	78	77.0211	215.9	5363	234	834.8	248.40	104.6
1899	117 31 25.96	79	217.3201	216.9	5728	599	1199.8	29.48	226.4

Constant subtracted from $L = 47' 40''$.

Mean Longitude, Arguments, &c., for Washington Mean Noon of Jan. 0 in common years, Jan. 1 in bissextile years.

Year.	VIII.	IX.	X.	XI.	XII.	XIII.	XIV.	Log. sin *i*.	360° − ☊.
	d	d							° ′ ″
1850	186.5	55.53	5.12	19.57	7.6	25.67	1.2	8.7722149	284 40 6.9
1851	110.3	183.53	38.37	167.22	27.2	28.78	2.0	2163	39 34.4
1852 *B.*	35.2	75.55	44.89	222.51	6.5	35.00	3.5	2176	39 1.8
1853	179.6	203.56	51.41	37.80	45.7	41.23	5.0	2190	38 29.3
1854	103.5	94.57	21.67	185.41	5.4	44.34	5.8	2203	37 56.8
1855	27.4	222.58	31.19	0.73	44.6	50.56	7.3	8.7722217	284 37 24.3
1856 *B.*	172.8	111.60	37.70	56.02	23.9	56.78	8.8	2230	36 51.8
1857	96.7	5.61	10.96	203.67	43.5	59.90	9.5	2244	36 19.3
1858	20.5	133.62	17.48	18.96	22.7	6.12	11.0	2257	35 46.8
1859	165.0	24.61	50.74	166.60	42.4	9.23	11.8	2271	35 14.3
1860 *B.*	89.8	153.65	57.25	221.89	21.6	15.45	13.3	8.7722284	284 34 41.7
1861	13.7	41.66	3.77	37.18	0.9	21.68	14.8	2298	34 9.2
1862	158.1	172.67	37.03	184.82	20.5	24.79	15.5	2311	33 36.7
1863	82.0	63.69	43.55	0.11	59.7	31.01	17.0	2325	33 4.2
1864 *B.*	6.9	192.70	50.07	55.40	39.0	37.23	18.5	2339	32 31.6
1865	151.3	83.71	23.32	203.05	58.6	40.35	19.3	8.7722352	284 31 59.1
1866	75.2	211.72	29.84	18.34	37.9	46.57	20.8	2366	31 26.6
1867	219.6	102.74	3.10	165.98	57.5	49.69	21.5	2379	30 54.1
1868 *B.*	141.5	231.71	9.62	221.27	36.7	55.91	23.0	2393	30 21.5
1869	68.3	122.76	16.13	36.56	16.0	2.13	24.5	2406	29 49.0
1870	212.8	13.78	49.39	184.21	35.6	5.24	25.3	8.7722420	284 29 16.5
1871	136.6	141.78	55.91	239.49	14.9	11.47	26.8	2433	28 44.0
1872 *B.*	61.5	33.80	2.43	51.79	54.1	17.69	28.3	2447	28 11.5
1873	205.9	161.81	35.69	202.43	13.7	20.80	29.1	2460	27 39.0
1874	129.8	52.83	42.20	17.72	53.0	27.03	30.6	2474	27 6.5
1875	53.7	180.83	15.46	165.36	12.6	30.14	31.3	8.7722487	284 26 34.0
1876 *B.*	199.1	72.85	21.98	220.65	51.9	36.36	32.8	2501	26 1.4
1877	123.0	200.86	28.50	35.94	31.1	42.59	34.3	2515	25 28.9
1878	46.9	91.87	1.76	183.59	50.7	45.70	35.1	2528	24 56.4
1879	191.3	219.88	8.27	238.88	30.0	51.92	0.6	2542	24 23.9
1880 *B.*	116.2	111.90	14.79	54.17	9.2	58.14	2.1	8.7722555	284 23 51.3
1881	40.0	2.91	48.05	201.81	28.9	1.26	2.8	2569	23 18.8
1882	184.5	130.92	51.57	17.10	8.1	7.48	4.3	2582	22 46.3
1883	108.3	21.94	27.82	164.75	27.7	10.59	5.1	2596	22 13.8
1884 *B.*	33.2	150.95	34.34	220.04	7.0	16.81	6.6	2609	21 41.2
1885	177.6	41.96	40.86	35.33	46.2	23.04	8.1	8.7722623	284 21 8.7
1886	101.5	169.97	14.12	182.97	5.9	26.15	8.8	2636	20 36.2
1887	25.4	60.99	20.63	238.26	45.1	32.37	10.4	2650	20 3.7
1888 *B.*	170.8	189.99	27.15	53.55	24.4	38.60	11.9	2664	19 31.1
1889	94.7	81.01	0.41	201.19	44.0	41.71	12.6	2677	18 58.6
1890	18.5	209.02	6.93	16.48	23.2	47.93	14.1	8.7722691	284 18 26.1
1891	163.0	100.04	40.19	164.13	42.9	51.04	14.9	2704	17 53.6
1892 *B.*	87.8	229.04	46.70	219.42	22.1	57.27	16.4	2718	17 21.0
1893	11.7	120.06	53.22	34.71	1.4	3.49	17.9	2731	16 48.5
1894	156.1	11.08	26.18	182.35	21.0	6.60	18.6	2745	16 15.9
1895	80.0	139.08	33.00	237.64	0.2	12.83	20.1	8.7722758	284 15 43.4
1896 *B.*	4.9	31.10	39.51	52.93	39.5	19.05	21.6	2772	15 10.8
1897	149.3	159.11	12.77	200.58	59.1	22.16	22.4	2785	14 38.3
1898	73.2	50.12	19.29	15.87	38.4	28.39	23.9	2799	14 5.8
1899	217.6	178.13	52.55	163.51	58.0	31.50	24.6	8.7722812	284 13 33.3

TABLE VI.

Mean Longitude, Arguments, &c., for Washington Mean Noon of Jan. 0 in common years, Jan. 1 in bissextile years.

Year.	L.	m.	I.	II.	III.	IV.	V.	VI.	VII.
	° ′ ″		d	y	d	d	d	d	d
1900	242 18 55.61	81	132.9188	217.9	6093	964	109.9	391.48	105.1
1901	207 6 25.31	83	48.5173	218.9	6458	1329	474.9	175.55	226.9
1902	71 53 51.99	84	188.8165	219.9	6823	1694	839.9	540.55	105.6
1903	296 41 21.67	86	104.1150	220.9	7188	2059	1204.9	321.63	227.4
1904 *B.*	163 5 2.15	88	21.0131	221.9	7554	2425	116.0	103.71	107.1
1905	27 52 31.83	89	161.3127	222.9	7919	2790	481.0	468.71	228.9
1906	252 40 1.51	91	76.9111	223.9	8284	196	846.0	249.79	107.6
1907	117 27 31.19	92	217.2104	224.9	8649	561	1211.0	30.87	229.5
1908 *B.*	343 51 8.67	94	133.8088	225.9	9015	927	122.0	396.87	109.1
1909	208 38 38.35	96	49.4073	226.9	9380	1292	487.0	177.95	231.0
1910	73 26 8.03	97	189.7065	227.9	9745	1657	852.0	542.95	109.6
1911	298 13 37.71	99	105.3050	228.9	10110	2022	1217.0	324.03	231.5
1912 *B.*	164 37 15.20	101	21.9034	229.9	10476	2388	128.1	106.10	111.1
1913	29 24 41.88	102	162.2027	230.9	10841	2753	493.1	471.10	233.0
1914	254 12 14.56	104	77.8011	231.9	11206	158	858.1	252.18	111.6
1915	118 59 44.24	105	218.1004	232.9	11571	523	1223.1	33.26	233.5
1916 *B.*	345 23 21.73	107	134.6988	233.9	11937	889	134.2	399.26	113.1
1917	210 10 51.41	109	50.2973	234.9	315	1254	499.2	180.34	235.0
1918	174 58 21.09	110	190.5965	235.9	680	1619	864.2	545.34	113.6
1919	299 45 50.77	112	106.1950	236.9	1045	1984	1229.2	326.42	235.5
1920 *B.*	166 9 28.26	114	22.7935	237.9	1411	2350	140.2	108.50	115.2
1921	30 56 57.95	115	163.0927	238.9	1776	2715	505.2	473.50	237.0
1922	255 44 27.63	117	78.6912	1.0	2141	121	870.2	254.58	115.7
1923	120 31 57.31	118	218.9904	2.0	2506	486	1235.2	35.65	237.5
1924 *B.*	346 55 34.80	120	135.5889	3.0	2872	852	146.3	401.65	117.2
1925	211 43 4.49	122	51.1873	4.0	3237	1217	511.3	182.73	239.0
1926	76 30 34.17	123	191.4866	5.0	3602	1582	876.3	547.73	117.7
1927	301 18 3.86	125	107.0850	6.0	3967	1947	1241.3	328.81	239.5
1928 *B.*	167 41 41.35	127	23.6835	7.0	4333	2313	152.4	110.89	119.2
1929	32 29 11.04	128	163.9827	8.0	4698	2678	517.4	475.89	241.0
1930	257 16 40.72	130	79.5812	9.0	5063	84	882.4	256.97	119.7
1931	122 4 10.41	131	219.8804	10.0	5428	449	1247.4	38.05	241.5
1932 *B.*	348 27 47.90	133	136.4789	11.0	5794	815	158.4	404.05	121.2
1933	213 15 17.59	135	52.0774	12.0	6159	1180	523.4	185.13	243.0
1934	78 2 47.27	136	192.3766	13.0	6524	1545	888.4	550.13	121.7
1935	302 50 16.96	138	107.9751	14.0	6889	1910	1253.4	331.20	0.4
1936 *B.*	169 13 54.46	140	24.5735	15.0	7255	2276	164.5	113.28	123.2
1937	34 1 24.15	141	164.8728	16.0	7620	2641	529.5	478.28	1.9
1938	258 48 53.83	143	80.4712	17.0	7985	47	894.5	259.36	123.7
1939	123 36 23.52	144	220.7705	18.0	8350	412	1259.5	40.44	2.4
1940 *B.*	350 0 1.02	146	137.3690	19.0	8716	778	170.5	406.44	125.2
1941	214 47 30.71	148	52.9674	20.0	9081	1143	535.5	187.52	3.9
1942	79 35 0.40	149	193.2667	21.0	9446	1508	900.5	552.52	125.7
1943	304 22 30.09	151	108.8651	22.0	9811	1873	1265.5	333.60	4.4
1944 *B.*	170 46 7.59	153	25.4636	23.0	10177	2239	176.6	115.68	127.2
1945	35 33 37.28	154	165.7628	24.0	10542	2604	541.6	480.68	5.9
1946	260 21 6.97	156	81.3613	25.0	10907	10	906.6	261.76	127.7
1947	125 8 36.66	157	221.6606	26.0	11272	375	1271.6	42.83	6.4
1948 *B.*	351 32 14.16	159	138.2590	27.0	11638	741	182.7	408.83	129.2
1949	216 19 43.85	161	53.8575	28.0	15	1106	547.7	189.91	7.9

Constant subtracted from $L = 47' 40''$.

Mean Longitude, Arguments, &c., for Washington Mean Noon of Jan. 0 in common years, Jan. 1 in bissextile years.

Year.	VIII.	IX.	X.	XI.	XII.	XIII.	XIV.	Log. sin *i*.	360° − ☊.
	d	d							° ′ ″
1900	141.5	69.15	59.07	248.80	37.2	37.72	26.1	8.7722824	284 13 0.8
1901	65.3	197.16	5.58	31.09	16.5	43.94	27.6	2837	12 28.3
1902	209.8	88.17	38.81	181.73	36.1	47.06	28.4	2851	11 55.8
1903	133.6	216.18	45.36	237.02	15.4	53.28	29.9	2864	11 23.3
1904 *B*.	58.5	108.20	51.88	52.31	54.6	59.50	31.4	2878	10 50.7
1905	202.9	236.21	25.13	199.96	14.3	2.62	32.2	8.7722891	284 10 18.2
1906	126.8	127.22	31.65	15.25	53.5	8.84	33.7	2905	9 45.7
1907	50.7	18.24	4.91	162.89	13.1	11.95	34.4	2918	9 13.2
1908 *B*.	196.1	147.25	11.43	218.18	52.4	18.17	35.9	2932	8 40.6
1909	120.0	38.26	17.95	33.47	31.6	21.40	1.5	2945	8 8.1
1910	43.8	166.27	51.20	181.12	51.3	27.51	2.2	8.7722959	284 7 35.6
1911	188.3	57.29	57.72	236.41	30.5	33.73	3.7	2972	7 3.0
1912 *B*.	113.1	186.29	4.24	51.70	9.8	39.96	5.2	2986	6 30.4
1913	37.0	77.31	37.50	199.31	29.4	43.07	5.9	2999	5 57.9
1914	181.4	205.32	44.01	14.63	8.6	49.29	7.4	3012	5 25.4
1915	105.3	96.33	17.27	162.27	28.3	52.40	8.2	8.7723026	284 4 52.9
1916 *B*.	30.2	225.34	23.79	217.56	7.5	58.63	9.7	3039	4 20.3
1917	174.6	116.36	30.31	32.85	46.8	4.85	11.2	3053	3 47.8
1918	98.5	7.38	3.57	180.50	6.4	7.96	11.9	3066	3 15.3
1919	22.3	135.38	10.08	235.79	45.6	14.19	13.4	3080	2 42.8
1920 *B*.	167.8	27.40	16.60	51.08	24.9	20.41	15.0	8.7723093	284 2 10.2
1921	91.6	155.41	49.86	198.72	44.5	23.52	15.7	3107	1 37.6
1922	15.5	46.42	56.38	14.01	23.8	29.75	17.2	3120	1 5.1
1923	159.9	174.43	29.63	161.66	43.4	32.86	18.0	3134	0 32.6
1924 *B*.	84.8	66.45	36.15	216.95	22.6	39.08	19.5	3147	284 0 0.0
1925	8.7	194.46	42.67	32.24	1.9	45.30	21.0	8.7723160	283 59 27.5
1926	153.1	85.47	15.93	179.88	21.5	48.42	21.7	3174	58 55.0
1927	77.0	213.48	22.45	235.17	0.8	51.64	23.2	3187	58 22.5
1928 *B*.	1.9	105.50	28.96	50.46	40.0	0.86	24.7	3201	57 49.9
1929	146.3	233.50	2.22	198.10	59.6	3.97	25.5	3214	57 17.3
1930	70.2	124.52	8.74	13.39	38.9	10.20	27.0	8.7723228	283 56 44.8
1931	214.6	15.54	42.00	161.04	58.5	13.31	27.7	3241	56 12.3
1932 *B*.	139.5	144.55	48.51	216.33	37.8	19.53	29.2	3255	55 39.7
1933	63.3	35.56	55.03	31.62	17.0	25.76	30.7	3268	55 7.2
1934	207.8	163.57	28.29	179.26	36.6	28.87	31.5	3282	54 34.7
1935	131.6	54.59	34.81	234.55	15.9	35.09	33.0	8.7723295	283 54 2.1
1936 *B*.	56.5	183.59	41.32	49.81	55.1	41.32	34.5	3309	53 29.5
1937	200.9	74.61	14.58	197.49	14.8	44.43	35.3	3322	52 57.0
1938	124.8	202.62	21.10	12.78	54.0	50.65	0.8	3335	52 24.5
1939	48.7	93.63	54.36	160.42	13.6	53.76	1.5	3349	51 52.0
1940 *B*.	194.1	222.64	0.88	215.71	52.9	59.99	3.0	8.7723362	283 51 19.4
1941	118.0	113.66	7.39	31.00	32.1	6.21	4.5	3376	50 46.9
1942	41.8	4.67	40.65	178.64	51.8	9.32	5.3	3389	50 14.3
1943	186.3	132.68	47.17	233.93	31.0	15.55	6.8	3403	49 41.8
1944 *B*.	111.1	24.70	53.69	49.22	10.3	21.77	8.3	3416	49 9.2
1945	35.0	152.71	26.95	196.87	29.9	24.88	9.0	8.7723430	283 48 36.7
1946	179.4	43.72	33.46	12.16	9.1	31.10	10.5	3443	48 4.2
1947	103.3	171.73	6.72	159.80	28.8	34.22	11.3	3457	47 31.6
1948 *B*.	28.2	63.75	13.24	215.09	8.0	40.44	12.8	3470	46 59.0
1949	172.6	191.76	19.76	30.38	47.3	46.66	14.3	8.7723484	283 46 26.5

TABLE VII.

Motion of mean Longitude and of $-$ ☊; and Fraction of Year.

Common Year.	Bissextile Year.	Motion of Mean Longitude.	Motion of 360° — ☊	Fract. of Year.	Year.	Motion of Mean Longitude.	Motion of 360° — ☊	Fract. of Year.
		° ′ ″	″			° ′ ″	″	
Jan. 0	Jan. 1	0 0 0.00	— 0.0	0.000	Mar. 1	96 7 48.44	— 5.3	0.164
1	2	1 36 7.81	0.1	0.003	2	97 43 56.25	5.4	0.167
2	3	3 12 15.61	0.2	0.005	3	99 20 4.05	5.5	0.170
3	4	4 48 23.42	0.3	0.008	4	100 56 11.86	5.6	0.173
4	5	6 24 31.23	— 0.4	0.011	5	102 32 19.67	— 5.7	0.175
5	6	8 0 39.04	0.4	0.014	6	104 8 27.48	5.8	0.178
6	7	9 36 46.84	0.5	0.016	7	105 44 35.29	5.9	0.181
7	8	11 12 54.65	0.6	0.019	8	107 20 43.09	6.0	0.183
8	9	12 49 2.46	— 0.7	0.022	9	108 56 50.90	— 6.1	0.186
9	10	14 25 10.27	0.8	0.025	10	110 32 58.70	6.1	0.189
10	11	16 1 18.07	0.9	0.027	11	112 9 6.51	6.2	0.192
11	12	17 37 25.88	1.0	0.030	12	113 45 14.32	6.3	0.194
12	13	19 13 33.69	— 1.1	0.033	13	115 21 22.13	— 6.4	0.197
13	14	20 49 41.50	1.2	0.036	14	116 57 29.93	6.5	0.200
14	15	22 25 49.30	1.2	0.038	15	118 33 37.74	6.6	0.203
15	16	24 1 57.11	1.3	0.041	16	120 9 45.55	6.7	0.205
16	17	25 38 4.92	— 1.4	0.044	17	121 45 53.36	— 6.8	0.208
17	18	27 14 12.72	1.5	0.047	18	123 22 1.16	6.9	0.211
18	19	28 50 20.53	1.6	0.049	19	124 58 8.97	6.9	0.214
19	20	30 26 28.34	1.7	0.052	20	126 34 16.78	7.0	0.216
20	21	32 2 36.15	— 1.8	0.055	21	128 10 24.59	— 7.1	0.219
21	22	33 38 43.95	1.9	0.057	22	129 46 32.39	7.2	0.222
22	23	35 14 51.76	2.0	0.060	23	131 22 40.20	7.3	0.225
23	24	36 50 59.57	2.0	0.063	24	132 58 48.01	7.4	0.227
24	25	38 27 7.38	— 2.1	0.066	25	134 34 55.81	— 7.5	0.230
25	26	40 3 15.18	2.2	0.068	26	136 11 3.62	7.6	0.233
26	27	41 39 22.99	2.3	0.071	27	137 47 11.43	7.7	0.236
27	28	43 15 30.80	2.4	0.074	28	139 23 19.24	7.7	0.238
28	29	44 51 38.60	— 2.5	0.077	29	140 59 27.04	— 7.8	0.241
29	30	46 27 46.41	2.6	0.079	30	142 35 34.85	7.9	0.244
30	31	48 3 54.22	2.7	0.082	31	144 11 42.66	8.0	0.246
31	Feb. 1	49 40 2.03	2.8	0.085	Apr. 1	145 47 50.47	8.1	0.249
Feb. 1	2	51 16 9.83	— 2.8	0.088	2	147 23 58.27	— 8.2	0.252
2	3	52 52 17.64	2.9	0.090	3	149 0 6.08	8.3	0.255
3	4	54 28 25.45	3.0	0.093	4	150 36 13.89	8.4	0.257
4	5	56 4 33.26	3.1	0.096	5	152 12 21.69	8.5	0.260
5	6	57 40 41.06	— 3.2	0.099	6	153 48 29.50	— 8.5	0.263
6	7	59 16 48.87	3.3	0.101	7	155 24 37.31	8.6	0.266
7	8	60 52 56.68	3.4	0.104	8	157 0 45.12	8.7	0.268
8	9	62 29 4.49	3.5	0.107	9	158 36 52.92	8.8	0.271
9	10	64 5 12.29	— 3.6	0.110	10	160 13 0.73	— 8.9	0.274
10	11	65 41 20.10	3.6	0.112	11	161 49 8.54	9.0	0.277
11	12	67 17 27.91	3.7	0.115	12	163 25 16.35	9.1	0.278
12	13	68 53 35.71	3.8	0.118	13	165 1 24.15	9.2	0.282
13	14	70 29 43.52	— 3.9	0.120	14	166 37 31.96	— 9.3	0.285
14	15	72 5 51.33	4.0	0.123	15	168 13 39.77	9.3	0.288
15	16	73 41 59.14	4.1	0.126	16	169 49 47.58	9.4	0.290
16	17	75 18 6.94	4.2	0.129	17	171 25 55.38	9.5	0.293
17	18	76 54 14.75	— 4.3	0.131	18	173 2 3.19	— 9.6	0.296
18	19	78 30 22.56	4.4	0.134	19	174 38 11.00	9.7	0.298
19	20	80 6 30.37	4.5	0.137	20	176 14 18.80	9.8	0.301
20	21	81 42 38.17	4.5	0.140	21	177 50 26.61	9.9	0.304
21	22	83 18 45.98	— 4.6	0.142	22	179 26 34.42	—10.0	0.307
22	23	84 54 53.79	4.7	0.145	23	181 2 42.23	10.1	0.309
23	24	86 31 1.60	4.8	0.148	24	182 38 50.03	10.1	0.312
24	25	88 7 9.40	4.9	0.151	25	184 14 57.84	10.2	0.315
25	26	89 43 17.21	— 5.0	0.153	26	185 51 5.65	—10.3	0.318
26	27	91 19 25.02	5.1	0.156	27	187 27 13.46	10.4	0.320
27	28	92 55 32.82	5.2	0.159	28	189 3 21.26	10.5	0.323
28	29	94 31 40.63	— 5.3	0.161	29	190 39 29.07	—10.6	0.326

Motion of Mean Longitude and of − ☊; and Fraction of Year.

Year.	Motion of Mean Longitude.	Motion of 360° − ☊	Fraction of Year.	Year.	Motion of Mean Longitude.	Motion of 360° − ☊	Fraction of Year.
	° ′ ″	″			° ′ ″	″	
April 30	192 15 36.88	−10.7	0.329	June 29	288 23 25.32	−16.0	0.493
May 1	193 51 44.69	10.8	0.331	30	289 59 33.12	16.1	0.496
2	195 27 52.49	10.9	0.334	July 1	291 35 40.93	16.2	0.498
3	197 4 0.30	10.9	0.337	2	293 11 48.74	16.3	0.501
4	198 40 8.11	−11.0	0.340	3	294 47 56.55	−16.4	0.504
5	200 16 15.91	11.1	0.342	4	296 24 4.35	16.5	0.507
6	201 52 23.72	11.2	0.345	5	298 0 12.16	16.6	0.509
7	203 28 31.53	11.3	0.348	6	299 36 19.97	16.7	0.512
8	205 4 39.34	−11.4	0.350	7	301 12 27.78	−16.7	0.515
9	206 40 47.14	11.5	0.353	8	302 48 35.58	16.8	0.518
10	208 16 54.95	11.6	0.356	9	304 24 43.39	16.9	0.520
11	209 53 2.76	11.7	0.359	10	306 0 51.20	17.0	0.523
12	211 29 10.57	−11.8	0.361	11	307 36 59.00	−17.1	0.526
13	213 5 18.37	11.8	0.364	12	309 13 6.81	17.2	0.528
14	214 41 26.18	11.9	0.367	13	310 49 14.62	17.3	0.531
15	216 17 33.99	12.0	0.370	14	312 25 22.43	17.4	0.534
16	217 53 41.79	−12.1	0.372	15	314 1 30.23	−17.4	0.537
17	219 29 49.60	12.2	0.375	16	315 37 38.04	17.5	0.539
18	221 5 57.41	12.3	0.378	17	317 13 45.85	17.6	0.542
19	222 42 5.22	12.4	0.381	18	318 49 53.66	17.7	0.545
20	224 18 13.02	−12.5	0.383	19	320 26 1.46	−17.8	0.548
21	225 54 20.83	12.6	0.386	20	322 2 9.27	17.9	0.550
22	227 30 28.64	12.6	0.389	21	323 38 17.08	18.0	0.553
23	229 6 36.45	12.7	0.392	22	325 14 24.88	18.1	0.556
24	230 42 44.25	−12.8	0.394	23	326 50 32.69	−18.2	0.559
25	232 18 52.06	12.9	0.397	24	328 26 40.50	18.2	0.561
26	233 54 59.87	13.0	0.400	25	330 2 48.31	18.3	0.564
27	235 31 7.68	13.1	0.403	26	331 38 56.11	18.4	0.567
28	237 7 15.48	−13.2	0.405	27	333 15 3.92	−18.5	0.570
29	238 43 23.29	13.3	0.408	28	334 51 11.73	18.6	0.572
30	240 19 31.10	13.4	0.411	29	336 27 19.54	18.7	0.575
31	241 55 38.90	13.4	0.413	30	338 3 27.34	18.8	0.578
June 1	243 31 46.71	−13.5	0.416	31	339 39 35.15	−18.9	0.580
2	245 7 54.52	13.6	0.419	Aug. 1	341 15 42.96	19.0	0.583
3	246 44 2.33	13.7	0.422	2	342 51 50.77	19.1	0.586
4	248 20 10.13	13.8	0.424	3	344 27 58.57	19.1	0.589
5	249 56 17.94	−13.9	0.427	4	346 4 6.38	−19.2	0.591
6	251 32 25.75	14.0	0.430	5	347 40 14.19	19.3	0.594
7	253 8 33.56	14.1	0.433	6	349 16 21.99	19.4	0.597
8	254 44 41.36	14.2	0.435	7	350 52 29.80	19.5	0.600
9	256 20 49.17	−14.2	0.438	8	352 28 37.61	−19.6	0.602
10	257 56 56.98	14.3	0.441	9	354 4 45.42	19.7	0.605
11	259 33 4.79	14.4	0.444	10	355 40 53.22	19.8	0.608
12	261 9 12.59	14.5	0.446	11	357 17 1.03	19.9	0.611
13	262 45 20.40	−14.6	0.449	12	358 53 8.84	−19.9	0.613
14	264 21 28.21	14.7	0.452	13	0 29 16.65	20.0	0.616
15	265 57 36.01	14.8	0.455	14	2 5 24.45	20.1	0.619
16	267 33 43.82	14.9	0.457	15	3 41 32.26	20.2	0.622
17	269 9 51.63	−15.0	0.460	16	5 17 40.07	−20.3	0.624
18	270 45 59.44	15.0	0.463	17	6 53 47.88	20.4	0.627
19	272 22 7.24	15.1	0.465	18	8 29 55.68	20.5	0.630
20	273 58 15.05	15.2	0.468	19	10 6 3.49	20.6	0.632
21	275 34 22.86	−15.3	0.471	20	11 42 11.30	−20.7	0.635
22	277 10 30.67	15.4	0.474	21	13 18 19.10	20.7	0.638
23	278 46 38.47	15.5	0.476	22	14 54 26.91	20.8	0.641
24	280 22 46.28	15.6	0.479	23	16 30 34.72	20.9	0.643
25	281 58 54.09	−15.7	0.482	24	18 6 42.53	−21.0	0.646
26	283 35 1.89	15.8	0.485	25	19 42 50.33	21.1	0.649
27	285 11 9.70	15.8	0.487	26	21 18 58.14	21.2	0.652
28	286 47 17.51	−15.9	0.490	27	22 55 5.95	−21.3	0.654

TABLE VII.

Motion of Mean Longitude and of − ☊; and Fraction of Year.

Year.	Motion of Mean Longitude.	Motion of 360°−☊	Fraction of Year.	Year.	Motion of Mean Longitude.	Motion of 360°−☊	Fraction of Year.
Aug. 28	24° 31′ 13″.76	−21″.4	0.657	Nov. 4	133° 28′ 4″.65	−27″.4	0.843
29	26 7 21.56	21.5	0.660	5	135 4 12.46	27.5	0.846
30	27 43 29.37	21.5	0.663	6	136 40 20.27	27.6	0.849
31	29 19 37.18	21.6	0.665	7	138 16 28.07	27.7	0.852
Sept. 1	30 55 44.98	−21.7	0.668	8	139 52 35.88	−27.8	0.854
2	32 31 52.79	21.8	0.671	9	141 28 43.69	27.9	0.857
3	34 8 0.60	21.9	0.674	10	143 4 51.50	28.0	0.860
4	35 44 8.41	22.0	0.676	11	144 40 59.30	28.0	0.862
5	37 20 16.21	−22.1	0.679	12	146 17 7.11	−28.1	0.865
6	38 56 24.02	22.2	0.682	13	147 53 14.92	28.2	0.868
7	40 32 31.83	22.3	0.685	14	149 29 22.73	28.3	0.871
8	42 8 39.64	22.3	0.687	15	151 5 30.53	28.4	0.873
9	43 44 47.44	−22.4	0.690	16	152 41 38.34	−28.5	0.876
10	45 20 55.25	22.5	0.693	17	154 17 46.15	28.6	0.879
11	46 57 3.06	22.6	0.695	18	155 53 53.96	28.7	0.882
12	48 33 10.87	22.7	0.698	19	157 30 1.76	28.8	0.884
13	50 9 18.67	−22.8	0.701	20	159 6 9.57	−28.8	0.887
14	51 45 26.48	22.9	0.704	21	160 42 17.38	28.9	0.890
15	53 21 34.29	23.0	0.706	22	162 18 25.18	29.0	0.893
16	54 57 42.09	23.1	0.709	23	163 54 32.99	29.1	0.895
17	56 33 49.90	−23.1	0.712	24	165 30 40.80	−29.2	0.898
18	58 9 57.71	23.2	0.715	25	167 6 48.61	29.3	0.901
19	59 46 5.52	23.3	0.717	26	168 42 56.41	29.4	0.904
20	61 22 13.32	23.4	0.720	27	170 19 4.22	29.5	0.906
21	62 58 21.13	−23.5	0.723	28	171 55 12.03	−29.6	0.909
22	64 34 28.94	23.6	0.726	29	173 31 19.84	29.6	0.912
23	66 10 36.75	23.7	0.728	30	175 7 27.64	29.7	0.914
24	67 46 44.55	23.8	0.731	Dec. 1	176 43 35.45	29.8	0.917
25	69 22 52.36	−23.9	0.734	2	178 19 43.26	−29.9	0.920
26	70 59 0.17	23.9	0.737	3	179 55 51.07	30.0	0.923
27	72 35 7.98	24.0	0.739	4	181 31 58.87	30.1	0.925
28	74 11 15.78	24.1	0.742	5	183 8 6.68	30.2	0.928
29	75 47 23.59	−24.2	0.745	6	184 44 14.49	−30.3	0.931
30	77 23 31.40	24.3	0.747	7	186 20 22.29	30.4	0.934
Oct. 1	78 59 39.20	24.4	0.750	8	187 56 30.10	30.4	0.936
2	80 35 47.01	24.5	0.753	9	189 32 37.91	30.5	0.939
3	82 11 54.82	−24.6	0.756	10	191 8 45.72	−30.6	0.942
4	83 48 2.63	24.7	0.758	11	192 44 53.52	30.7	0.945
5	85 24 10.43	24.7	0.761	12	194 21 1.33	30.8	0.947
6	87 0 18.24	24.8	0.764	13	195 57 9.14	30.9	0.950
7	88 36 26.05	−24.9	0.767	14	197 33 16.95	−31.0	0.953
8	90 12 33.86	25.0	0.769	15	199 9 24.75	31.1	0.956
9	91 48 41.66	25.1	0.772	16	200 45 32.56	31.2	0.958
10	93 24 49.47	25.2	0.775	17	202 21 40.37	31.2	0.961
11	95 0 57.28	−25.3	0.778	18	203 57 48.17	−31.3	0.964
12	96 37 5.08	25.4	0.780	19	205 33 55.98	31.4	0.967
13	98 13 12.89	25.5	0.783	20	207 10 3.79	31.5	0.969
14	99 49 20.70	25.6	0.786	21	208 46 11.60	31.6	0.972
15	101 25 28.51	−25.6	0.789	22	210 22 19.40	−31.7	0.975
16	103 1 36.31	25.7	0.791	23	211 58 27.21	31.8	0.977
17	104 37 44.12	25.8	0.794	24	213 34 35.02	31.9	0.980
18	106 13 51.93	25.9	0.797	25	215 10 42.83	32.0	0.983
19	107 49 59.74	−26.0	0.800	26	216 46 50.63	−32.0	0.986
20	109 26 7.54	26.1	0.802	27	218 22 58.44	32.1	0.988
21	111 2 15.35	26.2	0.805	28	219 59 6.25	32.2	0.991
22	112 38 23.16	26.3	0.808	29	221 35 14.06	32.3	0.994
23	114 14 30.97	−26.4	0.810	30	223 11 21.86	−32.4	0.997
24	115 50 38.77	26.4	0.813	31	224 47 29.67	32.5	0.999
25	117 26 46.58	26.5	0.816	32	226 23 37.48	32.6	1.002
26	119 2 54.39	26.6	0.819	33	227 59 45.28	32.7	1.005
27	120 39 2.19	−26.7	0.821	34	229 35 53.09	−32.8	1.008
28	122 15 10.00	26.8	0.824	35	231 12 0.90	32.8	1.010
29	123 51 17.81	26.9	0.827	36	232 48 8.71	32.9	1.013
30	125 27 25.62	27.0	0.830	37	234 24 16.51	−33.0	1.016
31	127 3 33.42	−27.1	0.832				
Nov. 1	128 39 41.23	27.2	0.835				
2	130 15 49.04	27.2	0.838				
3	131 51 56.85	−27.3	0.841				

TABLE VIII.

Motion of Mean Longitude.

Hours.	For Hours.	Minutes or Seconds.	For Minutes.	For Seconds.	Minutes or Seconds.	For Minutes.	For Seconds.
	° ′ ″		′ ″	″		′ ″	″
1	0 4 0.325	1	0 4.005	0.067	31	2 4.168	2.069
2	0 8 0.651	2	0 8.011	0.134	32	2 8.173	2.136
3	0 12 0.976	3	0 12.016	0.200	33	2 12.179	2.203
4	0 16 1.301	4	0 16.022	0.267	34	2 16.184	2.270
5	0 20 1.627	5	0 20.027	0.334	35	2 20.190	2.336
6	0 24 1.952	6	0 24.033	0.401	36	2 24.195	2.403
7	0 28 2.277	7	0 28.038	0.467	37	2 28.201	2.470
8	0 32 2.602	8	0 32.043	0.534	38	2 32.206	2.537
9	0 36 2.928	9	0 36.049	0.601	39	2 36.211	2.604
10	0 40 3.253	10	0 40.054	0.668	40	2 40.217	2.670
11	0 44 3.578	11	0 44.060	0.734	41	2 44.222	2.737
12	0 48 3.904	12	0 48.065	0.801	42	2 48.228	2.804
13	0 52 4.229	13	0 52.070	0.868	43	2 52.233	2.871
14	0 56 4.554	14	0 56.076	0.935	44	2 56.239	2.937
15	1 0 4.880	15	1 0.081	1.001	45	3 0.244	3.004
16	1 4 5.205	16	1 4.087	1.068	46	3 4.249	3.071
17	1 8 5.530	17	1 8.092	1.135	47	3 8.255	3.138
18	1 12 5.856	18	1 12.098	1.202	48	3 12.260	3.204
19	1 16 6.181	19	1 16.103	1.268	49	3 16.266	3.271
20	1 20 6.506	20	1 20.108	1.335	50	3 20.271	3.338
21	1 24 6.831	21	1 24.114	1.402	51	3 24.277	3.405
22	1 28 7.157	22	1 28.119	1.469	52	3 28.282	3.471
23	1 32 7.482	23	1 32.125	1.535	53	3 32.287	3.538
24	1 36 7.807	24	1 36.130	1.602	54	3 36.293	3.605
		25	1 40.136	1.669	55	3 40.298	3.672
		26	1 44.141	1.736	56	3 44.304	3.738
		27	1 48.146	1.802	57	3 48.309	3.805
		28	1 52.152	1.869	58	3 52.314	3.872
		29	1 56.157	1.936	50	3 56.320	3.939
		30	2 0.163	2.003	60	4 0.325	4.005

Days.	Motion of M. L.	Days.	Motion of M. L.	Days.	Motion of M. L.
	° ′ ″		′ ″		″
0.1	0 9 36.781	0.01	0 57.678	0.001	5.768
0.2	0 19 13.561	0.02	1 55.356	0.002	11.536
0.3	0 28 50.342	0.03	2 53.034	0.003	17.303
0.4	0 38 27.123	0.04	3 50.712	0.004	23.071
0.5	0 48 3.904	0.05	4 48.390	0.005	28.839
0.6	0 57 40.684	0.06	5 46.068	0.006	34.607
0.7	1 7 17.465	0.07	6 43.746	0.007	40.375
0.8	1 16 54.246	0.08	7 41.425	0.008	46.142
0.9	1 26 31.027	0.09	8 39.103	0.009	51.910
1.0	1 36 7.807	0.10	9 36.781	0.010	57.678

TABLE IX.

Factor of a small Correction to be multiplied by the fraction of the year and then added to L.

Year.	Factor.	Year.	Factor.	Year.	Factor.	Year.	Factor.
	″		″		″		″
1750	−0.018	1800	−0.011	1850	−0.005	1900	+0.007
1760	0.016	1810	0.010	1860	0.003	1910	0.010
1770	0.015	1820	0.009	1870	−0.001	1920	0.013
1780	0.014	1830	0.007	1880	+0.001	1930	0.016
1790	0.012	1840	0.006	1890	0.004	1940	0.020
1800	−0.011	1850	−0.005	1900	+0.007	1950	+0.023

EQUATION OF THE CENTRE, FOR m = 0.

Constant added 47′ 3″.5. Period = 224^{d}.7008.

Arg. I.	0^{d}.0	Diff. for 0^{d}.1	0^{d}.1	Diff. for 0^{d}.1	0^{d}.2	Diff. for 0^{d}.1	0^{d}.3	Diff. for 0^{d}.1	0^{d}.4	Diff. for 0^{d}.1
d	° ′ ″	″	′ ″	″	′ ″	″	′ ″	″	′ ″	″
0	0 47 3.50	+7.96	47 11.46	+7.96	47 19.42	+7.96	47 27.38	+7.96	47 35.35	+7.96
1	0 48 23.11	7.96	48 31.07	7.96	48 39.03	7.96	48 46.98	7.96	48 54.94	7.95
2	0 49 42.65	7.95	49 50.60	7.95	49 58.55	7.95	50 6.50	7.94	50 14.44	7.94
3	0 51 2.07	7.93	51 10.00	7.93	51 17.93	7.93	51 25.86	7.93	51 33.79	7.93
4	0 52 21.30	7.91	52 29.21	7.91	52 37.11	7.91	52 45.02	7.90	52 52.92	7.90
5	0 53 40.27	7.88	53 48.15	7.88	53 56.02	7.88	54 3.90	7.87	54 11.77	7.87
6	0 54 58.92	7.85	55 6.77	7.84	55 14.61	7.84	55 22.44	7.84	55 30.28	7.83
7	0 56 17.19	7.81	56 25.00	7.80	56 32.79	7.80	56 40.59	7.79	56 48.38	7.79
8	0 57 35.02	7.76	57 42.78	7.75	57 50.53	7.75	57 58.27	7.74	58 6.01	7.74
9	0 58 52.34	7.70	59 0.04	7.70	59 7.74	7.69	59 15.43	7.69	59 23.11	7.68
10	1 0 9.09	7.64	0 16.74	7.64	0 24.37	7.63	0 32.00	7.63	0 39.62	7.62
11	1 1 25.22	7.58	1 32.79	7.57	1 40.36	7.56	1 47.92	7.56	1 55.48	7.55
12	1 2 40.65	7.51	2 48.15	7.50	2 55.65	7.49	3 3.11	7.48	3 10.62	7.48
13	1 3 55.33	7.43	4 2.76	7.42	4 10.17	7.41	4 17.58	7.40	4 24.98	7.40
14	1 5 9.20	7.34	5 16.54	7.34	5 23.88	7.33	5 31.20	7.32	5 38.51	7.31
15	1 6 22.21	7.25	6 29.46	7.24	6 36.70	7.24	6 43.93	7.23	6 51.15	7.22
16	1 7 34.28	7.16	7 41.44	7.15	7 48.58	7.14	7 55.71	7.13	8 2.84	7.12
17	1 8 45.37	7.06	8 52.43	7.05	8 59.47	7.04	9 6.50	7.03	9 13.52	7.01
18	1 9 55.42	6.95	10 2.37	6.94	10 9.30	6.93	10 16.22	6.92	10 23.14	6.91
19	1 11 4.37	6.84	11 11.20	6.83	11 18.03	6.82	11 24.83	6.80	11 31.63	6.79
20	1 12 12.17	6.72	12 18.89	6.71	12 25.59	6.70	12 32.28	6.68	12 38.96	6.67
21	1 13 18.77	6.60	13 25.36	6.59	13 31.94	6.57	13 38.50	6.56	13 45.06	6.55
22	1 14 24.10	6.47	14 30.57	6.46	14 37.02	6.44	14 43.45	6.43	14 49.87	6.42
23	1 15 28.13	6.34	15 34.46	6.32	15 40.78	6.31	15 47.08	6.29	15 53.36	6.28
24	1 16 30.80	6.20	16 36.99	6.19	16 43.16	6.17	16 49.32	6.16	16 55.47	6.14
25	1 17 32.05	6.05	17 38.10	6.04	17 44.13	6.02	17 50.15	6.01	17 56.15	6.00
26	1 18 31.85	5.90	18 37.75	5.89	18 43.63	5.87	18 49.50	5.86	18 55.35	5.84
27	1 19 30.15	5.75	19 35.89	5.74	19 41.62	5.72	19 47.33	5.71	19 53.03	5.69
28	1 20 26.89	5.59	20 32.47	5.58	20 38.05	5.56	20 43.60	5.55	20 49.14	5.53
29	1 21 22.04	5.43	21 27.46	5.42	21 32.87	5.40	21 38.26	5.38	21 43.64	5.37
30	1 22 15.55	5.27	22 20.81	5.25	22 26.05	5.23	22 31.27	5.21	22 36.48	5.20
31	1 23 7.38	5.10	23 12.47	5.08	23 17.54	5.06	23 22.59	5.05	23 27.63	5.03
32	1 23 57.49	4.92	24 2.40	4.90	24 7.30	4.89	24 12.18	4.87	24 17.04	4.85
33	1 24 45.84	4.75	24 50.58	4.73	24 55.29	4.71	25 0.00	4.69	25 4.68	4.67
34	1 25 32.39	4.56	25 36.95	4.55	25 41.49	4.53	25 46.00	4.51	25 50.50	4.49
35	1 26 17.12	4.38	26 21.49	4.36	26 25.84	4.34	26 30.17	4.32	26 34.49	4.30
36	1 26 59.97	4.18	27 4.15	4.17	27 8.32	4.15	27 12.46	4.13	27 16.59	4.11
37	1 27 40.93	4.00	27 44.92	3.98	27 48.89	3.96	27 52.84	3.94	27 56.77	3.92
38	1 28 19.96	3.80	28 23.75	3.78	28 27.53	3.77	28 31.28	3.75	28 35.02	3.73
39	1 28 57.02	3.61	29 0.62	3.59	29 4.20	3.57	29 7.76	3.55	29 11.29	3.53
40	1 29 32.10	3.41	29 35.50	3.39	29 38.87	3.37	29 42.22	3.35	29 45.57	3.33
41	1 30 5.16	3.20	30 8.36	3.18	30 11.53	3.16	30 14.69	3.14	30 17.82	3.12
42	1 30 36.19	3.00	30 39.18	2.98	30 42.14	2.96	30 45.09	2.94	30 48.02	2.92
43	1 31 5.15	2.79	31 7.93	2.77	31 10.69	2.75	31 13.43	2.73	31 16.15	2.71
44	1 31 32.02	2.58	31 34.59	2.56	31 37.15	2.54	31 39.68	2.52	31 42.18	2.50
45	1 31 56.80	2.37	31 59.16	2.35	32 1.50	2.33	32 3.81	2.31	32 6.11	2.29
46	1 32 19.45	2.16	32 21.59	2.14	32 23.72	2.12	32 25.83	2.09	32 27.91	2.07
47	1 32 39.96	1.94	32 41.89	1.92	32 43.80	1.90	32 45.69	1.87	32 47.56	1.85
48	1 32 58.32	1.73	33 0.04	1.71	33 1.73	1.68	33 3.40	1.66	33 5.06	1.64
49	1 33 14.51	1.51	33 16.01	1.49	33 17.49	1.47	33 18.95	1.44	33 20.38	1.42
50	1 33 28.53	1.29	33 29.81	1.27	33 31.07	1.25	33 32.30	1.23	33 33.52	1.20
51	1 33 40.36	1.08	33 41.42	1.05	33 42.46	1.03	33 43.48	1.01	33 44.47	0.99
52	1 33 49.99	0.85	33 50.83	0.83	33 51.65	0.81	33 52.45	0.79	33 53.23	0.76
53	1 33 57.43	0.63	33 58.05	0.61	33 58.65	0.59	33 59.23	0.56	33 59.78	0.54
54	1 34 2.06	0.41	34 3.06	0.39	34 3.41	0.37	34 3.80	0.35	34 4.13	0.32
55	1 34 5.68	+0.19	34 5.86	+0.17	34 6.02	+0.15	34 6.15	+0.13	34 6.27	+0.10

EQUATION OF THE CENTRE, FOR m = 0.

Constant added 47′ 3″.5. Period = 224^{d}.7008.

Arg. I.	0^{d}.5	Diff. for 0^{d}.1	0^{d}.6	Diff. for 0^{d}.1	0^{d}.7	Diff. for 0^{d}.1	0^{d}.8	Diff. for 0^{d}.1	0^{d}.9	Diff. for 0^{d}.1
d	° ′ ″	″	′ ″	″	′ ″	″	′ ″	″	′ ″	″
0	0 47 43.31	+7.96	47 51.27	+7.96	47 59.23	+7.96	48 7.19	+7.96	48 15.15	+7.96
1	0 49 2.89	7.95	49 10.85	7.95	49 18.80	7.95	49 26.75	7.95	49 34.70	7.95
2	0 50 22.38	7.94	50 30.32	7.94	50 38.26	7.94	50 46.20	7.94	50 54.14	7.93
3	0 51 41.71	7.92	51 49.63	7.92	51 57.55	7.92	52 5.47	7.92	52 13.38	7.91
4	0 53 0.82	7.90	53 8.71	7.89	53 16.61	7.89	53 24.50	7.88	53 32.38	7.88
5	0 54 19.64	7.86	54 27.50	7.86	54 35.36	7.86	54 43.22	7.85	54 51.07	7.85
6	0 55 38.11	7.83	55 45.93	7.82	55 53.75	7.82	56 1.57	7.81	56 9.38	7.81
7	0 56 56.16	7.78	57 3.95	7.78	57 11.72	7.77	57 19.49	7.77	57 27.26	7.76
8	0 58 13.75	7.73	58 21.48	7.73	58 29.20	7.72	58 36.92	7.72	58 44.63	7.71
9	0 59 30.79	7.67	59 38.46	7.67	59 46.13	7.66	59 53.79	7.66	60 1.44	7.65
10	1 0 47.24	7.61	0 54.85	7.61	1 2.45	7.60	1 10.05	7.59	1 17.64	7.58
11	1 2 3.02	7.54	2 10.36	7.54	2 18.10	7.53	2 25.62	7.52	2 33.14	7.51
12	1 3 18.00	7.47	3 25.55	7.46	3 33.01	7.45	3 40.46	7.44	3 47.90	7.44
13	1 4 32.37	7.39	4 39.76	7.38	4 47.13	7.37	4 54.50	7.36	5 1.85	7.35
14	1 5 45.82	7.30	5 53.11	7.29	6 0.40	7.28	6 7.68	7.27	6 14.95	7.26
15	1 6 58.36	7.21	7 5.57	7.20	7 12.70	7.19	7 19.94	7.18	7 27.12	7.17
16	1 8 9.95	7.11	8 17.06	7.10	8 24.15	7.09	8 31.24	7.08	8 38.31	7.07
17	1 9 20.53	7.00	9 27.53	6.99	9 34.52	6.98	9 41.50	6.97	9 48.47	6.96
18	1 10 30.04	6.90	10 36.93	6.88	10 43.81	6.87	10 50.67	6.86	10 57.53	6.85
19	1 11 38.42	6.78	11 45.19	6.77	11 51.96	6.76	11 58.71	6.74	12 5.45	6.73
20	1 12 45.63	6.66	12 52.28	6.65	12 58.92	6.63	13 5.55	6.60	13 12.17	6.61
21	1 13 51.60	6.53	13 58.12	6.52	14 4.61	6.51	14 11.14	6.50	14 17.63	6.48
22	1 14 56.28	6.40	15 2.68	6.39	15 9.06	6.38	15 15.43	6.36	15 21.79	6.35
23	1 15 59.61	6.27	16 5.90	6.25	16 12.14	6.24	16 18.38	6.22	16 24.59	6.21
24	1 17 1.60	6.13	17 7.72	6.11	17 13.83	6.10	17 19.92	6.08	17 25.99	6.07
25	1 18 2.14	5.98	18 8.11	5.96	18 14.07	5.95	18 20.01	5.93	18 25.94	5.92
26	1 19 1.19	5.83	19 7.01	5.81	19 12.82	5.80	19 18.61	5.78	19 24.39	5.77
27	1 19 58.71	5.67	20 4.38	5.66	20 10.03	5.64	20 15.67	5.63	20 21.29	5.61
28	1 20 54.66	5.50	21 0.17	5.50	21 5.66	5.48	21 11.14	5.47	21 16.60	5.45
29	1 21 49.00	5.35	21 54.34	5.33	21 59.67	5.32	22 4.98	5.30	22 10.27	5.28
30	1 22 41.67	5.18	22 46.85	5.16	22 52.01	5.15	22 57.15	5.13	23 2.27	5.11
31	1 23 32.65	5.01	23 37.65	4.99	23 42.64	4.98	23 47.60	4.96	23 52.55	4.94
32	1 24 21.88	4.83	24 26.71	4.82	24 31.52	4.80	24 36.31	4.78	24 41.08	4.76
33	1 25 9.34	4.66	25 13.99	4.64	25 18.62	4.62	25 23.23	4.60	25 27.82	4.58
34	1 25 54.90	4.47	25 59.45	4.45	26 3.80	4.43	26 8.32	4.42	26 12.73	4.39
35	1 26 38.78	4.28	26 43.06	4.27	26 47.31	4.25	26 51.55	4.23	26 55.77	4.21
36	1 27 20.09	4.09	27 24.78	4.08	27 28.84	4.06	27 32.89	4.04	27 36.92	4.02
37	1 28 0.09	3.90	28 4.58	3.88	28 8.45	3.86	28 12.31	3.84	28 16.14	3.82
38	1 28 38.74	3.71	28 42.43	3.69	28 46.11	3.67	28 49.77	3.65	28 53.40	3.63
39	1 29 14.81	3.51	29 18.31	3.49	29 21.79	3.47	29 25.25	3.45	29 28.68	3.43
40	1 29 48.88	3.31	29 52.18	3.29	29 55.46	3.27	29 58.71	3.25	30 1.95	3.22
41	1 30 20.93	3.10	30 24.03	3.08	30 27.09	3.06	30 30.15	3.04	30 33.18	3.02
42	1 30 50.93	2.90	30 53.81	2.88	30 56.68	2.85	30 59.52	2.83	31 2.34	2.81
43	1 31 18.85	2.68	31 21.52	2.67	31 24.18	2.65	31 26.81	2.62	31 29.43	2.60
44	1 31 44.67	2.48	31 47.14	2.46	31 49.59	2.44	31 52.01	2.41	31 54.41	2.39
45	1 32 8.39	2.27	32 10.64	2.24	32 12.88	2.22	32 15.09	2.20	32 17.28	2.18
46	1 32 29.97	2.05	32 32.01	2.03	32 34.03	2.01	32 36.03	1.99	32 38.00	1.97
47	1 32 49.41	1.83	32 51.23	1.81	32 53.04	1.79	32 54.82	1.77	32 56.58	1.75
48	1 33 6.69	1.62	33 8.29	1.60	33 9.88	1.58	33 11.45	1.55	33 12.99	1.53
49	1 33 21.79	1.40	33 23.18	1.38	33 24.55	1.36	33 25.90	1.33	33 27.22	1.31
50	1 33 34.71	1.18	33 35.89	1.16	33 37.04	1.14	33 38.16	1.12	33 39.27	1.10
51	1 33 45.45	0.96	33 46.40	0.94	33 47.33	0.92	33 48.24	0.90	33 49.13	0.88
52	1 33 53.98	0.74	33 54.72	0.72	33 55.43	0.70	33 56.11	0.67	33 56.78	0.65
53	1 34 0.32	0.52	34 0.83	0.50	34 1.32	0.48	34 1.79	0.46	34 2.21	0.43
54	1 34 4.44	0.30	34 4.73	0.28	34 5.00	0.26	34 5.25	0.24	34 5.48	+0.21
55	1 34 6.36	+0.08	34 6.43	+0.06	34 6.48	+0.04	34 6.50	+0.01	34 6.51	−0.01

TABLE X.

EQUATION OF THE CENTRE, FOR m = 0.

Constant added 47′ 3″.5. Period = $224^{d}.7008$.

Arg. I.	d 0.0	Diff. for 0d.1	d 0.1	Diff. for 0d.1	d 0.2	Diff. for 0d.1	d 0.3	Diff. for 0d.1	d 0.4	Diff. for 0d.1
d	° ′ ″	″	′ ″	″	′ ″	″	′ ″	″	′ ″	″
56	1 34 6.49	−0.03	34 6.45	−0.05	34 6.39	−0.07	34 6.31	−0.09	34 6.20	−0.12
57	1 34 5.10	0.25	34 4.84	0.27	34 4.56	0.29	34 4.25	0.32	34 3.92	0.34
58	1 34 1.50	0.47	34 1.02	0.49	34 0.52	0.51	33 59.99	0.54	33 59.45	0.56
59	1 33 55.71	0.69	33 55.01	0.71	33 54.28	0.73	33 53.54	0.75	33 52.77	0.78
60	1 33 47.72	0.91	33 46.80	0.93	33 45.86	0.95	33 44.89	0.97	33 43.91	1.00
61	1 33 37.54	1.13	33 36.40	1.15	33 35.24	1.17	33 34.06	1.19	33 32.86	1.21
62	1 33 25.19	1.34	33 23.83	1.37	33 22.45	1.39	33 21.06	1.41	33 19.64	1.43
63	1 33 10.67	1.56	33 9.10	1.58	33 7.51	1.60	33 5.89	1.62	33 4.26	1.65
64	1 32 54.00	1.77	32 52.21	1.80	32 50.41	1.82	32 48.58	1.84	32 46.73	1.86
65	1 32 35.19	1.99	32 33.19	2.01	32 31.17	2.03	32 29.13	2.05	32 27.07	2.07
66	1 32 14.26	2.20	32 12.05	2.22	32 9.82	2.24	32 7.57	2.26	32 5.29	2.28
67	1 31 51.22	2.41	31 48.80	2.43	31 46.37	2.45	31 43.91	2.47	31 41.42	2.49
68	1 31 26.10	2.62	31 23.48	2.64	31 20.83	2.66	31 18.16	2.68	31 15.47	2.70
69	1 30 58.92	2.82	30 56.09	2.84	30 53.23	2.86	30 50.36	2.88	30 47.47	2.90
70	1 30 29.69	3.02	30 26.66	3.04	30 23.60	3.06	30 20.53	3.08	30 17.43	3.10
71	1 29 58.45	3.22	29 55.21	3.24	29 51.96	3.26	29 48.68	3.28	29 45.39	3.30
72	1 29 25.21	3.42	29 21.78	3.44	29 18.33	3.46	29 14.86	3.48	29 11.37	3.50
73	1 28 50.01	3.62	28 46.38	3.64	28 42.74	3.66	28 39.07	3.68	28 35.39	3.69
74	1 28 12.87	3.81	28 9.05	3.83	28 5.22	3.85	28 1.36	3.87	27 57.48	3.89
75	1 27 33.81	4.00	27 29.82	4.02	27 25.79	4.04	27 21.75	4.05	27 17.68	4.07
76	1 26 52.91	4.18	26 48.71	4.20	26 44.50	4.22	26 40.27	4.24	26 36.02	4.26
77	1 26 10.14	4.37	26 5.77	4.38	26 1.37	4.40	25 56.96	4.42	25 52.53	4.44
78	1 25 25.57	4.55	25 21.02	4.56	25 16.44	4.58	25 11.85	4.60	25 7.24	4.62
79	1 24 39.23	4.72	24 34.50	4.74	24 29.75	4.76	24 24.98	4.77	24 20.20	4.79
80	1 23 51.14	4.89	23 46.24	4.91	23 41.32	4.93	23 36.39	4.94	23 31.43	4.96
81	1 23 1.36	5.06	22 56.29	5.08	22 51.21	5.09	22 46.10	5.11	22 40.98	5.13
82	1 22 9.92	5.23	22 4.69	5.24	21 59.44	5.26	21 54.17	5.27	21 48.89	5.29
83	1 21 16.86	5.39	21 11.47	5.40	21 6.06	5.42	21 0.63	5.43	20 55.19	5.45
84	1 20 22.23	5.54	20 16.68	5.56	20 11.12	5.57	20 5.54	5.59	19 59.94	5.60
85	1 19 26.06	5.69	19 20.36	5.71	19 14.64	5.72	19 8.91	5.74	19 3.17	5.75
86	1 18 28.39	5.84	18 22.55	5.85	18 16.69	5.87	18 10.81	5.88	18 4.92	5.90
87	1 17 29.29	5.98	17 23.30	5.99	17 17.30	6.01	17 11.28	6.02	17 5.25	6.04
88	1 16 28.78	6.12	16 22.65	6.13	16 16.51	6.15	16 10.36	6.16	16 4.19	6.18
89	1 15 26.92	6.25	15 20.66	6.26	15 14.39	6.28	15 8.10	6.29	15 1.81	6.30
90	1 14 23.75	6.38	14 17.37	6.39	14 10.97	6.40	14 4.56	6.42	13 58.13	6.43
91	1 13 19.33	6.50	13 12.82	6.51	13 6.30	6.53	12 59.77	6.54	12 53.22	6.55
92	1 12 13.70	6.62	12 7.08	6.63	12 0.44	6.64	11 53.79	6.66	11 47.13	6.67
93	1 11 6.92	6.73	11 0.18	6.75	10 53.43	6.76	10 46.67	6.77	10 39.89	6.78
94	1 9 59.03	6.84	9 52.19	6.85	9 45.33	6.86	9 38.46	6.87	9 31.58	6.88
95	1 8 50.09	6.94	8 43.14	6.95	8 36.18	6.96	8 29.22	6.97	8 22.24	6.98
96	1 7 40.16	7.04	7 33.11	7.05	7 26.05	7.06	7 18.99	7.07	7 11.91	7.08
97	1 6 29.27	7.13	6 22.14	7.14	6 14.99	7.15	6 7.83	7.16	6 0.67	7.17
98	1 5 17.50	7.22	5 10.28	7.23	5 3.05	7.24	4 55.80	7.24	4 48.56	7.25
99	1 4 4.89	7.30	3 57.59	7.31	3 50.28	7.32	3 42.96	7.32	3 35.63	7.33
100	1 2 51.51	7.38	2 44.13	7.38	2 36.74	7.39	2 29.35	7.40	2 21.94	7.40
101	1 1 37.39	7.45	1 29.95	7.45	1 22.49	7.46	1 15.03	7.46	1 7.56	7.47
102	0 60 22.62	7.51	60 15.11	7.51	60 7.59	7.52	60 0.06	7.53	59 52.53	7.53
103	0 59 7.23	7.57	58 59.66	7.57	58 52.08	7.58	58 44.50	7.58	58 36.91	7.59
104	0 57 51.29	7.62	57 43.67	7.62	57 36.04	7.63	57 28.41	7.63	57 20.77	7.64
105	0 56 34.86	7.67	56 27.19	7.67	56 19.52	7.67	56 11.84	7.68	56 4.16	7.68
106	0 55 17.99	7.71	55 10.28	7.71	55 2.56	7.71	54 54.85	7.72	54 47.13	7.72
107	0 54 0.74	7.74	53 53.00	7.74	53 45.25	7.75	53 37.50	7.75	53 29.75	7.75
108	0 52 43.18	7.77	52 35.40	7.77	52 27.63	7.77	52 19.85	7.78	52 12.07	7.78
109	0 51 25.35	7.79	51 17.56	7.79	51 9.76	7.80	51 1.96	7.80	50 54.16	7.80
110	0 50 7.33	7.81	49 59.52	7.81	49 51.71	7.81	49 43.89	7.81	49 36.08	7.82
111	0 48 49.17	−7.82	48 41.34	−7.82	48 33.52	−7.82	48 25.70	−7.83	48 17.87	−7.82

EQUATION OF THE CENTRE, FOR m = 0.

Constant added 47′ 30″.5. Period = $221^{d}.7008$.

Arg. I	d 0.5	Diff. for $0^{d}.1$	d 0.6	Diff. for $0^{d}.1$	d 0.7	Diff. for $0^{d}.1$	d 0.8	Diff. for $0^{d}.1$	d 0.9	Diff. for $0^{d}.1$
d 56	° 1 34′ 6.07″	″ −0.14	34′ 5.92″	″ −0.16	34′ 5.75″	″ −0.18	34′ 5.56″	″ −0.21	34′ 5.34″	″ −0.23
57	1 34 3.58	0.36	34 3.21	0.38	34 2.81	0.40	34 2.40	0.43	34 1.96	0.45
58	1 33 58.88	0.58	33 58.20	0.60	33 57.48	0.62	33 57.04	0.65	33 56.28	0.67
59	1 33 51.99	0.80	33 51.18	0.83	33 50.34	0.84	33 49.49	0.86	33 48.61	0.89
60	1 33 42.90	1.02	33 41.87	1.04	33 40.82	1.06	33 39.75	1.08	33 38.66	1.10
61	1 33 31.63	1.24	33 30.39	1.26	33 29.12	1.28	33 27.83	1.30	33 26.52	1.32
62	1 33 18.20	1.45	33 16.73	1.47	33 15.25	1.49	33 13.74	1.52	33 12.22	1.54
63	1 33 2.60	1.67	33 0.92	1.69	32 59.22	1.71	32 57.50	1.73	32 55.76	1.75
64	1 32 44.85	1.88	32 42.97	1.90	32 41.05	1.92	32 39.12	1.94	32 37.17	1.97
65	1 32 24.90	2.09	32 22.88	2.11	32 20.76	2.14	32 18.61	2.16	32 16.45	2.18
66	1 32 3.00	2.30	32 0.69	2.32	31 58.35	2.35	31 56.00	2.37	31 53.62	2.39
67	1 31 38.92	2.51	31 36.40	2.53	31 33.86	2.55	31 31.29	2.57	31 24.71	2.59
68	1 31 12.77	2.72	31 10.04	2.74	31 7.29	2.76	31 4.52	2.78	31 1.73	2.80
69	1 30 44.56	2.92	30 41.63	2.94	30 38.67	2.96	30 35.70	2.98	30 32.71	3.00
70	1 30 14.32	3.12	30 11.19	3.14	30 8.03	3.16	30 4.86	3.18	30 1.66	3.20
71	1 29 42.08	3.32	29 38.74	3.34	29 35.39	3.36	29 32.02	3.38	29 28.63	3.40
72	1 29 7.86	3.52	29 4.33	3.54	29 0.78	3.56	28 57.21	3.58	28 53.62	3.60
73	1 28 31.68	3.71	28 27.96	3.73	28 24.22	3.75	28 20.46	3.77	28 16.68	3.79
74	1 27 53.59	3.90	27 49.67	3.92	27 45.74	3.94	27 41.79	3.96	27 37.82	3.98
75	1 27 13.60	4.09	27 9.50	4.11	27 5.38	4.13	27 1.24	4.15	26 57.08	4.17
76	1 26 31.75	4.28	26 27.47	4.29	26 23.16	4.31	26 18.84	4.33	26 14.50	4.35
77	1 25 48.08	4.46	25 43.62	4.47	25 39.13	4.49	25 34.63	4.51	25 30.11	4.53
78	1 25 2.62	4.63	24 57.98	4.65	24 53.31	4.67	24 48.64	4.69	24 43.94	4.70
79	1 24 15.40	4.81	24 10.58	4.83	24 5.75	4.84	24 0.90	4.86	23 56.03	4.88
80	1 23 26.46	4.98	23 21.48	4.99	23 16.47	5.01	23 11.45	5.03	23 6.42	5.04
81	1 22 35.85	5.14	22 30.70	5.16	22 25.53	5.18	22 20.34	5.19	22 15.14	5.21
82	1 21 43.59	5.31	21 38.28	5.32	21 32.95	5.34	21 27.60	5.35	21 22.24	5.37
83	1 20 49.74	5.47	20 44.27	5.48	20 38.78	5.50	20 33.28	5.51	20 27.76	5.53
84	1 19 54.33	5.61	19 48.71	5.63	19 43.07	5.64	19 37.41	5.66	19 31.74	5.67
85	1 18 57.41	5.77	18 51.63	5.78	18 45.85	5.80	18 40.04	5.81	18 34.23	5.82
86	1 17 59.02	5.91	17 53.10	5.93	17 47.17	5.94	17 41.22	5.95	17 35.26	5.97
87	1 16 59.20	6.05	16 53.15	6.06	16 47.07	6.08	16 40.99	6.09	16 34.89	6.10
88	1 15 58.01	6.19	15 51.82	6.20	15 45.62	6.21	15 39.40	6.23	15 33.16	6.24
89	1 14 55.50	6.32	14 49.17	6.33	14 42.84	6.34	14 36.49	6.35	14 30.13	6.37
90	1 13 51.70	6.44	13 45.25	6.45	13 38.79	6.46	13 32.31	6.48	13 25.83	6.49
91	1 12 46.66	6.56	12 40.10	6.57	12 33.52	6.59	12 26.92	6.60	12 20.32	6.61
92	1 11 40.45	6.68	11 33.77	6.69	11 27.07	6.70	11 20.37	6.71	11 13.65	6.72
93	1 10 33.11	6.79	10 26.32	6.80	10 19.51	6.82	10 12.70	6.83	10 5.87	6.84
94	1 9 24.69	6.89	9 17.79	6.90	9 10.88	6.91	9 3.97	6.92	8 57.04	6.93
95	1 8 15.25	6.99	8 8.25	7.00	8 1.24	7.01	7 54.22	7.02	7 47.19	7.03
96	1 7 4.83	7.09	6 57.74	7.10	6 50.64	7.11	6 43.52	7.12	6 36.40	7.12
97	1 5 53.50	7.18	5 46.31	7.19	5 39.12	7.19	5 31.93	7.20	5 24.72	7.21
98	1 4 41.30	7.26	4 34.03	7.27	4 26.76	7.28	4 19.48	7.29	4 12.19	7.29
99	1 3 28.30	7.34	3 20.95	7.35	3 13.60	7.36	3 6.24	7.36	2 58.88	7.37
100	1 2 14.54	7.41	2 7.12	7.42	1 59.70	7.42	1 52.27	7.43	1 44.84	7.44
101	1 1 0.09	7.48	0 52.60	7.48	0 45.12	7.49	0 37.62	7.50	0 30.12	7.50
102	0 59 44.99	7.54	59 37.45	7.54	59 29.91	7.55	59 22.35	7.56	59 14.79	7.56
103	0 58 29.32	7.60	58 21.73	7.60	58 14.12	7.60	58 6.52	7.61	57 58.91	7.61
104	0 57 13.13	7.64	57 5.49	7.65	56 57.83	7.65	56 50.18	7.66	56 42.52	7.66
105	0 55 56.47	7.69	55 48.78	7.69	55 41.09	7.69	55 33.39	7.70	55 25.69	7.70
106	0 54 39.11	7.72	54 31.68	7.73	54 23.95	7.73	54 16.22	7.73	54 8.48	7.74
107	0 53 21.99	7.76	53 14.23	7.76	53 6.47	7.76	52 58.71	7.78	52 50.94	7.77
108	0 52 4.29	7.78	51 56.51	7.78	51 48.72	7.79	51 40.93	7.79	51 33.14	7.79
109	0 50 46.36	7.80	50 38.56	7.80	50 30.75	7.81	50 22.95	7.81	50 15.14	7.81
110	0 49 28.26	7.82	49 20.45	7.82	49 12.63	7.82	49 4.81	7.82	48 56.99	7.82
111	0 48 10.05	−7.82	48 2.23	−7.82	47 54.40	−7.83	47 46.57	−7.83	47 38.75	−7.83

TABLE X.

EQUATION OF THE CENTRE, FOR m = 0.

Constant added 47′ 3″.5. Period = 221ᵈ.7008.

Arg. l.	0ᵈ.0	Diff. for 0ᵈ.1	0ᵈ.1	Diff. for 0ᵈ.1	0ᵈ.2	Diff. for 0ᵈ.1	0ᵈ.3	Diff. for 0ᵈ.1	0ᵈ.4	Diff. for 0ᵈ.1
d	° ′ ″	″	′ ″	″	′ ″	″	′ ″	″	′ ″	″
112	0 47 30.92	−7.83	47 23.10	−7.83	47 15.27	−7.83	47 7.44	−7.83	46 59.62	−7.83
113	0 46 12.66	7.82	46 4.83	7.82	45 57.01	7.82	45 49.19	7.82	45 41.36	7.82
114	0 44 54.43	7.82	44 46.61	7.82	44 38.80	7.82	44 30.98	7.81	44 23.17	7.81
115	0 43 36.31	7.81	43 28.50	7.80	43 20.70	7.80	43 12.90	7.80	43 5.10	7.80
116	0 42 18.34	7.79	42 10.55	7.78	42 2.77	7.78	41 54.99	7.78	41 47.21	7.78
117	0 41 0.59	7.76	40 52.82	7.76	40 45.07	7.76	40 37.31	7.75	40 29.56	7.75
118	0 39 43.11	7.73	39 35.38	7.73	39 27.65	7.72	39 19.93	7.72	39 12.21	7.72
119	0 38 25.97	7.69	38 18.28	7.69	38 10.59	7.69	38 2.90	7.68	37 55.22	7.68
120	0 37 9.23	7.65	37 1.58	7.65	36 53.93	7.64	36 46.29	7.64	36 38.65	7.63
121	0 35 52.93	7.60	35 45.33	7.60	35 37.74	7.59	35 30.14	7.60	35 22.56	7.58
122	0 34 37.15	7.55	34 29.61	7.54	34 22.06	7.54	34 14.53	7.53	34 7.00	7.53
123	0 33 21.94	7.49	33 14.46	7.48	33 6.97	7.48	32 59.50	7.47	32 52.03	7.46
124	0 32 7.36	7.42	31 59.94	7.42	31 52.52	7.41	31 45.12	7.40	31 37.71	7.40
125	0 30 53.46	7.35	30 46.11	7.35	30 38.77	7.34	30 31.43	7.33	30 24.11	7.32
126	0 29 40.30	7.28	29 33.03	7.27	29 25.76	7.26	29 18.51	7.25	29 11.26	7.24
127	0 28 27.94	7.19	28 20.75	7.19	28 13.57	7.18	28 6.39	7.17	27 59.23	7.16
128	0 27 16.43	7.11	27 9.32	7.10	27 2.23	7.09	26 55.15	7.08	26 48.07	7.07
129	0 26 5.82	7.01	25 58.81	7.00	25 51.81	6.99	25 44.83	6.98	25 37.85	6.97
130	0 24 56.18	6.91	24 49.27	6.90	24 42.37	6.89	24 35.48	6.88	24 28.60	6.87
131	0 23 47.55	6.81	23 40.75	6.80	23 33.95	6.79	23 27.17	6.78	23 20.39	6.77
132	0 22 39.99	6.70	22 33.29	6.69	22 26.61	6.68	22 19.94	6.67	22 13.27	6.66
133	0 21 33.55	6.59	21 26.97	6.57	21 20.40	6.56	21 13.84	6.55	21 7.30	6.54
134	0 20 28.28	6.47	20 21.82	6.45	20 15.37	6.44	20 8.93	6.43	20 2.51	6.42
135	0 19 24.23	6.34	19 17.89	6.33	19 11.57	6.32	19 5.26	6.30	18 58.96	6.29
136	0 18 21.45	6.21	18 15.24	6.20	18 9.05	6.19	18 2.87	6.17	17 56.70	6.16
137	0 17 19.99	6.08	17 13.92	6.06	17 7.86	6.05	17 1.82	6.04	16 55.79	6.02
138	0 16 19.90	5.94	16 13.96	5.92	16 8.05	5.91	16 2.14	5.90	15 56.25	5.88
139	0 15 21.22	5.80	15 15.43	5.78	15 9.66	5.77	15 3.90	5.75	14 58.15	5.74
140	0 14 24.00	5.65	14 18.36	5.63	14 12.73	5.62	14 7.12	5.61	14 1.53	5.59
141	0 13 28.28	5.49	13 22.79	5.48	13 17.32	5.46	13 11.87	5.45	13 6.43	5.43
142	0 12 34.12	5.34	12 28.79	5.32	12 23.47	5.31	12 18.17	5.29	12 12.89	5.27
143	0 11 41.54	5.18	11 36.37	5.17	11 31.22	5.15	11 26.08	5.13	11 20.96	5.11
144	0 10 50.59	5.01	10 45.59	5.00	10 40.60	4.98	10 35.63	4.96	10 30.68	4.94
145	0 10 1.32	4.84	9 56.48	4.83	9 51.66	4.81	9 46.86	4.79	9 42.08	4.77
146	0 9 13.75	4.67	9 9.09	4.65	9 4.45	4.63	8 59.82	4.62	8 55.21	4.60
147	0 8 27. 3	4.49	8 23.45	4.47	8 18.98	4.46	8 14.54	4.44	8 10.11	4.42
148	0 7 43.90	4.31	7 39.60	4.29	7 35.31	4.28	7 31.04	4.26	7 26.80	4.24
149	0 7 1.69	4.13	6 57.57	4.11	6 53.47	4.09	6 49.38	4.07	6 45.32	4.05
150	0 6 21.33	3.94	6 17.39	3.92	6 13.48	3.90	6 9.59	3.89	6 5.71	3.87
151	0 5 42.85	3.75	5 39.11	3.73	5 35.38	3.71	5 31.68	3.69	5 28.00	3.68
152	0 5 6.29	3.56	5 2.74	3.54	4 59.21	3.52	4 55.70	3.50	4 52.21	3.48
153	0 4 31.68	3.36	4 28.32	3.34	4 24.99	3.33	4 21.68	3.30	4 18.38	3.28
154	0 3 59.04	3.16	3 55.88	3.14	3 52.75	3.13	3 49.63	3.10	3 46.54	3.08
155	0 3 28.40	2.96	3 25.44	2.94	3 22.51	2.92	3 19.60	2.90	3 16.70	2.88
156	0 2 59.78	2.76	2 57.03	2.74	2 54.30	2.72	2 51.59	2.70	2 48.90	2.68
157	0 2 33.21	2.55	2 30.67	2.53	2 28.14	2.51	2 25.64	2.49	2 23.16	2.47
158	0 2 8.71	2.35	2 6.38	2.32	2 4.06	2.30	2 1.77	2.28	1 59.50	2.26
159	0 1 46.31	2.13	1 44.18	2.11	1 42.08	2.09	1 40.00	2.07	1 37.94	2.05
160	0 1 26.01	1.92	1 24.10	1.90	1 22.21	1.88	1 20.34	1.86	1 18.49	1.84
161	0 1 7.84	1.71	1 6.14	1.69	1 4.47	1.67	1 2.81	1.65	1 1.17	1.62
162	0 0 51.81	1.49	0 50.33	1.47	0 48.87	1.45	0 47.43	1.43	0 46.01	1.41
163	0 0 37.94	1.28	0 36.68	1.26	0 35.43	1.23	0 34.21	1.21	0 33.00	1.19
164	0 0 26.24	1.06	0 25.19	1.04	0 24.16	1.02	0 23.16	1.00	0 22.17	0.97
165	0 0 16.72	0.84	0 15.89	0.82	0 15.08	0.80	0 14.29	0.78	0 13.53	0.76
166	0 0 9.39	0.62	0 8.77	0.60	0 8.18	0.58	0 7.61	0.56	0 7.07	0.54
167	0 0 4.25	−0.40	0 3.86	−0.38	0 3.49	−0.36	0 3.14	−0.34	0 2.81	−0.32

EQUATION OF THE CENTRE, FOR m = 0.

Constant added 47′ 3″.5. Period = 221ᵈ.7008.

Arg. I.	0ᵈ.5	Diff. for 0ᵈ.1	0ᵈ.6	Diff. for 0ᵈ.1	0ᵈ.7	Diff. for 0ᵈ.1	0ᵈ.8	Diff. for 0ᵈ.1	0ᵈ.9	Diff. for 0ᵈ.1
d	° ′ ″	″	′ ″	″	′ ″	″	′ ″	″	′ ″	″
112	0 46 51.79	−7.83	46 43.96	−7.83	46 36.14	−7.83	46 28.31	−7.83	46 20.49	−7.83
113	0 45 33.54	7.82	45 25.72	7.82	45 17.90	7.82	45 10.07	7.82	45 2.25	7.82
114	0 44 15.35	7.81	44 7.51	7.81	43 59.73	7.81	43 51.92	7.81	43 44.11	7.81
115	0 42 57.30	7.80	42 49.50	7.79	42 41.71	7.79	42 33.92	7.79	42 26.13	7.79
116	0 41 39.43	7.77	41 31.66	7.77	41 23.89	7.77	41 16.12	7.77	41 8.35	7.76
117	0 40 21.81	7.75	40 14.06	7.74	40 6.32	7.74	39 58.58	7.74	39 50.84	7.74
118	0 39 4.50	7.71	38 56.78	7.71	38 49.08	7.71	38 41.37	7.70	38 33.67	7.70
119	0 37 47.55	7.67	37 39.87	7.67	37 32.21	7.67	37 24.54	7.66	37 16.88	7.66
120	0 36 31.02	7.63	36 23.39	7.62	36 15.77	7.62	36 8.15	7.61	36 0.54	7.61
121	0 35 14.98	7.58	35 7.40	7.57	34 59.83	7.57	34 52.27	7.56	34 44.71	7.56
122	0 33 59.47	7.52	33 51.96	7.51	33 44.44	7.51	33 36.94	7.50	33 29.44	7.50
123	0 32 44.57	7.46	32 37.11	7.45	32 29.67	7.45	32 22.22	7.44	32 14.79	7.43
124	0 31 30.32	7.39	31 22.94	7.38	31 15.56	7.38	31 8.18	7.37	31 0.82	7.36
125	0 30 16.79	7.32	30 9.47	7.31	30 2.17	7.30	29 54.87	7.29	29 47.58	7.28
126	0 29 4.02	7.24	28 56.78	7.23	28 49.56	7.22	28 42.34	7.21	28 35.11	7.20
127	0 27 52.07	7.15	27 44.92	7.14	27 37.79	7.13	27 30.66	7.12	27 23.54	7.10
128	0 26 41.01	7.06	26 33.95	7.05	26 26.91	7.04	26 19.87	7.03	26 12.84	7.02
129	0 25 30.88	6.96	25 23.92	6.95	25 16.97	6.94	25 10.03	6.93	25 3.10	6.92
130	0 24 21.73	6.86	24 14.88	6.85	24 8.03	6.84	24 1.19	6.83	23 54.37	6.82
131	0 23 13.63	6.76	23 6.88	6.75	23 0.14	6.73	22 53.41	6.72	22 46.69	6.71
132	0 22 6.62	6.64	21 59.99	6.63	21 53.36	6.62	21 46.74	6.61	21 40.14	6.60
133	0 21 0.76	6.53	20 54.24	6.51	20 47.73	6.50	20 41.24	6.49	20 34.75	6.48
134	0 19 56.10	6.40	19 49.70	6.39	19 43.31	6.38	19 36.94	6.37	19 30.58	6.35
135	0 18 52.68	6.28	18 46.40	6.27	18 40.14	6.26	18 33.90	6.24	18 27.67	6.23
136	0 17 50.55	6.15	17 44.41	6.13	17 38.28	6.12	17 32.17	6.11	17 26.07	6.09
137	0 16 49.77	6.01	16 43.77	5.99	16 37.78	5.98	16 31.80	5.97	16 25.84	5.95
138	0 15 50.38	5.87	15 44.52	5.86	15 38.67	5.84	15 32.84	5.82	15 27.02	5.81
139	0 14 52.42	5.72	14 46.71	5.71	14 41.01	5.69	14 35.32	5.68	14 29.65	5.66
140	0 13 55.95	5.57	13 50.38	5.56	13 44.84	5.54	13 39.30	5.53	13 33.78	5.51
141	0 13 1.00	5.42	12 55.59	5.40	12 50.20	5.39	12 44.82	5.37	12 39.46	5.36
142	0 12 7.63	5.26	12 2.38	5.24	11 57.14	5.23	11 51.92	5.21	11 46.72	5.19
143	0 11 15.86	5.09	11 10.77	5.08	11 5.70	5.06	11 0.65	5.04	10 55.61	5.03
144	0 10 25.74	4.93	10 20.82	4.91	10 15.92	4.90	10 11.04	4.88	10 6.17	4.86
145	0 9 37.32	4.76	9 32.57	4.74	9 27.84	4.72	9 23.12	4.70	9 18.43	4.69
146	0 8 50.62	4.58	8 46.05	4.56	8 41.49	4.55	8 36.96	4.53	8 32.44	4.51
147	0 8 5.69	4.40	8 1.30	4.39	7 56.92	4.37	7 52.56	4.35	7 48.22	4.33
148	0 7 22.56	4.22	7 18.35	4.20	7 14.16	4.18	7 9.98	4.17	7 5.83	4.15
149	0 6 41.27	4.04	6 37.25	4.02	6 33.24	4.00	6 29.25	3.98	6 25.28	3.96
150	0 6 1.85	3.85	5 58.01	3.83	5 54.20	3.81	5 50.40	3.79	5 46.61	3.77
151	0 5 24.33	3.66	5 20.68	3.64	5 17.06	3.62	5 13.45	3.60	5 9.86	3.58
152	0 4 48.74	3.46	4 45.29	3.44	4 41.85	3.42	4 38.44	3.40	4 35.05	3.38
153	0 4 15.11	3.26	4 11.85	3.24	4 8.62	3.22	4 5.41	3.20	4 2.21	3.18
154	0 3 43.46	3.06	3 40.41	3.04	3 37.38	3.02	3 34.37	3.00	3 31.37	2.98
155	0 3 13.83	2.86	3 10.98	2.84	3 8.15	2.82	3 5.34	2.80	3 2.55	2.78
156	0 2 46.21	2.66	2 43.59	2.64	2 40.97	2.62	2 38.36	2.59	2 35.78	2.57
157	0 2 20.70	2.45	2 18.26	2.43	2 15.84	2.41	2 13.45	2.39	2 11.07	2.37
158	0 1 57.25	2.24	1 55.02	2.22	1 52.82	2.20	1 50.63	2.18	1 48.45	2.16
159	0 1 35.90	2.03	1 33.88	2.01	1 31.88	1.99	1 29.90	1.97	1 27.95	1.94
160	0 1 16.66	1.82	1 14.85	1.80	1 13.07	1.77	1 11.30	1.75	1 9.56	1.73
161	0 0 59.56	1.60	0 57.97	1.59	0 56.40	1.56	0 54.85	1.54	0 53.32	1.52
162	0 0 44.61	1.39	0 43.21	1.37	0 41.88	1.34	0 40.54	1.32	0 39.23	1.30
163	0 0 31.82	1.17	0 30.66	1.15	0 29.53	1.13	0 28.41	1.10	0 27.32	1.08
164	0 0 21.21	0.95	0 20.27	0.93	0 19.35	0.91	0 18.45	0.89	0 17.57	0.86
165	0 0 12.78	0.72	0 12.06	0.71	0 11.36	0.69	0 10.68	0.67	0 10.02	0.65
166	0 0 6.51	0.51	0 6.01	0.49	0 5.56	0.47	0 5.10	0.45	0 4.66	0.43
167	0 0 2.51	−0.29	0 2.22	−0.27	0 1.96	−0.25	0 1.73	−0.23	0 1.51	−0.21

EQUATION OF THE CENTRE, FOR m = 0.

Constant added 47′ 3″.5. Period = 224^{d}.7008.

Arg. I	0^{d}.0	Diff. for 0^{d}.1	0^{d}.1	Diff. for 0^{d}.1	0^{d}.2	Diff. for 0^{d}.1	0^{d}.3	Diff. for 0^{d}.1	0^{d}.4	Diff. for 0^{d}.1
d	° ′ ″	″	′ ″	″	′ ″	″	′ ″	″	′ ″	″
168	0 0 1.31	−0.18	0 1.14	−0.16	0 0.99	−0.14	0 0.86	−0.12	0 0.76	−0.10
169	0 0 0.58	+0.04	0 0.63	+0.06	0 0.70	+0.08	0 0.79	+0.10	0 0.91	+0.13
170	0 0 2.06	0.26	0 2.33	0.28	0 2.62	0.30	0 2.93	0.32	0 3.27	0.35
171	0 0 5.74	0.48	0 6.23	0.50	0 6.75	0.52	0 7.28	0.54	0 7.84	0.57
172	0 0 11.64	0.70	0 12.35	0.72	0 13.08	0.74	0 13.83	0.76	0 14.61	0.79
173	0 0 19.73	0.92	0 20.66	0.94	0 21.61	0.96	0 22.59	0.98	0 23.58	1.01
174	0 0 30.02	1.14	0 31.17	1.16	0 32.34	1.18	0 33.54	1.20	0 34.75	1.22
175	0 0 42.51	1.36	0 43.88	1.38	0 45.27	1.40	0 46.68	1.42	0 48.11	1.44
176	0 0 57.18	1.58	0 58.76	1.60	1 0.37	1.62	0 2.00	1.64	0 3.65	1.66
177	0 1 14.02	1.79	1 15.82	1.81	1 17.65	1.84	1 19.50	1.86	1 21.36	1.88
178	0 1 33.03	2.01	1 35.04	2.03	1 37.08	2.05	1 39.15	2.07	1 41.23	2.09
179	0 1 54.18	2.22	1 56.41	2.24	1 58.67	2.26	2 0.94	2.29	2 3.24	2.31
180	0 2 17.47	2.43	2 19.91	2.46	2 22.38	2.48	2 24.87	2.50	2 27.38	2.52
181	0 2 42.87	2.65	2 45.53	2.67	2 48.20	2.69	2 50.90	2.71	2 53.62	2.73
182	0 3 10.37	2.85	3 13.24	2.87	3 16.12	2.90	3 19.03	2.92	3 21.96	2.94
183	0 3 39.05	3.06	3 43.02	3.08	3 46.12	3.10	3 49.21	3.12	3 52.36	3.14
184	0 4 11.59	3.27	4 14.87	3.29	4 18.16	3.31	4 21.48	3.33	4 24.82	3.35
185	0 4 45.26	3.47	4 48.74	3.49	4 52.23	3.51	4 55.75	3.53	4 59.29	3.55
186	0 5 20.93	3.67	5 24.61	3.69	5 28.31	3.71	5 32.02	3.73	5 35.76	3.75
187	0 5 58.59	3.86	6 2.46	3.88	6 6.36	3.90	6 10.27	3.92	6 14.20	3.94
188	0 6 38.20	4.06	6 42.26	4.08	6 46.35	4.10	6 50.46	4.11	6 54.58	4.13
189	0 7 19.73	4.25	7 23.98	4.27	7 28.26	4.29	7 32.55	4.30	7 36.87	4.32
190	0 8 3.14	4.43	8 7.50	4.45	8 12.05	4.47	8 16.53	4.49	8 21.03	4.51
191	0 8 48.42	4.62	8 53.05	4.64	8 57.69	4.65	9 2.36	4.67	9 7.04	4.69
192	0 9 35.51	4.80	9 40.32	4.82	9 45.15	4.83	9 49.99	4.85	9 54.85	4.87
193	0 10 24.40	4.98	10 29.38	4.99	10 34.38	5.01	10 39.40	5.03	10 44.44	5.04
194	0 11 15.02	5.15	11 20.18	5.17	11 25.35	5.19	11 30.55	5.20	11 35.75	5.22
195	0 12 7.33	5.32	12 12.68	5.33	12 18.03	5.35	12 23.39	5.37	12 28.76	5.38
196	0 13 1.36	5.48	13 6.85	5.50	13 12.36	5.51	13 17.88	5.53	13 23.42	5.55
197	0 13 56.99	5.64	14 2.64	5.66	14 8.31	5.67	14 13.99	5.69	14 19.69	5.71
198	0 14 54.20	5.80	15 0.01	5.81	15 5.83	5.83	15 11.67	5.84	15 17.52	5.86
199	0 15 52.95	5.96	15 58.91	5.98	16 4.88	5.97	16 10.87	5.99	16 16.87	6.01
200	0 16 53.19	6.10	16 59.29	6.11	17 5.41	6.13	17 11.54	6.14	17 17.69	6.15
201	0 17 54.87	6.24	18 1.12	6.25	18 7.38	6.27	18 13.65	6.28	18 19.94	6.29
202	0 18 57.95	6.38	19 4.33	6.39	19 10.72	6.40	19 17.13	6.42	19 23.56	6.43
203	0 20 2.37	6.51	20 8.88	6.52	20 15.41	6.53	20 21.95	6.55	20 28.50	6.56
204	0 21 8.09	6.63	21 14.73	6.65	21 21.38	6.66	21 28.05	6.67	21 34.72	6.68
205	0 22 15.04	6.76	22 21.81	6.77	22 28.58	6.78	22 35.37	6.79	22 42.16	6.80
206	0 23 23.19	6.87	23 30.07	6.88	23 36.96	6.89	23 43.86	6.91	23 50.77	6.92
207	0 24 32.48	6.98	24 39.47	6.99	24 46.46	7.00	24 53.47	7.02	25 0.50	7.03
208	0 25 42.84	7.09	25 49.93	7.10	25 57.04	7.11	26 4.15	7.12	26 11.28	7.13
209	0 26 54.23	7.19	27 1.42	7.20	27 8.62	7.21	27 15.84	7.22	27 23.06	7.23
210	0 28 6.59	7.28	28 13.87	7.29	28 21.17	7.30	28 28.47	7.31	28 35.79	7.32
211	0 29 19.85	7.37	29 27.23	7.38	29 34.61	7.39	29 42.00	7.40	29 49.40	7.40
212	0 30 33.97	7.45	30 41.43	7.46	30 48.89	7.47	30 56.36	7.48	31 3.84	7.48
213	0 31 48.89	7.53	31 56.41	7.54	32 3.95	7.54	32 11.50	7.55	32 19.05	7.56
214	0 33 4.52	7.60	33 12.13	7.61	33 19.74	7.61	33 27.35	7.62	33 34.97	7.63
215	0 34 20.84	7.66	34 28.51	7.67	34 36.18	7.67	34 43.86	7.68	34 51.54	7.69
216	0 35 37.77	7.72	35 45.49	7.73	35 53.22	7.73	36 0.95	7.74	36 8.69	7.74
217	0 36 55.24	7.77	37 3.02	7.78	37 10.80	7.78	37 18.58	7.79	37 26.37	7.79
218	0 38 13.21	7.82	38 21.03	7.82	38 28.85	7.83	38 36.68	7.83	38 44.51	7.83
219	0 39 31.60	7.86	39 39.46	7.86	39 47.32	7.87	39 55.19	7.87	40 3.06	7.87
220	0 40 50.35	7.89	40 58.24	7.89	41 6.13	7.90	41 14.03	7.90	41 21.93	7.90
221	0 42 9.40	7.92	42 17.32	7.92	42 25.24	7.92	42 33.16	7.93	42 41.09	7.93
222	0 43 28.68	7.94	43 36.62	7.94	43 44.56	7.94	43 52.51	7.94	44 0.45	7.94
223	0 44 48.14	7.95	44 56.10	7.95	45 4.05	7.95	45 12.00	7.96	45 19.96	7.96
224	0 46 7.71	+7.96	46 15.67	+7.96	46 23.63	+7.96	46 31.59	+7.96	46 39.55	+7.96

EQUATION OF THE CENTRE, FOR m = 0.

Constant added 47′ 39″.5. Period = 221^{d}.7008.

Arg 1.	0^{d}.5	Diff. for 0^{d}.1	0^{d}.6	Diff. for 0^{d}.1	0^{d}.7	Diff. for 0^{d}.1	0^{d}.8	Diff. for 0^{d}.1	0^{d}.9	Diff. for 0^{d}.1
d	° ′ ″	″	′ ″	″	′ ″	″	′ ″	″	′ ″	″
168	0 0 0.67	−0.07	0 0.61	−0.05	0 0.57	−0.03	0 0.55	−0.01	0 0.56	+0.01
169	0 0 1.05	+0.15	0 1.20	+0.17	0 1.38	+0.19	0 1.59	+0.21	0 1.81	0.23
170	0 0 3.61	0.37	0 4.01	0.39	0 4.41	0.41	0 4.83	0.43	0 5.28	0.46
171	0 0 8.11	0.59	0 9.01	0.61	0 9.64	0.63	0 10.28	0.65	0 10.95	0.68
172	0 0 15.41	0.81	0 16.21	0.83	0 17.07	0.85	0 17.93	0.88	0 18.82	0.90
173	0 0 24.60	1.03	0 25.61	1.05	0 26.70	1.07	0 27.79	1.09	0 28.89	1.12
174	0 0 35.89	1.25	0 37.25	1.27	0 38.53	1.29	0 39.81	1.31	0 41.16	1.34
175	0 0 49.57	1.47	0 51.05	1.49	0 52.55	1.51	0 54.07	1.53	0 55.61	1.55
176	0 1 5.33	1.68	1 7.02	1.71	1 8.74	1.73	1 10.48	1.75	1 12.24	1.77
177	0 1 23.25	1.90	1 25.16	1.92	1 27.10	1.94	1 29.05	1.96	1 31.02	1.99
178	0 1 43.33	2.12	1 45.16	2.14	1 47.61	2.16	1 49.78	2.18	1 51.97	2.20
179	0 2 5.56	2.33	2 7.90	2.35	2 10.26	2.37	2 12.64	2.39	2 15.04	2.41
180	0 2 29.91	2.54	2 32.46	2.56	2 35.03	2.58	2 37.62	2.60	2 40.24	2.62
181	0 2 56.36	2.75	2 59.12	2.77	3 1.91	2.79	3 4.71	2.81	3 7.53	2.83
182	0 3 24.91	2.96	3 27.87	2.98	3 30.86	3.00	3 33.87	3.02	3 36.90	3.04
183	0 3 55.52	3.16	3 58.69	3.18	4 1.88	3.20	4 5.10	3.22	4 8.33	3.25
184	0 4 28.17	3.37	4 31.55	3.39	4 34.95	3.41	4 38.36	3.43	4 41.80	3.45
185	0 5 2.85	3.57	5 6.42	3.59	5 10.02	3.61	5 13.64	3.63	5 17.28	3.65
186	0 5 39.52	3.77	5 43.29	3.79	5 47.09	3.81	5 50.90	3.82	5 54.74	3.84
187	0 6 18.15	3.96	6 22.12	3.98	6 26.11	4.00	6 30.12	4.02	6 34.15	4.04
188	0 6 58.72	4.15	7 2.89	4.17	7 7.07	4.19	7 11.27	4.21	7 15.49	4.23
189	0 7 41.20	4.34	7 45.55	4.36	7 49.92	4.38	7 54.31	4.40	7 58.72	4.42
190	0 8 25.55	4.53	8 30.09	4.54	8 34.64	4.56	8 39.21	4.58	8 43.81	4.60
191	0 9 11.74	4.71	9 16.46	4.73	9 21.20	4.75	9 25.95	4.76	9 30.72	4.78
192	0 9 59.73	4.89	10 4.63	4.91	10 9.55	4.92	10 14.48	4.94	10 19.43	4.96
193	0 10 49.49	5.06	10 54.57	5.08	10 59.65	5.10	11 4.76	5.12	11 9.88	5.13
194	0 11 40.98	5.23	11 46.22	5.25	11 51.48	5.27	11 56.76	5.28	12 2.05	5.30
195	0 12 34.15	5.40	12 39.56	5.42	12 44.99	5.43	12 50.43	5.45	12 55.89	5.47
196	0 13 28.98	5.56	13 34.55	5.58	13 40.13	5.59	13 45.74	5.61	13 51.36	5.63
197	0 14 25.40	5.72	14 31.13	5.74	14 36.88	5.75	14 42.64	5.77	14 48.41	5.78
198	0 15 23.39	5.88	15 29.27	5.89	15 35.17	5.90	15 41.08	5.92	15 47.01	5.93
199	0 16 22.88	6.02	16 28.92	6.04	16 34.96	6.05	16 41.02	6.07	16 47.10	6.08
200	0 17 23.85	6.17	17 30.03	6.18	17 36.22	6.20	17 42.42	6.21	17 48.64	6.22
201	0 18 26.24	6.31	18 32.55	6.32	18 38.88	6.33	18 45.22	6.35	18 51.58	6.36
202	0 19 29.99	6.44	19 36.44	6.46	19 42.90	6.47	19 49.38	6.48	19 55.87	6.49
203	0 20 35.07	6.57	20 41.65	6.58	20 48.24	6.60	20 54.84	6.61	21 1.46	6.62
204	0 21 41.41	6.70	21 48.12	6.71	21 54.83	6.72	22 1.56	6.73	22 8.29	6.74
205	0 22 48.97	6.81	22 55.79	6.83	23 2.63	6.84	23 9.47	6.85	23 16.33	6.86
206	0 23 57.70	6.93	24 4.63	6.94	24 11.57	6.95	24 18.53	6.96	24 25.50	6.97
207	0 25 7.53	7.04	25 14.57	7.05	25 21.62	7.06	25 28.69	7.07	25 35.76	7.08
208	0 26 18.41	7.14	26 25.55	7.15	26 32.71	7.16	26 39.87	7.17	26 47.05	7.18
209	0 27 30.29	7.24	27 37.53	7.24	27 44.78	7.25	27 52.04	7.26	27 59.31	7.27
210	0 28 43.11	7.33	28 50.44	7.34	28 57.78	7.34	29 5.13	7.35	29 12.49	7.36
211	0 29 56.81	7.41	30 4.23	7.42	30 11.65	7.43	30 19.08	7.44	30 26.52	7.44
212	0 31 11.33	7.49	31 18.83	7.50	31 26.33	7.51	31 33.84	7.51	31 41.36	7.52
213	0 32 26.61	7.56	32 34.18	7.57	32 41.76	7.58	32 49.34	7.59	32 56.93	7.59
214	0 33 42.60	7.63	33 50.24	7.64	33 57.88	7.64	34 5.53	7.65	34 13.18	7.66
215	0 34 59.23	7.69	35 6.93	7.70	35 14.63	7.70	35 22.34	7.71	35 30.05	7.72
216	0 36 16.44	7.75	36 24.19	7.75	36 31.95	7.76	36 39.71	7.76	36 47.47	7.77
217	0 37 34.17	7.80	37 41.97	7.80	37 49.77	7.81	37 57.58	7.81	38 5.39	7.81
218	0 38 52.35	7.84	39 0.19	7.84	39 8.04	7.85	39 15.89	7.85	39 23.74	7.85
219	0 40 10.93	7.87	40 18.81	7.88	40 26.69	7.88	40 34.57	7.88	40 42.46	7.89
220	0 41 29.84	7.91	41 37.74	7.91	41 45.65	7.91	41 53.57	7.91	42 1.48	7.92
221	0 42 49.02	7.93	42 56.95	7.93	43 4.88	7.93	43 12.81	7.93	43 20.75	7.94
222	0 44 8.40	7.95	44 16.34	7.95	44 24.29	7.95	44 32.24	7.95	44 40.19	7.95
223	0 45 27.92	7.96	45 35.87	7.96	45 43.83	7.96	45 51.79	7.96	45 59.75	7.96
224	0 46 47.52	+7.96	46 55.48	+7.96	47 3.44	+7.96	47 11.40	+7.96	47 19.36	+7.96

TABLE XI.

Perturbations of the Longitude.

Factor to be multiplied by the integer **m**; and its Logarithm.

TABLE XII.

Pert. of the Long.

Fact. to be $\times \left(\frac{m}{100}\right)^2$

Arg. I.	Factor.	Log. Fac.	Arg. I.	Factor.	Log. Fac.	Arg. I.	Factor.	Log. Fac.	Arg. I.	Factor.	Log. Fac.	Arg. I.	Fact.	L. Fac.
d 0	— 0.000	n ∞	d 60	—12.596	n1.1002	d 120	+ 2.640	0.4231	d 180	+12.109	1.0831	d 0	+0.00	∞
1	0.361	9.5575	61	12.547	1.0985	121	2.990	0.4757	181	11.996	1.0790	4	0.22	9.349
2	0.721	9.8579	62	12.488	1.0965	122	3.328	0.5222	182	11.875	1.0746	8	0.44	9.648
3	1.081	0.0338	63	12.421	1.0942	123	3.663	0.5638	183	11.744	1.0698	12	0.66	9.820
4	— 1.411	n0.1587	64	—12.343	n1.0914	124	+ 3.997	0.6017	184	+11.604	1.0646	16	+0.87	9.938
5	1.790	0.2559	65	12.256	1.0883	125	4.326	0.6361	185	11.454	1.0590	20	1.06	0.027
6	2.155	0.3334	66	12.159	1.0849	126	4.652	0.6676	186	11.295	1.0529	24	1.25	0.096
7	2.500	0.3995	67	12.053	1.0811	127	4.976	0.6969	187	11.128	1.0464	28	1.42	0.151
8	— 2.862	n0.4567	68	—11.938	n1.0769	128	+ 5.295	0.7239	188	+10.952	1.0395	32	+1.56	0.194
9	3.212	0.5068	69	11.813	1.0724	129	5.611	0.7490	189	10.766	1.0321	36	1.69	0.229
10	3.563	0.5514	70	11.680	1.0674	130	5.922	0.7725	190	10.571	1.0241	40	1.80	0.256
11	3.904	0.5915	71	11.536	1.0621	131	6.230	0.7945	191	10.369	1.0157	44	1.89	0.277
12	— 4.246	n0.6280	72	—11.385	n1.0563	132	+ 6.532	0.8150	192	+10.158	1.0068	48	+1.95	0.291
13	4.584	0.6612	73	11.226	1.0502	133	6.829	0.8341	193	9.039	0.9973	52	1.99	0.299
14	4.918	0.6918	74	11.056	1.0436	134	7.121	0.8525	194	9.712	0.9873	56	2.01	0.302
15	5.250	0.7202	75	10.879	1.0366	135	7.408	0.8697	195	9.478	0.9767	60	1.99	0.300
16	— 5.575	n0.7462	76	—10.694	n1.0291	136	+ 7.680	0.8859	196	+ 9.235	0.9654	64	+1.96	0.292
17	5.896	0.7706	77	10.501	1.0212	137	7.965	0.9012	197	8.985	0.9535	68	1.90	0.278
18	6.213	0.7933	78	10.299	1.0128	138	8.235	0.9157	198	8.727	0.9409	72	1.81	0.258
19	6.524	0.8145	79	10.090	1.0039	139	8.498	0.9293	199	8.463	0.9275	76	1.71	0.232
20	— 6.830	n0.8344	80	— 9.873	n0.9944	140	+ 8.756	0.9423	200	+ 8.191	0.9133	80	+1.58	0.198
21	7.131	0.8531	81	9.648	0.9844	141	9.006	0.9545	201	7.914	0.8984	84	1.43	0.155
22	7.426	0.8707	82	9.417	0.9739	142	9.249	0.9661	202	7.629	0.8825	88	1.26	0.101
23	7.715	0.8873	83	9.177	0.9627	143	9.486	0.9771	203	7.338	0.8656	92	1.08	0.034
24	— 7.997	n0.9029	84	— 8.932	n0.9509	144	+ 9.716	0.9875	204	+ 7.042	0.8477	96	+0.88	9.947
25	8.273	0.9177	85	8.679	0.9385	145	9.939	0.9973	205	6.739	0.8286	100	0.68	9.832
26	8.542	0.9316	86	8.421	0.9254	146	10.153	1.0066	206	6.431	0.8083	104	0.46	9.667
27	8.805	0.9447	87	8.155	0.9114	147	10.360	1.0154	207	6.118	0.7866	108	0.24	9.386
28	— 9.060	n0.9571	88	— 7.883	n0.8967	148	+10.559	1.0236	208	+ 5.801	0.7635	112	+0.02	p8.293
29	9.308	0.9689	89	7.606	0.8812	149	10.730	1.0314	209	5.478	0.7386	116	—0.20	n9.310
30	9.548	0.9799	90	7.323	0.8647	150	10.933	1.0387	210	5.150	0.7118	120	0.42	9.629
31	9.781	0.9904	91	7.035	0.8473	151	11.108	1.0456	211	4.819	0.6830	124	0.64	9.807
32	—10.005	n1.0002	92	— 6.741	n0.8287	152	+11.274	1.0521	212	+ 4.484	0.6517	128	—0.85	n9.929
33	10.229	1.0096	93	6.442	0.8090	153	11.432	1.0581	213	4.145	0.6175	132	1.05	0.023
34	10.431	1.0183	94	6.138	0.7880	154	11.581	1.0637	214	3.802	0.5800	136	1.23	0.091
35	10.631	1.0266	95	5.830	0.7657	155	11.721	1.0690	215	3.457	0.5387	140	1.40	0.146
36	—10.823	n1.0343	96	— 5.517	n0.7417	156	+11.851	1.0738	216	+ 3.108	0.4925	144	—1.55	n0.191
37	11.005	1.0416	97	5.200	0.7160	157	11.972	1.0782	217	2.757	0.4404	148	1.68	0.226
38	11.179	1.0484	98	4.879	0.6883	158	12.085	1.0822	218	2.404	0.3809	152	1.80	0.254
39	11.344	1.0548	99	4.555	0.6585	159	12.189	1.0860	219	2.049	0.3115	156	1.89	0.275
40	—11.500	n1.0607	100	— 4.227	n0.6260	160	+12.283	1.0893	220	+ 1.691	0.2281	160	—1.95	n0.290
41	11.647	1.0662	101	3.897	0.5907	161	12.367	1.0923	221	1.333	0.1248	164	1.99	0.299
42	11.784	1.0713	102	3.563	0.5518	162	12.442	1.0949	222	0.974	9.9886	168	2.01	0.302
43	11.913	1.0760	103	3.227	0.5088	163	12.507	1.0972	223	0.613	9.7875	172	2.00	0.300
44	—12.031	n1.0803	104	— 2.888	n0.4606	164	+12.563	1.0991	224	+ 0.253	p9.4031	176	—1.96	n0.293
45	12.140	1.0842	105	2.547	0.4060	165	12.609	1.1007	225	— 0.108	n9.0334	180	1.90	0.280
46	12.239	1.0877	106	2.205	0.3434	166	12.645	1.1019	226	0.469	9.6712	184	1.82	0.260
47	12.329	1.0909	107	1.860	0.2695	167	12.671	1.1028	227	0.829	9.9185	188	1.72	0.234
48	—12.408	n1.0937	108	— 1.514	n0.1801	168	+12.687	1.1034	228	— 1.189	n0.0752	192	—1.59	n0.201
49	12.479	1.0962	109	1.167	0.0671	169	12.693	1.1036	229	1.548	0.1898	196	1.44	0.159
50	12.540	1.0983	110	0.819	9.9133	170	12.690	1.1035	230	1.906	0.2801	200	1.28	0.106
51	12.590	1.1000	111	0.471	9.6730	171	12.676	1.1030	231	2.262	0.3545	204	1.10	0.040
52	—12.630	n1.1011	112	— 0.122	n9.0864	172	+12.653	1.1022	232	— 2.615	n0.4175	208	—0.90	n9.956
53	12.660	1.1024	113	+ 0.227	p9.3560	173	12.619	1.1010	233	2.967	0.4723	212	0.70	9.843
54	12.681	1.1032	114	0.575	9.7597	174	12.576	1.0995	234	3.317	0.5207	216	0.48	9.684
55	12.692	1.1035	115	0.923	9.9652	175	12.522	1.0977	235	3.664	0.5640	220	0.26	9.420
56	—12.692	n1.1035	116	+ 1.271	0.1041	176	+12.459	1.0955	236	— 4.007	n0.6028	224	—0.04	n8.591
57	12.683	1.1032	117	1.617	0.2087	177	12.386	1.0929	237	4.348	0.6383	228	+0.18	p9.267
58	12.664	1.1026	118	1.963	0.2929	178	12.304	1.0900	238	4.685	0.6707	232	0.41	9.619
59	12.635	1.1016	119	2.307	0.3639	179	12.211	1.0868	239	5.018	0.7005	236	0.62	9.795
60	—12.596	n1.1002	120	+ 2.640	0.4231	180	+12.109	1.0831	240	— 5.349	n0.7283	240	+0.83	9.920

The perturbations are expressed in hundredths of a second of arc.

TABLE XIII.

Pert. of the Longitude by the Earth.

Arg. II.	Equa.	Arg II.
0^{y}	0	240^{y}
2	0	238
4	1	236
6	3	234
8	5	232
10	9	230
12	13	228
14	17	226
16	23	224
18	29	222
20	36	220
22	44	218
24	52	216
26	61	214
28	70	212
30	80	210
32	91	208
34	102	206
36	114	204
38	126	202
40	139	200
42	152	198
44	165	196
46	179	194
48	193	192
50	207	190
52	221	188
54	236	186
56	250	184
58	265	182
60	280	180
62	295	178
64	310	176
66	324	174
68	339	172
70	353	170
72	368	168
74	382	166
76	395	164
78	409	162
80	422	160
82	434	158
84	447	156
86	459	154
88	470	152
90	481	150
92	491	148
94	501	146
96	510	144
98	518	142
100	526	140
102	533	138
104	539	136
106	545	134
108	550	132
110	554	130
112	558	128
114	560	126
116	562	124
118	564	122
120	564	120

TABLE XIV.

Pert. of the Longitude, by Mars.

Arg. III.	Equa.
0^{d}	226
200	220
400	213
600	204
800	194
1000	183
1200	171
1400	158
1600	145
1800	131
2000	117
2200	103
2400	90
2600	76
2800	64
3000	52
3200	41
3400	32
3600	23
3800	16
4000	10
4200	5
4400	2
4600	0
4800	0
5000	0
5200	2
5400	5
5600	9
5800	14
6000	20
6200	26
6400	34
6600	42
6800	50
7000	59
7200	69
7400	78
7600	88
7800	99
8000	109
8200	120
8400	131
8600	141
8800	152
9000	162
9200	172
9400	182
9600	192
9800	200
10000	208
10200	216
10400	222
10600	227
10800	231
11000	234
11200	235
11400	235
11600	233
11800	230
12000	226

TABLE XV.

Perturbation of the Longitude, by the Earth.

Arg. IV.	Equa.	Arg. IV.
0^{d}	0	2960^{d}
40	1	2920
80	3	2880
120	5	2840
160	9	2800
200	14	2760
240	19	2720
280	26	2680
320	34	2640
360	42	2600
400	51	2560
440	61	2520
480	71	2480
520	83	2440
560	94	2400
600	106	2360
640	118	2320
680	131	2280
720	144	2240
760	156	2200
800	169	2160
840	181	2120
880	194	2080
920	206	2040
960	217	2000
1000	228	1960
1040	239	1920
1080	249	1880
1120	258	1840
1160	266	1800
1200	274	1760
1240	280	1720
1280	286	1680
1320	291	1640
1360	295	1600
1400	297	1560
1440	299	1520
1480	300	1480

TABLE XVI.

Perturbation of the Longitude, by the Earth.

Arg. V.	Equa.	Arg. V.	Equa.
0^{d}	2	736^{d}	707
16	5	752	708
32	9	768	708
48	15	784	707
64	23	800	703
80	32	816	698
96	43	832	691
112	55	848	683
128	68	864	672
144	83	880	660
160	98	896	647
176	115	912	632
192	132	928	615
208	151	944	597
224	170	960	577
240	190	976	556
256	210	992	534
272	231	1008	511
288	252	1024	486
304	273	1040	461
320	295	1056	436
336	317	1072	410
352	339	1088	383
368	360	1104	356
384	382	1120	329
400	404	1136	303
416	425	1152	276
432	446	1168	250
448	467	1184	225
464	487	1200	200
480	507	1216	177
496	527	1232	154
512	545	1248	133
528	563	1264	113
544	581	1280	94
560	597	1296	77
576	613	1312	61
592	628	1328	47
608	641	1344	35
624	654	1360	25
640	666	1376	17
656	676	1392	10
672	685	1408	5
688	692	1424	3
704	699	1440	2
720	703	1456	3
736	707	1472	5

Constant added in Table	XIII.	2.82.
" " " "	XIV.	1.15.
" " " "	XV.	1.50.
" " " "	XVI.	3.60.

Period of Argument	II.	238^{y}.92.
" " "	III.	11987^{d}.4.
" " "	IV.	2050^{d}.4.
" " "	V.	1454^{d}.9.

The perturbations are expressed in hundredths of a second of arc.

TABLE XVII.

Perturbation of the Longitude by the Earth.

Constant added 16″.65. Period of Argument VI., 5834.92.

Arg. VI.	Equa.	Arg. VI.	Equa.	Arg. VI.	Equa.	Arg. VI.	Equa.	Arg. VI.	Equa.	Arg. VI.	Equa.
0^{d}	1668	104^{d}	47	208^{d}	2720	312^{d}	912	416^{d}	2093	520^{d}	2456
2	1671	106	31	210	2772	314	846	418	2172	522	2405
4	1675	108	18	212	2821	316	783	420	2249	524	2354
6	1677	110	8	214	2866	318	722	422	2326	526	2303
8	1679	112	3	216	2908	320	664	424	2400	528	2254
10	1680	114	0	218	2946	322	609	426	2473	530	2205
12	1678	116	2	220	2979	324	557	428	2544	532	2158
14	1676	118	7	222	3009	326	509	430	2613	534	2112
16	1671	120	16	224	3035	328	464	432	2680	536	2068
18	1664	122	28	226	3057	330	423	434	2744	538	2025
20	1655	124	45	228	3074	332	385	436	2805	540	1985
22	1643	126	65	230	3087	334	352	438	2863	542	1946
24	1628	128	90	232	3095	336	322	440	2918	544	1910
26	1611	130	118	234	3099	338	296	442	2971	546	1875
28	1591	132	149	236	3099	340	275	444	3020	548	1843
30	1569	134	185	238	3095	342	258	446	3065	550	1813
32	1544	136	224	240	3086	344	245	448	3108	552	1786
34	1517	138	266	242	3073	346	237	450	3147	554	1762
36	1486	140	312	244	3055	348	233	452	3182	556	1740
38	1454	142	361	246	3033	350	233	454	3214	558	1721
40	1419	144	414	248	3007	352	237	456	3241	560	1704
42	1382	146	470	250	2977	354	246	458	3265	562	1690
44	1343	148	528	252	2943	356	259	460	3285	564	1679
46	1302	150	590	254	2905	358	277	462	3302	566	1670
48	1259	152	654	256	2864	360	299	464	3314	568	1663
50	1214	154	720	258	2818	362	325	466	3323	570	1659
52	1168	156	789	260	2770	364	355	468	3328	572	1656
54	1120	158	860	262	2717	366	389	470	3329	574	1655
56	1071	160	933	264	2662	368	426	472	3327	576	1656
58	1022	162	1008	266	2604	370	468	474	3320	578	1658
60	971	164	1084	268	2542	372	514	476	3311	580	1661
62	920	166	1162	270	2479	374	563	478	3297	582	1664
64	868	168	1241	272	2412	376	615	480	3280	584	1668
66	816	170	1321	274	2344	378	671	482	3260	586	1671
68	764	172	1402	276	2273	380	729	484	3237	588	1675
70	712	174	1483	278	2201	382	791	486	3211	590	1677
72	660	176	1564	280	2127	384	855	488	3182	592	1679
74	609	178	1646	282	2051	386	923	490	3150	594	1680
76	559	180	1727	284	1975	388	991	492	3116	596	1678
78	510	182	1808	286	1897	390	1063	494	3079	598	1676
80	462	184	1888	288	1819	392	1137	496	3039	600	1671
82	415	186	1967	290	1740	394	1212	498	2998	602	1664
84	370	188	2046	292	1661	396	1289	500	2954	604	1655
86	327	190	2123	294	1582	398	1367	502	2909	606	1642
88	285	192	2198	296	1504	400	1446	504	2862	608	1627
90	246	194	2272	298	1426	402	1527	506	2814	610	1610
92	210	196	2343	300	1348	404	1607	508	2764	612	1590
94	175	198	2413	302	1272	406	1689	510	2714	614	1568
96	144	200	2479	304	1197	408	1770	512	2663	616	1543
98	115	202	2544	306	1123	410	1851	514	2612	618	1516
100	89	204	2603	308	1051	412	1932	516	2560	620	1485
102	67	206	2664	310	980	414	2013	518	2508	622	1453
104	47	208	2720	312	912	416	2093	520	2456	624	1418

The perturbations are expressed in hundredths of a second of arc.

TABLE XVIII.

Pert. of the Longitude by the Earth.

Arg. VII.	Equa.	Arg. VII.
d 0	0	d 248
4	0	244
8	2	240
12	5	236
16	10	232
20	16	228
24	25	224
28	34	220
32	45	216
36	57	212
40	71	208
44	85	204
48	100	200
52	116	196
56	132	192
60	149	188
64	165	184
68	182	180
72	198	176
76	215	172
80	230	168
84	245	164
88	259	160
92	272	156
96	283	152
100	294	148
104	303	144
108	310	140
112	316	136
116	321	132
120	323	128
124	324	124

TABLE XIX.

Pert. of the Longitude by Mars.

Arg. VIII.	Equa.	Arg. VIII.
d 0	0	d 224
4	0	220
8	1	216
12	3	212
16	6	208
20	9	204
24	13	200
28	18	196
32	23	192
36	29	188
40	36	184
44	42	180
48	50	176
52	57	172
56	64	168
60	72	164
64	79	160
68	86	156
72	93	152
76	100	148
80	106	144
84	112	140
88	117	136
92	121	132
96	125	128
100	128	124
104	130	120
108	131	116
112	132	112

TABLE XX.

Perturbation of the Longitude by Jupiter.

Arg. IX.	Equa.	Arg. IX.	Equa.	Arg. IX.	Equa.
d 0	332	d 80	7	d 160	671
2	327	82	12	162	672
4	321	84	19	164	672
6	315	86	28	166	670
8	309	88	38	168	667
10	303	90	49	170	663
12	296	92	62	172	658
14	289	94	77	174	651
16	281	96	93	176	643
18	273	98	110	178	634
20	264	100	128	180	624
22	255	102	148	182	613
24	245	104	168	184	602
26	235	106	190	186	590
28	224	108	212	188	577
30	213	110	235	190	564
32	201	112	259	192	551
34	188	114	283	194	538
36	176	116	307	196	524
38	163	118	332	198	511
40	150	120	356	200	498
42	137	122	381	202	485
44	123	124	405	204	472
46	110	126	428	206	460
48	98	128	452	208	448
50	85	130	474	210	436
52	73	132	496	212	425
54	62	134	517	214	415
56	51	136	537	216	405
58	41	138	556	218	396
60	32	140	573	220	388
62	23	142	590	222	380
64	16	144	605	224	372
66	10	146	618	226	365
68	6	148	630	228	359
70	2	150	641	230	352
72	0	152	650	232	346
74	0	154	658	234	341
76	0	156	664	236	335
78	3	158	668	238	330
80	7	160	671	240	324

Constant added in Table XVIII. 1.62.
Constant added in Table XIX. 0.66.
Constant added in Table XX. 3.35.

Period of Argument VII. 243.16.
Period of Argument VIII. 220.57.
Period of Argument IX. 236.90.

The perturbations are expressed in hundredths of a second of arc.

TABLE XXI.

Perturbation of the Longitude by Mercury.

Horizontal Argument = I.

Constant added 0″.85. Period of Argument I., 224ᵈ.7.

Arg. X.	0^{d}	8^{d}	16^{d}	24^{d}	32^{d}	40^{d}	48^{d}	56^{d}	64^{d}	72^{d}	80^{d}	88^{d}	96^{d}	104^{d}	112^{d}
0	132	131	131	132	135	137	138	138	138	141	146	152	158	162	162
1	128	127	128	129	132	134	134	135	136	139	144	151	156	158	158
2	123	122	122	124	127	129	130	131	132	136	142	148	152	153	152
3	116	115	116	118	121	124	125	125	128	132	138	143	147	146	143
4	107	107	109	112	115	117	118	120	122	127	133	138	139	138	134
5	99	99	102	105	108	111	112	113	117	122	127	131	131	128	123
6	90	91	94	98	102	104	105	107	111	116	121	123	122	118	112
7	81	84	87	92	95	97	99	101	105	110	114	115	112	107	100
8	74	77	81	86	89	92	93	96	100	104	107	107	102	96	89
9	67	72	76	81	85	87	88	91	95	99	100	99	93	85	78
10	63	68	73	78	81	83	85	87	91	94	94	91	81	76	68
11	69	65	71	75	79	80	82	85	88	90	89	84	76	67	60
12	59	65	70	75	77	79	81	83	86	86	84	78	69	60	53
13	60	66	72	76	78	79	80	83	84	84	80	73	63	55	48
14	64	70	73	78	80	81	82	83	84	82	77	69	59	51	45
15	69	75	79	82	83	83	84	85	85	81	75	66	57	49	43
16	75	81	85	86	87	87	87	87	86	81	74	65	56	49	44
17	84	88	91	92	92	91	91	91	88	82	74	65	56	50	46
18	93	97	99	98	97	96	96	94	90	84	75	65	57	52	50
19	102	105	106	105	103	102	100	98	93	85	76	67	60	56	55
20	112	114	113	111	109	107	105	101	95	87	78	69	64	61	60
21	121	122	120	117	114	112	108	104	98	89	80	72	68	66	66
22	130	129	126	122	119	115	112	107	99	90	81	75	72	71	72
23	137	135	131	126	122	118	114	108	100	91	83	78	76	77	78
24	143	139	134	129	124	120	115	108	100	91	84	80	80	81	83
25	147	142	136	130	125	120	114	108	99	91	85	82	83	85	88
26	148	142	135	129	123	118	113	105	97	89	84	83	85	88	91
27	147	140	133	126	120	115	109	101	93	87	83	83	87	90	93
28	144	136	128	121	116	110	104	96	89	83	81	83	87	90	93
29	138	130	122	115	109	104	97	90	83	79	78	81	86	89	92
30	130	122	113	107	101	96	89	82	77	74	75	78	83	87	89
31	120	112	104	98	92	87	80	74	69	68	70	75	80	83	85
32	100	100	93	87	82	77	71	65	62	62	65	70	75	78	80
33	96	88	81	75	71	66	61	56	54	56	60	65	70	73	74
34	82	74	64	64	60	55	51	47	46	49	54	60	64	66	68
35	68	61	56	52	49	45	41	39	39	43	49	54	58	60	61
36	54	48	41	41	38	35	32	31	33	38	44	49	52	53	54
37	41	36	33	31	29	26	24	25	28	33	39	44	46	47	47
38	29	26	24	22	21	19	18	19	24	30	36	39	41	41	42
39	19	17	16	15	14	13	13	16	21	27	33	36	37	37	37
40	11	10	10	10	10	10	11	14	20	26	31	34	34	34	34
41	5	5	6	7	8	8	10	15	21	27	31	33	32	32	32
42	2	3	5	7	8	9	12	17	23	29	32	33	32	32	33
43	2	4	6	9	10	12	15	21	27	32	35	35	34	34	35
44	4	7	10	12	14	17	21	27	33	37	39	39	37	37	39
45	8	12	16	19	21	24	29	35	40	44	44	43	42	43	45
46	16	20	24	27	29	33	38	43	48	51	51	50	49	50	53
47	25	30	34	36	39	43	48	53	58	59	59	57	57	58	62
48	36	41	45	47	50	54	59	64	68	68	67	66	66	68	72
49	48	53	57	59	62	66	71	75	78	78	77	75	76	79	84
50	61	65	69	71	74	78	82	86	88	88	86	85	87	91	96
51	74	78	81	83	86	90	94	97	98	97	96	96	98	103	108
52	87	91	93	95	97	101	105	107	108	106	105	106	109	115	120
53	99	102	104	105	108	111	114	116	116	115	114	116	120	126	132
54	110	112	113	114	117	120	123	124	124	122	122	125	130	136	142
55	119	121	121	122	124	127	130	131	130	129	130	133	139	145	150
56	126	127	127	128	130	133	135	135	135	134	136	140	146	153	157
57	131	131	131	132	134	137	138	139	138	138	141	145	152	158	162
58	134	131	133	134	136	139	140	140	139	140	144	149	156	161	164
59	134	133	133	134	137	139	140	140	140	141	146	152	158	163	164
60	132	131	131	132	135	137	138	138	138	141	146	152	158	162	162

The perturbations are expressed in hundredths of a second of arc.

Perturbation of the Longitude by Mercury.

Horizontal Argument = I.

Constant added 0″.85. Period of Argument X, 60.

Arg. X.	120^d	128^d	136^d	144^d	152^d	160^d	168^d	176^d	184^d	192^d	200^d	208^d	216^d	224^d	232^d
0	162	160	159	158	156	151	145	138	130	124	118	111	103	93	85
1	156	154	152	150	147	141	134	125	118	111	105	97	89	79	72
2	149	146	143	140	136	129	120	112	104	97	91	83	74	65	59
3	140	136	133	129	123	115	106	97	90	83	76	68	60	51	46
4	129	125	121	116	109	100	91	82	75	69	62	54	46	39	34
5	118	113	108	102	95	85	76	68	61	55	48	41	34	27	24
6	106	101	95	89	80	71	62	54	48	42	36	29	23	18	15
7	94	88	82	75	67	57	48	41	36	31	25	19	14	10	9
8	82	76	70	63	54	45	37	30	26	21	16	11	7	5	5
9	71	66	59	51	43	34	27	22	18	14	10	6	3	2	3
10	62	56	49	42	33	25	19	15	12	10	6	3	2	2	4
11	53	48	41	34	26	19	14	12	10	8	5	3	3	5	8
12	47	42	35	28	21	16	12	11	10	8	7	6	7	10	14
13	42	37	31	25	18	14	12	12	12	12	11	11	13	18	22
14	40	35	30	24	19	16	15	16	17	17	17	19	22	27	32
15	39	35	30	25	21	20	20	22	24	25	26	29	33	38	43
16	40	37	32	28	26	26	28	31	33	34	36	40	45	50	55
17	43	40	37	34	32	34	37	40	43	45	48	52	57	63	68
18	48	45	42	41	41	43	47	51	54	57	60	65	71	76	81
19	53	51	49	49	50	54	58	63	66	69	73	78	84	89	93
20	59	58	57	57	60	65	70	74	78	81	85	91	96	101	104
21	65	65	65	66	70	76	81	86	89	92	97	102	107	112	114
22	72	72	73	75	80	86	91	96	99	103	107	112	117	120	122
23	79	79	81	84	89	95	101	105	108	111	116	120	125	127	128
24	84	85	88	92	97	103	108	112	115	118	122	127	130	132	132
25	89	90	93	98	104	110	114	118	120	123	127	131	133	134	134
26	92	94	98	103	109	114	118	121	123	126	129	132	134	134	133
27	94	96	100	105	112	117	120	122	123	126	129	131	132	132	131
28	95	97	101	107	112	117	119	120	122	124	126	128	129	127	126
29	94	96	101	106	111	114	116	117	118	120	122	123	123	121	120
30	91	94	98	103	108	110	111	111	112	114	115	116	115	114	113
31	87	90	94	99	103	104	105	104	105	106	107	108	107	105	105
32	82	85	89	93	96	97	97	96	97	98	99	99	98	97	97
33	76	79	83	86	88	88	88	87	88	89	89	89	89	88	89
34	69	72	76	79	80	79	78	78	78	80	80	80	80	80	81
35	62	65	68	70	71	70	69	68	70	71	72	72	71	72	75
36	55	58	61	63	63	61	60	60	61	63	64	64	63	66	70
37	49	51	54	55	55	53	52	53	55	56	57	58	59	62	66
38	43	46	48	49	48	46	46	47	49	52	53	54	56	59	64
39	39	41	43	43	43	42	42	43	46	49	50	52	55	60	64
40	36	38	40	40	39	38	39	42	45	48	50	52	56	61	66
41	34	37	38	38	38	38	39	42	46	50	52	55	60	64	70
42	35	37	39	39	38	39	42	46	50	54	56	59	64	70	75
43	37	40	41	42	42	43	47	51	56	60	63	66	71	77	82
44	42	44	46	46	47	50	54	59	64	68	71	75	79	85	90
45	48	51	52	53	55	58	63	69	73	77	80	84	89	95	99
46	56	59	61	62	64	68	74	80	84	88	91	95	100	105	107
47	66	69	71	73	75	80	86	92	96	99	102	106	110	114	116
48	77	80	82	84	88	93	99	104	108	111	114	117	121	124	124
49	88	92	94	97	101	106	112	117	120	123	125	128	130	132	131
50	101	104	106	110	114	119	125	129	132	133	135	137	139	139	137
51	113	116	119	122	127	132	137	140	142	142	143	145	145	144	141
52	125	128	130	134	138	144	148	150	150	150	150	150	150	148	143
53	136	138	141	145	149	153	156	157	157	155	155	154	152	148	143
54	146	148	150	154	157	161	163	163	161	159	157	155	153	147	140
55	154	156	158	161	164	166	167	165	162	159	157	154	149	143	136
56	160	161	163	165	168	169	168	165	161	157	154	150	144	137	129
57	164	164	166	167	169	169	166	162	157	152	148	143	137	128	120
58	165	166	166	167	167	165	162	156	150	145	140	134	127	118	109
59	165	164	164	164	163	160	155	148	141	135	130	123	115	106	98
60	162	160	159	158	156	151	145	138	130	124	118	111	103	93	85

Add 33.96 to Arg. X. when 224ᵈ.7 is subtracted from Arg. I.

TABLE XXII.

Perturbations of the Longitude by the Earth.

Horizontal Argument = I.

Constant added 1''.40. Period of Argument I. 224d.7.

Arg. XI.	0d	8d	16d	24d	32d	40d	48d	56d	64d	72d	80d	88d	96d	104d	112d
0	71	80	88	94	98	100	102	105	110	117	127	140	153	165	177
1	63	71	79	85	88	90	92	95	99	105	115	126	139	152	164
2	55	63	71	76	79	81	82	85	88	94	102	113	126	138	151
3	49	56	63	68	71	72	73	75	77	82	91	101	113	126	138
4	44	50	56	60	63	64	65	66	68	72	80	90	101	114	126
5	40	45	50	54	56	57	57	58	59	63	70	79	90	102	115
6	39	42	47	50	51	52	51	51	52	55	61	70	81	92	105
7	39	42	45	47	48	48	47	47	47	49	54	62	72	84	95
8	42	43	46	47	47	47	45	44	43	45	49	56	65	76	87
9	47	47	48	49	49	48	45	43	42	42	45	51	60	70	81
10	54	53	53	54	53	51	49	45	43	42	44	49	56	65	75
11	63	61	61	60	59	57	53	49	46	44	45	48	54	62	71
12	73	71	70	69	67	64	61	56	51	49	47	49	53	69	67
13	84	82	81	80	77	74	70	64	59	55	52	52	55	59	66
14	95	94	92	91	89	85	80	74	68	62	58	57	58	61	65
15	107	106	104	103	101	97	92	85	78	72	66	63	62	63	66
16	118	117	116	115	114	109	104	97	89	82	75	70	68	67	69
17	129	128	128	127	125	121	116	108	100	92	84	78	74	73	73
18	139	138	138	137	136	132	127	119	111	102	94	87	82	79	78
19	146	146	146	146	145	141	136	129	121	112	103	95	90	86	83
20	153	153	153	153	152	148	144	137	129	120	111	103	97	93	90
21	158	158	158	158	157	154	150	144	136	127	118	110	104	100	97
22	163	162	162	162	161	158	154	148	140	133	124	116	111	106	103
23	166	165	164	163	162	160	156	150	143	136	128	121	115	112	109
24	168	166	165	164	163	160	156	151	145	138	130	124	119	116	114
25	170	167	165	164	162	160	156	151	144	138	131	125	121	119	117
26	172	168	165	163	161	158	154	149	143	136	130	124	121	119	119
27	174	169	166	163	160	157	152	147	140	134	128	123	120	119	119
28	176	171	167	164	160	156	151	144	138	131	125	120	117	116	117
29	179	174	169	165	161	156	150	143	136	128	122	116	113	112	114
30	183	177	172	167	162	157	150	143	135	126	118	112	109	107	109
31	187	181	176	171	166	159	152	144	134	125	116	109	104	102	103
32	190	185	181	176	170	163	155	146	135	125	114	106	100	97	97
33	194	190	186	182	176	169	160	150	138	126	114	104	96	92	91
34	198	195	192	188	183	176	166	156	143	129	115	104	94	88	86
35	201	200	198	195	190	183	174	162	149	134	110	105	94	86	82
36	204	204	203	202	197	191	182	170	156	140	124	108	95	86	80
37	205	208	208	207	204	199	191	179	164	148	131	114	99	87	80
38	205	208	211	212	211	206	199	188	174	157	139	121	105	92	83
39	204	209	213	216	216	213	207	198	184	167	149	130	113	98	88
40	201	208	214	218	220	219	215	206	194	178	160	141	123	107	95
41	197	205	213	219	223	224	221	215	203	189	171	153	134	118	105
42	192	202	211	219	225	229	226	222	213	200	183	165	147	130	116
43	186	197	208	217	225	230	231	220	221	211	196	178	161	143	129
44	179	192	203	214	224	231	235	234	229	221	207	191	175	158	143
45	172	185	198	210	222	231	237	239	236	230	219	204	188	172	157
46	165	178	192	206	218	230	238	242	242	238	229	216	201	186	171
47	157	171	186	200	214	227	238	245	217	245	238	227	213	199	184
48	150	163	178	194	209	224	236	246	250	250	246	237	224	211	196
49	142	156	171	187	204	220	234	245	252	254	252	245	234	222	208
50	134	147	162	179	197	214	230	243	252	257	256	251	242	231	218
51	126	139	154	170	189	207	225	239	250	257	259	255	248	238	226
52	117	129	144	161	180	199	218	234	246	256	259	258	252	243	232
53	108	119	133	150	169	189	209	226	241	252	257	258	254	247	237
54	99	109	122	138	157	178	198	217	233	245	253	256	254	240	240
55	90	98	110	125	144	164	185	205	223	237	247	251	252	248	242
56	81	87	97	111	129	149	170	191	210	226	238	245	248	246	241
57	72	76	84	96	113	133	154	175	196	213	227	236	241	242	239
58	63	64	70	81	96	115	136	158	179	198	214	225	233	236	235
59	55	54	57	66	79	97	117	139	161	181	199	212	222	228	230
60	49	45	45	51	63	79	98	119	141	163	182	198	210	218	223

The perturbations are expressed in hundredths of a second of arc.

Perturbations of the Longitude by the Earth.

Horizontal Argument = I.

Constant added 1".40. Period of Argument XI, 240 units.

Arg XI.	120d	128d	136d	144d	152d	160d	168d	176d	184d	192d	200d	208d	216d	224d	232d
0	188	195	201	204	205	206	206	207	209	211	213	214	214	211	235
1	175	183	189	193	195	197	198	201	204	208	212	215	216	215	211
2	162	170	177	182	185	187	190	193	198	203	209	213	217	218	215
3	149	159	166	171	174	178	181	185	191	197	204	211	216	219	218
4	138	147	155	160	164	168	172	177	183	190	199	207	214	218	219
5	127	136	144	150	155	158	163	168	175	183	193	202	210	216	219
6	116	127	134	141	145	149	154	159	166	176	186	196	206	214	218
7	107	117	125	132	137	140	145	151	158	168	179	190	201	211	217
8	99	109	117	124	129	132	137	142	150	159	171	183	196	208	215
9	92	101	109	116	120	124	128	134	141	151	164	177	191	204	214
10	85	95	102	108	112	116	120	125	133	143	156	170	186	200	212
11	80	89	96	101	105	109	113	117	124	135	148	161	180	196	211
12	76	84	90	95	99	102	105	110	117	127	141	157	175	192	209
13	73	80	85	91	93	95	99	102	109	119	134	150	169	188	207
14	71	77	81	85	87	89	92	95	102	112	126	143	163	184	204
15	71	75	78	81	83	84	86	89	95	105	119	136	157	179	201
16	72	75	77	79	80	80	82	84	89	98	111	129	150	174	197
17	74	76	77	78	78	77	78	79	83	92	105	122	143	167	192
18	78	78	79	79	78	76	76	76	79	86	98	115	136	160	185
19	83	83	82	81	79	77	75	74	76	82	92	108	128	151	177
20	89	88	86	85	82	79	76	73	74	78	87	101	119	142	168
21	95	94	92	90	87	83	78	74	73	75	82	94	111	132	157
22	102	101	99	96	92	87	82	77	74	74	78	88	103	122	146
23	108	107	105	103	99	93	87	81	75	73	75	83	95	112	134
24	114	113	112	110	105	100	93	85	78	74	73	78	87	102	122
25	118	118	117	116	111	106	98	90	82	76	72	74	81	93	110
26	120	121	122	121	117	112	104	95	86	78	73	72	76	85	99
27	121	123	125	125	122	117	110	101	90	81	74	71	72	78	90
28	120	123	126	127	125	121	115	106	95	84	76	71	69	73	82
29	117	121	125	127	127	124	119	110	99	88	78	72	68	69	76
30	113	117	122	126	127	126	121	113	103	92	81	74	69	67	71
31	107	112	118	123	125	125	121	115	106	96	85	77	70	67	69
32	100	106	112	118	122	123	121	117	108	99	88	80	72	68	68
33	94	99	106	113	118	121	120	117	110	101	92	83	76	71	69
34	88	92	99	107	113	117	118	117	111	104	95	87	79	74	71
35	83	86	93	101	108	113	116	116	112	106	98	91	83	77	74
36	79	82	88	96	103	110	114	115	113	108	102	95	87	82	78
37	78	79	85	92	100	107	112	114	113	110	105	99	92	86	82
38	78	79	83	90	98	105	111	114	115	112	108	103	96	91	86
39	82	81	84	90	98	105	111	115	117	115	111	107	100	95	91
40	88	85	87	93	100	107	113	118	119	118	115	111	105	100	95
41	96	92	93	97	104	110	117	121	123	122	119	115	109	104	99
42	106	101	101	103	109	115	121	126	127	127	124	120	114	109	104
43	118	111	110	112	116	122	127	131	133	133	129	125	119	114	109
44	131	123	120	121	125	130	135	138	139	139	136	131	125	119	114
45	144	136	132	132	134	138	142	145	146	146	142	137	131	125	120
46	158	149	144	142	144	147	151	153	154	153	149	144	138	132	126
47	171	161	155	153	153	156	159	160	161	160	156	151	145	139	133
48	184	173	166	163	163	164	167	168	169	167	163	158	152	146	140
49	195	184	176	172	171	172	174	175	176	174	170	165	159	153	149
50	205	194	185	181	179	179	180	181	182	180	177	172	166	160	155
51	213	202	193	188	185	185	186	187	187	186	183	178	172	167	162
52	220	209	200	194	191	190	191	192	192	191	188	184	178	173	168
53	226	215	206	200	196	195	195	196	196	195	192	188	183	178	173
54	230	220	211	205	201	199	199	199	200	199	196	192	187	182	177
55	233	224	215	209	205	202	202	203	202	201	198	195	190	184	179
56	234	226	218	213	208	206	204	205	205	203	200	197	191	186	181
57	234	227	221	215	211	209	207	208	207	205	202	198	192	186	180
58	232	227	222	218	214	212	210	210	209	207	203	198	192	185	179
59	229	226	223	219	216	214	213	212	211	208	204	198	191	184	177
60	224	224	222	220	218	216	215	215	213	210	205	198	191	183	171

Add 147.64 to Arg. XI. when 2244.7 is subtracted from Arg. I.

TABLE XXII.

Perturbations of the Longitude by the Earth.

Horizontal Argument = I.

Constant added 1″.40. Period of Argument I., 224d.7.

Arg. XI.	0^d	8^d	16^d	24^d	32^d	40^d	48^d	56^d	64^d	72^d	80^d	88^d	96^d	104^d	112^d
60	49	45	45	51	63	79	98	119	141	163	182	198	210	218	223
61	44	37	35	38	47	62	79	99	122	143	164	182	196	207	214
62	41	31	26	27	33	44	60	80	102	124	146	164	181	194	203
63	41	28	21	18	21	30	44	62	83	105	127	147	164	179	191
64	43	28	18	12	12	18	30	45	65	86	108	128	147	164	177
65	47	31	18	10	7	10	18	32	40	60	90	111	130	147	162
66	54	36	21	11	5	4	10	21	36	54	74	94	113	131	147
67	63	44	28	15	6	3	6	14	26	42	60	79	97	115	131
68	73	54	37	23	12	6	5	10	20	33	48	66	83	99	115
69	85	67	49	33	21	12	9	10	16	27	40	55	70	85	100
70	97	80	63	46	32	21	15	13	16	24	34	46	60	73	87
71	110	94	78	61	45	33	24	20	20	24	31	41	52	63	75
72	123	109	93	76	69	47	36	29	26	27	31	38	46	55	65
73	134	122	108	92	76	62	49	40	35	33	34	38	44	51	58
74	144	135	122	107	92	77	64	53	43	41	40	41	44	48	54
75	153	143	135	122	107	92	78	66	57	51	47	46	47	49	52
76	160	155	146	134	121	107	93	80	69	62	56	53	52	52	53
77	165	162	155	145	133	120	106	93	82	73	66	69	59	57	56
78	169	167	162	153	144	131	118	106	94	85	77	71	67	64	61
79	171	170	167	160	152	141	129	117	106	96	88	81	76	71	67
80	172	172	170	165	158	149	138	127	116	107	99	91	85	80	73
81	172	172	171	168	163	155	146	136	126	117	108	101	95	89	83
82	171	172	171	169	166	160	152	144	134	126	118	110	104	97	90
83	170	171	171	170	167	163	157	150	142	134	126	119	112	105	98
84	169	169	169	169	168	165	161	155	148	141	134	126	120	112	105
85	169	168	168	168	168	166	163	158	153	147	140	133	126	119	111
86	168	166	166	167	167	167	165	161	157	152	145	139	132	124	116
87	167	165	164	166	166	167	166	163	160	156	150	143	136	129	120
88	167	164	163	165	164	166	166	165	163	159	153	147	140	133	123
89	167	163	161	162	163	165	166	166	164	161	156	151	144	136	126
90	167	162	160	160	162	163	165	166	165	163	159	154	147	139	129
91	168	162	159	158	159	161	164	165	165	164	161	156	150	142	132
92	168	161	157	156	157	159	162	164	165	165	162	158	153	145	136
93	168	160	156	153	154	156	159	162	164	165	163	161	156	148	139
94	168	160	154	151	151	152	156	159	162	164	164	163	158	152	144
95	169	159	153	149	148	149	152	156	160	163	165	164	162	157	149
96	169	159	152	147	145	146	149	153	158	162	165	166	165	161	154
97	170	159	151	145	143	143	145	150	155	161	165	168	168	166	160
98	171	160	151	145	141	140	143	147	153	159	165	169	171	171	167
99	172	162	152	145	140	139	140	145	151	158	164	171	174	175	174
100	174	164	154	146	141	138	139	143	150	157	165	172	177	180	180
101	176	167	158	149	143	140	140	143	149	157	165	173	180	184	186
102	179	171	162	153	146	142	141	144	149	157	166	175	183	189	191
103	182	175	166	158	151	146	144	146	151	158	167	176	185	192	196
104	184	179	171	163	156	151	149	149	153	160	169	178	187	195	200
105	187	183	177	170	163	157	154	154	157	163	171	180	189	198	203
106	188	186	181	176	169	164	160	159	161	166	173	182	191	200	206
107	188	188	185	181	176	170	167	165	166	169	175	184	193	201	208
108	186	189	188	185	181	176	173	170	170	173	178	186	194	203	210
109	182	187	189	188	185	181	178	175	175	176	180	187	195	203	211
110	177	184	188	188	187	184	181	170	178	179	182	188	195	204	212
111	170	178	183	186	186	185	183	181	180	180	183	189	195	203	211
112	161	171	177	182	183	184	182	181	180	181	183	188	194	202	210
113	150	161	168	174	177	179	179	179	179	179	181	186	192	201	209
114	138	149	157	164	169	172	174	175	175	176	178	183	189	198	206
115	125	136	145	153	158	163	166	168	169	171	174	179	185	193	203
116	112	122	131	140	146	152	156	159	162	161	168	173	179	188	198
117	99	108	117	125	132	139	144	149	152	156	163	165	172	181	192
118	87	95	102	110	118	125	132	137	142	146	151	157	164	174	184
119	76	82	89	96	104	111	119	125	131	136	141	148	155	164	175
120	67	71	77	83	90	98	106	113	119	125	131	138	145	154	165

The perturbations are expressed in hundredths of a second of arc.

Perturbations of the Longitude by the Earth.

Horizontal Argument = I.

Constant added 1″.40. Period of Argument XI, 240 units.

Arg. XI.	120^d	128^d	136^d	144^d	152^d	160^d	168^d	176^d	184^d	192^d	200^d	208^d	216^d	224^d	232^d
60	224	221	222	220	218	216	215	215	213	210	205	198	191	183	174
61	218	219	219	219	218	218	217	217	215	211	206	199	190	181	171
62	209	213	216	217	218	218	219	218	217	213	207	200	190	180	170
63	199	206	210	214	216	218	219	220	218	215	209	201	191	180	168
64	188	196	203	208	213	216	218	220	219	216	211	203	193	180	168
65	175	185	194	201	207	212	216	220	220	218	213	205	195	183	169
66	160	172	183	192	200	207	213	218	220	219	215	208	198	186	172
67	145	158	170	181	191	200	208	215	218	219	217	211	202	190	177
68	130	143	156	168	180	191	201	210	216	219	217	214	206	195	182
69	115	128	142	155	168	181	193	204	212	217	219	217	210	201	189
70	100	114	127	141	155	169	184	196	207	215	219	219	214	206	195
71	87	100	113	127	142	157	173	188	201	211	218	220	218	211	202
72	76	87	100	114	129	145	162	178	194	206	215	220	220	216	209
73	67	77	88	101	116	133	151	168	185	200	211	219	221	220	214
74	61	68	78	90	105	121	139	158	176	193	207	216	221	222	218
75	57	63	71	81	95	110	128	148	167	185	201	212	219	222	220
76	55	59	65	74	86	101	118	137	157	177	194	207	216	220	221
77	56	58	61	69	79	93	109	128	148	167	185	200	211	217	219
78	60	60	62	67	75	87	102	119	138	158	177	192	204	212	215
79	65	63	63	66	72	81	95	111	129	149	167	183	196	205	210
80	70	67	65	66	70	77	80	103	120	139	157	173	187	197	203
81	77	73	69	67	69	75	84	96	112	129	147	163	177	188	194
82	84	78	73	69	69	72	79	90	104	120	137	152	166	177	185
83	90	84	77	72	69	70	75	84	96	111	126	141	156	167	175
84	97	89	81	74	70	68	71	77	88	101	116	130	145	156	164
85	102	93	84	76	70	66	67	72	80	92	106	119	134	145	154
86	106	97	86	77	70	64	63	66	73	83	96	109	123	134	143
87	110	100	89	78	69	62	59	60	65	74	86	98	112	123	133
88	113	102	90	78	68	60	55	54	58	65	76	88	101	113	122
89	116	104	91	79	67	58	52	49	51	57	67	78	91	102	112
90	118	106	93	80	67	56	49	45	45	50	58	68	81	92	102
91	121	109	95	81	67	56	46	42	40	43	51	60	71	82	92
92	124	112	98	83	69	56	45	39	36	38	44	52	63	73	83
93	128	116	102	87	71	58	46	38	34	33	38	45	55	65	74
94	133	121	107	91	76	61	48	38	33	31	34	39	48	57	66
95	139	127	113	97	81	66	52	41	33	30	31	35	42	50	58
96	146	134	121	105	89	73	58	45	36	31	30	32	38	45	51
97	153	142	129	114	97	81	65	51	41	34	31	31	35	40	46
98	161	151	139	124	107	91	74	59	47	39	34	32	35	38	43
99	169	160	149	134	118	101	84	68	55	45	39	35	36	38	42
100	177	169	159	145	129	113	95	78	64	53	45	40	40	40	42
101	184	178	169	156	141	124	107	90	75	61	54	47	45	44	45
102	191	187	178	166	152	136	119	101	86	73	63	55	52	50	51
103	197	194	187	176	163	147	130	113	97	84	73	65	61	58	58
104	203	201	195	185	173	158	141	125	109	96	84	76	71	68	67
105	207	206	202	193	181	167	152	135	120	106	96	87	82	79	78
106	210	211	207	200	189	176	162	145	131	118	107	99	94	91	89
107	214	215	212	206	197	184	171	155	141	129	118	111	106	102	101
108	216	218	217	211	203	192	179	164	151	139	128	122	117	114	113
109	217	220	220	216	209	198	186	173	160	149	139	132	128	125	124
110	218	222	223	220	214	205	193	180	169	157	148	142	137	135	135
111	218	223	225	223	218	210	200	189	176	165	156	150	146	144	143
112	218	224	227	226	223	215	206	195	183	173	164	157	153	151	151
113	217	224	228	229	227	220	212	201	190	179	170	163	159	157	156
114	215	223	229	231	230	225	217	207	196	185	176	169	164	161	161
115	213	221	228	232	232	229	222	212	202	191	182	174	168	165	163
116	208	218	227	232	234	232	226	217	207	196	187	178	172	167	165
117	203	214	224	230	234	233	229	221	212	201	191	182	175	170	167
118	196	208	219	227	232	234	231	224	216	205	195	185	177	172	168
119	188	200	212	222	229	232	231	226	219	209	198	189	180	174	169
120	178	191	204	215	224	228	230	227	220	212	202	192	183	176	170

Add 147.64 to Arg. XI. when 224^d.7 is subtracted from Arg. I.

TABLE XXII.

Perturbations of the Longitude by the Earth.

Horizontal Argument = I.

Constant added 1″.40. Period of Argument I., 224ᵈ.7.

Arg. XI.	0ᵈ	8ᵈ	16ᵈ	24ᵈ	32ᵈ	40ᵈ	48ᵈ	56ᵈ	64ᵈ	72ᵈ	80ᵈ	88ᵈ	96ᵈ	104ᵈ	112ᵈ
120	67	71	77	83	90	98	106	113	119	125	131	138	145	154	165
121	59	62	66	71	78	86	93	101	108	114	121	127	134	143	154
122	53	55	57	62	67	75	82	90	98	104	110	117	124	132	142
123	50	51	51	54	59	65	73	80	88	94	101	107	113	121	131
124	48	47	47	49	53	58	65	72	80	86	92	99	104	111	119
125	48	46	45	46	48	53	59	66	73	79	85	91	96	101	108
126	49	46	45	44	46	49	55	61	68	74	80	84	89	93	99
127	52	49	46	45	45	48	52	58	65	70	76	80	83	87	91
128	56	52	49	46	46	47	51	57	62	68	73	77	80	82	86
129	60	56	52	49	47	48	51	56	62	67	72	76	78	80	82
130	65	61	56	52	50	49	52	56	61	67	72	76	79	80	81
131	70	66	61	56	53	51	53	57	62	68	74	78	80	82	83
132	76	71	65	60	56	54	55	58	63	69	75	80	83	85	86
133	82	76	70	64	59	56	56	59	64	70	77	83	87	90	91
134	89	82	75	68	62	58	58	60	65	72	79	86	92	95	97
135	96	88	80	73	66	61	60	62	66	73	81	90	96	101	104
136	103	95	86	77	70	64	62	63	67	75	83	92	101	107	111
137	112	103	93	83	74	68	65	65	69	76	85	95	104	112	117
138	121	111	100	90	80	72	68	67	70	77	86	97	107	116	123
139	131	120	109	97	86	77	72	70	72	78	87	98	109	119	127
140	141	130	118	106	94	84	76	73	74	79	87	98	110	121	130
141	152	141	128	115	102	91	82	78	76	80	87	98	109	121	131
142	163	151	138	125	111	99	89	83	80	81	87	97	108	119	130
143	173	162	149	136	121	108	96	88	84	83	88	96	106	117	128
144	183	173	161	147	132	117	104	94	88	86	88	94	103	114	125
145	193	183	171	158	142	127	113	101	93	88	89	93	100	110	121
146	201	193	181	168	153	137	122	109	98	92	90	92	98	106	116
147	208	201	190	178	163	147	130	117	104	95	91	91	95	102	111
148	213	207	198	186	172	156	139	124	110	100	94	92	93	99	107
149	217	212	205	194	180	164	147	131	116	105	97	92	93	96	103
150	219	216	210	200	187	172	155	138	123	110	100	94	92	94	100
151	219	218	214	205	194	179	162	146	130	115	104	97	94	94	98
152	218	219	216	209	199	185	169	153	136	121	109	100	96	94	97
153	217	219	218	213	204	191	176	159	143	128	115	105	99	96	97
154	214	218	219	216	208	197	183	166	151	135	122	111	103	99	99
155	211	217	220	218	212	202	189	174	158	143	129	118	109	103	102
156	208	215	220	220	217	208	196	182	167	152	138	125	116	109	106
157	204	214	221	223	221	215	204	191	177	161	147	134	124	116	111
158	200	212	221	226	226	221	212	200	187	172	158	144	133	123	117
159	197	211	222	229	231	228	221	210	198	183	169	155	143	132	125
160	193	209	222	232	236	236	230	221	209	196	182	167	154	142	133
161	189	207	223	235	242	243	240	232	221	208	194	180	166	153	143
162	185	204	223	237	246	250	249	242	233	221	207	193	179	165	154
163	179	201	221	238	250	256	257	253	245	234	221	206	192	178	165
164	173	197	219	238	252	261	264	262	255	245	233	219	205	191	178
165	167	191	215	236	252	263	269	269	264	256	245	232	219	204	191
166	159	184	209	232	250	264	272	274	271	265	256	244	231	218	204
167	150	176	201	225	246	261	271	276	276	272	264	254	243	230	217
168	141	166	192	217	239	256	269	276	278	276	270	263	253	242	230
169	131	155	181	206	229	249	263	272	277	277	274	269	261	252	242
170	120	144	168	194	217	238	254	266	272	276	275	272	267	260	252
171	110	132	155	180	204	225	243	256	265	271	273	272	270	266	260
172	100	119	141	165	189	210	229	244	255	263	267	270	270	268	265
173	91	108	128	150	173	194	213	230	242	252	259	264	267	268	268
174	84	97	115	135	157	178	197	214	228	239	248	255	261	265	267
175	77	88	103	121	141	161	180	197	212	224	235	244	252	258	263
176	72	80	93	109	127	145	163	180	195	208	220	230	239	248	256
177	69	75	84	98	114	130	147	163	177	191	203	214	225	235	245
178	67	71	78	89	103	117	132	147	160	173	185	197	209	220	231
179	68	69	74	82	94	106	119	132	144	156	167	179	191	203	215
180	69	68	71	78	87	97	108	119	129	140	150	161	172	185	198

The perturbations are expressed in hundredths of a second of arc.

Perturbations of the Longitude by the Earth.

Horizontal Argument = I.

Constant added 1″.40. Period of Argument XI., 240 units.

Arg. XI.	120ᵈ	128ᵈ	136ᵈ	144ᵈ	152ᵈ	160ᵈ	168ᵈ	176ᵈ	184ᵈ	192ᵈ	200ᵈ	208ᵈ	216ᵈ	224ᵈ	232ᵈ
120	178	191	204	215	224	228	230	227	230	212	202	192	183	176	170
121	167	180	193	206	216	223	226	225	224	213	204	195	186	179	173
122	155	168	182	195	207	216	221	221	219	214	206	198	189	182	176
123	142	155	169	183	196	206	213	216	217	213	207	200	193	186	180
124	129	141	155	169	183	195	204	210	212	211	208	202	196	190	184
125	117	128	141	155	170	183	194	202	207	208	207	203	199	194	189
126	106	116	128	142	156	170	182	192	199	203	204	204	201	198	194
127	97	105	116	129	142	157	170	182	191	197	201	203	202	201	199
128	90	96	105	117	130	144	158	171	182	191	197	201	203	203	203
129	85	90	97	107	119	133	146	161	173	184	192	198	202	205	206
130	83	86	92	100	110	123	137	151	164	176	186	194	200	205	208
131	83	85	89	95	104	115	128	142	155	168	179	189	197	204	209
132	86	87	89	93	100	110	121	134	147	160	173	184	193	202	208
133	91	91	91	94	99	106	116	127	140	153	166	177	188	198	206
134	97	97	96	97	100	105	113	122	134	146	159	171	182	193	203
135	105	104	103	101	103	106	111	119	129	140	152	164	176	188	199
136	112	112	110	108	107	108	112	117	125	134	145	157	169	181	193
137	120	120	118	115	113	112	113	116	122	130	139	150	162	175	187
138	126	127	126	123	119	116	116	114	120	126	133	144	155	167	180
139	132	134	133	130	125	121	119	117	118	122	128	137	147	160	173
140	136	139	139	135	131	126	122	118	117	119	123	131	140	152	165
141	138	142	143	140	135	130	124	119	116	116	119	125	133	144	158
142	138	144	145	143	139	133	126	120	116	114	115	119	126	136	149
143	137	143	146	145	141	134	128	120	115	111	110	114	119	128	141
144	134	141	145	145	142	135	128	121	114	109	106	109	111	120	132
145	130	137	142	143	141	135	128	123	113	106	102	102	104	111	122
146	125	133	139	141	139	135	128	119	111	104	98	96	97	103	112
147	120	128	135	137	137	133	127	118	110	101	94	91	89	93	101
148	115	123	130	134	134	131	126	117	109	99	91	86	82	84	91
149	110	118	125	130	132	130	124	117	108	97	89	81	75	75	79
150	106	114	121	126	129	128	123	116	107	96	85	76	69	67	68
151	103	110	117	123	126	126	123	116	107	96	84	73	61	59	57
152	101	107	114	120	124	125	122	117	108	96	83	71	59	52	48
153	100	106	112	118	123	124	122	117	109	97	83	70	57	47	40
154	101	105	111	117	121	124	123	118	110	99	85	71	55	43	34
155	102	105	110	116	121	123	123	120	113	102	88	73	56	42	30
156	105	107	111	115	120	123	124	121	115	105	92	76	59	43	29
157	109	109	112	116	120	123	124	123	118	109	96	81	64	46	31
158	113	112	113	117	120	123	125	125	121	114	102	87	70	52	35
159	119	116	116	118	120	123	126	126	124	118	108	95	78	60	42
160	126	122	119	119	121	124	126	128	126	122	114	103	89	70	52
161	134	128	124	122	123	125	127	129	129	127	121	111	98	82	64
162	143	135	130	126	125	126	128	130	132	131	127	120	108	94	77
163	154	144	136	131	129	128	130	132	134	135	133	128	119	107	91
164	165	154	145	138	133	132	132	134	137	139	139	136	129	119	105
165	178	165	155	146	140	137	136	137	140	142	144	143	138	131	119
166	190	178	166	156	148	143	141	141	143	146	148	149	147	141	131
167	204	191	179	167	158	151	147	145	147	149	152	155	154	150	142
168	218	205	192	179	169	160	154	151	151	153	156	159	159	157	152
169	231	218	206	192	181	171	163	158	156	157	159	162	163	163	159
170	242	232	220	206	194	183	173	166	162	161	162	165	166	167	165
171	252	244	233	220	207	195	184	175	169	166	166	167	168	170	169
172	260	254	241	233	220	207	195	184	176	171	169	169	170	171	171
173	266	260	254	244	232	219	206	194	184	176	172	171	170	171	172
174	268	266	261	253	243	230	216	203	191	182	175	172	171	171	172
175	267	267	265	260	251	239	226	212	198	187	179	174	171	170	171
176	262	266	266	263	257	246	233	219	205	193	182	175	171	170	169
177	254	260	264	263	259	251	239	226	211	198	186	177	171	169	168
178	242	251	257	260	258	253	243	230	216	202	189	179	172	168	167
179	228	239	248	254	255	252	241	233	219	205	192	181	173	168	165
180	211	224	236	244	248	248	243	231	222	207	195	183	174	167	164

Add 147.64 to Arg. XI. when 224ᵈ.7 is subtracted from Arg. I.

TABLE XXII.

Perturbations of the Longitude by the Earth.

Horizontal Argument = I.

Constant added 1″.40. Period of Argument I. 224d.7.

Arg. XI.	d 0	d 8	d 16	d 24	d 32	d 40	d 48	d 56	d 64	d 72	d 80	d 88	d 96	d 104	d 112
180	69	68	71	78	87	97	108	119	129	140	150	161	172	185	198
181	72	70	71	75	82	90	99	107	116	125	133	143	154	166	179
182	75	72	72	74	79	85	91	98	105	111	118	126	136	147	160
183	79	75	74	75	78	82	86	90	95	99	104	110	119	129	141
184	83	79	77	77	78	80	82	85	87	89	93	96	103	112	123
185	87	83	80	79	79	80	80	81	81	82	83	85	89	97	107
186	92	87	84	82	81	80	80	78	77	76	75	75	78	83	93
187	96	92	88	86	84	82	80	77	75	72	69	68	69	73	81
188	101	96	93	89	87	85	82	78	74	70	66	63	62	64	71
189	105	100	97	94	91	88	85	80	75	69	64	60	57	58	63
190	110	105	101	98	95	92	88	83	77	71	64	58	55	54	58
191	115	110	106	103	100	96	92	87	81	74	66	59	54	52	54
192	121	116	112	108	105	102	97	92	85	78	70	62	56	52	52
193	127	122	117	114	111	108	104	98	91	83	74	66	58	54	52
194	133	129	124	121	118	114	111	105	98	90	81	71	62	56	53
195	140	136	131	128	125	122	118	113	106	98	88	77	67	60	55
196	147	143	138	136	133	130	127	121	115	106	96	84	73	64	58
197	154	150	146	143	140	138	135	131	124	115	104	92	80	69	61
198	161	157	153	150	148	146	144	140	134	124	113	100	87	75	65
199	168	164	160	157	156	154	152	149	143	134	122	109	94	81	69
200	173	170	166	164	163	161	160	157	151	143	131	117	102	87	74
201	178	174	171	169	168	167	167	164	159	151	139	125	109	94	79
202	182	178	174	172	172	172	172	170	166	158	147	133	117	100	84
203	184	180	176	174	174	174	175	174	171	164	154	140	124	107	90
204	185	180	176	174	174	175	176	176	174	168	159	146	130	113	96
205	184	180	175	173	173	173	175	176	175	171	162	151	136	119	101
206	184	178	173	170	169	170	172	174	174	171	165	155	141	124	107
207	182	175	170	165	164	165	167	170	171	170	165	157	144	129	112
208	181	173	166	160	158	163	162	165	167	167	164	157	147	133	117
209	179	170	162	156	153	153	155	159	162	164	162	157	148	136	120
210	178	168	159	152	148	147	149	153	156	159	159	156	148	137	124
211	179	167	157	149	144	142	142	146	150	154	155	153	148	138	126
212	180	167	156	146	140	137	137	141	145	148	151	150	146	138	127
213	182	169	157	146	139	135	134	136	140	143	147	148	144	138	128
214	186	172	160	148	139	134	132	133	137	141	144	145	143	137	128
215	190	177	164	152	142	136	133	133	135	139	142	143	141	136	128
216	196	183	170	157	147	139	135	134	136	138	141	142	141	136	129
217	202	190	177	164	153	145	140	138	138	140	142	143	141	137	129
218	207	197	185	172	161	152	146	143	143	143	145	145	143	139	131
219	213	204	193	181	170	160	154	150	149	148	149	149	146	142	135
220	217	210	200	189	179	169	162	158	156	155	155	154	151	147	139
221	220	215	207	197	187	178	171	166	164	162	162	161	158	153	146
222	222	219	212	204	195	186	180	175	172	171	170	169	166	161	154
223	221	220	216	209	201	193	187	183	181	179	179	178	175	171	163
224	219	220	217	212	205	199	194	190	188	187	187	187	185	181	174
225	215	218	217	213	208	202	198	195	194	194	195	196	195	192	186
226	210	214	214	211	208	204	201	199	199	200	202	204	204	202	198
227	202	208	209	208	206	203	201	201	202	205	208	211	213	213	209
228	194	200	203	203	202	200	200	201	204	208	213	217	221	222	220
229	184	192	195	197	197	196	197	199	203	208	215	221	226	230	229
230	174	182	187	189	190	190	192	195	200	207	216	223	230	235	237
231	163	172	177	181	182	183	186	190	196	204	214	223	231	238	241
232	153	161	167	172	173	175	178	183	190	199	210	220	230	239	243
233	142	151	157	162	164	167	170	175	183	192	204	215	227	236	243
234	131	140	147	152	155	158	161	167	174	184	196	209	221	232	240
235	120	130	137	142	145	148	152	157	163	175	187	200	213	225	234
236	110	119	127	132	136	139	142	147	155	165	177	190	203	215	225
237	99	109	117	123	126	129	132	137	144	153	165	178	192	204	215
238	89	99	107	113	117	119	122	127	133	142	153	166	179	192	203
239	80	89	97	103	107	110	112	116	122	130	140	153	166	179	191
240	71	80	88	94	98	100	102	104	110	117	127	140	153	165	177

The perturbations are expressed in hundredths of a second of arc.

Perturbations of the Longitude by the Earth.

Horizontal Argument = I.

Constant added 1''.40. Period of Argument XI, 240 units.

Arg. XI	120d	128d	136d	144d	152d	160d	168d	176d	184d	192d	200d	208d	216d	224d	232d
180	211	224	236	244	248	248	243	233	222	207	195	183	174	167	164
181	193	208	221	232	239	242	239	232	222	209	197	185	175	167	163
182	175	190	205	218	228	233	234	229	222	210	198	186	176	168	163
183	156	172	188	203	216	224	227	225	220	210	199	187	176	168	162
184	138	154	171	188	202	213	219	220	217	209	199	188	177	168	162
185	121	137	155	172	188	201	210	214	213	208	199	188	178	168	161
186	106	121	139	157	175	190	201	207	209	205	198	189	179	169	160
187	92	107	123	141	162	179	192	201	204	203	197	189	179	169	160
188	81	95	112	131	150	168	183	194	200	200	196	189	179	169	160
189	72	85	101	120	140	159	175	187	195	197	195	189	180	170	160
190	65	77	92	111	131	150	167	181	190	194	194	188	181	171	161
191	60	71	85	103	122	142	160	175	185	191	192	188	182	172	162
192	57	66	79	96	115	135	153	169	181	188	190	188	183	174	164
193	55	63	75	90	108	128	147	163	176	185	189	188	184	176	166
194	55	60	71	85	102	121	140	157	171	181	187	188	185	179	169
195	55	59	67	80	96	115	133	151	166	177	185	188	186	181	174
196	55	58	64	76	90	108	127	144	160	173	182	186	187	184	178
197	57	57	62	72	85	101	119	137	153	167	178	185	187	186	182
198	59	57	60	68	79	95	112	129	146	161	173	182	187	188	185
199	61	58	58	64	74	88	104	121	139	154	168	178	185	188	188
200	64	58	57	60	69	81	97	113	130	146	161	173	182	187	189
201	67	59	56	57	61	75	89	105	122	138	153	166	177	184	188
202	71	61	56	55	60	69	82	97	113	129	145	159	170	179	185
203	75	64	57	54	57	61	75	89	104	120	135	150	162	172	180
204	80	67	58	54	55	61	69	82	96	111	126	140	153	164	173
205	85	71	61	55	54	58	65	75	88	101	116	129	142	154	164
206	90	76	64	57	54	56	61	70	81	92	105	118	131	142	152
207	95	80	68	60	56	56	59	66	74	84	96	107	119	129	140
208	100	85	72	63	57	56	57	62	69	77	87	96	107	116	126
209	105	90	77	67	60	57	56	60	65	71	78	86	95	103	112
210	109	94	81	70	62	58	56	58	61	66	71	77	84	91	98
211	112	97	84	73	65	60	57	57	59	62	65	69	74	79	86
212	114	100	87	76	67	61	58	57	57	59	61	62	66	69	74
213	115	102	90	79	69	63	59	57	56	56	57	57	59	61	65
214	116	104	91	80	71	64	60	57	56	55	55	54	55	55	57
215	117	105	93	81	72	65	60	58	56	55	54	52	52	51	51
216	118	106	94	82	73	66	61	58	57	55	54	51	50	49	48
217	119	107	95	84	75	67	62	59	58	57	55	52	50	48	46
218	121	109	97	86	76	69	64	61	59	58	57	54	52	49	46
219	124	113	100	89	79	71	66	63	61	61	59	57	55	52	48
220	129	117	104	93	83	75	69	66	64	63	62	60	58	55	51
221	135	123	111	99	88	79	74	70	68	68	67	64	62	59	55
222	143	131	118	106	95	86	80	75	73	72	72	69	67	64	60
223	153	141	128	116	104	94	87	82	80	79	77	75	73	69	61
224	164	153	140	127	115	105	97	91	87	85	84	81	79	75	69
225	177	166	153	140	128	117	108	101	97	95	92	89	85	81	75
226	190	180	167	154	142	130	120	113	107	103	100	96	92	87	80
227	203	193	182	169	156	144	134	125	119	114	110	105	100	94	86
228	215	207	196	184	171	159	148	139	131	125	120	114	108	101	93
229	226	219	209	198	186	173	162	152	144	137	131	124	117	109	100
230	234	230	221	211	199	187	176	166	157	149	142	134	127	118	109
231	241	238	231	222	211	200	189	178	169	161	153	145	137	128	117
232	245	244	238	231	221	210	200	190	181	172	165	156	148	138	127
233	246	246	242	236	228	218	209	200	191	183	175	167	158	149	137
234	244	246	244	239	232	224	216	207	200	192	185	177	169	159	148
235	240	243	242	239	233	227	220	213	206	200	194	187	179	170	159
236	233	237	238	236	232	227	221	216	211	206	201	196	189	180	170
237	224	229	231	230	228	224	220	217	214	211	207	203	197	190	180
238	213	219	222	223	222	220	217	216	214	212	211	208	204	198	190
239	201	207	211	214	214	213	212	212	211	213	213	212	210	205	198
240	188	195	201	204	205	206	206	207	209	211	213	214	214	211	205

Add 147.64 to Arg. XI. when 224d.7 is subtracted from Arg. I.

TABLE XXIII.

Perturbations of the Longitude by Mars.

Horizontal Argument = I.

Constant added 0''.15. Period of Argument I., 224d.7.

Arg. XII.	0^d	8^d	16^d	24^d	32^d	40^d	48^d	56^d	64^d	72^d	80^d	88^d	96^d	104^d	112^d
0	3	4	6	9	12	15	17	20	23	24	26	26	26	26	24
1	1	2	3	5	8	11	14	17	20	22	24	26	26	26	26
2	1	1	1	3	5	8	10	14	17	19	22	24	25	26	26
3	2	1	1	1	3	5	7	10	13	16	19	21	23	24	25
4	4	2	1	1	2	3	5	8	10	13	16	18	20	22	23
5	6	4	3	2	2	2	4	6	8	11	13	16	18	20	21
6	8	6	4	3	3	2	3	5	7	9	11	14	16	18	20
7	11	8	6	5	4	3	4	5	6	8	10	13	15	16	18
8	12	10	8	6	5	4	4	5	6	7	9	12	14	16	18
9	14	12	10	7	6	5	5	5	5	7	9	11	13	15	17
10	15	13	11	9	7	6	5	5	5	6	8	10	12	15	17
11	17	15	13	11	8	7	5	5	5	5	7	9	11	14	16
12	18	17	15	12	10	8	6	5	5	5	6	7	9	12	15
13	20	19	17	15	12	10	8	6	5	5	5	6	8	10	13
14	21	21	19	17	15	13	10	8	6	5	5	5	6	8	10
15	22	22	21	19	17	15	13	10	8	7	6	5	6	7	9
16	21	22	22	21	19	18	15	13	11	9	7	6	6	6	8
17	20	21	21	21	20	19	18	15	13	11	9	8	7	7	7
18	17	19	20	23	20	20	19	17	15	13	11	10	9	8	8
19	15	16	18	19	19	19	19	17	16	15	13	11	10	9	9
20	13	15	15	16	17	18	18	17	16	15	14	12	11	10	10
21	12	13	14	15	15	16	16	16	15	14	13	12	11	11	10
22	12	13	13	14	14	15	15	14	14	14	13	12	11	10	10
23	13	13	14	14	14	14	14	14	13	13	12	11	10	9	9
24	15	15	15	15	15	15	14	14	13	12	12	10	9	8	8
25	16	16	16	16	16	16	16	15	14	13	12	11	9	8	7
26	16	17	17	17	17	17	17	17	16	15	13	12	10	9	7
27	16	16	17	18	18	19	19	18	18	17	15	14	12	10	8
28	14	15	16	17	18	19	19	19	19	19	18	16	14	13	11
29	12	13	14	15	16	18	19	20	20	20	19	18	17	15	13
30	10	11	11	13	14	16	17	19	20	20	20	20	19	17	15
31	9	9	9	10	12	13	15	17	18	19	20	20	19	18	17
32	9	9	8	9	9	11	12	14	16	17	18	19	19	19	18
33	11	9	8	8	8	9	10	12	13	15	16	17	18	18	18
34	13	11	9	8	8	8	9	10	11	12	14	15	16	16	17
35	15	13	11	10	9	8	8	9	10	11	12	13	14	15	15
36	18	16	13	11	10	9	9	9	10	10	11	12	13	14	14
37	20	18	16	14	12	10	10	10	10	10	11	12	13	14	14
38	22	20	18	15	14	12	11	11	10	11	11	12	13	14	14
39	23	21	19	17	15	13	12	11	11	11	12	13	13	14	15
40	24	23	21	18	17	15	13	12	11	11	12	13	13	14	15
41	25	24	22	20	18	16	14	13	12	11	12	12	13	14	15
42	26	25	24	22	20	18	15	14	12	12	11	12	13	14	15
43	28	27	26	24	22	20	17	15	13	12	11	12	12	13	14
44	28	28	28	26	24	22	20	17	15	13	12	11	11	12	13
45	28	29	29	28	27	25	23	20	17	15	13	12	11	11	12
46	27	28	29	29	28	27	25	23	20	18	16	14	13	12	12
47	24	26	28	29	29	28	27	25	23	20	18	16	14	13	12
48	21	24	26	27	28	28	28	26	25	23	21	19	16	15	14
49	18	20	23	25	26	27	27	27	26	24	22	20	19	17	15
50	16	17	20	22	24	25	26	26	25	25	23	22	20	18	17
51	13	15	17	19	21	23	24	24	24	24	23	22	21	19	18
52	12	14	16	17	19	21	22	23	23	23	22	21	20	19	18
53	12	13	15	17	18	20	21	21	22	22	21	21	20	19	17
54	12	14	15	17	18	19	20	21	21	21	21	20	19	18	17
55	12	14	15	17	18	20	21	21	21	21	20	20	19	18	16
56	12	14	15	17	19	20	21	22	22	22	22	21	20	18	17
57	10	12	14	17	19	20	22	23	23	24	23	22	21	20	18
58	8	10	12	15	17	20	21	23	24	25	25	24	23	22	20
59	5	7	9	12	15	17	20	22	24	25	26	26	25	24	22
60	3	4	6	9	12	15	17	21	23	24	26	26	26	26	24

The perturbations are expressed in hundredths of a second of arc.

Perturbations of the Longitude by Mars.

Horizontal Argument = I.

Constant added 0″.15. Period of Argument XII., 60 units.

Arg. XII.	120ᵈ	128ᵈ	136ᵈ	144ᵈ	152ᵈ	160ᵈ	168ᵈ	176ᵈ	184ᵈ	192ᵈ	200ᵈ	208ᵈ	216ᵈ	224ᵈ	232ᵈ
0	23	21	19	17	15	13	12	11	10	10	10	11	12	14	15
1	25	23	21	19	17	15	14	12	11	11	11	11	11	12	13
2	25	24	23	22	20	18	16	15	13	12	12	11	12	12	13
3	25	25	24	23	21	20	18	17	15	14	13	13	13	13	13
4	24	24	24	23	22	21	19	18	17	16	15	14	14	14	14
5	22	23	23	22	23	20	19	18	17	17	16	16	15	15	15
6	21	21	21	21	20	20	19	18	17	16	16	16	16	16	16
7	20	20	20	20	20	19	18	17	16	16	15	15	15	16	16
8	19	20	20	20	19	18	17	16	15	14	14	14	14	15	15
9	19	20	20	20	19	18	17	16	15	14	13	12	12	13	14
10	19	20	21	21	21	20	18	17	15	13	12	11	11	11	11
11	18	20	21	22	22	21	20	18	16	14	13	11	10	9	10
12	17	19	21	23	23	23	22	21	19	16	14	12	11	9	9
13	16	18	21	23	24	24	24	23	21	19	17	14	12	10	9
14	13	16	19	21	23	24	25	24	23	21	19	17	14	12	10
15	11	14	17	20	22	24	25	25	25	23	22	20	17	15	12
16	10	12	15	18	20	22	24	25	25	25	24	22	20	17	15
17	9	11	13	16	18	21	23	24	25	25	25	24	22	19	17
18	9	10	12	14	17	19	21	23	25	25	25	25	23	21	19
19	9	10	11	13	15	18	20	22	24	24	25	25	24	23	21
20	10	10	11	13	15	17	19	21	23	25	25	26	25	24	22
21	10	10	11	12	14	16	19	21	23	24	25	26	25	25	24
22	9	10	11	12	13	15	18	20	22	24	25	27	27	26	25
23	9	9	9	10	12	14	16	18	22	23	25	27	27	27	27
24	7	7	8	9	10	12	15	17	20	22	24	26	28	28	28
25	6	6	6	6	8	10	12	14	17	20	22	25	27	28	29
26	6	5	5	5	5	7	9	11	14	17	20	23	25	27	28
27	7	5	5	4	4	5	6	8	11	14	16	20	22	25	27
28	8	7	5	4	4	4	4	6	8	10	13	16	19	22	24
29	11	9	7	5	4	4	4	5	6	8	10	13	16	19	21
30	13	11	9	8	6	5	4	5	5	6	8	10	13	16	18
31	15	14	12	10	8	7	6	5	5	6	7	9	11	13	16
32	17	15	13	12	10	9	8	7	7	7	7	8	10	12	14
33	17	16	14	13	12	10	9	8	8	8	8	9	10	12	13
34	16	15	14	13	12	11	10	9	9	9	9	10	11	12	13
35	15	15	14	13	12	11	10	9	9	9	9	10	11	12	14
36	14	14	13	12	11	10	9	9	8	8	9	9	10	12	14
37	14	13	13	12	11	9	8	8	7	7	7	8	9	11	13
38	14	14	13	12	11	9	8	7	6	5	5	6	7	9	11
39	15	15	14	13	11	10	8	6	5	4	4	4	5	6	8
40	16	16	15	14	13	11	9	7	5	4	3	2	3	3	5
41	16	17	17	16	15	13	11	9	7	5	3	2	1	2	3
42	16	17	17	17	17	15	14	12	9	7	5	3	2	1	1
43	15	17	18	18	18	17	16	14	12	9	7	5	3	1	1
44	14	16	17	18	19	18	18	17	15	12	10	7	5	3	2
45	13	14	16	17	18	19	19	18	17	15	12	10	7	5	3
46	12	13	15	16	17	18	19	18	18	16	15	12	10	8	5
47	13	13	14	15	16	18	18	18	18	17	16	14	12	10	8
48	13	13	14	15	16	17	18	18	18	18	17	16	14	12	10
49	15	14	14	15	16	17	17	18	18	18	18	17	16	13	11
50	16	15	15	15	16	17	17	18	19	19	19	18	17	15	13
51	17	16	16	16	16	17	18	18	19	19	19	19	18	17	14
52	17	16	16	16	16	17	18	19	19	20	20	20	19	18	16
53	17	16	16	15	16	17	17	18	20	20	21	21	21	20	18
54	16	15	15	15	15	16	17	17	19	20	21	21	22	21	20
55	15	14	15	13	13	14	15	16	17	19	20	21	22	22	21
56	15	14	13	12	12	12	13	14	15	17	18	20	21	22	22
57	16	14	13	12	11	11	11	12	13	15	16	18	19	21	21
58	18	16	14	13	11	11	10	10	11	12	14	15	17	18	19
59	20	18	16	14	13	11	10	10	10	11	11	13	14	16	17
60	23	21	19	17	15	13	12	11	10	10	10	11	12	14	15

Add 10.6 to Arg. XII. when 224ᵈ.7 is subtracted from Arg. I.

TABLE XXIV.

Perturbations of the Longitude by Jupiter.

Horizontal Argument = I.

Constant added 2″.35. Period of Argument I. 224d.7.

Arg. XIII.	d 0	d 8	d 16	d 24	d 32	d 40	d 48	d 56	d 64	d 72	d 80	d 88	d 96	d 104	d 112
0	205	209	216	226	237	248	259	268	275	278	280	279	276	271	268
1	185	184	188	194	204	214	226	236	245	253	257	259	258	256	254
2	169	164	163	166	173	182	192	204	215	224	231	237	239	240	238
3	158	147	142	141	144	151	160	171	183	194	204	212	218	221	222
4	150	136	126	121	120	123	130	140	151	163	175	186	195	201	204
5	145	128	115	105	100	100	104	111	121	133	146	158	170	179	185
6	143	125	108	95	86	82	82	86	94	104	117	131	144	156	161
7	143	123	105	89	77	68	61	65	70	79	90	104	118	132	143
8	143	124	105	87	72	61	53	50	52	57	67	79	93	108	121
9	143	126	108	89	72	58	47	40	38	40	47	58	71	85	100
10	142	128	111	93	75	59	46	36	30	29	32	40	51	65	79
11	140	129	115	99	81	65	49	37	28	23	23	27	36	47	61
12	136	129	119	105	89	73	57	42	31	23	19	20	25	34	45
13	130	128	121	111	98	83	67	52	38	28	21	18	19	25	34
14	124	125	122	116	106	94	79	64	50	37	27	21	19	21	27
15	116	120	122	120	114	105	92	78	64	50	38	29	24	22	24
16	109	115	120	122	120	115	106	94	80	66	53	42	34	28	27
17	102	110	117	123	125	124	119	100	98	85	71	58	48	40	35
18	96	105	114	122	129	131	130	124	116	104	91	78	65	55	47
19	92	101	111	122	131	137	140	138	133	124	112	99	85	73	63
20	91	99	103	121	132	142	149	151	149	142	133	121	108	94	82
21	92	99	108	120	133	146	156	161	163	160	153	143	131	117	104
22	95	101	109	121	135	149	161	170	176	177	173	165	154	141	128
23	100	105	112	123	136	151	166	178	187	191	190	186	177	165	152
24	108	111	118	127	139	154	170	184	196	204	206	205	199	189	177
25	117	120	125	133	144	158	174	190	203	214	220	222	219	211	201
26	128	130	134	141	150	163	178	194	210	223	232	237	237	232	224
27	139	142	145	151	159	170	184	199	215	230	241	249	252	251	245
28	151	155	158	163	169	178	190	205	220	236	249	260	266	267	264
29	164	168	171	175	180	188	198	211	226	241	255	268	277	281	281
30	177	181	185	189	194	199	207	218	231	246	261	274	285	292	296
31	190	196	200	204	208	212	218	227	238	251	265	279	291	301	307
32	204	210	215	219	222	226	230	237	245	256	269	283	296	307	316
33	219	224	229	234	237	240	243	248	254	263	273	286	299	311	322
34	235	239	244	249	252	255	257	260	264	270	278	289	301	314	326
35	251	254	259	263	267	269	271	273	275	278	284	292	303	315	327
36	268	270	274	278	281	284	286	286	287	288	291	297	305	315	327
37	287	287	289	292	296	298	300	300	299	299	299	302	307	316	326
38	306	304	305	306	309	311	313	313	312	310	308	308	311	316	325
39	326	322	321	321	322	324	325	325	324	321	318	316	316	318	321
40	346	341	337	335	335	336	337	337	336	333	328	324	321	321	324
41	366	359	354	350	348	347	348	348	346	343	339	333	329	325	325
42	386	378	370	365	361	358	358	357	356	353	348	343	336	331	327
43	405	396	387	379	373	369	367	366	364	362	357	351	344	337	331
44	422	413	403	394	386	380	375	373	371	369	365	359	352	344	336
45	436	428	418	408	398	390	383	379	376	374	371	366	359	351	341
46	447	440	431	420	409	399	391	384	381	378	375	371	365	357	347
47	454	450	441	431	419	408	398	390	384	381	378	374	369	362	353
48	457	455	449	439	428	415	404	394	387	382	378	375	371	365	357
49	455	456	452	444	433	421	409	398	388	382	378	374	371	367	360
50	448	452	451	446	436	425	412	400	389	381	376	372	369	366	361
51	436	443	445	442	435	426	413	401	389	380	373	368	365	363	359
52	419	429	434	434	430	423	412	400	388	377	369	363	360	358	355
53	397	410	418	421	421	416	407	396	384	373	364	357	353	350	349
54	372	386	397	404	406	404	398	389	378	368	358	350	345	342	341
55	344	359	372	381	386	388	385	379	370	360	351	342	336	332	331
56	315	329	343	354	362	367	368	365	358	350	341	333	326	322	320
57	285	298	312	324	335	342	346	346	343	337	330	323	315	310	307
58	256	267	279	292	304	313	320	324	324	321	316	310	304	298	295
59	229	237	247	259	271	281	291	297	301	301	299	296	290	285	282
60	205	209	216	226	237	248	259	268	275	278	280	279	276	271	268

The perturbations are expressed in hundredths of a second of arc.

Perturbations of the Longitude by Jupiter.

Horizontal Argument = I.

Constant added 2″.35. Period of Argument XIII, 60 units.

Arg. XIII.	120^d	128^d	136^d	144^d	152^d	160^d	168^d	176^d	184^d	192^d	200^d	208^d	216^d	224^d	232^d
0	265	264	265	266	267	266	262	254	242	226	208	189	172	157	147
1	251	250	250	251	252	253	251	246	236	222	205	187	169	150	136
2	236	235	234	235	236	237	237	235	228	217	202	185	166	146	129
3	221	220	219	219	220	221	222	221	218	210	198	183	164	145	126
4	205	205	204	203	203	205	206	207	205	201	192	179	163	145	125
5	188	189	189	188	189	189	190	191	191	189	184	175	161	145	126
6	171	174	174	174	173	173	174	175	176	176	174	168	158	144	128
7	152	157	161	160	160	159	158	159	161	162	162	159	153	143	129
8	132	140	145	147	147	146	145	145	146	148	149	149	147	140	130
9	113	123	130	134	135	134	132	132	132	134	136	138	138	136	130
10	93	105	115	121	123	123	122	120	120	121	123	127	129	130	128
11	75	89	100	108	112	114	113	111	110	110	112	115	120	123	124
12	59	73	85	95	101	104	105	103	102	101	102	105	110	115	119
13	46	59	72	83	91	96	98	97	95	91	94	97	101	107	114
14	36	48	60	72	81	88	92	92	91	89	89	90	94	101	109
15	31	40	51	62	73	81	86	88	88	87	85	86	89	95	104
16	30	36	45	56	66	75	82	85	86	86	84	84	87	92	100
17	34	37	43	52	61	71	78	83	86	86	85	85	87	90	98
18	43	42	45	51	59	68	76	82	86	88	88	88	89	92	98
19	56	52	52	55	60	68	75	82	87	91	92	93	93	95	100
20	73	66	62	62	65	70	77	84	90	95	97	98	99	101	105
21	93	83	77	73	73	76	81	87	94	99	103	105	107	109	112
22	115	103	94	88	85	85	88	93	99	105	110	113	116	118	121
23	139	126	115	106	100	98	98	101	106	112	118	122	126	129	131
24	163	150	137	127	118	113	111	112	116	121	127	132	136	140	143
25	188	175	162	150	139	132	127	126	128	132	137	142	149	152	156
26	213	200	187	174	162	153	146	143	142	141	149	154	159	165	169
27	236	225	212	199	187	176	167	162	159	159	162	166	172	178	183
28	258	248	237	224	212	200	190	183	178	176	177	181	186	191	197
29	277	270	260	249	237	225	214	206	199	195	194	196	200	205	211
30	295	290	282	273	262	250	240	230	222	216	213	213	216	220	226
31	309	307	302	295	286	275	265	255	246	239	234	232	233	236	240
32	321	322	320	315	308	299	289	280	270	262	256	252	251	253	256
33	330	334	335	333	329	321	313	304	295	286	279	274	271	270	272
34	336	342	347	348	346	341	335	328	319	311	303	296	291	290	289
35	339	348	355	359	361	360	355	350	342	334	327	319	313	308	306
36	340	351	360	368	372	374	373	369	364	357	350	342	334	329	324
37	338	351	362	372	380	385	387	386	383	378	372	364	356	349	343
38	336	349	361	374	384	392	398	400	400	397	392	386	378	370	362
39	333	345	358	372	385	396	404	410	413	413	410	405	398	389	381
40	330	340	353	368	382	396	407	416	422	425	425	422	416	408	399
41	328	336	347	361	376	392	406	418	427	434	436	435	431	424	416
42	327	332	340	353	368	384	401	416	428	437	443	445	444	438	430
43	328	329	334	345	358	375	392	409	424	437	446	451	452	449	442
44	330	328	329	337	348	363	380	399	416	431	443	452	456	455	451
45	333	328	326	330	339	351	367	385	404	421	436	448	455	458	456
46	338	330	325	324	329	338	352	370	388	407	424	439	449	455	456
47	343	333	325	321	321	327	338	353	371	390	408	425	438	447	451
48	347	337	327	319	315	317	324	336	352	370	389	407	422	434	441
49	351	341	329	319	312	309	312	320	332	348	367	385	402	416	426
50	353	344	332	321	311	304	302	305	314	327	343	360	378	394	406
51	353	346	335	323	311	301	295	293	297	306	319	335	351	368	382
52	351	345	336	324	312	299	290	284	283	287	296	309	324	340	355
53	346	342	335	325	313	299	287	277	271	270	275	283	295	310	325
54	339	337	332	324	313	299	285	273	262	257	256	260	269	280	293
55	330	329	326	320	311	299	284	270	257	247	241	240	244	252	262
56	319	319	318	314	307	297	283	268	253	239	229	223	222	225	231
57	306	307	307	305	301	293	281	266	250	234	221	210	204	202	205
58	293	294	295	295	292	287	277	264	248	231	214	200	190	183	182
59	280	279	280	281	281	278	271	260	245	228	210	193	179	169	162
60	265	264	265	266	267	266	262	254	242	226	208	189	172	157	147

Add 3.11 to Arg. XIII. when 224^d.7 is subtracted from Arg. I.

TABLE XXV.

Perturbations of the Longitude by Saturn.

Horizontal Argument = I.

Constant added 0″.40. Period of Argument I., 224^{d}.7.

Arg. XIV.	0^{d}	8^{d}	16^{d}	24^{d}	32^{d}	40^{d}	48^{d}	56^{d}	64^{d}	72^{d}	80^{d}	88^{d}	96^{d}	104^{d}	112^{d}
0	39	43	47	54	60	66	72	77	80	81	81	80	78	75	72
1	37	30	43	48	54	61	67	72	77	79	80	80	79	76	74
2	36	36	39	43	48	54	61	67	72	76	78	79	78	77	74
3	36	35	35	38	42	47	54	60	66	71	75	77	77	76	74
4	36	34	33	34	36	40	46	52	59	64	69	73	74	75	73
5	37	34	31	30	31	34	39	44	51	57	63	67	70	71	71
6	38	34	31	28	28	29	32	37	42	49	55	60	65	67	68
7	38	34	31	27	25	25	27	30	34	40	46	52	59	62	64
8	39	34	31	27	24	22	22	24	27	33	38	44	50	55	59
9	37	34	31	27	23	21	19	19	21	25	30	35	42	47	52
10	35	33	30	26	23	19	17	16	16	18	22	27	33	39	45
11	33	31	29	26	22	19	16	14	13	14	16	20	25	31	37
12	30	29	27	25	22	19	15	12	11	10	11	14	18	24	29
13	27	26	25	23	21	18	15	12	9	8	8	9	12	17	22
14	25	24	23	22	20	18	15	12	9	7	6	6	8	11	16
15	23	22	21	20	19	17	15	12	9	7	5	4	5	7	11
16	23	21	20	19	18	16	15	13	10	8	5	4	3	4	7
17	24	21	19	18	17	16	15	13	11	8	6	4	3	3	4
18	26	23	20	19	17	16	15	13	12	10	7	5	4	3	3
19	29	26	23	20	19	17	16	15	13	11	9	7	5	4	3
20	33	30	26	23	21	19	18	16	15	13	11	9	7	5	4
21	38	34	31	27	25	22	20	19	17	16	14	12	10	8	6
22	42	39	36	32	29	26	24	22	20	19	17	15	13	11	9
23	46	44	42	38	35	32	29	27	24	22	21	19	17	15	13
24	50	50	47	44	41	38	34	32	29	27	25	23	21	19	17
25	54	54	53	50	47	44	41	38	35	32	30	28	26	24	22
26	56	58	57	56	54	51	47	44	41	38	36	34	31	29	27
27	58	60	61	61	59	57	54	51	48	44	42	39	37	35	32
28	58	62	64	65	65	63	60	57	54	51	48	45	43	41	38
29	58	63	66	68	69	68	66	63	60	57	54	51	49	47	44
30	57	62	67	70	72	72	71	69	66	63	60	57	55	52	50
31	54	61	66	70	73	75	75	74	71	69	66	63	60	57	55
32	52	58	64	69	74	76	77	77	76	73	71	68	65	62	60
33	48	55	61	67	72	76	79	79	79	77	75	72	69	67	64
34	45	51	57	64	69	74	78	80	81	80	78	76	73	70	68
35	42	47	52	59	65	71	76	79	81	81	80	78	76	73	70
36	39	43	47	54	60	66	72	77	80	81	81	80	78	75	72

The perturbations are expressed in hundredths of a second of arc.

TABLE XXV.

Perturbations of the Longitude by Saturn.

Horizontal Argument = I

Constant added 0″.40. Period of Argument XIV., 36 units.

Arg. XIV.	120ᵈ	128ᵈ	136ᵈ	144ᵈ	152ᵈ	160ᵈ	168ᵈ	176ᵈ	184ᵈ	192ᵈ	200ᵈ	208ᵈ	216ᵈ	224ᵈ	232ᵈ
0	70	68	66	63	61	59	56	52	48	45	41	38	37	37	40
1	71	69	67	65	63	61	58	55	51	47	44	40	38	36	37
2	72	69	67	65	63	61	59	57	54	50	46	43	39	36	35
3	72	69	67	64	63	61	59	57	55	52	48	44	40	36	34
4	71	69	66	64	62	60	58	57	55	52	49	45	41	37	34
5	70	68	65	62	60	58	56	55	53	52	49	46	42	38	34
6	68	66	64	61	58	56	54	53	51	50	48	46	42	39	35
7	65	64	62	59	57	54	52	50	48	47	46	44	42	38	35
8	60	61	60	58	55	52	49	47	46	44	43	42	40	38	34
9	55	57	57	55	53	50	47	45	43	41	40	39	38	36	34
10	49	52	53	53	51	49	46	43	40	38	37	36	35	34	32
11	42	46	49	50	49	47	45	42	38	36	34	33	31	31	29
12	35	40	44	46	47	46	44	41	38	35	32	30	28	28	27
13	28	33	38	42	43	44	43	40	37	34	31	29	27	26	24
14	21	27	32	37	40	41	41	40	37	34	32	28	25	24	23
15	15	21	27	32	36	39	40	39	38	35	32	28	25	23	21
16	11	16	21	27	32	36	38	39	38	36	33	30	27	24	22
17	7	11	16	22	28	32	36	38	39	38	35	32	29	26	23
18	5	8	13	18	23	29	33	37	38	39	37	35	32	29	25
19	4	6	10	15	20	25	31	35	38	40	40	38	36	32	29
20	4	6	8	12	17	23	28	33	36	40	41	41	40	37	33
21	6	6	8	11	15	20	26	32	37	40	43	44	43	41	38
22	8	8	9	11	14	19	24	30	35	40	44	46	47	45	43
23	11	10	10	12	14	18	23	28	34	39	44	47	49	49	48
24	15	13	13	13	15	18	22	27	33	39	44	48	51	53	53
25	19	17	16	16	16	18	22	26	32	38	43	49	53	55	56
26	24	22	20	19	19	20	22	26	31	36	43	48	53	57	59
27	30	27	25	23	22	22	23	26	30	35	41	47	53	58	61
28	35	33	30	28	26	25	25	27	30	34	40	46	52	58	62
29	41	39	36	33	30	29	28	28	30	34	38	44	50	57	62
30	47	44	41	38	35	33	31	30	31	33	37	42	48	55	60
31	53	50	47	44	41	38	35	33	33	34	36	40	46	52	58
32	57	55	52	49	46	42	39	36	35	34	36	39	43	49	55
33	63	60	57	54	51	47	44	40	38	36	36	37	41	45	51
34	65	63	61	58	55	52	48	45	41	39	37	37	39	42	47
35	68	66	64	61	59	56	53	49	45	41	39	37	38	39	43
36	70	68	66	63	61	59	56	52	48	45	41	38	37	37	40

Add 0.8 to Arg. XIV. when 224ᵈ.7 is subtracted from Arg. I.

Logarithm of the Elliptic Radius Vector for **m** = 0.

Constant subtracted 0.0000257. *Period of Argument* I. $224^{d}.7008$.

Arg. I.	$0^{d}.0$	$0^{d}.1$	$0^{d}.2$	$0^{d}.3$	$0^{d}.4$	$0^{d}.5$	$0^{d}.6$	$0^{d}.7$	$0^{d}.8$	$0^{d}.9$	Diff. for $0^{d}.1$.
0^{d}	9.8563298	63298	63298	63299	63300	63301	63302	63304	63305	63307	+1
1	63310	63312	63315	63318	63321	63324	63328	63332	63336	63341	4
2	63345	63350	63355	63360	63366	63372	63378	63384	63391	63397	6
3	63404	63412	63419	63427	63435	63443	63451	63460	63469	63478	8
4	63487	63497	63507	63517	63527	63538	63548	63559	63571	63582	11
5	63594	63606	63618	63630	63643	63656	63669	63682	63696	63710	13
6	63724	63738	63752	63767	63782	63797	63813	63828	63844	63860	15
7	63877	63893	63910	63927	63945	63962	63980	63998	64016	64035	18
8	64053	64072	64092	64111	64131	64150	64171	64191	64211	64232	20
9	64253	64274	64296	64317	64339	64362	64384	64407	64429	64452	22
10	64476	64499	64523	64547	64571	64595	64620	64645	64670	64695	25
11	64721	64747	64773	64799	64825	64852	64879	64906	64933	64961	27
12	64989	65017	65045	65073	65102	65131	65160	65189	65219	65249	29
13	65279	65309	65340	65370	65401	65432	65464	65495	65527	65559	31
14	65591	65624	65656	65689	65722	65756	65789	65823	65857	65891	33
15	65925	65960	65995	66030	66065	66100	66136	66172	66208	66244	36
16	66281	66318	66354	66392	66429	66467	66504	66542	66581	66619	38
17	66658	66697	66736	66775	66814	66854	66894	66934	66974	67015	40
18	67055	67096	67137	67179	67220	67262	67304	67346	67388	67431	42
19	67474	67517	67560	67603	67647	67691	67734	67779	67823	67868	44
20	67912	67957	68002	68048	68093	68139	68185	68231	68278	68324	46
21	68371	68418	68465	68512	68560	68609	68656	68704	68752	68800	48
22	68849	68898	68947	68996	69046	69095	69145	69195	69245	69296	50
23	69346	69397	69448	69499	69550	69602	69654	69706	69758	69810	52
24	69862	69915	69968	70021	70074	70127	70181	70234	70288	70342	53
25	70396	70451	70505	70560	70615	70670	70726	70781	70837	70893	55
26	70949	71005	71061	71118	71174	71231	71288	71345	71403	71460	57
27	71518	71576	71634	71692	71751	71809	71868	71927	71986	72045	59
28	72105	72164	72224	72284	72344	72404	72464	72525	72586	72646	60
29	72707	72769	72830	72891	72953	73015	73077	73139	73201	73264	62
30	73326	73389	73452	73515	73578	73642	73705	73769	73833	73897	63
31	73961	74025	74089	74154	74219	74284	74349	74414	74479	74544	65
32	74610	74676	74742	74808	74874	74940	75007	75073	75140	75207	66
33	75274	75341	75408	75476	75543	75611	75679	75747	75815	75883	68
34	75951	76020	76089	76157	76226	76295	76364	76434	76503	76573	69
35	76642	76712	76782	76852	76922	76993	77063	77134	77204	77275	70
36	77346	77417	77488	77560	77631	77703	77774	77846	77918	77990	72
37	78062	78134	78207	78279	78352	78425	78497	78570	78643	78716	73
38	78790	78863	78937	79010	79084	79158	79232	79306	79380	79454	74
39	79528	79603	79677	79752	79827	79902	79977	80052	80127	80202	75
40	80277	80352	80428	80504	80580	80656	80732	80808	80884	80960	76
41	81036	81113	81189	81266	81343	81419	81496	81573	81650	81727	77
42	81805	81882	81959	82037	82114	82192	82270	82348	82425	82503	78
43	82582	82660	82738	82816	82895	82973	83052	83130	83209	83288	78
44	83366	83445	83524	83603	83682	83762	83841	83920	84000	84079	79
45	84159	84238	84318	84398	84477	84557	84637	84717	84797	84877	80
46	84958	85038	85118	85199	85279	85359	85440	85521	85601	85682	81
47	9.8585763	85844	85924	86005	86086	86167	86249	86330	86411	86492	+81

TABLE XXVI.

Logarithm of the Elliptic Radius Vector for m = 0.

Constant subtracted 0.0000257. Period of Argument I, 22^d.7008.

Arg. I.	0^d.0	0^d.1	0^d.2	0^d.3	0^d.4	0^d.5	0^d.6	0^d.7	0^d.8	0^d.9	Diff. for 0^d.1.
48^d	9.8586573	86655	86736	86817	86899	86980	87062	87144	87225	87307	+82
49	87389	87471	87552	87634	87716	87798	87880	87962	88044	88126	82
50	88208	88290	88373	88455	88537	88619	88702	88784	88867	88949	82
51	89031	89114	89196	89279	89362	89444	89527	89609	89692	89775	83
52	89857	89940	90023	90106	90189	90271	90354	90437	90520	90603	83
53	90686	90769	90852	90934	91017	91100	91183	91266	91349	91432	83
54	91516	91599	91682	91765	91848	91931	92014	92097	92180	92263	83
55	92346	92429	92513	92596	92679	92762	92845	92928	93011	93094	83
56	93177	93260	93344	93427	93510	93593	93676	93759	93842	93925	83
57	94008	94091	94174	94257	94340	94423	94506	94589	94672	94755	83
58	94838	94921	95004	95086	95169	95252	95335	95418	95500	95583	83
59	95666	95749	95831	95914	95996	96079	96162	96244	96327	96409	83
60	96492	96574	96656	96739	96821	96903	96986	97068	97150	97232	82
61	97314	97396	97478	97560	97642	97724	97806	97888	97970	98052	82
62	98134	98215	98297	98378	98460	98542	98623	98705	98786	98867	82
63	98949	99030	99111	99192	99273	99354	99435	99516	99597	99678	81
64	9.8599759	99839	99920	:00001	00081	00162	00242	00323	00403	00483	80
65	9.8600563	00643	00724	00804	00884	00963	01043	01123	01203	01282	80
66	01362	01442	01521	01600	01680	01759	01838	01917	01996	02075	79
67	02154	02233	02311	02390	02469	02547	02626	02704	02782	02860	78
68	02938	03016	03094	03172	03250	03328	03405	03483	03560	03638	78
69	03715	03792	03869	03946	04023	04100	04177	04254	04330	04407	77
70	04483	04560	04636	04712	04788	04864	04940	05016	05091	05167	76
71	05242	05318	05393	05468	05543	05618	05693	95768	05843	05917	75
72	05992	06066	06140	06215	06289	06363	06436	06510	06584	06657	74
73	06731	06804	06877	06950	07023	07096	07169	07242	07314	07387	73
74	07459	07531	07603	07675	07747	07819	07891	07962	08034	08105	72
75	08176	08247	08318	08389	08460	08530	08601	08671	08741	08811	71
76	08881	08951	09021	09090	09160	09229	09298	09367	09436	09505	69
77	09574	09642	09711	09779	09847	09915	09983	10051	10118	10186	68
78	10253	10321	10388	10455	10522	10588	10655	10721	10788	10854	67
79	10920	10986	11051	11117	11182	11248	11313	11378	11443	11507	65
80	11572	11636	11701	11765	11829	11893	11956	12020	12083	12146	64
81	12210	12273	12335	12398	12461	12523	12585	12647	12709	12771	62
82	12832	12894	12955	13016	13077	13138	13199	13259	13319	13380	61
83	13440	13500	13559	13619	13678	13738	13797	13856	13914	13973	59
84	14031	14090	14148	14206	14263	14321	14378	14436	14493	14550	58
85	14606	14663	14720	14776	14832	14888	14943	14999	15054	15110	56
86	15165	15220	15275	15329	15384	15438	15492	15546	15599	15653	54
87	15706	15759	15812	15865	15918	15970	16023	16075	16127	16178	52
88	16230	16281	16333	16384	16434	16485	16536	16586	16636	16686	51
89	16736	16785	16835	16884	16933	16982	17031	17079	17127	17175	49
90	17223	17271	17319	17366	17413	17460	17507	17553	17600	17646	47
91	17692	17738	17783	17829	17874	17919	17964	18009	18053	18098	45
92	18142	18186	18229	18273	18316	18359	18402	18445	18488	18530	43
93	18572	18614	18656	18697	18739	18780	18821	18862	18902	18943	41
94	18983	19023	19063	19102	19142	19181	19220	19258	19297	19335	39
95	9.8619373	19411	19449	19487	19524	19561	19598	19635	19671	19708	+37

TABLE XXVI.

Logarithm of the Elliptic Radius Vector for **m** = 0.

Constant subtracted 0.0000257. Period of Argument I. 224d.7008.

Arg. I.	0d.0	0d.1	0d.2	0d.3	0d.4	0d.5	0d.6	0d.7	0d.8	0d.9	Diff. for 0d.1.
96d	9.8619744	19780	19815	19851	19886	19921	19956	19991	20025	20060	+35
97	20091	20127	20161	20194	20228	20261	20294	20326	20359	20391	33
98	20423	20454	20486	20517	20548	20579	20610	20641	20671	20701	31
99	20731	20760	20790	20819	20848	20877	20905	20934	20962	20990	29
100	21017	21045	21072	21099	21126	21153	21179	21205	21231	21257	27
101	21282	21308	21333	21358	21382	21407	21431	21455	21479	21502	24
102	21526	21549	21572	21595	21617	21639	21662	21683	21705	21726	22
103	21748	21769	21789	21810	21830	21850	21870	21890	21909	21928	20
104	21947	21966	21984	22003	22021	22039	22056	22074	22091	22108	18
105	22124	22141	22157	22173	22189	22205	22220	22235	22250	22265	16
106	22280	22294	22308	22322	22335	22349	22362	22375	22388	22400	13
107	22412	22424	22436	22448	22459	22470	22481	22492	22502	22512	11
108	22522	22532	22542	22551	22560	22569	22577	22586	22594	22602	9
109	22610	22617	22625	22632	22639	22645	22651	22658	22663	22669	6
110	22675	22680	22685	22690	22694	22699	22703	22707	22710	22714	4
111	22717	22720	22723	22725	22727	22729	22731	22733	22734	22735	+2
112	22736	22737	22737	22737	22737	22737	22737	22736	22735	22734	0
113	22733	22731	22729	22727	22725	22722	22720	22717	22714	22710	−3
114	22706	22703	22698	22694	22690	22685	22680	22675	22669	22663	5
115	22657	22651	22645	22638	22632	22624	22617	22610	22602	22594	7
116	22586	22577	22569	22560	22551	22542	22532	22522	22512	22502	9
117	22492	22481	22470	22459	22448	22436	22424	22412	22400	22387	12
118	22375	22362	22349	22335	22322	22308	22294	22279	22265	22250	14
119	22235	22220	22205	22189	22173	22157	22141	22124	22108	22091	16
120	22074	22056	22039	22021	22003	21984	21966	21947	21928	21909	18
121	21890	21870	21850	21830	21810	21789	21769	21748	21726	21705	21
122	21683	21662	21639	21617	21595	21572	21549	21526	21503	21479	23
123	21455	21431	21407	21383	21358	21333	21308	21283	21257	21231	25
124	21205	21179	21153	21126	21099	21072	21045	21017	20990	20962	27
125	20934	20905	20877	20848	20819	20790	20760	20731	20701	20671	29
126	20640	20610	20579	20548	20517	20486	20455	20423	20391	20359	31
127	20326	20294	20261	20228	20195	20161	20128	20094	20060	20026	34
128	19991	19956	19921	19886	19851	19816	19780	19744	19708	19672	36
129	19635	19598	19561	19524	19487	19449	19412	19374	19335	19297	38
130	19258	19220	19181	19141	19102	19063	19023	18983	18943	18902	40
131	18862	18821	18780	18739	18697	18656	18614	18572	18530	18488	42
132	18445	18402	18359	18316	18273	18230	18186	18142	18098	18054	44
133	18009	17964	17919	17874	17829	17784	17738	17692	17646	17600	46
134	17554	17507	17460	17413	17366	17319	17271	17224	17176	17128	47
135	17079	17031	16982	16933	16884	16835	16785	16736	16686	16636	49
136	16586	16536	16485	16435	16384	16333	16282	16230	16179	16127	51
137	16075	16023	15971	15918	15865	15813	15760	15706	15653	15600	53
138	15546	15492	15438	15384	15329	15275	15220	15165	15110	15055	55
139	14999	14944	14888	14832	14776	14720	14663	14607	14550	14493	56
140	14436	14379	14321	14264	14206	14148	14090	14031	13973	13914	58
141	13856	13797	13738	13679	13619	13560	13500	13440	13380	13320	60
142	13259	13199	13138	13077	13016	12955	12894	12833	12771	12709	61
143	9.8612647	12585	12523	12461	12398	12336	12273	12210	12147	12083	−63

Logarithm of the Elliptic Radius Vector for m = 0.

Constant subtracted 0.0000257. Period of Argument I. 224d.7008.

Arg. I.	0d.0	0d.1	0d.2	0d.3	0d.4	0d.5	0d.6	0d.7	0d.8	0d.9	Diff. for 0d.1.
144d	9.8612020	11956	11893	11829	11765	11701	11636	11572	11507	11443	−64
145	11378	11313	11248	11182	11117	11051	10986	10920	10854	10788	66
146	10721	10655	10588	10522	10455	10388	10321	10254	10186	10119	67
147	10051	09983	09916	09848	09779	09711	09643	09574	09505	09437	68
148	09368	09299	09229	09160	09091	09021	08951	08882	08812	08741	70
149	08671	08601	08531	08460	08389	08318	08248	08176	08105	08034	71
150	07963	07891	07819	07748	07676	07604	07532	07459	07387	07315	72
151	07242	07169	07097	07024	06951	06878	06804	06731	06658	06584	73
152	06511	06437	06363	06289	06215	06141	06066	05992	05917	05843	74
153	05768	05693	05619	05544	05468	05393	05318	05243	05167	05091	75
154	05016	04940	04864	04788	04712	04636	04560	04484	04407	04331	76
155	04254	04177	04101	04024	03947	03870	03793	03715	03638	03561	77
156	03483	03406	03328	03251	03173	03095	03017	02939	02861	02783	78
157	02704	02626	02548	02469	02390	02312	02233	02154	02075	01997	79
158	01918	01838	01759	01680	01601	01521	01442	01363	01283	01203	79
159	01124	01044	00964	00884	00804	00724	00644	00564	00484	00403	80
160	9.8600323	00243	00162	00082	00001	:99921	99840	99759	99678	99598	81
161	9.8599517	99436	99355	99274	99193	99111	99030	98949	98868	98786	81
162	98705	98624	98542	98461	98379	98297	98216	98134	98052	97971	82
163	97889	97807	97725	97643	97561	97479	97397	97315	97233	97151	82
164	97068	96986	96904	96822	96739	96657	96575	96492	96410	96327	82
165	96245	96162	96080	95997	95914	95832	95749	95666	95584	95501	83
166	95418	95335	95253	95170	95087	95004	94921	94838	94756	94673	83
167	94590	94507	94424	94341	94258	94175	94092	94009	93926	93843	83
168	93760	93677	93594	93510	93427	93344	93261	93178	93095	93012	83
169	92929	92846	92763	92679	92596	92513	92430	92347	92264	92181	83
170	92098	92015	91932	91848	91765	91682	91599	91516	91433	91350	83
171	91267	91184	91101	91018	90935	90852	90769	90686	90603	90521	83
172	90438	90355	90272	90189	90106	90024	89941	89858	89775	89693	83
173	89610	89527	89445	89362	89280	89197	89115	89032	88950	88867	83
174	88785	88703	88620	88538	88456	88373	88291	88209	88127	88045	82
175	87963	87881	87798	87717	87635	87553	87471	87389	87308	87226	82
176	87144	87063	86981	86900	86818	86737	86655	86574	86493	86412	81
177	86330	86249	86168	86087	86006	85925	85844	85763	85683	85602	81
178	85521	85441	85360	85280	85199	85119	85039	84959	84878	84798	80
179	84718	84638	84558	84478	84399	84319	84239	84159	84080	84000	80
180	83921	83842	83762	83683	83604	83525	83446	83367	83288	83210	79
181	83131	83052	82974	82895	82817	82739	82661	82582	82504	82426	78
182	82348	82271	82193	82115	82038	81960	81883	81806	81728	81651	77
183	81574	81497	81421	81344	81267	81190	81114	81038	80961	80885	77
184	80809	80733	80657	80581	80505	80430	80354	80278	80203	80128	76
185	80053	79978	79903	79828	79753	79678	79604	79529	79455	79381	75
186	79307	79233	79159	79085	79011	78938	78864	78791	78717	78644	74
187	78571	78498	78426	78353	78280	78208	78135	78063	77991	77919	72
188	77847	77775	77704	77632	77561	77489	77418	77347	77276	77205	71
189	77135	77064	76994	76923	76853	76783	76713	76643	76574	76504	70
190	76435	76365	76296	76227	76158	76090	76021	75952	75884	75816	69
191	9.8575748	75680	75612	75544	75477	75409	75342	75275	75208	75141	−67

TABLE XXVI.

Logarithm of the Elliptic Radius Vector for [illegible] = 0.

Constant subtracted 0.0000257. Period of Argument I. 224ᵈ.7008.

Arg. I.	0ᵈ.0	0ᵈ.1	0ᵈ.2	0ᵈ.3	0ᵈ.4	0ᵈ.5	0ᵈ.6	0ᵈ.7	0ᵈ.8	0ᵈ.9	Diff. for 0ᵈ.1.
192ᵈ	9.8575074	75008	74941	74875	74809	74743	74677	74611	74545	74480	−66
193	74415	74350	74285	74220	74155	74090	74026	73962	73898	73834	64
194	73770	73706	73643	73579	73516	73453	73390	73327	73265	73202	63
195	73140	73078	73016	72954	72893	72831	72770	72709	72648	72587	61
196	72526	72465	72405	72345	72285	72225	72165	72106	72046	71987	60
197	71928	71869	71810	71752	71693	71635	71577	71519	71462	71404	58
198	71347	71289	71232	71175	71119	71062	71006	70950	70894	70838	56
199	70782	70727	70671	70616	70561	70507	70452	70398	70343	70289	55
200	70236	70182	70128	70075	70022	69969	69916	69863	69811	69759	53
201	69707	69655	69603	69552	69500	69449	69398	69347	69297	69246	51
202	69196	69146	69096	69047	69899	68948	68899	68850	68801	68753	49
203	68705	68657	68609	68561	68514	68466	68419	68372	68326	68279	47
204	68233	68186	68140	68095	68049	68004	67959	67914	67869	67824	45
205	67780	67736	67692	67648	67605	67561	67518	67475	67432	67390	43
206	67347	67305	67263	67222	67180	67139	67098	67057	67016	66975	41
207	66935	66895	66855	66815	66776	66737	66698	66659	66620	66582	39
208	66544	66506	66468	66430	66393	66356	66319	66282	66246	66209	37
209	66173	66137	66102	66066	66031	65996	65961	65927	65892	65858	35
210	65824	65790	65757	65724	65690	65658	65625	65592	65560	65528	33
211	65496	65465	65434	65403	65372	65341	65310	65280	65250	65220	31
212	65191	65162	65133	65104	65075	65046	65018	64990	64962	64935	28
213	64907	64880	64853	64827	64800	64774	64748	64722	64697	64672	26
214	64646	64622	64597	64573	64548	64524	64501	64477	64454	64431	24
215	64408	64385	64363	64341	64319	64297	64276	64255	64234	64213	22
216	64192	64172	64152	64132	64112	64093	64074	64055	64036	64018	19
217	63999	63981	63964	63946	63929	63912	63895	63878	63862	63846	17
218	63830	63814	63799	63784	63769	63754	63739	63725	63711	63697	15
219	63684	63670	63657	63644	63632	63619	63607	63595	63584	63572	12
220	63561	63550	63539	63528	63518	63508	63498	63489	63479	63470	10
221	63461	63453	63444	63436	63428	63420	63413	63406	63399	63392	8
222	63386	63379	63373	63367	63362	63357	63351	63347	63342	63338	5
223	63333	63330	63326	63322	63319	63316	63314	63311	63309	63307	3
224	9.8563305	63303	63302	63301	63300	63300	63299	63299	63299	63300	− 0

TABLE XXVII.

Perturbations of Log. r..

Factor to be multiplied by m, and its logarithm. Period of Argument I. = 224d.7008.

Arg. I.	Factor.	log. fac.	Arg. I.	Factor.	log. fac.	Arg. I.	Factor.	log. fac.	Arg. I.	Factor.	log. fac.
0	+13.45	1.1288	60	− 1.61	n0.2057	120	−12.98	n1.1132	180	+ 4.06	0.6083
1	13.45	1.1286	61	1.97	0.2956	121	12.90	1.1105	181	4.41	0.6449
2	13.43	1.1281	62	2.34	0.3696	122	12.81	1.1074	182	4.77	0.6784
3	13.40	1.1272	63	2.71	0.4325	123	12.71	1.1040	183	5.12	0.7093
4	+13.36	1.1260	64	− 3.07	n0.4871	124	−12.59	n1.1002	184	+ 5.47	0.7377
5	13.32	1.1244	65	3.43	0.5354	125	12.48	1.0961	185	5.81	0.7642
6	13.26	1.1224	66	3.79	0.5784	126	12.35	1.0915	186	6.15	0.7888
7	13.19	1.1201	67	4.14	0.6172	127	12.21	1.0866	187	6.48	0.8118
8	+13.10	1.1174	68	− 4.49	n0.6521	128	−12.06	n1.0813	188	+ 6.81	0.8333
9	13.01	1.1144	69	4.81	0.6847	129	11.90	1.0757	189	7.13	0.8534
10	12.91	1.1110	70	5.18	0.7144	130	11.74	1.0696	190	7.45	0.8723
11	12.80	1.1072	71	5.52	0.7419	131	11.56	1.0630	191	7.77	0.8902
12	+12.68	1.1030	72	− 5.85	n0.7674	132	11.38	n1.0561	192	+ 8.07	0.9070
13	12.54	1.0984	73	6.18	0.7912	133	11.19	1.0487	193	8.37	0.9229
14	12.40	1.0935	74	6.51	0.8134	134	10.98	1.0408	194	8.67	0.9379
15	12.25	1.0880	75	6.83	0.8342	135	10.77	1.0324	195	8.95	0.9520
16	+12.08	1.0822	76	− 7.14	n0.8538	136	−10.56	n1.0235	196	+ 9.23	0.9653
17	11.91	1.0760	77	7.45	0.8720	137	10.33	1.0141	197	9.51	0.9780
18	11.73	1.0693	78	7.75	0.8893	138	10.10	1.0041	198	9.77	0.9899
19	11.54	1.0622	79	8.05	0.9056	139	9.85	0.9936	199	10.03	1.0013
20	+11.34	1.0546	80	− 8.33	n0.9209	140	− 9.60	n0.9825	200	+10.28	1.0119
21	11.13	1.0465	81	8.62	0.9354	141	9.35	0.9707	201	10.52	1.0220
22	10.91	1.0379	82	8.89	0.9491	142	9.08	0.9583	202	10.75	1.0315
23	10.68	1.0287	83	9.16	0.9621	143	8.81	0.9451	203	10.98	1.0405
24	+10.45	1.0190	84	− 9.43	n0.9743	144	− 8.53	n0.9311	204	+11.19	1.0489
25	10.20	1.0088	85	9.68	0.9859	145	8.25	0.9164	205	11.40	1.0569
26	9.95	0.9979	86	9.93	0.9969	146	7.96	0.9009	206	11.60	1.0644
27	9.69	0.9864	87	10.17	1.0072	147	7.66	0.8842	207	11.79	1.0714
28	+ 9.43	0.9743	88	−10.40	n1.0170	148	− 7.36	n0.8666	208	+11.96	1.0779
29	9.15	0.9614	89	10.62	1.0262	149	7.05	0.8480	209	12.13	1.0840
30	8.87	0.9478	90	10.84	1.0349	150	6.73	0.8281	210	12.29	1.0897
31	8.58	0.9335	91	11.05	1.0432	151	6.41	0.8069	211	12.44	1.0950
32	+ 8.28	0.9182	92	−11.24	n1.0509	152	− 6.08	n0.7842	212	+12.58	1.0999
33	7.98	0.9021	93	11.43	1.0582	153	5.75	0.7600	213	12.71	1.1043
34	7.67	0.8850	94	11.61	1.0650	154	5.42	0.7339	214	12.83	1.1083
35	7.36	0.8668	95	11.79	1.0714	155	5.08	0.7050	215	12.94	1.1120
36	+ 7.04	0.8476	96	−11.95	n1.0774	156	− 4.73	n0.6753	216	+13.04	1.1153
37	6.71	0.8270	97	12.10	1.0830	157	4.39	0.6422	217	13.13	1.1183
38	6.38	0.8051	98	12.25	1.0881	158	4.04	0.6059	218	13.21	1.1208
39	6.05	0.7816	99	12.39	1.0930	159	3.68	0.5660	219	13.28	1.1231
40	+ 5.71	0.7566	100	−12.51	n1.0974	160	− 3.32	n0.5215	220	+13.33	1.1249
41	5.36	0.7296	101	12.63	1.1014	161	2.96	0.4716	221	13.38	1.1264
42	5.02	0.7004	102	12.74	1.1050	162	2.60	0.4146	222	13.41	1.1275
43	4.66	0.6648	103	12.83	1.1083	163	2.23	0.3487	223	13.44	1.1283
44	+ 4.31	0.6344	104	−12.92	n1.1113	164	− 1.86	n0.2707	224	+13.45	1.1287
45	3.95	0.5966	105	13.00	1.1139	165	1.49	0.1746	225	13.45	1.1288
46	3.59	0.5550	106	13.07	1.1162	166	1.12	0.0511	226	13.44	1.1285
47	3.22	0.5085	107	13.13	1.1182	167	0.75	9.8762	227	13.42	1.1279
48	+ 2.86	0.4562	108	−13.17	n1.1198	168	− 0.38	n9.5786	228	+13.39	1.1269
49	2.49	0.3961	109	13.21	1.1210	169	− 0.01	n7.7853	229	13.35	1.1256
50	2.12	0.3265	110	13.24	1.1220	170	+ 0.37	p9.5658	230	13.30	1.1239
51	1.75	0.2430	111	13.26	1.1225	171	0.74	9.8704	231	13.21	1.1218
52	+ 1.38	0.1380	112	−13.27	n1.1228	172	+ 1.12	0.0477	232	+13.17	1.1193
53	1.00	0.0017	113	13.27	1.1228	173	1.49	0.1726	233	13.08	1.1165
54	0.63	9.7993	114	13.26	1.1224	174	1.86	0.2695	234	12.99	1.1131
55	+ 0.26	p9.4082	115	13.23	1.1217	175	2.23	0.3487	235	12.88	1.1099
56	− 0.12	n9.0710	116	−13.20	n1.1207	176	+ 2.60	0.4151	236	+12.77	1.1063
57	0.49	9.6911	117	13.16	1.1193	177	2.97	0.4725	237	12.64	1.1017
58	0.86	9.9360	118	13.11	1.1176	178	3.33	0.5239	238	12.50	1.0970
59	1.23	0.0917	119	13.05	1.1156	179	3.70	0.5680	239	12.36	1.0919
60	− 1.61	n0.2057	120	−12.98	n1.1132	180	+ 4.06	0.6083	240	+12.20	1.0863

TABLE XXVIII.

Pert. of Log. r.

Fact. to be × $\left(\frac{m}{100}\right)^2$

Arg. I.	Factor.
0	− 2.1
4	2.1
8	2.0
12	2.0
16	− 1.9
20	1.8
24	1.6
28	1.5
32	− 1.3
36	1.1
40	0.9
44	0.7
48	− 0.5
52	− 0.2
56	0.0
60	+ 0.2
64	+ 0.5
68	0.7
72	0.9
76	1.1
80	+ 1.3
84	1.5
88	1.6
92	1.8
96	+ 1.9
100	2.0
104	2.0
108	2.1
112	+ 2.1
116	2.1
120	2.0
124	2.0
128	+ 1.9
132	1.8
136	1.7
140	1.5
144	+ 1.3
148	1.1
152	0.9
156	0.7
160	+ 0.5
164	0.3
168	+ 0.0
172	− 0.2
176	− 0.4
180	0.7
184	0.9
188	1.1
192	− 1.3
196	1.5
200	1.6
204	1.8
208	− 1.9
212	2.0
216	2.0
220	2.1
224	− 2.1
228	2.1
232	2.1
236	2.0
240	− 1.9

The perturbations are in units of the eighth decimal place.

TABLE XXIX.

Perturbations of Log. r, by the Earth.

Constant added 1594. Period of Argument VI., 583^{d}.02.

Arg. VI.	Equa.	Arg. VI.	Equa.	Arg. VI.	Equa.	Arg. VI.	Equa.	Arg. VI.	Equa.	Arg. VI.	Equa.
0^{d}	1716	104^{d}	1859	208^{d}	550	312^{d}	2856	416^{d}	45	520^{d}	2527
2	1718	106	1795	210	614	314	2811	418	64	522	2524
4	1725	108	1729	212	681	316	2762	420	87	524	2518
6	1736	110	1662	214	751	318	2709	422	114	526	2509
8	1751	112	1593	216	822	320	2653	424	145	528	2496
10	1769	114	1523	218	896	322	2594	426	179	530	2480
12	1792	116	1452	220	972	324	2531	428	216	532	2460
14	1818	118	1381	222	1049	326	2466	430	258	534	2438
16	1846	120	1310	224	1128	328	2397	432	302	536	2413
18	1878	122	1238	226	1209	330	2326	434	350	538	2385
20	1912	124	1166	228	1290	332	2253	436	401	540	2356
22	1948	126	1095	230	1372	334	2178	438	454	542	2323
24	1985	128	1024	232	1455	336	2101	440	510	544	2290
26	2024	130	955	234	1538	338	2022	442	569	546	2253
28	2064	132	886	236	1621	340	1942	444	629	548	2216
30	2103	134	818	238	1704	342	1861	446	692	550	2177
32	2143	136	752	240	1787	344	1780	448	757	552	2138
34	2183	138	687	242	1869	346	1697	450	823	554	2098
36	2221	140	624	244	1950	348	1614	452	891	556	2059
38	2259	142	563	246	2030	350	1531	454	960	558	2019
40	2294	144	505	248	2108	352	1449	456	1029	560	1981
42	2329	146	449	250	2185	354	1365	458	1100	562	1944
44	2361	148	395	252	2260	356	1283	460	1171	564	1908
46	2391	150	345	254	2333	358	1202	462	1243	566	1874
48	2418	152	297	256	2404	360	1123	464	1315	568	1843
50	2443	154	253	258	2472	362	1044	466	1386	570	1814
52	2465	156	212	260	2538	364	967	468	1457	572	1789
54	2484	158	174	262	2600	366	891	470	1528	574	1767
56	2500	160	140	264	2659	368	818	472	1598	576	1749
58	2513	162	109	266	2715	370	746	474	1666	578	1734
60	2522	164	83	268	2767	372	677	476	1733	580	1724
62	2528	166	60	270	2815	374	610	478	1799	582	1718
64	2531	168	41	272	2860	376	546	480	1863	584	1716
66	2530	170	27	274	2901	378	485	482	1924	586	1718
68	2525	172	17	276	2938	380	427	484	1984	588	1725
70	2517	174	11	278	2970	382	372	486	2041	590	1737
72	2505	176	9	280	2999	384	321	488	2095	592	1752
74	2490	178	12	282	3023	386	273	490	2147	594	1770
76	2471	180	19	284	3043	388	229	492	2196	596	1793
78	2449	182	31	286	3058	390	188	494	2242	598	1819
80	2423	184	46	288	3069	392	152	496	2285	600	1847
82	2393	186	66	290	3076	394	119	498	2324	602	1879
84	2360	188	91	292	3078	396	91	500	2361	604	1913
86	2323	190	120	294	3075	398	67	502	2393	606	1950
88	2284	192	153	296	3068	400	47	504	2422	608	1987
90	2241	194	189	298	3057	402	32	506	2448	610	2026
92	2194	196	230	300	3041	404	20	508	2470	612	2066
94	2145	198	275	302	3020	406	14	510	2489	614	2105
96	2093	200	323	304	2996	408	11	512	2503	616	2145
98	2039	202	375	306	2967	410	13	514	2515	618	2185
100	1981	204	430	308	2934	412	20	516	2523	620	2223
102	1921	206	488	310	2897	414	30	518	2527	622	2261
104	1859	208	530	312	2856	416	45	520	2527	624	2295

The perturbations are in units of the eighth decimal place.

TABLE XXX.

Perturbations of Log. r, by the Earth.

Constant added 162. Period of Arg. VII. 243ᵈ.16.

Arg. VII.	Equa.	Arg. VII.	Equa.
d 0	171	d 128	180
4	154	132	197
8	137	136	213
12	121	140	228
16	105	144	243
20	90	148	257
24	75	152	270
28	61	156	282
32	49	160	293
36	37	164	302
40	27	168	310
44	19	172	316
48	12	176	320
52	6	180	323
56	2	184	324
60	0	188	324
64	0	192	321
68	1	196	317
72	4	200	311
76	9	204	304
80	15	208	295
84	23	212	285
88	33	216	273
92	43	220	261
96	56	224	247
100	69	228	232
104	83	232	216
108	98	236	200
112	114	240	184
116	130	244	167
120	146	248	151
124	163	252	134
128	180	256	118

TABLE XXXI.

Perturbations of Log. r, by Jupiter.

Constant added 445. Period of Arg. IX., 236ᵈ.99.

Arg. IX.	Equa.	Arg. IX.	Equa.	Arg. IX.	Equa.
d 0	585	d 80	321	d 160	363
2	585	82	295	162	389
4	586	84	269	164	414
6	588	86	244	166	438
8	591	88	219	168	462
10	594	90	194	170	484
12	598	92	171	172	506
14	603	94	148	174	526
16	608	96	127	176	545
18	613	98	106	178	563
20	618	100	88	180	579
22	623	102	71	182	593
24	629	104	55	184	606
26	633	106	41	186	617
28	638	108	29	188	627
30	642	110	19	190	635
32	645	112	12	192	641
34	647	114	6	194	646
36	648	116	2	196	649
38	648	118	1	198	651
40	647	120	1	200	651
42	644	122	4	202	651
44	640	124	9	204	649
46	635	126	16	206	646
48	628	128	25	208	642
50	619	130	36	210	638
52	608	132	49	212	633
54	596	134	64	214	628
56	583	136	81	216	623
58	567	138	99	218	617
60	551	140	118	220	612
62	532	142	139	222	607
64	513	144	162	224	602
66	492	146	185	226	597
68	470	148	209	228	593
70	447	150	234	230	590
72	423	152	259	232	588
74	398	154	285	234	586
76	373	156	311	236	585
78	347	158	337	238	585
80	321	160	363	240	586

The perturbations are in units of the eighth decimal place.

Perturbations of Log. r, by Mercury.

Horizontal Argument = 1.

Constant added 34. Period of Argument 1., 224d.7.

Arg. X.	0d	8d	16d	24d	32d	40d	48d	56d	64d	72d	80d	88d	96d	104d	112d
0	18	21	30	39	45	44	40	36	34	35	36	34	28	23	23
1	19	24	32	41	45	43	38	34	34	35	37	34	29	25	27
2	20	25	34	42	44	41	36	33	33	35	37	35	30	27	31
3	21	27	36	42	43	39	34	32	33	36	38	35	31	30	36
4	21	28	37	42	42	37	32	31	34	37	39	36	33	34	42
5	22	29	37	41	39	34	30	31	34	38	40	37	35	38	48
6	22	30	37	40	37	32	29	31	35	39	41	39	38	42	53
7	22	30	36	38	34	30	29	32	37	40	42	41	41	46	58
8	22	30	36	36	32	28	28	33	39	42	44	43	44	51	63
9	22	30	34	34	30	27	29	35	41	44	45	45	47	55	67
10	22	29	33	32	28	27	30	37	43	46	47	47	51	59	70
11	22	29	32	30	27	27	32	39	45	48	48	49	54	63	72
12	22	29	31	29	27	28	34	42	48	50	50	52	57	66	74
13	23	30	31	29	27	30	37	45	50	52	51	54	59	68	75
14	25	30	31	29	28	33	41	49	53	53	53	56	61	69	75
15	26	31	31	29	30	36	45	52	55	55	54	58	63	69	73
16	28	32	32	31	33	40	49	55	57	56	55	59	64	69	71
17	31	34	34	33	37	44	53	58	59	57	56	59	65	68	68
18	34	36	36	36	41	49	57	61	61	58	56	60	65	67	65
19	38	39	38	40	45	54	61	63	62	58	57	60	64	65	61
20	42	42	42	44	50	59	64	65	62	58	57	60	63	62	56
21	46	46	45	48	55	63	68	66	62	57	57	59	61	59	51
22	50	50	50	53	60	67	70	67	62	57	56	59	59	55	47
23	55	53	54	58	65	71	71	67	61	56	55	58	57	51	42
24	59	57	58	63	69	73	72	66	59	55	54	56	54	47	38
25	63	61	62	67	73	75	72	64	57	54	53	54	51	43	35
26	67	65	66	71	75	76	71	62	55	52	52	51	47	39	32
27	70	68	70	74	77	76	69	60	53	50	51	49	44	36	30
28	73	71	73	76	78	75	66	57	51	48	49	47	41	34	28
29	75	73	75	78	78	72	63	54	48	46	47	45	38	32	27
30	76	75	76	78	76	69	59	50	45	44	45	42	36	30	27
31	77	75	77	77	74	65	55	46	42	42	44	40	34	29	28
32	77	75	76	75	70	60	50	42	40	41	42	38	33	29	29
33	75	74	74	72	66	55	45	38	38	39	41	36	32	29	31
34	73	72	72	69	63	49	40	35	36	38	39	35	31	30	33
35	71	69	68	64	54	44	35	32	34	37	38	35	31	31	35
36	67	66	64	58	48	38	31	30	33	36	37	34	31	32	38
37	63	62	59	52	42	32	26	29	32	36	36	34	32	34	40
38	58	57	53	46	35	27	23	26	31	35	35	33	33	36	43
39	53	52	47	39	29	22	21	25	31	34	34	33	34	38	45
40	48	46	41	32	23	18	19	25	31	34	34	33	35	40	46
41	42	40	35	26	18	15	18	25	32	34	34	34	36	41	46
42	37	35	29	20	14	13	17	25	32	35	34	35	38	42	46
43	32	29	23	15	10	11	18	26	33	35	34	35	39	43	45
44	27	24	18	11	8	11	19	28	34	35	34	36	40	43	44
45	23	19	13	7	6	12	21	30	35	36	35	36	40	42	42
46	19	15	9	5	6	13	23	32	36	36	35	37	41	42	40
47	15	12	6	4	7	15	25	34	37	36	35	37	41	41	37
48	13	9	4	3	8	18	28	35	38	37	35	38	41	40	34
49	11	7	3	4	11	21	31	37	38	37	36	38	40	38	31
50	9	5	3	5	14	25	34	39	39	37	36	38	39	35	27
51	8	5	4	8	17	29	37	40	39	37	36	38	38	32	24
52	8	5	5	11	21	32	39	41	39	37	36	38	37	30	21
53	9	6	7	14	25	36	41	41	39	37	36	37	36	28	18
54	9	7	10	18	30	39	43	41	38	36	36	37	34	26	16
55	10	9	13	22	33	41	44	40	38	36	36	36	32	24	15
56	12	12	17	26	37	43	44	40	37	35	36	35	31	22	15
57	13	14	20	30	40	45	44	39	36	35	36	35	30	21	16
58	15	16	24	34	42	45	43	38	35	35	36	34	29	21	17
59	16	19	27	37	44	45	42	37	34	35	36	34	28	22	19
60	18	21	30	39	45	44	40	36	34	35	36	34	28	23	23

The perturbations are in units of the eighth decimal place.

Perturbations of Log. r, by Mercury.

Horizontal Argument = I.

Constant added 34. Period of Argument X., 60 units.

Arg. X.	120^{d}	128^{d}	136^{d}	144^{d}	152^{d}	160^{d}	168^{d}	176^{d}	184^{d}	192^{d}	200^{d}	208^{d}	216^{d}	224^{d}	232^{d}
0	27	37	48	55	58	60	65	75	85	93	94	88	81	75	74
1	33	44	55	60	63	65	71	81	90	95	93	86	79	73	72
2	39	51	61	65	67	70	76	85	93	96	92	83	75	70	69
3	45	57	66	69	71	73	79	88	95	95	89	79	71	66	65
4	52	63	71	73	74	76	82	90	95	93	85	74	66	62	61
5	58	68	74	75	76	78	84	91	93	89	80	68	61	57	56
6	64	73	77	77	77	79	85	90	90	84	73	62	55	52	50
7	68	76	78	78	77	79	85	88	86	78	66	55	49	47	44
8	72	78	79	77	76	79	83	85	80	70	58	48	43	41	39
9	75	79	79	75	74	77	80	80	73	62	50	41	37	36	33
10	77	79	77	73	72	74	76	74	66	54	42	34	31	31	28
11	78	78	74	70	69	71	72	68	58	45	34	28	26	26	23
12	78	75	70	66	65	67	67	61	50	37	27	22	22	22	19
13	77	72	66	62	61	62	61	53	42	29	21	17	18	18	15
14	74	68	61	57	57	57	55	46	34	22	15	13	15	15	11
15	70	63	57	53	53	52	49	39	27	16	10	10	13	12	9
16	66	58	52	48	49	48	42	32	20	10	7	8	11	10	7
17	61	53	47	44	45	43	36	26	14	6	5	7	10	10	6
18	56	48	42	40	41	38	31	20	9	3	4	7	10	9	5
19	51	43	38	37	37	34	26	15	5	2	3	8	10	9	6
20	46	38	34	34	34	30	21	11	3	1	4	9	11	9	7
21	41	34	32	32	32	27	17	8	2	1	6	11	12	10	8
22	37	31	30	31	30	24	15	6	2	3	9	13	13	11	10
23	33	28	29	30	28	22	13	6	3	6	12	15	14	12	12
24	30	26	28	29	27	21	12	6	5	9	14	17	16	14	14
25	28	26	28	30	27	20	12	7	7	12	17	19	17	15	16
26	26	26	29	30	27	19	12	8	10	16	20	21	19	17	19
27	25	27	30	31	27	19	13	10	13	19	23	22	19	18	21
28	25	28	32	32	27	20	14	13	17	22	25	23	20	19	24
29	26	30	34	33	28	20	16	15	20	25	26	23	20	20	26
30	28	32	36	34	28	21	17	18	23	27	27	23	20	21	27
31	30	35	38	35	28	21	19	20	25	28	27	22	19	21	28
32	33	38	39	35	28	22	20	23	27	28	26	21	18	21	29
33	35	40	40	35	27	22	21	24	28	28	24	19	17	21	29
34	38	42	41	35	27	22	22	25	28	27	22	17	16	21	29
35	40	44	41	34	26	21	22	25	27	25	19	14	15	21	29
36	43	45	41	33	25	21	22	25	25	22	16	12	14	21	29
37	45	45	40	31	23	20	22	24	23	19	13	10	13	21	29
38	46	45	38	28	21	19	21	22	20	15	9	8	13	21	29
39	46	43	35	25	19	18	19	20	17	11	6	7	14	22	29
40	46	41	32	22	17	16	17	18	14	8	4	6	14	23	29
41	45	38	28	19	14	14	15	15	10	5	3	6	15	24	30
42	44	35	24	15	12	12	14	12	7	2	2	7	17	26	31
43	41	31	20	12	10	10	12	9	5	1	2	9	20	28	33
44	38	27	16	9	8	9	10	7	3	0	3	12	23	31	35
45	34	23	12	6	6	8	9	6	2	0	5	16	27	35	37
46	30	18	9	4	5	8	8	5	2	2	9	21	32	39	40
47	26	14	6	3	5	8	8	5	3	5	14	27	37	43	43
48	22	11	4	3	6	8	8	5	5	9	20	33	42	47	47
49	18	8	3	3	7	9	9	7	8	14	27	39	48	51	51
50	15	6	2	4	9	12	11	10	13	21	34	46	54	56	55
51	12	4	3	6	12	15	14	14	18	29	42	53	60	60	59
52	10	4	5	10	15	18	18	19	25	36	50	60	65	64	62
53	9	5	7	14	19	22	23	25	33	44	58	67	70	68	66
54	8	7	11	19	24	27	28	32	41	53	66	73	74	71	69
55	9	10	16	24	29	32	34	39	49	62	73	78	77	74	72
56	11	14	22	30	35	38	40	46	57	70	80	83	80	76	74
57	14	19	28	36	41	43	47	53	65	77	86	86	82	77	75
58	17	24	35	43	47	49	53	61	73	84	90	88	83	77	75
59	22	30	42	49	53	55	59	68	80	89	93	89	82	76	75
60	27	37	48	55	58	60	65	75	85	93	94	88	81	75	74

When $224^{d}.7$ is subtracted from Arg. I., add 33.26 to Arg. X.

TABLE XXXIII.

Perturbations of Log. r, by the Earth.

Horizontal Argument = I.

Constant added 150. Period of Argument I., $224^d.7$.

Arg. XI.	0^d	8^d	16^d	24^d	32^d	40^d	48^d	56^d	64^d	72^d	80^d	88^d	96^d	104^d	112^d
0	206	207	211	216	220	224	225	223	219	214	209	204	202	202	205
2	210	210	213	217	222	225	227	226	222	218	212	207	204	202	204
4	213	213	214	218	221	224	226	225	222	217	212	206	202	200	200
6	216	214	214	217	219	222	223	222	218	214	209	203	198	195	194
8	214	212	212	214	216	218	219	218	215	210	205	198	193	190	188
10	209	207	207	200	211	213	214	214	211	207	201	195	190	185	184
12	199	196	197	200	203	206	209	210	208	205	200	194	188	183	181
14	184	182	183	187	192	197	202	204	204	202	199	193	189	184	180
16	167	166	167	172	178	185	192	196	199	198	197	192	188	183	180
18	151	150	151	156	162	170	179	185	180	191	191	188	184	181	178
20	140	137	137	141	147	155	164	171	176	180	180	179	176	173	171
22	133	129	127	130	134	141	149	156	161	165	167	165	163	160	159
24	130	126	123	123	126	131	137	143	147	150	152	150	148	145	144
26	129	125	121	121	122	126	130	134	137	139	139	136	133	129	127
28	127	125	121	122	123	125	128	131	133	134	132	128	123	118	114
30	121	122	122	123	125	128	131	134	135	135	133	128	120	113	106
32	109	114	118	122	126	131	136	140	142	143	140	134	126	115	105
34	92	101	108	116	124	132	140	146	151	153	152	146	137	125	112
36	74	84	95	106	117	128	140	150	157	162	163	159	150	138	123
38	55	66	79	92	106	120	134	147	158	167	170	169	162	150	136
40	41	51	62	76	90	106	123	138	152	164	171	172	169	160	147
42	33	39	48	60	74	90	107	124	140	155	165	170	170	164	154
44	31	33	38	47	58	72	89	107	124	140	153	162	166	164	157
46	36	32	33	37	45	56	72	88	106	124	138	150	158	160	156
48	45	36	32	31	35	44	56	71	89	107	124	138	148	153	153
50	58	45	35	30	30	35	44	57	73	91	109	125	137	145	149
52	75	58	44	35	29	30	36	47	61	77	95	111	126	135	142
54	96	76	58	44	34	31	32	39	50	65	81	98	113	124	132
56	121	100	79	61	46	36	33	34	42	53	69	83	98	110	120
58	150	129	106	83	64	49	39	35	37	44	55	68	81	94	104
60	181	160	137	112	89	69	53	42	38	39	46	55	66	77	87
62	211	193	171	145	120	95	74	58	47	42	43	47	55	64	72
64	236	223	203	180	154	127	102	82	65	54	49	48	51	57	63
66	253	245	231	212	188	163	136	113	93	77	67	61	59	60	63
68	261	259	251	238	219	197	173	149	127	109	94	84	78	75	73
70	259	263	263	256	244	228	207	186	165	146	129	116	106	100	94
72	251	260	265	265	261	251	236	219	201	183	166	152	141	131	122
74	241	252	261	267	269	265	257	245	231	216	201	187	175	164	154
76	233	244	254	263	269	271	268	262	253	242	229	217	206	196	186
78	228	237	247	257	264	270	271	270	265	259	249	240	231	223	214
80	229	233	241	249	257	264	268	270	270	266	261	255	250	243	237
82	231	232	236	242	249	256	262	267	269	269	268	265	262	259	255
84	236	233	233	237	242	248	254	261	265	268	270	271	271	270	269
86	236	232	231	232	234	240	246	253	259	265	270	273	276	278	279
88	235	230	227	226	227	231	237	244	252	260	267	273	279	283	287
90	229	225	221	219	219	222	226	233	242	251	260	269	277	284	290
92	220	218	214	211	209	210	214	220	228	237	248	259	269	278	286
94	210	209	206	203	199	198	199	203	210	218	229	241	253	265	276
96	198	199	197	194	189	185	184	185	189	195	205	217	229	243	257
98	183	188	188	184	179	173	169	166	167	170	178	188	201	216	231
100	167	174	176	174	169	162	155	150	147	147	152	159	171	185	202
102	147	156	161	162	158	151	143	136	130	127	129	133	142	155	171
104	122	135	143	146	145	140	133	126	118	113	111	112	118	128	143
106	95	110	121	128	130	128	123	117	109	103	98	97	99	106	118
108	68	84	97	106	112	114	112	107	101	94	88	85	85	89	97
110	45	59	73	84	92	97	98	96	92	86	80	75	73	74	79
112	28	40	52	63	72	79	83	83	80	76	70	65	61	63	62
114	21	29	37	46	54	61	65	67	66	64	59	53	49	46	46
116	23	26	30	36	41	46	50	52	52	51	47	42	37	33	31
118	32	30	31	32	31	37	39	41	41	39	36	32	27	22	19
120	45	41	38	35	33	33	33	34	34	33	30	27	22	17	12

The perturbations are in units of the eighth decimal place.

Perturbations of Log. r, by the Earth.

Horizontal Argument = I.

Constant added 150. Period of Argument XI., 240 units.

Arg. XI.	120^d	128^d	136^d	144^d	152^d	160^d	168^d	176^d	184^d	192^d	200^d	208^d	216^d	224^d	232^d
0	210	217	224	231	235	238	239	238	237	236	236	239	244	252	262
2	207	212	218	223	227	229	230	229	227	226	227	230	236	245	256
4	202	206	211	215	218	220	221	219	217	216	216	219	225	234	246
6	196	199	202	206	209	210	210	209	206	204	204	206	211	220	232
8	189	191	194	197	199	199	199	196	193	190	188	190	194	203	215
10	183	184	186	188	189	188	186	183	178	174	171	171	173	181	193
12	179	180	180	181	180	178	174	169	162	156	150	148	149	156	166
14	178	177	176	176	174	170	164	156	147	138	130	125	124	128	139
16	177	176	175	173	170	165	157	148	136	124	113	105	101	102	100
18	175	174	173	172	169	164	156	145	131	117	102	91	83	81	84
20	170	169	170	170	168	164	158	147	134	118	101	87	75	68	67
22	159	160	163	165	167	166	162	153	142	126	109	92	76	65	69
24	144	147	151	157	162	165	166	161	152	139	122	105	87	72	62
26	128	130	136	144	153	169	165	165	161	151	137	121	103	86	73
28	113	114	120	128	138	140	158	163	164	160	150	137	120	103	88
30	102	100	104	111	121	133	145	154	169	161	156	147	134	119	104
32	98	92	91	96	104	115	128	139	149	154	155	150	142	130	118
34	100	93	85	84	89	98	109	122	133	142	147	147	143	136	128
36	108	95	85	79	79	84	93	104	116	127	135	139	140	137	133
38	119	103	90	83	75	76	82	91	102	114	123	130	134	135	134
40	131	113	98	86	78	75	77	81	93	104	114	122	128	131	133
42	140	121	108	91	84	78	78	82	80	98	107	116	123	127	130
44	146	132	117	103	92	85	82	84	89	96	104	112	118	123	127
46	149	137	124	111	100	92	88	87	90	95	102	108	114	119	122
48	140	141	129	118	107	99	93	91	92	95	100	105	110	113	116
50	147	141	133	123	113	104	98	94	94	95	98	101	105	107	109
52	143	140	133	125	116	108	101	97	95	95	96	98	101	102	103
54	136	135	131	125	117	111	105	100	98	98	98	98	99	100	99
56	125	127	125	122	117	112	108	105	103	103	103	103	102	101	99
58	112	115	116	116	113	111	110	109	109	110	111	111	111	108	104
60	96	104	105	107	108	108	110	112	115	118	121	123	123	120	115
62	81	87	92	96	99	102	107	112	119	125	131	135	136	135	129
64	70	75	80	84	89	94	100	108	117	127	136	144	148	149	145
66	66	70	73	76	79	84	91	100	111	123	135	146	155	159	158
68	73	72	72	73	74	76	81	90	109	114	129	142	155	163	166
70	89	85	81	77	74	73	75	81	90	103	118	133	148	161	168
72	114	107	99	91	84	78	76	77	83	93	107	123	140	155	166
74	144	134	123	112	101	92	84	82	83	90	101	115	132	148	162
76	176	165	153	140	126	114	103	96	93	95	102	114	128	144	150
78	205	195	183	170	156	142	129	118	111	109	112	120	131	145	159
80	230	222	212	200	187	172	158	145	136	130	129	133	141	151	162
82	250	244	237	227	215	202	188	174	163	154	150	150	155	161	170
84	266	263	258	250	240	228	214	200	188	178	171	168	169	173	179
86	270	278	274	268	260	249	236	222	208	197	189	184	183	184	189
88	289	288	287	292	274	264	252	238	225	212	202	196	193	194	197
90	293	295	295	291	285	275	263	250	236	221	213	205	201	200	203
92	293	297	298	296	291	283	272	259	245	232	221	212	206	205	206
94	285	292	296	297	294	287	277	265	252	239	227	218	212	209	210
96	269	279	288	291	291	288	280	270	258	245	233	223	216	213	212
98	246	260	272	280	284	283	279	271	261	249	237	228	220	215	213
100	219	236	251	262	270	273	272	267	259	248	238	229	220	215	212
102	189	207	225	240	251	254	259	257	251	242	233	221	216	210	207
104	160	178	197	214	227	237	241	212	238	231	222	214	206	201	198
106	133	150	169	186	201	213	219	222	220	214	207	199	192	187	185
108	109	125	142	159	174	187	196	200	200	196	189	182	175	170	169
110	88	101	116	133	149	162	173	179	180	178	173	166	159	155	153
112	68	73	92	108	121	139	151	163	164	163	159	153	147	142	139
114	50	58	75	84	101	117	131	142	149	151	150	145	139	134	130
116	32	39	49	62	78	96	112	125	135	140	142	140	135	130	126
118	18	22	30	42	57	74	92	107	121	129	135	136	133	129	125
120	10	11	16	21	37	53	71	87	103	115	124	128	129	127	125

When $224^d.7$ is subtracted from Arg. I., add 147.64 to Arg. XI.

TABLE XXXIII.

Perturbations of Log. r, by the Earth.

Horizontal Argument = I.

Constant added 150. Period of Argument I., 224d.7.

Arg. XI.	0d	8d	16d	24d	32d	40d	48d	56d	64d	72d	80d	88d	96d	104d	112d
120	45	41	38	35	33	33	33	34	34	33	30	27	22	17	12
122	60	54	48	43	38	36	34	33	33	32	30	28	23	18	13
124	74	68	61	55	48	44	40	38	38	37	36	35	31	26	20
126	88	82	76	68	61	55	50	47	46	45	46	46	44	40	34
128	102	98	91	83	75	68	62	58	56	55	56	58	57	55	51
130	118	114	108	100	92	83	76	69	66	65	66	68	69	69	68
132	138	135	129	120	111	100	93	82	76	73	73	75	78	80	81
134	162	158	152	144	133	120	107	96	87	81	79	80	83	87	91
136	187	184	178	169	158	144	128	114	101	91	86	84	86	91	97
138	211	209	205	197	185	170	153	136	120	106	97	92	92	95	101
140	232	232	229	223	213	199	182	164	145	128	115	106	102	103	108
142	247	249	251	247	240	229	213	195	175	157	139	127	119	116	117
144	255	260	264	265	263	255	243	227	208	188	169	153	141	134	131
146	256	264	271	277	279	277	268	256	240	221	201	182	167	156	149
148	252	262	273	282	288	291	288	279	266	250	230	211	193	179	168
150	244	256	268	281	291	297	299	295	286	272	255	237	218	201	187
152	233	245	259	273	286	297	302	303	298	288	274	257	239	222	206
154	219	231	246	261	276	289	298	303	303	297	286	272	255	239	222
156	201	213	228	244	261	276	289	298	301	300	293	283	269	254	238
158	178	190	205	222	240	259	275	287	295	298	296	290	280	267	253
160	152	163	178	196	216	236	255	272	284	292	296	294	288	279	267
162	121	133	148	166	187	210	232	252	269	281	289	293	292	287	279
164	98	105	118	135	156	183	204	227	247	263	276	285	289	289	286
166	77	81	91	106	125	148	173	197	219	239	256	269	277	282	284
168	66	65	70	81	98	118	141	164	188	208	227	243	256	265	272
170	65	59	59	65	77	93	112	133	154	174	193	211	225	238	250
172	74	63	58	58	64	75	89	106	124	141	158	175	190	204	219
174	88	75	65	61	61	66	75	87	100	114	127	141	155	169	184
176	105	90	78	71	67	68	71	78	87	96	105	114	125	136	149
178	120	106	94	85	79	77	77	80	84	89	93	98	104	111	120
180	131	120	109	100	94	90	89	90	91	92	92	93	93	94	93
182	136	128	120	114	109	106	104	104	103	102	100	96	92	88	86
184	137	133	128	124	121	119	119	119	118	116	112	105	97	88	81
186	135	134	132	131	129	129	130	130	131	129	124	116	106	94	81
188	131	133	133	133	134	135	137	138	139	138	134	126	114	101	85
190	127	130	132	133	135	137	139	142	144	143	140	133	122	108	91
192	123	126	129	131	133	135	138	142	145	146	144	139	129	115	98
194	118	122	124	126	129	131	135	140	144	147	147	143	135	122	106
196	113	115	118	120	123	126	131	136	142	146	148	147	141	130	115
198	106	108	110	112	115	119	124	131	138	144	149	150	147	139	126
200	101	102	103	104	106	111	117	124	133	141	147	152	151	146	136
202	98	98	97	97	99	102	108	115	124	134	142	149	152	150	142
204	102	99	96	94	93	94	98	104	113	123	133	142	147	148	144
206	109	105	100	95	91	89	90	94	101	111	120	130	138	142	141
208	122	117	110	102	95	89	86	86	91	98	107	117	125	132	134
210	137	132	124	114	104	94	87	84	84	89	96	105	114	121	125
212	151	148	140	130	118	106	96	88	85	86	90	98	106	113	119
214	160	160	155	146	134	121	109	99	93	92	93	98	105	112	118
216	163	167	166	160	150	138	126	116	108	104	104	107	112	118	123
218	160	169	171	170	161	154	144	134	126	121	120	122	126	131	135
220	154	166	173	176	173	167	159	151	144	139	137	139	143	147	152
222	148	162	172	178	179	176	171	164	158	151	153	154	158	161	168
224	145	159	171	178	182	181	178	173	168	164	164	166	170	177	183
226	147	160	171	179	184	184	182	177	173	170	169	172	177	185	193
228	154	165	175	182	187	187	185	181	177	173	172	174	180	188	198
230	164	173	181	187	191	192	189	185	180	175	174	175	180	189	200
232	176	182	189	194	198	198	194	191	185	180	177	178	182	189	200
234	186	191	196	201	205	205	203	199	193	188	184	183	185	191	200
236	195	198	203	208	212	213	212	208	203	197	193	190	190	194	202
238	201	204	208	213	217	221	220	217	212	207	202	198	197	199	204
240	206	207	211	216	220	224	225	223	219	214	209	204	202	202	205

The perturbations are in units of the eighth decimal place.

Perturbations of Log. r, by the Earth.

Horizontal Argument = I.

Constant added 150. Period of Argument XI., 240 units.

Arg. XI.	120^{d}	128^{d}	136^{d}	144^{d}	152^{d}	160^{d}	168^{d}	176^{d}	184^{d}	192^{d}	200^{d}	208^{d}	216^{d}	224^{d}	232^{d}
120	10	11	16	21	37	53	71	87	103	115	121	128	129	127	125
122	8	6	6	12	21	31	49	66	82	96	108	116	121	122	122
124	14	9	6	6	10	19	30	44	59	74	87	97	106	111	115
126	27	20	13	9	8	11	17	26	38	51	64	76	86	95	103
128	44	37	28	20	14	11	11	15	23	32	43	54	66	76	86
130	63	56	47	37	28	21	16	15	16	21	28	36	47	57	69
132	80	76	69	60	49	40	31	25	21	20	22	27	34	42	52
134	92	92	89	83	74	64	53	44	36	29	27	26	28	33	40
136	102	105	106	104	98	90	79	69	58	48	40	34	31	30	33
138	109	115	120	121	119	114	106	96	83	71	59	49	40	35	32
140	115	123	130	135	137	135	129	121	109	95	81	67	54	44	35
142	123	130	138	145	150	152	149	142	132	119	104	87	71	56	44
144	133	139	146	154	160	164	164	161	153	141	126	109	91	73	57
146	147	149	154	160	167	173	176	175	171	161	148	132	113	94	75
148	162	160	162	167	174	180	186	188	187	181	171	156	139	118	97
150	178	173	172	174	180	187	194	199	201	199	193	182	166	147	125
152	193	185	181	182	186	192	200	208	213	215	214	206	195	178	157
154	208	198	191	189	192	197	205	213	222	228	231	228	221	207	189
156	224	212	202	198	197	200	207	216	226	235	241	244	242	233	219
158	239	226	215	207	204	204	208	215	224	235	244	251	254	251	243
160	255	242	229	219	212	208	208	212	219	229	240	250	258	260	257
162	269	257	244	232	222	214	210	210	214	221	231	241	253	259	263
164	279	269	258	246	234	223	215	211	210	214	221	230	242	252	261
166	282	276	260	258	247	235	225	217	211	211	214	221	231	242	253
168	275	275	273	267	258	248	237	228	219	214	213	216	224	233	244
170	258	264	268	268	265	258	250	241	232	224	220	218	222	228	237
172	232	243	253	260	263	263	260	254	246	238	231	226	225	228	233
174	199	214	230	242	243	259	262	261	257	250	243	236	232	230	232
176	164	181	199	216	232	245	254	260	260	257	252	245	239	235	232
178	132	147	165	184	204	222	236	248	254	255	253	248	242	237	233
180	106	117	132	150	171	191	210	226	238	245	217	215	241	236	231
182	87	92	103	117	136	157	178	198	214	226	233	236	234	231	227
184	76	75	79	80	105	123	144	166	186	202	214	221	223	223	225
186	71	64	63	67	78	93	113	135	156	176	192	203	210	212	211
188	71	69	52	51	57	68	85	106	128	150	169	184	194	200	201
190	74	59	47	41	42	49	63	81	102	121	145	161	177	186	190
192	80	62	47	37	33	35	44	59	78	100	122	142	158	169	176
194	88	69	51	37	28	26	29	40	57	76	97	118	135	149	159
196	98	78	58	41	28	21	20	25	36	52	71	91	110	126	138
198	109	88	69	49	32	20	14	14	20	31	47	65	83	99	114
200	121	101	81	60	40	25	13	8	0	15	26	40	56	72	87
202	130	113	94	73	52	34	19	9	4	5	11	21	34	48	63
204	135	122	105	86	65	46	30	17	9	5	6	11	19	30	42
206	136	126	113	97	79	61	44	31	20	13	10	11	14	21	29
208	133	127	118	105	91	76	61	48	37	28	23	20	19	21	25
210	127	125	119	110	100	88	76	65	55	46	40	35	31	30	29
212	122	122	120	114	106	98	88	80	72	61	58	53	47	43	38
214	121	123	121	117	111	105	97	91	85	79	74	69	63	58	52
216	127	128	127	122	117	111	104	99	95	90	87	83	78	72	66
218	138	139	136	132	126	119	113	107	103	100	97	94	91	86	80
220	151	154	152	147	139	132	124	118	113	110	107	106	103	100	95
222	172	173	170	165	158	149	140	133	127	123	121	120	118	116	112
224	188	190	190	186	179	171	161	153	147	142	139	138	136	135	131
226	200	205	207	206	201	194	186	177	170	165	161	160	159	157	154
228	207	216	221	223	221	216	209	202	196	190	186	185	184	182	179
230	211	222	230	235	236	234	230	224	218	213	210	209	208	207	205
232	212	224	234	242	246	246	244	240	236	232	229	228	228	229	228
234	212	223	235	243	249	251	251	249	245	242	241	241	243	245	247
236	211	222	232	241	247	251	251	250	247	245	245	246	249	254	259
238	211	220	229	237	242	246	247	246	244	243	242	245	249	256	264
240	210	217	224	231	235	238	239	238	237	236	236	239	244	252	262

When $224^{d}.7$ is subtracted from Arg. I., add 147.61 to Arg. XI.

TABLE XXXIV.

Perturbations of Log. r, by Mars.

Horizontal Argument = I.

Constant added 80. Period of Argument I., $224^{d}.7$.

Arg. XII.	0^d	8^d	16^d	24^d	32^d	40^d	48^d	56^d	64^d	72^d	80^d	88^d	96^d	104^d	112^d
0	122	106	88	71	51	38	25	15	8	5	6	11	20	32	46
1	138	124	109	93	76	60	44	30	18	10	7	8	11	18	29
2	149	140	129	115	99	82	65	49	35	24	15	10	9	11	17
3	152	149	142	132	118	103	87	71	55	40	28	19	14	11	12
4	150	152	150	144	134	122	108	92	76	61	46	33	24	17	13
5	140	147	150	148	143	135	125	113	97	82	67	52	39	29	21
6	125	136	143	147	147	144	138	128	115	102	88	73	58	45	34
7	106	120	131	140	145	146	144	139	131	121	107	93	78	64	50
8	85	101	115	126	135	142	145	144	139	132	123	112	99	84	71
9	64	79	94	108	120	130	138	142	143	140	134	126	116	104	91
10	45	59	73	88	102	115	126	134	139	141	140	136	129	120	109
11	30	41	54	68	82	97	110	120	129	135	139	139	137	132	124
12	19	27	37	49	61	75	90	103	115	125	132	137	139	137	133
13	16	19	25	33	44	56	69	83	96	108	119	127	133	137	137
14	18	17	18	22	30	40	51	64	77	90	102	114	123	130	135
15	28	22	19	19	22	27	35	45	57	70	83	96	108	118	126
16	43	33	26	21	19	21	25	31	40	51	63	76	89	101	112
17	59	47	37	29	23	20	20	23	28	36	46	58	70	84	96
18	80	67	54	43	33	26	21	20	21	25	31	40	51	62	75
19	101	87	74	60	48	38	30	24	21	20	22	27	35	45	56
20	119	106	92	79	66	53	43	33	26	21	19	20	24	31	40
21	133	122	111	90	86	73	59	47	37	29	23	19	18	29	26
22	142	136	128	118	105	92	79	65	53	42	32	24	19	17	18
23	144	143	130	132	122	111	99	86	72	58	46	35	26	20	16
24	141	144	144	141	135	127	117	105	92	78	63	51	39	29	21
25	132	139	143	144	143	138	131	122	111	98	85	70	56	43	31
26	117	127	135	141	144	144	142	136	127	117	105	91	76	61	47
27	98	111	122	132	139	143	145	143	139	132	122	110	96	82	66
28	78	93	106	118	128	137	143	146	145	142	137	128	117	103	88
29	58	71	86	99	112	124	134	142	146	147	146	141	133	122	109
30	41	52	65	79	93	107	120	130	139	145	148	148	144	137	127
31	29	37	47	60	73	88	102	115	127	137	145	149	150	148	141
32	20	24	31	42	53	67	82	96	110	123	134	144	150	152	151
33	19	18	21	26	36	47	63	75	90	105	119	131	141	149	152
34	25	20	17	18	23	32	42	55	69	85	100	115	128	139	148
35	35	27	20	16	16	20	27	37	49	63	79	95	111	125	136
36	51	39	29	21	16	15	17	23	31	43	57	73	89	105	120
37	69	55	43	32	22	16	13	15	19	27	38	52	67	84	100
38	90	76	61	48	34	24	16	13	12	16	23	33	46	61	78
39	110	97	82	66	51	38	27	18	13	11	13	19	29	41	56
40	128	116	102	87	72	56	42	29	19	13	10	11	16	25	36
41	140	131	121	108	93	78	61	46	32	22	14	10	10	13	21
42	148	144	137	128	114	99	83	66	50	36	24	15	10	8	11
43	149	150	148	142	132	119	105	89	71	54	39	27	17	11	8
44	141	148	150	150	145	136	124	110	94	77	59	44	31	20	12
45	130	140	148	152	152	147	140	130	116	99	82	64	49	35	23
46	112	127	139	147	153	154	151	144	133	120	104	87	69	53	38
47	90	108	123	136	146	152	155	153	147	138	126	109	92	75	58
48	68	88	104	119	133	145	152	155	154	149	141	129	114	97	81
49	46	62	81	98	115	130	142	151	156	156	152	144	133	119	103
50	27	41	57	76	93	111	127	139	149	155	156	154	147	136	123
51	13	23	36	53	70	89	107	122	136	146	154	156	155	150	140
52	3	9	19	32	48	63	84	102	118	133	144	152	156	156	150
53	1	2	7	15	28	44	60	79	97	114	129	141	149	154	155
54	6	2	1	4	12	24	39	55	73	92	109	125	137	146	153
55	18	9	3	1	3	10	21	35	50	68	87	104	120	133	143
56	35	21	11	4	1	3	9	18	31	46	63	82	99	115	128
57	54	39	25	14	6	2	2	7	16	27	42	59	76	94	110
58	79	61	44	30	18	9	4	3	6	13	24	38	54	70	87
59	102	84	67	49	33	21	12	6	4	6	12	22	35	49	65
60	122	106	88	71	54	38	25	15	8	5	6	11	20	32	46

The perturbations are in units of the eighth decimal place.

Perturbations of Log. r, by Mars.

Horizontal Argument = I.

Constant added 60. Period of Argument XII., 60 units.

Arg. XII.	120d	128d	136d	144d	152d	160d	168d	176d	184d	192d	200d	208d	216d	224d	232d
0	61	76	92	107	121	131	139	145	148	147	142	134	125	113	100
1	42	56	71	86	102	116	127	135	141	145	146	143	137	128	118
2	26	37	51	65	80	95	109	121	131	138	143	145	143	140	133
3	17	24	34	47	60	74	89	102	115	126	135	141	144	144	142
4	12	15	21	31	42	55	69	83	97	110	121	131	138	143	144
5	16	15	16	21	29	38	50	62	76	90	103	115	126	134	140
6	25	20	17	17	20	26	34	45	57	69	83	96	110	122	131
7	39	30	23	19	18	19	24	31	41	52	64	77	91	105	117
8	57	45	35	27	22	20	20	22	28	36	46	57	70	84	98
9	78	64	52	41	32	26	22	20	21	25	32	40	51	63	78
10	96	83	70	57	46	37	29	23	20	20	23	29	36	46	58
11	114	102	90	78	65	53	43	34	27	22	20	21	25	32	41
12	127	118	108	97	84	71	59	47	37	29	23	20	20	22	28
13	135	130	123	114	103	90	78	65	53	42	33	26	21	19	23
14	137	136	133	127	119	108	97	85	71	58	47	37	28	22	19
15	132	136	137	135	130	124	115	104	92	78	65	53	41	31	23
16	122	129	135	137	136	133	128	120	110	98	85	71	58	45	34
17	108	118	126	133	137	137	136	132	125	115	104	91	77	63	50
18	88	101	113	123	131	137	139	139	136	130	122	111	98	84	69
19	69	82	95	108	120	129	136	140	141	140	135	127	117	105	91
20	51	63	76	89	103	115	125	134	140	142	142	138	132	122	110
21	34	45	56	69	84	98	111	122	132	140	144	144	142	137	128
22	22	29	38	50	63	77	92	106	119	130	139	144	146	145	141
23	16	18	24	33	44	57	71	86	101	115	127	137	144	148	149
24	16	13	14	19	27	38	51	65	81	96	111	125	136	144	149
25	22	16	13	13	16	23	33	44	59	75	91	106	121	133	143
26	34	24	16	11	10	12	18	27	39	53	69	85	102	118	131
27	52	39	27	18	12	9	10	15	23	34	48	63	80	98	114
28	71	55	42	29	18	11	7	7	11	18	29	42	58	75	93
29	94	77	61	46	32	20	12	6	5	7	14	24	37	52	70
30	114	99	83	66	50	36	23	13	7	4	5	11	20	32	47
31	131	119	105	89	71	55	40	26	15	7	3	3	8	16	27
32	145	136	125	110	94	76	59	43	28	16	7	3	2	5	13
33	152	148	141	130	115	99	82	64	47	32	19	9	3	1	4
34	153	153	151	145	134	120	104	87	69	51	35	21	11	4	1
35	146	152	155	154	147	137	125	110	93	74	57	40	26	14	5
36	134	144	152	155	154	140	141	129	114	97	79	61	44	29	16
37	116	130	141	150	155	155	152	144	133	119	102	85	66	49	34
38	94	111	126	139	149	155	156	153	146	137	124	107	90	72	54
39	72	90	107	123	137	147	154	156	154	149	140	127	111	95	77
40	50	66	84	101	118	132	143	152	156	156	151	142	131	116	100
41	32	46	62	79	97	114	128	140	149	155	155	151	144	134	120
42	18	28	41	57	74	92	109	124	137	146	152	154	151	146	137
43	10	15	24	37	52	68	86	103	119	133	143	150	153	152	148
44	9	8	12	21	33	48	64	81	98	114	128	140	147	151	151
45	14	9	8	12	19	29	43	58	75	93	109	123	135	143	149
46	25	16	10	8	10	16	26	39	54	70	87	103	118	130	140
47	43	30	19	12	9	9	15	24	36	50	65	81	98	113	126
48	63	47	34	23	14	10	10	13	21	31	45	60	76	92	106
49	86	69	53	38	26	17	12	10	13	19	29	41	55	70	86
50	107	91	74	57	42	30	22	13	11	12	17	26	37	50	65
51	127	112	97	80	63	48	35	24	17	13	13	16	24	34	46
52	142	130	117	102	85	68	53	39	28	20	15	15	17	22	31
53	151	144	134	122	106	90	74	58	44	33	23	17	15	16	21
54	155	152	147	138	126	111	96	80	64	49	37	27	21	17	17
55	150	153	152	148	140	129	117	102	86	70	56	43	33	25	20
56	140	147	151	151	147	141	132	120	106	91	76	61	48	37	29
57	124	136	144	150	151	148	143	135	124	111	97	82	67	54	43
58	103	118	131	140	146	149	149	145	138	129	117	103	89	75	60
59	82	98	113	126	137	143	148	148	146	140	132	121	108	95	81
60	61	76	92	107	121	131	139	145	148	147	142	134	125	113	100

When 224d.7 is subtracted from Arg. I., add 10.6 to Arg. XII.

Perturbations of Log. r, by Jupiter.

Horizontal Argument = I.

Constant added 80. Period of Argument I., 224d.7.

Arg. XIII.	d 0	d 8	d 16	d 24	d 32	d 40	d 48	d 56	d 64	d 72	d 80	d 88	d 96	d 104	d 112
0	81	61	46	35	28	27	31	39	50	61	72	80	85	88	88
1	100	81	62	47	35	29	28	32	39	49	60	69	76	80	82
2	119	100	80	62	46	34	28	27	31	38	48	57	66	72	76
3	136	119	99	79	60	44	33	27	26	30	38	46	55	63	69
4	150	136	118	97	76	57	42	31	26	25	30	37	45	54	61
5	159	149	134	115	94	73	54	39	29	24	25	29	36	45	53
6	165	160	148	132	112	90	69	50	36	27	23	21	29	37	45
7	165	165	158	145	128	107	85	64	47	33	25	22	24	30	38
8	161	165	163	155	141	123	102	80	60	43	31	24	23	25	32
9	153	161	164	161	151	137	117	96	75	56	40	29	24	24	28
10	142	154	160	161	157	147	131	112	91	71	52	38	29	25	26
11	129	142	152	158	158	153	141	125	106	86	67	50	37	30	27
12	114	127	140	149	155	154	148	136	120	101	82	63	48	37	31
13	99	112	125	138	147	151	150	143	131	115	97	78	62	48	39
14	85	96	109	123	135	143	147	146	139	127	111	94	76	61	49
15	72	82	93	107	120	132	140	144	142	135	123	108	91	75	61
16	61	67	77	90	104	118	129	138	141	139	132	121	106	90	75
17	54	56	63	74	87	101	116	128	136	140	137	130	119	104	89
18	48	48	51	59	70	84	100	114	127	135	139	136	129	118	104
19	46	42	42	46	55	67	83	99	114	127	135	138	136	128	117
20	45	39	36	37	42	52	66	82	99	115	128	136	139	136	128
21	47	39	33	31	32	39	50	66	83	101	118	130	138	140	136
22	49	40	32	27	25	29	37	50	67	86	104	121	133	140	141
23	51	43	34	27	22	21	26	36	51	70	80	108	125	136	142
24	54	47	37	28	21	18	19	26	37	54	73	94	113	129	140
25	56	49	41	32	23	17	15	18	26	40	58	78	99	118	133
26	57	53	45	37	27	19	14	14	18	29	44	63	84	105	123
27	57	55	49	42	33	24	17	13	14	20	32	49	68	90	110
28	57	56	52	46	39	30	22	15	13	15	23	37	54	74	95
29	57	56	55	51	45	37	28	20	15	14	18	27	41	59	80
30	56	57	56	54	50	44	36	27	20	16	16	21	31	46	64
31	56	57	57	57	55	50	43	35	27	21	17	18	24	35	50
32	56	56	58	59	58	56	51	44	36	28	22	19	21	27	39
33	58	58	58	60	61	61	58	52	45	37	29	23	21	23	30
34	62	60	59	61	63	64	64	60	54	46	37	30	24	22	24
35	67	63	62	63	65	68	69	67	63	56	47	38	30	24	22
36	74	68	65	65	67	70	72	73	71	66	58	48	39	30	24
37	83	75	70	68	70	72	76	78	77	74	68	59	49	38	28
38	91	83	77	73	73	75	78	82	83	82	77	70	59	48	36
39	100	91	84	80	78	79	81	85	87	88	85	80	70	59	46
40	108	100	93	87	84	83	85	88	91	93	92	88	81	70	57
41	114	108	102	95	91	89	80	91	94	97	97	96	90	81	68
42	118	115	110	104	99	95	94	95	97	100	102	102	98	91	80
43	120	120	117	112	107	102	99	99	100	102	105	106	104	99	90
44	117	122	122	119	115	110	106	104	104	105	107	109	109	106	99
45	111	120	124	124	121	117	113	109	108	108	109	111	112	111	107
46	102	115	123	126	126	123	119	115	112	111	111	112	114	114	112
47	91	108	119	126	129	128	125	121	117	114	113	113	115	116	116
48	77	96	111	122	129	131	129	126	121	117	115	114	115	116	117
49	62	82	101	115	125	131	132	129	125	121	117	115	115	116	118
50	48	69	88	105	118	127	131	131	128	124	119	116	115	115	117
51	34	53	74	93	109	121	128	131	130	126	121	117	114	113	115
52	23	40	60	79	97	112	122	128	129	127	122	118	114	112	112
53	16	29	46	65	84	100	113	122	126	125	122	118	113	110	110
54	12	21	34	51	69	87	102	113	120	122	121	117	112	109	107
55	14	17	26	39	56	73	89	102	112	116	117	115	111	107	104
56	20	17	21	31	44	59	75	89	101	108	112	111	109	105	102
57	30	23	21	25	34	47	61	76	89	98	104	106	105	102	99
58	44	32	25	24	28	37	49	62	76	87	95	99	100	98	96
59	62	46	34	27	26	30	39	50	62	74	84	90	93	94	92
60	81	61	46	35	28	27	31	39	50	61	72	80	85	88	88

The perturbations are in units of the eighth decimal place.

TABLE XXXV.

Perturbations of Log. r, by Jupiter.

Horizontal Argument = I.

Constant added 80. Period of Argument XIII., 60 units.

Arg. XIII.	120^d	128^d	136^d	144^d	152^d	160^d	168^d	176^d	184^d	192^d	200^d	208^d	216^d	224^d	232^d
0	87	86	86	89	96	105	116	129	141	150	156	156	150	139	123
1	83	82	82	84	89	97	108	121	135	147	156	160	159	152	139
2	78	79	79	80	84	90	100	112	126	140	152	160	163	161	152
3	73	75	75	77	79	84	92	103	116	130	144	156	163	165	161
4	67	70	72	73	75	79	85	94	106	120	134	148	159	165	165
5	60	65	69	71	72	74	79	86	96	108	123	137	150	160	165
6	53	60	65	68	70	71	74	79	87	98	111	125	139	151	160
7	46	54	60	65	67	69	71	74	80	88	99	112	126	140	151
8	40	48	56	62	65	68	69	71	74	80	88	99	112	126	139
9	35	43	51	58	63	66	68	69	70	73	79	87	98	111	125
10	31	38	46	54	61	65	67	68	68	69	71	77	85	96	109
11	30	35	43	51	58	63	66	67	66	66	66	68	74	82	93
12	30	34	40	47	55	61	65	67	66	65	63	63	65	70	79
13	34	34	38	45	52	59	64	66	66	64	62	59	58	60	65
14	41	38	39	43	50	57	62	65	66	65	62	57	54	53	55
15	50	44	42	44	48	55	61	63	66	66	62	57	52	48	47
16	62	52	47	46	48	53	59	63	66	66	63	58	52	46	42
17	75	63	54	50	50	52	57	61	65	66	64	60	53	46	40
18	89	75	64	57	53	53	56	60	63	65	65	61	55	47	40
19	103	89	76	66	59	56	56	58	61	64	64	62	57	50	41
20	117	103	89	76	67	61	58	58	60	62	62	62	59	52	44
21	128	116	102	88	76	67	61	59	59	61	61	62	60	55	47
22	137	127	115	101	87	75	67	61	59	59	60	61	60	56	50
23	142	137	126	113	99	85	74	66	60	59	59	59	59	57	53
24	144	143	136	124	110	96	83	72	64	60	58	58	58	58	55
25	142	145	142	134	121	107	92	79	69	62	58	57	57	57	55
26	136	144	145	141	131	118	103	88	75	66	60	57	56	56	57
27	127	138	144	144	138	127	113	98	84	72	63	58	56	56	56
28	114	130	140	144	142	134	122	108	93	80	68	61	57	56	56
29	100	118	132	140	142	139	130	117	102	88	75	65	60	57	56
30	84	103	120	132	139	140	134	124	111	98	84	72	64	59	58
31	69	88	106	121	132	137	136	130	119	106	92	80	70	63	60
32	54	72	90	107	122	131	134	132	124	114	101	89	77	69	64
33	41	57	74	92	108	121	128	130	127	120	109	97	86	76	69
34	31	43	59	75	93	108	119	126	127	123	116	106	95	85	76
35	25	32	44	59	86	92	107	117	123	123	120	113	103	93	84
36	22	24	32	44	59	76	92	105	115	120	121	117	110	102	93
37	22	20	24	31	44	59	75	91	104	113	119	119	116	110	102
38	26	20	18	22	30	43	58	75	90	103	113	118	118	116	110
39	33	23	17	16	20	29	42	58	75	90	104	113	118	119	116
40	43	30	20	14	13	17	27	42	58	75	91	105	114	119	120
41	54	39	26	15	10	10	16	27	42	59	77	93	106	116	121
42	66	50	35	21	11	6	7	15	27	43	61	80	96	110	119
43	78	62	46	30	16	7	3	6	15	28	45	64	83	100	113
44	89	75	59	41	25	12	4	1	6	16	31	49	68	88	104
45	99	87	72	54	37	21	9	2	1	6	18	34	53	74	93
46	107	97	84	68	50	33	17	6	1	1	8	21	39	59	79
47	113	106	96	82	65	47	29	15	5	0	3	12	25	44	65
48	117	113	106	94	79	62	44	27	14	5	2	6	16	31	50
49	118	117	113	105	93	78	60	42	26	13	6	4	9	21	37
50	118	120	119	114	105	93	77	59	42	26	14	8	8	14	27
51	117	120	121	120	115	106	93	76	59	42	26	16	11	12	19
52	114	118	121	123	122	116	107	93	77	60	41	28	18	14	16
53	111	115	119	123	125	124	119	109	95	78	61	44	30	21	18
54	108	111	116	122	126	128	128	122	111	97	80	62	45	32	24
55	104	107	112	118	125	130	133	131	125	114	99	82	64	47	34
56	100	102	106	113	121	129	135	137	136	129	117	101	83	65	49
57	97	98	101	107	116	125	134	140	143	140	132	119	103	84	66
58	94	94	96	101	109	119	130	139	146	148	144	135	121	104	85
59	90	90	91	95	102	112	124	136	146	151	152	148	138	122	104
60	87	86	86	89	96	105	116	129	141	150	156	156	150	139	123

When 224^d.7 is subtracted from Arg. I., add 3.11 to Arg. XIII.

TABLE XXXVI.

Perturbations of Log. r, by Saturn.

Horizontal Argument = I.

Constant added 25. Period of Argument I., 224d.7.

Arg. XIV.	0d	8d	16d	24d	32d	40d	48d	56d	64d	72d	80d	88d	96d	104d	112d
0	13	8	4	1	0	0	3	6	11	17	22	27	31	35	37
1	18	13	8	4	1	0	1	3	7	12	18	23	28	32	35
2	23	18	12	7	3	1	0	1	4	9	13	18	24	28	32
3	28	22	17	11	7	3	1	1	2	5	9	14	19	24	29
4	32	27	22	16	11	6	3	1	1	3	6	10	15	20	25
5	35	31	26	21	15	10	6	3	1	2	4	7	12	16	21
6	37	34	30	25	20	15	10	6	3	2	2	5	8	13	18
7	39	36	33	29	24	19	14	9	5	3	2	3	6	9	14
8	39	38	36	32	28	23	18	13	8	5	3	3	4	7	11
9	39	39	37	35	32	27	22	17	12	8	5	3	3	5	8
10	39	39	38	36	34	32	26	21	16	11	8	5	4	4	6
11	38	38	38	37	36	33	29	25	20	15	11	7	5	4	5
12	37	38	38	38	36	35	32	28	24	19	14	10	7	5	4
13	37	37	37	37	37	36	34	31	27	23	18	13	9	6	5
14	37	37	37	37	37	36	35	33	30	26	21	17	12	8	6
15	37	37	37	37	37	37	36	34	32	29	25	20	15	11	8
16	37	37	37	37	37	37	36	35	33	31	27	23	19	14	10
17	37	37	37	37	37	37	37	36	35	33	30	26	22	17	13
18	37	38	38	37	37	37	37	36	35	34	32	29	25	20	16
19	37	38	38	38	38	37	37	37	36	35	33	31	28	24	19
20	36	37	38	38	38	38	38	37	37	36	35	33	30	27	22
21	34	36	38	39	39	39	38	38	37	37	36	34	32	29	25
22	31	35	37	39	39	39	39	38	38	37	37	36	34	32	28
23	28	32	36	38	39	40	40	39	39	38	38	37	36	34	31
24	24	29	33	36	39	40	40	40	40	39	39	38	37	35	33
25	20	25	30	34	37	39	40	40	40	40	40	39	38	37	35
26	15	20	26	31	35	38	39	40	41	41	40	40	39	38	37
27	10	16	21	26	31	35	38	40	41	41	41	41	40	40	39
28	6	11	16	22	27	32	36	39	40	41	41	41	41	40	40
29	3	7	12	17	23	28	33	36	39	40	41	42	41	41	41
30	1	3	7	12	18	23	29	33	37	39	41	41	42	42	41
31	0	1	3	8	13	18	24	29	34	37	39	41	41	42	42
32	0	0	1	4	8	13	19	25	30	34	37	39	41	41	42
33	2	0	0	1	4	9	14	20	25	30	34	37	39	41	42
34	5	1	0	0	2	5	10	15	21	26	31	34	37	39	41
35	9	4	1	0	0	2	6	10	16	21	27	31	35	37	39
36	13	8	4	1	0	0	3	6	11	17	22	27	31	35	37

The perturbations are in units of the eighth decimal place.

Perturbations of Log. r, by Saturn.

Horizontal Argument = I

Constant added 25. Period of Argument XIV., 36 units.

Arg. XIV.	120^d	128^d	136^d	144^d	152^d	160^d	168^d	176^d	184^d	192^d	200^d	208^d	216^d	224^d	232^d
0	39	40	41	41	42	42	41	41	39	37	33	28	23	17	12
1	37	39	40	41	41	42	42	41	40	39	36	33	28	22	17
2	35	37	39	40	40	41	41	41	41	40	38	36	32	27	22
3	32	35	37	39	39	40	41	41	41	41	40	38	35	31	26
4	29	33	35	37	38	39	40	40	41	41	40	39	37	34	31
5	26	30	33	35	37	38	39	40	40	40	40	40	39	37	34
6	22	27	30	33	35	37	38	39	39	40	40	40	40	38	36
7	19	23	28	31	34	36	37	38	38	39	39	40	40	39	38
8	15	20	25	29	32	34	36	37	38	38	39	39	39	39	39
9	12	17	21	26	29	32	34	36	37	37	38	38	38	39	39
10	9	13	18	23	27	30	33	35	36	37	37	37	38	38	38
11	7	10	15	19	24	28	31	34	35	36	37	37	37	38	38
12	5	8	12	16	21	25	29	32	34	36	36	37	37	37	37
13	5	6	9	13	18	22	26	30	33	35	36	36	37	37	37
14	4	5	7	10	14	19	23	28	31	34	35	36	37	37	37
15	5	4	5	8	11	16	20	25	29	32	34	36	37	37	37
16	7	5	4	6	8	12	17	21	26	30	33	35	37	37	37
17	9	6	4	5	6	9	13	18	23	27	31	34	36	37	37
18	12	8	5	4	5	7	10	14	19	24	28	32	35	37	38
19	15	10	7	5	4	5	7	11	15	20	25	30	33	36	37
20	18	13	9	6	4	4	5	8	12	16	22	26	31	34	36
21	21	16	12	8	5	3	3	5	8	12	17	23	28	32	35
22	24	20	15	10	7	4	3	3	5	9	13	18	24	28	33
23	27	23	19	14	9	6	3	2	3	5	9	14	19	25	29
24	30	27	22	17	12	8	5	2	2	3	6	10	15	20	26
25	33	30	26	21	16	11	7	4	2	1	3	6	10	16	21
26	35	33	29	25	20	15	10	6	3	1	1	3	6	11	16
27	37	35	32	29	24	19	14	9	5	2	1	1	3	7	12
28	39	37	35	32	28	23	18	13	8	4	1	0	1	3	7
29	40	39	37	35	32	27	23	17	12	7	3	1	0	1	4
30	41	40	39	37	35	31	27	22	16	11	6	2	0	0	1
31	42	41	40	39	37	35	31	26	21	16	10	5	2	0	0
32	42	42	41	41	39	37	34	30	26	20	15	9	5	1	0
33	42	42	42	41	41	39	37	34	30	25	20	14	9	4	1
34	41	42	42	42	41	41	39	37	34	30	24	19	13	8	4
35	40	41	42	42	42	41	41	39	37	33	29	24	18	13	7
36	39	40	41	41	42	42	41	41	39	37	33	28	23	17	12

When 224^d.7 is subtracted from Arg. I. add 0.8 to Arg. XIV.

TABLE XXXVII.

Perturbations of the Latitude, by the Earth.

Horizontal Argument = I.

Constant added 0″.62. Period of Argument I., 224ᵈ.7.

Arg. XI.	0ᵈ	8ᵈ	16ᵈ	24ᵈ	32ᵈ	40ᵈ	48ᵈ	56ᵈ	64ᵈ	72ᵈ	80ᵈ	88ᵈ	96ᵈ	104ᵈ	112ᵈ
0	48	43	30	36	34	35	37	41	45	51	58	63	71	77	81
2	55	48	42	38	35	34	34	36	40	45	50	57	64	70	75
4	62	55	48	42	38	34	33	34	36	39	44	50	56	62	68
6	70	62	55	48	43	38	35	34	34	36	39	44	49	55	61
8	78	70	63	55	49	43	38	36	34	34	36	40	44	49	54
10	84	77	70	62	55	49	43	39	36	35	35	37	40	44	48
12	89	83	77	69	62	55	49	44	40	37	36	36	38	40	43
14	94	89	83	76	69	62	55	49	44	40	37	36	37	38	40
16	97	93	88	82	76	69	62	55	49	44	40	38	37	36	37
18	98	96	93	88	82	76	68	62	55	49	44	41	38	36	36
20	98	97	96	92	87	82	75	69	62	55	50	45	41	38	36
22	96	97	97	95	92	88	82	76	69	63	56	51	45	41	38
24	92	95	96	96	95	92	88	83	77	70	64	58	51	46	41
26	86	90	93	94	95	94	92	88	84	78	72	66	59	53	47
28	78	82	87	90	92	94	93	92	89	85	80	74	68	61	55
30	69	73	78	83	87	90	91	92	91	89	86	81	76	70	64
32	60	64	69	73	78	83	87	89	91	91	89	87	83	77	73
34	52	55	59	63	68	74	79	83	87	89	90	90	88	84	80
36	47	47	50	53	58	64	69	75	80	84	87	89	90	89	86
38	44	43	43	45	48	53	59	65	71	77	81	85	88	90	89
40	45	41	39	38	40	43	48	54	61	67	73	79	84	88	90
42	48	41	37	34	34	35	39	44	51	57	64	71	78	84	88
44	53	44	38	33	30	30	32	35	41	47	55	62	70	77	83
46	59	49	41	34	29	26	26	28	32	38	45	53	61	70	77
48	67	55	45	36	29	24	22	22	25	30	36	44	52	61	70
50	75	63	51	41	32	25	21	18	19	22	27	35	43	52	61
52	83	71	59	47	36	27	21	17	16	17	20	26	34	42	52
54	92	80	67	55	43	32	24	18	14	13	15	19	25	33	42
56	100	88	76	63	50	39	29	21	15	12	12	14	19	25	33
58	106	96	84	72	59	47	36	27	19	14	12	12	15	19	26
60	111	102	92	81	69	56	44	34	26	19	15	13	13	16	20
62	112	106	97	87	76	65	53	43	34	26	20	16	15	15	18
64	111	107	100	92	82	72	62	52	42	35	28	23	19	18	18
66	107	104	100	94	86	77	68	60	51	43	36	30	26	24	22
68	100	100	97	93	87	80	73	65	58	51	45	39	34	32	28
70	93	93	92	89	85	80	75	69	63	57	52	47	42	39	35
72	84	86	86	84	82	79	75	70	66	62	58	54	50	46	43
74	76	78	79	79	77	75	73	70	67	64	62	59	56	53	50
76	67	70	71	72	72	71	69	68	66	65	64	62	61	59	57
78	58	62	64	66	66	66	65	65	64	65	65	64	63	63	62
80	50	54	56	59	60	61	61	61	62	63	64	65	66	67	67
82	41	45	48	51	53	55	55	57	58	60	63	65	68	69	71
84	32	36	40	43	46	48	49	51	54	57	60	64	67	71	73
86	23	28	32	35	38	40	42	45	48	52	56	61	66	70	75
88	16	20	24	28	30	33	35	38	41	45	50	56	62	67	74
90	11	15	18	21	23	26	28	30	34	38	43	50	57	64	72
92	8	11	13	16	18	19	21	23	26	30	36	43	50	59	67
94	7	9	11	13	14	15	16	17	20	23	28	35	42	51	60
96	9	10	11	12	12	12	13	13	14	17	21	27	34	43	53
98	13	13	13	13	13	12	11	11	11	13	15	21	27	35	45
100	19	18	17	17	16	14	12	11	10	10	12	15	21	28	37
102	25	24	23	21	20	17	15	12	10	9	10	12	16	22	31
104	33	31	30	28	25	22	19	15	13	10	9	10	13	18	25
106	42	40	38	35	32	28	25	20	16	13	10	10	11	15	21
108	51	49	47	44	40	36	32	26	21	17	13	12	11	14	18
110	61	59	57	54	50	45	40	34	28	23	18	15	13	13	16
112	70	69	67	64	61	56	50	44	37	30	24	20	16	15	16
114	78	78	76	75	72	67	62	55	48	40	33	27	22	19	18
116	84	85	85	85	83	79	74	67	60	52	44	36	30	25	23
118	86	90	92	93	92	90	86	80	72	64	56	48	40	34	30
120	85	91	95	98	99	99	96	91	85	77	69	60	52	45	39

The perturbations are expressed in hundredths of a second of arc.

Perturbations of the Latitude, by the Earth.

Horizontal Argument = I.

Constant added 0''.52. Period of Argument XI., 240 units.

Arg. XI.	120^d	128^d	136^d	144^d	152^d	160^d	168^d	176^d	184^d	192^d	200^d	208^d	216^d	224^d	232^d
0	85	87	88	87	84	81	76	70	64	57	51	46	41	37	36
2	80	83	86	86	85	83	80	76	71	65	59	54	48	44	41
4	73	78	81	83	84	84	82	81	76	71	67	62	56	52	48
6	66	71	75	78	81	82	82	82	79	76	72	68	64	60	56
8	59	64	69	72	76	78	79	80	80	78	76	74	71	67	63
10	53	57	62	66	70	73	76	78	79	79	78	77	75	73	70
12	47	51	56	60	63	67	71	74	76	77	79	79	78	77	76
14	43	46	50	53	57	61	65	69	72	75	78	79	80	81	80
16	39	41	44	48	51	55	59	64	68	71	75	78	81	82	83
18	36	37	40	42	45	49	53	58	62	67	72	76	80	83	85
20	34	35	36	37	40	43	47	51	56	61	67	73	78	82	86
22	35	34	33	33	35	37	40	44	49	55	61	68	74	80	86
24	37	35	32	31	31	32	34	37	42	47	54	61	69	76	83
26	42	38	34	31	29	28	29	31	35	40	46	53	61	70	78
28	49	43	38	33	29	27	26	27	29	32	38	45	52	61	71
30	57	51	44	38	33	29	26	24	24	27	31	36	43	52	62
32	66	60	53	46	39	33	28	25	23	25	25	29	34	43	52
34	75	69	62	55	48	41	34	29	25	23	23	25	28	36	44
36	83	78	72	65	57	50	42	35	29	26	24	23	25	30	36
38	88	85	80	74	67	59	52	44	37	31	27	25	24	26	31
40	90	89	87	82	76	69	62	54	46	39	33	29	26	25	29
42	90	91	91	88	84	78	71	63	55	48	41	35	31	28	28
44	88	91	92	92	89	85	80	73	65	57	50	42	37	33	30
46	84	89	92	94	93	91	87	81	74	67	59	51	44	39	35
48	78	84	90	94	96	95	93	89	83	76	68	60	53	46	41
50	70	78	86	91	95	97	97	94	90	84	77	70	62	55	48
52	61	71	80	87	93	97	99	98	96	92	86	79	72	64	57
54	52	62	72	81	88	94	98	100	100	97	93	87	81	73	66
56	43	53	63	73	82	89	95	99	101	101	98	94	89	82	75
58	34	43	53	63	73	82	90	96	99	101	101	99	95	90	84
60	27	35	44	54	64	73	82	90	95	99	101	101	99	96	91
62	22	29	37	45	54	64	73	81	88	94	97	100	100	98	96
64	21	25	32	38	46	55	64	72	80	88	92	95	98	98	98
66	23	25	29	34	40	47	55	63	71	78	84	89	93	95	96
68	27	27	29	32	36	42	48	55	62	69	75	81	86	89	92
70	33	32	32	33	36	39	44	50	55	61	67	73	78	82	86
72	40	38	37	37	37	39	42	46	50	55	60	65	70	75	78
74	47	45	43	41	41	41	42	44	47	50	54	58	63	67	71
76	54	52	49	47	45	44	44	44	45	47	50	53	57	61	65
78	61	58	56	53	51	48	47	46	45	46	47	49	52	55	60
80	66	65	62	59	57	54	51	48	47	46	46	46	48	50	53
82	71	70	69	66	63	59	56	52	49	47	45	45	45	46	48
84	75	75	75	72	70	66	62	57	53	49	46	45	43	43	44
86	78	80	80	79	77	73	69	64	59	54	49	46	43	41	41
88	79	82	84	85	83	80	76	71	65	59	54	49	45	41	39
90	78	83	87	89	89	87	83	79	73	66	60	54	48	44	40
92	75	82	87	91	93	92	90	86	81	74	67	61	54	48	42
94	70	78	85	91	94	96	95	92	88	82	75	69	61	54	47
96	63	72	81	88	94	98	98	97	94	89	83	77	69	61	54
98	55	65	75	84	91	96	99	99	98	95	90	84	77	69	62
100	47	58	68	78	86	93	97	100	100	98	95	90	84	77	69
102	40	50	61	71	81	88	94	98	100	100	98	95	90	84	77
104	33	43	54	64	74	83	90	95	99	100	100	98	94	89	83
106	28	37	47	57	68	77	84	91	96	99	100	100	97	94	88
108	24	32	41	51	61	70	79	86	92	96	99	100	99	97	93
110	21	28	36	45	54	64	72	80	87	92	96	99	100	98	96
112	19	25	31	39	48	57	66	74	81	87	92	96	98	99	98
114	20	23	28	35	43	51	59	67	74	81	87	91	95	97	98
116	22	24	27	32	39	46	53	60	67	74	80	85	90	93	95
118	25	28	29	32	37	42	48	54	60	66	72	78	82	87	91
120	30	34	33	35	37	41	45	49	54	59	64	69	74	79	84

When 224^d.7 is subtracted from Arg. I., add 147.64 to Arg. XI.

TABLE XXXVII.

Perturbations of the Latitude, by the Earth.

Horizontal Argument = I.

Constant added 0″.62. Period of Argument I., $224^d.7$.

Arg. XI.	0^d	8^d	16^d	24^d	32^d	40^d	48^d	56^d	64^d	72^d	80^d	88^d	96^d	104^d	112^d
120	85	91	95	98	99	99	96	91	85	77	69	60	52	45	39
122	82	89	96	100	103	105	104	101	96	89	81	73	64	57	51
124	76	85	93	99	105	108	110	108	105	99	93	85	77	70	63
126	69	78	88	96	103	108	112	112	111	107	102	95	84	81	75
128	61	71	81	91	99	106	112	114	114	112	109	104	98	92	86
130	54	64	74	84	94	103	109	113	115	115	113	109	104	100	94
132	47	57	67	77	88	97	105	110	114	116	115	113	109	106	101
134	41	50	60	70	81	91	99	107	112	114	115	114	112	110	106
136	36	44	53	63	74	84	94	101	108	112	114	114	113	112	110
138	32	39	47	56	67	77	87	95	103	108	111	113	113	112	111
140	29	35	41	50	59	70	79	89	97	102	107	110	111	111	111
142	28	32	37	44	53	62	72	81	89	96	101	105	107	109	109
144	30	30	35	40	47	56	64	73	82	89	94	99	102	105	106
146	33	32	35	38	43	50	58	66	74	81	87	92	96	98	100
148	38	37	36	38	41	47	53	60	67	73	79	84	88	91	94
150	45	43	41	41	42	46	50	55	61	67	72	76	80	84	85
152	53	50	47	45	45	47	49	53	57	62	66	69	73	77	78
154	61	57	54	51	50	50	51	53	56	59	62	64	67	69	70
156	68	61	61	58	56	55	55	55	56	58	60	61	62	63	64
158	73	71	68	65	62	61	59	59	59	59	59	59	59	59	59
160	77	76	74	72	69	67	65	63	62	61	60	59	57	56	55
162	80	80	79	77	75	73	70	68	66	63	62	59	57	54	52
164	83	83	83	83	81	79	76	74	71	68	65	61	58	54	50
166	83	66	87	87	87	85	83	80	77	73	69	64	60	54	50
168	83	87	90	91	92	91	89	87	83	79	74	68	63	56	50
170	80	86	90	94	96	96	95	94	90	86	80	74	67	60	52
172	75	83	89	94	98	100	100	100	97	93	88	81	73	65	56
174	69	77	85	92	98	102	104	105	103	100	95	89	81	72	62
176	60	70	79	87	95	101	105	108	108	106	103	97	89	80	69
178	51	61	71	80	89	97	103	108	110	110	108	104	97	88	78
180	42	52	61	72	81	91	98	105	110	112	112	109	104	96	87
182	35	43	52	62	72	82	91	99	106	110	112	111	108	102	94
184	29	35	43	52	62	72	82	91	99	105	109	111	110	106	100
186	26	31	36	44	53	62	72	82	90	98	104	107	108	107	103
188	26	28	32	38	45	53	62	72	81	89	96	101	104	106	103
190	29	28	30	34	39	46	54	62	71	80	87	94	98	101	101
192	33	31	30	32	35	40	47	54	61	70	78	85	91	94	97
194	40	35	33	32	34	37	41	46	53	61	68	75	82	87	91
196	47	41	37	35	34	35	37	41	46	52	59	66	72	78	83
198	56	48	43	39	36	35	35	37	40	45	50	56	62	68	74
200	65	57	51	45	41	38	36	35	36	39	43	47	53	59	65
202	74	67	60	53	47	42	39	36	35	35	37	40	44	49	54
204	83	76	69	62	55	49	44	39	36	34	34	35	37	41	45
206	91	85	78	71	64	58	51	45	40	37	34	33	33	35	37
208	96	92	86	80	74	67	60	53	47	42	37	33	31	31	31
210	99	96	92	88	82	76	69	62	55	49	43	37	33	30	29
212	98	97	96	93	89	84	78	72	64	58	50	44	38	33	29
214	94	96	96	95	92	89	85	79	73	67	59	52	45	38	33
216	89	91	93	94	93	92	89	86	81	75	68	61	53	46	39
218	82	85	88	90	92	92	91	89	86	81	76	69	62	55	47
220	74	78	82	85	88	90	91	91	89	86	82	77	70	63	55
222	67	71	75	79	83	86	88	90	90	89	86	82	77	70	63
224	60	64	68	73	77	81	84	87	89	89	88	86	82	77	70
226	55	58	62	66	71	75	80	84	87	88	89	88	86	82	76
228	50	52	55	60	65	69	74	79	83	86	89	89	88	86	82
230	46	47	50	54	58	63	68	74	79	83	87	89	89	88	86
232	43	43	45	48	52	57	62	68	74	79	84	87	89	90	88
234	41	40	41	43	46	50	55	61	67	73	79	83	87	89	90
236	41	39	38	39	40	44	48	54	60	66	73	79	83	87	89
238	44	40	37	36	36	39	42	47	52	59	65	72	78	83	86
240	48	43	39	36	34	35	37	41	45	51	58	65	71	77	81

The perturbations are expressed in hundredths of a second of arc.

TABLE XXXVII.

Perturbations of the Latitude, by the Earth.

Horizontal Argument = I.

Constant added 0″.62. Period of Argument XI, 240 units.

Arg. XI.	120^d	128^d	136^d	144^d	152^d	160^d	168^d	176^d	184^d	192^d	200^d	208^d	216^d	224^d	232^d
120	36	34	33	35	37	41	45	49	54	59	64	69	74	79	84
122	46	43	41	41	41	43	45	47	50	54	57	61	65	70	75
124	58	54	50	48	47	47	47	48	49	51	52	55	57	61	65
126	69	65	61	58	56	54	53	52	51	51	50	50	51	53	56
128	81	76	72	69	67	64	62	59	56	54	51	49	48	48	49
130	90	86	83	80	77	74	71	68	64	60	55	51	47	45	44
132	98	95	92	90	87	84	81	77	73	69	61	55	49	45	42
134	104	101	99	98	95	93	91	87	82	76	68	62	54	47	42
136	108	107	105	104	103	101	99	96	91	85	78	70	61	52	45
138	111	109	109	109	108	106	108	104	100	94	87	78	69	59	49
140	111	111	111	112	112	112	114	111	108	103	95	87	77	67	55
142	110	110	112	113	114	116	118	116	114	110	104	95	85	75	63
144	107	108	110	113	115	117	119	120	119	116	111	103	94	83	71
146	102	104	107	110	113	116	119	122	122	121	117	110	102	91	79
148	96	99	102	105	109	113	117	121	123	123	121	116	109	99	88
150	89	91	95	98	103	108	113	118	121	123	122	119	114	106	96
152	81	83	86	90	95	100	106	112	117	120	121	120	117	110	102
154	72	74	77	81	86	91	97	104	110	114	117	118	116	112	106
156	65	66	68	71	76	81	87	94	101	106	111	113	114	111	107
158	59	59	60	63	66	71	77	84	90	97	102	106	108	108	105
160	54	53	53	54	57	61	66	73	80	86	92	97	100	101	101
162	50	48	47	48	49	53	57	63	69	76	82	87	91	94	94
164	47	44	42	41	42	44	48	53	59	66	72	77	82	85	87
166	45	41	38	36	36	37	40	44	50	56	62	68	73	77	79
168	44	38	34	31	30	30	32	36	41	46	53	59	64	68	71
170	45	37	32	27	24	23	24	27	32	37	43	49	55	59	63
172	47	38	31	25	20	18	18	19	23	28	34	40	46	51	55
174	52	41	32	24	18	14	12	12	15	19	25	30	36	42	46
176	58	47	36	26	19	12	9	7	8	11	16	22	27	33	38
178	67	54	42	31	22	14	8	5	4	6	9	14	19	24	29
180	75	63	50	38	27	17	10	5	2	2	4	8	12	17	21
182	84	72	59	47	35	24	15	8	3	2	2	4	7	11	15
184	91	80	67	56	44	32	21	13	7	5	2	3	5	7	11
186	96	87	76	64	52	40	29	20	13	9	5	5	5	7	9
188	99	92	83	72	61	49	38	28	21	14	11	8	8	8	10
190	99	94	87	78	68	58	47	37	29	22	17	14	13	12	12
192	96	94	89	82	74	65	55	45	37	30	25	21	19	17	16
194	92	92	89	84	78	71	62	53	46	39	33	29	26	24	22
196	86	88	87	85	81	75	68	60	54	48	42	38	34	32	30
198	79	82	83	83	81	77	72	67	61	56	51	47	43	40	38
200	70	74	77	79	79	78	75	71	67	63	59	55	52	50	47
202	60	65	69	72	74	75	75	73	71	69	66	64	62	59	57
204	50	55	60	64	68	70	72	73	73	73	72	71	70	69	67
206	40	45	50	54	59	63	67	70	72	74	75	76	76	77	76
208	33	36	40	45	50	54	59	64	68	72	75	78	80	83	84
210	28	30	32	36	40	45	50	56	61	67	72	77	81	85	89
212	27	26	26	29	32	36	41	47	53	60	66	73	79	85	90
214	28	26	24	24	25	29	33	38	44	51	59	66	74	82	89
216	33	28	25	23	22	23	27	31	36	43	50	58	67	76	85
218	40	34	29	25	22	21	23	25	29	35	42	51	59	69	79
220	48	41	34	29	24	22	21	22	25	29	35	43	51	61	71
222	56	47	41	34	28	24	22	21	22	25	30	36	45	54	64
224	63	56	48	41	34	29	25	22	22	23	26	31	38	47	57
226	70	63	55	48	40	34	29	25	23	22	24	28	33	41	50
228	76	70	63	55	47	40	34	29	25	23	23	25	30	36	44
230	81	76	69	62	54	47	40	34	29	25	24	25	27	32	39
232	86	81	76	69	62	54	47	40	34	29	26	25	26	29	34
234	88	86	81	76	69	62	55	47	41	34	30	28	27	28	32
236	89	88	86	81	76	69	62	55	48	41	36	32	29	29	31
238	88	89	88	85	81	76	70	63	56	49	43	38	34	32	33
240	85	87	88	87	84	81	76	70	64	57	51	46	41	37	36

When $224^d.7$ is subtracted from Arg. I., add 147.64 to Arg. XI.

TABLE XXXVIII.

Perturbations of the Latitude, by Jupiter.

Horizontal Argument = I.

Constant added 0″.21. Period of Argument I., 224d.7.

Arg. XIII.	0d	8d	16d	24d	32d	40d	48d	56d	64d	72d	80d	88d	96d	104d	112d
0	17	14	11	9	7	6	5	5	6	6	8	10	12	15	18
1	21	18	15	12	9	7	6	5	4	5	5	7	9	12	15
2	25	22	18	15	12	9	7	5	4	4	4	5	6	9	11
3	29	26	22	19	15	12	9	7	5	4	3	3	4	6	8
4	32	29	26	22	19	15	12	9	6	5	3	3	3	4	6
5	35	32	29	26	22	19	15	12	9	6	4	3	3	3	4
6	37	35	32	29	26	22	18	15	11	8	6	4	3	3	3
7	38	37	35	32	29	26	22	18	15	11	8	6	4	3	3
8	39	38	37	34	32	29	25	22	18	14	11	9	6	5	4
9	39	38	38	36	34	31	28	25	21	18	15	12	9	7	5
10	37	38	38	37	35	33	31	29	24	21	18	15	12	10	8
11	36	37	37	37	36	34	32	30	27	24	21	18	15	13	11
12	33	35	36	36	36	35	34	32	30	27	24	22	19	16	14
13	30	32	34	35	35	35	34	33	31	29	27	25	22	20	17
14	27	29	31	32	33	34	34	34	33	31	29	27	25	23	21
15	23	26	28	30	31	32	33	33	33	32	31	30	28	26	24
16	20	23	25	27	28	30	31	32	33	33	32	31	30	29	27
17	17	19	21	23	25	27	29	31	32	32	33	33	32	31	30
18	14	16	18	20	22	24	27	29	30	32	33	33	33	33	32
19	11	13	15	17	19	21	24	26	28	30	32	33	34	34	34
20	9	10	12	14	16	18	21	23	26	28	30	32	34	34	35
21	8	8	9	11	13	15	18	20	23	26	28	31	33	34	35
22	7	7	7	9	10	12	15	18	20	23	26	29	32	34	35
23	7	6	6	7	8	10	12	15	18	21	24	27	30	32	34
24	7	6	5	6	6	8	10	12	15	18	21	25	28	31	33
25	8	6	5	5	5	6	8	10	13	15	19	22	25	28	31
26	9	7	6	5	5	5	6	8	10	13	16	19	23	26	29
27	11	9	7	6	5	5	5	6	8	11	14	17	20	24	27
28	14	11	8	7	5	5	5	6	7	9	12	15	18	21	24
29	16	13	10	8	6	5	5	5	6	8	10	12	15	18	22
30	19	16	13	10	8	6	6	5	6	7	8	10	13	16	19
31	21	18	15	12	10	8	7	6	6	6	7	9	11	14	16
32	24	21	18	15	12	10	8	7	7	6	7	8	10	12	14
33	27	24	21	18	15	13	11	9	8	7	7	7	9	10	12
34	29	26	24	21	18	15	13	11	9	8	7	7	8	9	10
35	31	29	26	24	21	18	16	14	11	10	9	8	8	8	9
36	33	31	29	27	24	22	19	16	14	12	10	9	8	7	7
37	34	33	31	30	27	25	22	19	17	14	12	10	9	8	7
38	35	34	33	32	30	28	25	23	20	17	15	12	10	8	7
39	35	35	35	34	33	31	29	26	23	20	18	15	12	10	8
40	35	36	36	36	35	34	32	29	27	24	21	17	15	12	9
41	34	35	36	37	37	36	34	32	30	27	24	20	17	14	11
42	32	34	36	37	38	38	37	35	33	30	27	24	20	17	13
43	30	33	35	37	39	39	39	37	36	33	31	27	24	20	16
44	28	31	34	36	38	39	40	39	38	36	34	30	27	23	19
45	25	28	32	35	37	39	40	40	40	39	36	34	30	26	22
46	22	25	29	33	36	38	40	41	41	40	39	36	33	30	26
47	18	22	26	30	34	37	39	41	41	41	40	38	36	33	29
48	15	19	23	27	31	35	37	40	41	41	41	40	38	35	32
49	12	16	20	24	28	32	35	38	40	41	41	41	39	37	35
50	9	12	16	20	25	28	32	35	38	40	41	41	40	39	37
51	6	9	13	17	21	25	29	32	35	38	39	40	40	39	38
52	5	7	10	14	17	21	25	29	32	35	37	38	39	39	39
53	4	5	8	11	14	17	21	25	28	31	34	36	38	38	38
54	3	4	6	8	11	14	17	21	24	27	30	33	35	37	38
55	4	4	5	6	8	11	14	17	20	23	27	30	32	34	36
56	5	4	4	5	7	8	11	13	16	19	23	26	28	31	33
57	7	6	5	5	5	7	8	10	13	15	18	21	24	27	30
58	10	8	6	6	5	5	6	8	9	12	14	17	20	23	26
59	13	11	9	7	6	5	5	6	7	9	11	14	16	19	22
60	17	14	11	9	7	6	5	5	5	6	8	10	12	15	18

The perturbations are expressed in hundredths of a second of arc.

Perturbations of the Latitude, by Jupiter.

Horizontal Argument = I.

Constant added 0″.21. Period of Argument XIII., 60 units.

Arg. XIII.	120ᵈ	128ᵈ	136ᵈ	144ᵈ	152ᵈ	160ᵈ	168ᵈ	176ᵈ	184ᵈ	192ᵈ	200ᵈ	208ᵈ	216ᵈ	224ᵈ	232ᵈ
0	22	25	28	31	33	35	37	38	38	37	36	35	32	29	26
1	18	21	25	28	31	34	36	37	38	38	38	37	35	33	30
2	14	18	21	25	28	31	34	36	38	39	39	39	37	35	33
3	11	14	17	21	25	28	31	34	36	38	39	39	39	37	35
4	8	11	14	17	21	25	28	32	34	37	38	39	39	38	37
5	6	8	11	14	18	21	25	29	32	34	37	38	39	39	38
6	4	6	8	11	14	18	22	25	29	32	34	36	38	38	39
7	3	5	6	9	12	15	18	22	25	29	32	34	36	37	38
8	4	4	5	7	9	12	15	19	22	25	28	31	33	35	36
9	5	4	5	6	8	10	13	16	19	22	25	28	30	32	34
10	6	6	5	6	7	9	11	13	16	19	22	24	27	29	32
11	9	7	7	7	7	8	9	11	13	16	18	21	24	26	28
12	12	10	9	8	8	8	8	10	11	13	15	18	20	23	25
13	15	13	11	10	9	8	8	9	10	11	13	15	17	19	22
14	18	16	14	12	11	10	9	9	9	10	11	12	14	16	18
15	22	19	17	15	13	12	10	10	9	9	10	10	12	13	15
16	25	23	21	18	16	14	12	11	10	9	9	9	10	11	12
17	28	26	24	22	19	17	15	13	11	10	9	8	8	9	10
18	31	29	27	25	22	20	17	15	13	11	9	8	8	7	8
19	33	32	30	28	26	23	20	18	15	13	11	9	7	7	7
20	35	34	32	31	29	26	23	20	17	15	12	10	8	7	6
21	35	35	34	33	31	29	26	23	20	17	14	11	9	7	6
22	36	36	36	35	33	31	29	26	23	20	16	13	11	8	7
23	36	36	37	36	35	33	31	28	26	22	19	16	13	10	8
24	35	36	37	37	37	35	33	31	28	25	22	18	15	12	9
25	34	35	37	37	37	36	35	33	30	27	24	21	17	14	11
26	32	34	36	37	37	37	36	34	32	29	27	23	20	17	14
27	30	32	34	36	37	37	37	35	34	31	29	25	22	19	16
28	27	30	33	35	36	37	37	36	35	33	31	28	25	22	19
29	25	28	30	33	35	36	36	36	36	34	32	30	27	25	21
30	22	25	28	30	32	34	35	36	36	35	34	32	30	27	24
31	19	22	25	28	30	32	34	35	35	35	34	33	31	29	27
32	17	19	22	25	28	30	32	33	34	35	35	34	33	31	29
33	14	17	19	22	25	27	29	31	33	34	35	34	34	33	31
34	12	14	16	19	22	24	27	29	31	33	34	34	34	34	33
35	10	11	13	16	18	21	24	26	29	31	32	34	34	35	34
36	8	9	11	13	15	18	21	23	26	28	31	32	34	35	35
37	7	8	9	10	12	15	17	20	23	25	28	31	33	34	36
38	6	6	7	8	10	11	14	17	20	23	26	29	31	33	35
39	6	6	6	6	7	9	11	13	16	19	23	26	29	32	34
40	7	6	5	4	5	6	8	10	13	16	20	23	26	30	33
41	8	6	5	4	3	4	5	7	10	13	16	20	23	27	31
42	10	7	5	3	3	3	3	5	7	10	13	16	20	24	28
43	12	9	6	4	3	2	2	3	4	7	10	13	17	21	25
44	15	11	8	5	3	2	1	1	2	4	7	10	14	18	22
45	18	14	10	7	4	2	1	1	1	2	4	7	11	14	18
46	22	17	13	10	6	4	2	1	0	1	2	5	8	11	15
47	25	21	17	13	9	6	3	2	1	1	1	3	5	8	12
48	28	24	20	16	12	9	6	3	2	1	1	2	4	6	9
49	31	28	24	19	15	12	8	6	4	2	1	2	3	4	7
50	34	31	27	23	19	15	12	9	6	4	3	2	2	3	5
51	36	33	30	27	23	19	16	12	9	7	5	4	3	3	4
52	37	35	33	30	26	23	19	16	13	10	8	6	4	4	4
53	38	37	35	33	30	27	23	20	17	14	11	9	7	6	5
54	38	37	36	35	33	30	27	24	21	18	15	12	10	8	6
55	37	37	37	36	35	33	30	28	25	22	19	16	13	11	8
56	35	36	37	37	36	35	33	31	29	26	23	20	17	14	11
57	32	34	36	36	37	36	35	34	32	30	27	24	21	18	15
58	29	32	34	35	36	37	37	36	35	33	31	28	25	22	19
59	26	29	31	34	35	37	37	37	37	35	34	31	29	26	22
60	22	25	28	31	33	35	37	38	38	37	36	35	32	29	26

When 224ᵈ.7 is subtracted from Arg. I., add 3.11 to Arg. XIII.

Values, for the beginning of the year, of K_x, K_y, &c., and of the Arguments of Nutation, for Washington Mean Noon of Jan. 0 in Common Years and Jan. 1 in Bissextile Years.

Year.	K_x.	K_y.	K_z.	Log k_x.	Log k_y.	Log k_z.	XV.	XVI.
							d	d
1750	89° 58′ 6″.44	1° 26′ 53″.89	352° 48′ 5″.43	9.9992934	9.9595611	9.6191304	1504.7	1.9
1751	6.48	54.03	3.51	2933	5633	1202	1869.7	1.7
1752 B.	6.53	54.17	352 48 1.60	2932	5655	1100	2235.7	2.4
1753	6.57	54.31	352 47 59.68	2932	5677	0997	2600.7	2.2
1754	6.61	54.45	57.77	2931	5699	0895	2965.7	2.0
1755	6.65	54.59	55.86	2931	5722	0793	3330.7	1.7
1756 B.	6.69	54.73	53.95	2930	5744	0691	3696.7	2.5
1757	6.73	54.87	52.01	2930	5766	0589	4061.7	2.2
1758	6.77	55.00	50.13	2929	5788	0486	4426.7	2.0
1759	6.81	55.14	48.22	2928	5810	0384	4791.7	1.7
1760 B.	6.86	55.28	46.31	2928	5832	0282	5157.7	2.5
1761	6.91	55.42	44.40	2927	5854	0180	5522.7	2.3
1762	6.96	55.56	42.49	2926	5876	9.6190077	5887.7	2.0
1763	7.02	55.70	40.58	2926	5899	9.6189975	6252.7	1.8
1764 B.	7.08	55.84	38.68	2925	5921	9873	6618.7	2.5
1765	7.13	55.97	36.77	2924	5943	9770	185.5	2.3
1766	7.18	56.11	34.87	2923	5965	9668	550.5	2.0
1767	7.24	56.25	32.96	2923	5987	9565	915.5	1.8
1768 B.	7.30	56.39	31.06	2922	6009	9463	1281.5	2.6
1769	7.35	56.52	29.15	2921	6031	9360	1646.5	2.3
1770	7.40	56.66	27.25	2920	6053	9258	2011.5	2.1
1771	7.44	56.80	25.35	2920	6076	9156	2376.5	1.8
1772 B.	7.48	56.94	23.44	2919	6098	9053	2742.5	2.6
1773	7.52	57.07	21.54	2919	6120	8951	3107.5	2.3
1774	7.57	57.21	19.64	2918	6142	8848	3472.5	2.1
1775	7.61	57.35	17.74	2918	6164	8746	3837.5	1.9
1776 B.	7.65	57.48	15.84	2917	6186	8644	4203.5	2.6
1777	7.69	57.62	13.94	2916	6208	8541	4568.5	2.4
1778	7.73	57.75	12.01	2916	6230	8439	4933.5	2.1
1779	7.78	57.89	10.14	2915	6252	8336	5298.5	1.9
1780 B.	7.83	58.03	8.24	2914	6275	8234	5664.5	2.6
1781	7.88	58.16	6.34	2914	6297	8132	6029.5	2.4
1782	7.94	58.30	4.44	2913	6319	8029	6394.5	2.2
1783	8.00	58.43	2.54	2912	6341	7927	6759.5	1.9
1784 B.	8.06	58.57	352 47 0.65	2911	6363	7824	327.2	2.7
1785	8.11	58.70	352 46 58.75	2911	6385	7722	692.2	2.4
1786	8.17	58.84	56.86	2910	6407	7619	1057.2	2.2
1787	8.23	58.97	54.96	2909	6429	7517	1422.2	1.9
1788 B.	8.28	59.11	53.07	2909	6452	7414	1788.2	2.7
1789	8.32	59.24	51.17	2908	6474	7312	2153.2	2.5
1790	8.36	59.38	49.28	2907	6496	7209	2518.2	2.2
1791	8.40	59.51	47.39	2907	6518	7106	2883.2	2.0
1792 B.	8.44	59.64	45.50	2906	6540	7004	3249.2	2.7
1793	8.48	59.78	43.60	2906	6562	6901	3614.2	2.5
1794	8.53	1 26 59.91	41.71	2905	6584	6799	3979.2	2.2
1795	8.57	1 27 0.05	39.82	2905	6606	6696	4344.2	2.0
1796 B.	8.61	0.18	37.93	2904	6629	6593	4710.2	2.8
1797	8.65	0.31	36.04	2903	6651	6491	5075.2	2.5
1798	8.70	0.45	34.15	2903	6673	6388	5440.2	2.3
1799	89 58 8.76	1 27 0.58	352 46 32.26	9.9992902	9.9596695	9.6186286	5805.2	2.0

From each of the quantities K_x, K_y and K_z the constant 20″.00 has been subtracted; and from log k_y the constant 0.0000089, and from log k_z the constant 0.0000560

TABLE XXXIX.

Values, for the beginning of the year, of K_x, K_y, &c., and of the Arguments of Nutation, for Washington Mean Noon of Jan. 0 in Common Years and Jan. 1 in Bissextile Years.

Year.	K_x.	K_y.	K_z.	Log k_x.	Log k_y.	Log k_z.	XV.	XVI.
1800	89° 58′ 8″.82	1° 27′ 0″.71	352° 46′ 30″.37	9.9992901	9.9596717	9.6186183	6170ᵈ.2	1ᵈ.8
1801	8.88	0.84	28.48	2900	6739	6080	6535.2	1.5
1802	8.93	0.98	26.59	2900	6761	5978	102.0	1.3
1803	8.98	1.11	24.70	2899	6783	5875	467.0	1.0
1804 *B.*	9.04	1.24	22.81	2898	6806	5773	833.0	1.8
1805	9.09	1.37	20.93	2897	6828	5670	1198.0	1.6
1806	9.15	1.51	19.04	2897	6850	5567	1563.0	1.3
1807	9.20	1.64	17.16	2896	6872	5464	1928.0	1.1
1808 *B.*	9.24	1.77	15.27	2896	6894	5362	2294.0	1.8
1809	9.29	1.90	13.39	2895	6916	5259	2659.0	1.6
1810	9.33	2.03	11.50	2894	6939	5156	3024.0	1.4
1811	9.37	2.16	9.62	2894	6961	5053	3389.0	1.1
1812 *B.*	9.41	2.30	7.74	2893	6983	4950	3755.0	1.9
1813	9.45	2.43	5.85	2893	7015	4848	4120.0	1.6
1814	9.49	2.56	3.97	2892	7037	4745	4485.0	1.4
1815	9.53	2.69	2.09	2892	7059	4642	4850.0	1.1
1816 *B.*	9.58	2.82	352 46 0.21	2891	7082	4539	5216.0	1.9
1817	9.63	2.95	352 45 58.33	2890	7104	4436	5581.0	1.7
1818	9.69	3.08	56.45	2890	7126	4334	5946.0	1.4
1819	9.75	3.21	54.57	2889	7148	4231	6311.0	1.2
1820 *B.*	9.80	3.34	52.69	2888	7170	4128	6677.0	1.9
1821	9.85	3.47	50.81	2887	7192	4025	243.7	1.7
1822	9.91	3.60	48.93	2887	7215	3922	608.7	1.4
1823	9.97	3.73	47.06	2886	7237	3820	973.7	1.2
1824 *B.*	10.03	3.86	45.18	2885	7259	3717	1339.7	2.0
1825	10.08	3.99	43.30	2885	7281	3614	1704.7	1.7
1826	10.13	4.12	41.43	2884	7303	3511	2069.7	1.5
1827	11.17	4.25	39.55	2883	7325	3408	2434.7	1.2
1828 *B.*	10.21	4.38	37.68	2883	7347	3305	2800.7	2.0
1829	10.25	4.51	35.80	2882	7370	3202	3165.7	1.7
1830	10.29	4.63	33.93	2882	7392	3099	3530.7	1.5
1831	10.33	4.76	32.06	2881	7414	2996	3805.7	1.3
1832 *B.*	10.37	4.89	30.19	2881	7436	2893	4261.7	2.0
1833	10.42	5.02	28.31	2880	7458	2790	4626.7	1.8
1834	10.46	5.15	26.44	2879	7480	2687	4991.7	1.5
1835	10.51	5.28	24.57	2879	7503	2584	5356.7	1.3
1836 *B.*	10.57	5.40	22.70	2878	7525	2481	5722.7	2.0
1837	10.62	5.53	20.83	2877	7547	2378	6087.7	1.8
1838	10.68	5.66	18.96	2877	7569	2275	6452.7	1.6
1839	10.73	5.79	17.09	2876	7591	2172	19.4	1.3
1840 *B.*	10.78	5.91	15.22	2875	7613	2069	385.4	2.1
1841	10.84	6.04	13.35	2875	7636	1966	750.4	1.8
1842	10.90	6.17	11.48	2874	7658	1863	1115.4	1.6
1843	10.95	6.30	9.62	2873	7680	1760	1480.4	1.3
1844 *B.*	11.01	6.42	7.75	2872	7702	1657	1846.4	2.1
1845	11.06	6.55	5.88	2872	7724	1554	2211.4	1.9
1846	11.10	6.67	4.01	2871	7746	1451	2576.4	1.6
1847	11.14	6.80	2.15	2871	7769	1348	2941.4	1.4
1848 *B.*	11.18	6.93	352 45 0.28	2870	7791	1245	3307.4	2.1
1849	89 58 11.22	1 27 7.05	352 44 58.42	9.9992870	9.9597813	9.6181142	3672.4	1.9

From each of the quantities K_x, K_y and K_z, the constant 20″.00 has been subtracted; and from log k_y the constant 0.0000080, and from log k_z the constant 0.0000560.

TABLE XXXIX.

Values, for the beginning of the year, of K_x, K_y, &c., and of the Arguments of Nutation, for Washington Mean Noon of Jan. 0 in Common Years and Jan. 1 in Bissextile Years.

Year.	K_x.	K_y.	K_z.	Log k_x.	Log k_y.	Log k_z.	XV.	XVI.
	° ′ ″	° ′ ″	° ′ ″				d	d
1850	89 58 11.27	1 27 7.18	352 44 56.55	9.9992869	9.9597825	9.6181039	4037.4	1.6
1851	11.31	7.31	54.69	2869	7847	0936	4402.4	1.4
1852 *B.*	11.35	7.43	52.83	2868	7869	0833	4768.4	2.2
1853	11.40	7.56	50.96	2867	7891	0729	5133.4	1.9
1854	11.44	7.68	49.10	2867	7914	0626	5498.4	1.7
1855	11.50	7.81	47.24	2866	7936	0523	5863.4	1.4
1856 *B.*	11.56	7.93	45.38	2865	7958	0420	6229.4	2.2
1857	11.62	8.06	43.52	2865	7980	0317	6594.4	1.9
1858	11.67	8.18	41.66	2864	8002	0213	161.2	1.7
1859	11.73	8.31	39.80	2863	8024	0110	526.2	1.5
1860 *B.*	11.79	8.43	37.94	2863	8046	9.6180007	892.2	2.2
1861	11.84	8.56	36.08	2862	8069	9.6179904	1257.2	2.0
1862	11.89	8.68	34.22	2861	8091	9801	1622.2	1.7
1863	11.94	8.80	32.37	2861	8113	9697	1987.2	1.5
1864 *B.*	11.99	8.93	30.51	2860	8135	9594	2353.2	2.2
1865	12.03	9.05	28.65	2859	8157	9491	2718.2	2.0
1866	12.07	9.18	26.79	2859	8179	9388	3083.2	1.8
1867	12.11	9.30	24.94	2858	8201	9285	3448.2	1.5
1868 *B.*	12.15	9.42	23.08	2858	8224	9181	3814.2	2.3
1869	12.19	9.55	21.23	2857	8246	9078	4179.2	2.0
1870	12.24	9.67	19.37	2857	8268	8975	4544.2	1.8
1871	12.28	9.79	17.52	2856	8290	8872	4909.2	1.5
1872 *B.*	12.33	9.92	15.67	2856	8312	8768	5275.2	2.3
1873	12.39	10.04	13.81	2855	8334	8665	5640.2	2.1
1874	12.44	10.16	11.96	2854	8356	8561	6005.2	1.8
1875	12.50	10.28	10.11	2854	8378	8458	6370.2	1.6
1876 *B.*	12.56	10.40	8.26	2853	8401	8355	6736.2	2.3
1877	12.62	10.53	6.41	2852	8423	8251	302.9	2.1
1878	12.67	10.65	4.56	2851	8445	8148	667.9	1.8
1879	12.73	10.77	2.71	2851	8467	8044	1032.9	1.6
1880 *B.*	12.78	10.89	352 44 0.86	2850	8489	7941	1398.9	2.4
1881	12.83	11.01	352 43 59.01	2849	8511	7838	1763.9	2.1
1882	12.88	11.14	57.16	2849	8533	7734	2128.9	1.9
1883	12.93	11.26	55.32	2848	8556	7631	2493.9	1.6
1884 *B.*	12.97	11.38	53.47	2848	8578	7528	2859.9	2.4
1885	13.01	11.50	51.62	2847	8600	7424	3224.9	2.1
1886	13.05	11.62	49.77	2847	8622	7321	3589.9	1.9
1887	13.09	11.74	47.93	2846	8644	7217	3954.9	1.7
1888 *B.*	13.13	11.86	46.08	2846	8666	7114	4330.9	2.4
1889	13.18	11.98	44.24	2845	8688	7010	4685.9	2.2
1890	13.22	12.10	42.39	2844	8711	6907	5050.9	1.9
1891	13.27	12.22	40.55	2844	8733	6804	5415.9	1.7
1892 *B.*	13.33	12.34	38.71	2843	8755	6700	5781.9	2.4
1893	13.39	12.46	36.86	2842	8777	6597	6146.9	2.2
1894	13.45	12.58	35.02	2842	8799	6493	6511.9	2.0
1895	13.50	12.70	33.18	2841	8821	6390	78.6	1.7
1896 *B.*	13.56	12.82	31.31	2840	8843	6286	444.6	2.5
1897	13.62	12.94	29.50	2840	8866	6183	809.6	2.2
1898	13.67	13.06	27.66	2839	8888	6079	1174.6	2.0
1899	89 58 13.73	1 27 13.18	352 43 25.82	9.9992838	9.9598910	9.6175976	1539.6	1.7

From each of the quantities K_x, K_y and K_z the constant 20″.00 has been subtracted; and from log k_y the constant 0.0000089, and from log k_z the constant 0.0000560

TABLE XXXIX.

Values, for the beginning of the year, of K_x, K_y, &c., and of the Arguments of Nutation, for Washington Mean Noon of Jan. 0 in Common Years and Jan. 1 in Bissextile Years.

Year.	K_x.	K_y.	K_z.	Log k_x.	Log k_y.	Log k_z.	XV.	XVI.
	° ′ ″	° ′ ″	° ′ ″				d	d
1900	89 58 13.78	1 27 13.30	352 43 23.98	9.9992838	9.9598932	9.6175872	1904.6	1.5
1901	13.82	13.42	22.14	2837	8954	5768	2269.6	1.3
1902	13.87	13.54	20.30	2837	8976	5665	2634.6	1.0
1903	13.91	13.65	18.47	2836	8998	5561	2999.6	0.8
1904*B*.	13.95	13.77	16.63	2836	9021	5458	3365.6	1.5
1905	13.99	13.89	14.79	2835	9043	5354	3730.6	1.3
1906	14.03	14.01	12.95	2835	9065	5250	4095.6	1.0
1907	14.08	14.13	11.12	2834	9087	5147	4460.6	0.8
1908*B*.	14.12	14.25	9.28	2833	9109	5043	4826.6	1.6
1909	14.17	14.36	7.45	2833	9131	4940	5191.6	1.3
1910	14.22	14.48	5.61	2832	9154	4836	5556.6	1.1
1911	14.28	14.60	3.78	2832	9176	4732	5921.6	0.8
1912*B*.	14.34	14.72	1.95	2831	9198	4629	6287.6	1.6
1913	14.40	14.83	352 43 0.11	2830	9220	4525	6652.6	1.3
1914	14.45	14.95	352 42 58.28	2829	9242	4422	219.4	1.1
1915	14.50	15.07	56.45	2829	9264	4318	584.4	0.9
1916*B*.	14.56	15.18	54.62	2828	9287	4214	950.4	1.6
1917	14.62	15.30	52.79	2827	9309	4110	1315.4	1.4
1918	14.67	15.42	50.96	2827	9331	4007	1680.4	1.1
1919	14.72	15.53	49.13	2826	9353	3903	2045.4	0.9
1920*B*.	14.76	15.65	47.30	2826	9375	3799	2411.4	1.6
1921	14.80	15.76	45.47	2825	9397	3695	2776.4	1.4
1922	14.84	15.88	43.64	2825	9420	3591	3141.4	1.2
1923	14.88	16.00	41.82	2824	9442	3488	3506.4	0.9
1924*B*.	14.93	16.11	39.99	2824	9464	3384	3872.4	1.7
1925	14.97	16.23	38.16	2823	9486	3280	4237.4	1.4
1926	15.02	16.34	36.33	2823	9508	3176	4602.4	1.2
1927	15.06	16.46	34.51	2822	9530	3072	4967.4	0.9
1928*B*.	15.11	16.57	32.68	2821	9552	2969	5333.4	1.7
1929	15.17	16.69	30.86	2821	9575	2865	5698.4	1.5
1930	15.22	16.80	29.03	2820	9597	2761	6063.4	1.2
1931	15.28	16.92	27.21	2819	9619	2657	6428.4	1.0
1932*B*.	15.34	17.03	25.38	2819	9641	2553	6794.4	1.7
1933	15.40	17.14	23.56	2818	9663	2450	361.1	1.5
1934	15.46	17.26	21.73	2817	9685	2346	726.1	1.3
1935	15.51	17.37	19.91	2817	9708	2242	1091.1	1.0
1936*B*.	15.57	17.49	18.09	2816	9730	2138	1457.1	1.8
1937	15.62	17.60	16.27	2815	9752	2034	1822.1	1.5
1938	15.66	17.71	14.45	2815	9774	1930	2187.1	1.3
1939	15.71	17.83	12.63	2814	9796	1826	2552.1	1.0
1940*B*.	15.75	17.94	10.81	2814	9818	1722	2918.1	1.8
1941	15.79	18.05	8.99	2813	9841	1618	3283.1	1.6
1942	15.83	18.17	7.17	2813	9863	1514	3648.1	1.3
1943	15.88	18.28	5.36	2812	9885	1410	4013.1	1.1
1944*B*.	15.92	18.39	3.54	2812	9907	1306	4379.1	1.8
1945	15.97	18.50	352 42 1.72	2811	9929	1202	4744.1	1.6
1946	16.02	18.62	352 41 59.91	2811	9951	1098	5109.1	1.3
1947	16.07	18.73	58.09	2810	9974	0994	5474.1	1.1
1948*B*.	16.12	18.84	56.28	2809	9.9599996	0890	5840.1	1.9
1949	89 58 16.18	1 27 18.95	352 41 54.46	9.9992809	9.9600018	9.6170786	6205.1	1.6

From each of the quantities K_x, K_y and K_z, the constant 20″.00 has been subtracted; and from log k_y the constant 0.0000[illegible]0, and from log k_z the constant 0.0000560.

TABLE XL.

Corrections of K_x, K_y, &c., due to Lunar Nutation, for 1850.

Period of Argument XV., 6798d.3.

Arg. XV.	△ K_x.	△ K_y.	△ K_z.	Var. in 100 yrs.	△ log k_y.	△ log k_z.	Arg. XV.	△ K_x.	△ K_y.	△ K_z.	Var. in 100 yrs.	△ log k_y.	△ log k_z.
d	″	″	″	″			d	″	″	″	″		
0	18.00	18.63	20.05	+0.03	1	850	2400	32.02	31.70	28.47	−0.02	118	140
50	18.78	19.42	20.79	0.03	1	847	2450	31.53	31.18	27.89	0.02	151	125
100	19.56	20.20	21.52	0.03	2	844	2500	31.00	30.63	27.28	0.02	154	111
150	20.34	20.98	22.25	0.03	3	840	2550	30.45	30.05	26.64	0.02	157	98
200	21.11	21.75	22.95	0.03	4	835	2600	29.87	29.45	25.99	0.03	160	86
250	21.87	22.50	23.65	+0.02	5	829	2650	29.26	28.82	25.32	−0.03	162	74
300	22.63	23.25	24.33	0.02	7	822	2700	28.63	28.17	24.63	0.03	164	63
350	23.38	24.00	25.00	0.02	8	814	2750	27.97	27.49	23.92	0.03	166	53
400	24.12	24.71	25.66	0.02	10	806	2800	27.29	26.78	23.19	0.03	168	41
450	24.85	25.46	26.30	0.02	12	797	2850	26.59	26.06	22.45	0.03	170	36
500	25.57	26.17	26.93	+0.02	14	787	2900	25.87	25.33	21.70	−0.03	172	28
550	26.27	26.86	27.53	0.02	16	777	2950	25.13	24.58	20.94	0.03	173	21
600	26.94	27.52	28.10	0.02	19	766	3000	24.38	23.81	20.17	0.03	174	16
650	27.60	28.17	28.65	0.02	21	754	3050	23.61	23.03	19.39	0.03	175	11
700	28.25	28.80	29.19	0.02	24	741	3100	22.83	22.23	18.60	0.03	176	7
750	28.87	29.41	29.69	+0.02	27	727	3150	22.04	21.43	17.81	−0.03	176	4
800	29.47	29.99	30.17	0.02	29	713	3200	21.24	20.62	17.02	0.03	177	2
850	30.05	30.55	30.62	0.01	32	699	3250	20.43	19.80	16.23	0.03	177	1
900	30.60	31.09	31.05	0.01	36	684	3300	19.62	18.99	15.45	0.03	177	0
950	31.13	31.60	31.45	0.01	39	668	3350	18.80	18.16	14.66	0.03	177	1
1000	31.63	32.08	31.81	+0.01	42	652	3400	17.98	17.34	13.88	−0.03	177	3
1050	32.10	32.53	32.14	0.01	46	635	3450	17.16	16.51	13.10	0.03	176	5
1100	32.55	32.95	32.45	0.01	49	618	3500	16.35	15.70	12.34	0.03	175	9
1150	32.97	33.34	32.73	0.01	53	600	3550	15.54	14.89	11.59	0.03	174	13
1200	33.35	33.70	32.97	+0.01	57	582	3600	14.73	14.09	10.84	0.03	173	18
1250	33.70	34.03	33.18	0.00	61	564	3650	13.93	13.29	10.11	−0.03	172	24
1300	34.02	34.32	33.35	0.00	64	545	3700	13.14	12.50	9.40	0.02	171	31
1350	34.31	34.58	33.49	0.00	68	526	3750	12.36	11.72	8.70	0.02	169	39
1400	34.56	34.81	33.60	0.00	72	507	3800	11.59	10.96	8.02	0.02	167	48
1450	34.78	35.00	33.67	0.00	76	488	3850	10.84	10.22	7.36	0.02	165	58
1500	34.96	35.16	33.70	0.00	80	469	3900	10.10	9.49	6.72	−0.02	163	68
1550	35.10	35.27	33.70	0.00	84	449	3950	9.38	8.78	6.11	0.02	160	80
1600	35.21	35.35	33.66	0.00	88	429	4000	8.68	8.10	5.52	0.02	158	92
1650	35.28	35.39	33.58	−0.01	93	410	4050	8.00	7.43	4.95	0.02	155	104
1700	35.32	35.40	33.48	0.01	97	390	4100	7.35	6.79	4.42	0.02	152	118
1750	35.32	35.37	33.34	−0.01	101	370	4150	6.72	6.18	3.91	−0.02	150	132
1800	35.29	35.31	33.17	0.01	105	351	4200	6.11	5.59	3.43	0.02	146	146
1850	35.21	35.20	32.96	0.01	109	332	4250	5.53	5.02	2.98	0.01	143	162
1900	35.10	35.06	32.71	0.01	113	313	4300	4.98	4.49	2.56	0.01	140	178
1950	34.95	34.88	32.42	0.01	117	294	4350	4.46	3.99	2.18	0.01	137	194
2000	34.77	34.67	32.11	−0.01	120	275	4400	3.96	3.52	1.82	−0.01	133	211
2050	34.55	34.42	31.76	0.02	124	257	4450	3.50	3.08	1.50	0.01	129	229
2100	34.29	34.14	31.38	0.02	128	239	4500	3.07	2.67	1.21	0.01	126	247
2150	34.00	33.82	30.97	0.02	132	221	4550	2.68	2.30	0.97	0.01	122	265
2200	33.67	33.46	30.53	0.02	135	204	4600	2.32	1.97	0.75	−0.01	118	284
2250	33.31	33.07	30.06	−0.02	139	187	4650	1.99	1.67	0.57	0.00	114	303
2300	32.91	32.64	29.55	0.02	142	171	4700	1.70	1.40	0.43	0.00	110	322
2350	32.48	32.18	29.02	0.02	145	155	4750	1.41	1.17	0.32	0.00	106	341
2400	32.02	31.70	28.47	−0.02	148	140	4800	1.22	0.98	0.25	0.00	102	360

△ log k_y and △ log k_z are in units of the seventh decimal place.

The constants added are, 18″.00 to △ K_x, 18″.00 to △ K_y, 17″.00 to △ K_z, 88 to △ log k_y, and 430 to △ log k_z.

TABLE XL.

Corrections of K_x, K_y, &c., due to Lunar Nutation, for 1850.

Period of Argument XV., 6798d.3.

Arg. XV.	△ K_x.	△ K_y.	△ K_z.	Var. in 100 yrs.	△ log k_y	△ log k_z
d 4800	″ 1.22	″ 0.98	″ 0.25	″ 0.00	102	360
4850	1.01	0.83	0.22	0.00	98	380
4900	0.89	0.71	0.22	0.00	94	400
4950	0.78	0.62	0.25	0.00	90	420
5000	0.71	0.58	0.33	+0.01	86	439
5050	0.68	0.58	0.44	+0.01	81	459
5100	0.68	0.61	0.58	0.01	77	479
5150	0.72	0.68	0.76	0.01	73	498
5200	0.79	0.78	0.97	0.01	69	517
5250	0.90	0.92	1.22	0.01	66	536
5300	1.05	1.10	1.50	+0.01	62	555
5350	1.23	1.31	1.81	0.01	58	573
5400	1.45	1.56	2.15	0.02	54	592
5450	1.70	1.81	2.52	0.02	50	609
5500	1.99	2.16	2.93	0.02	47	627
5550	2.31	2.51	3.36	+0.02	43	644
5600	2.67	2.89	3.83	0.02	40	660
5650	3.06	3.31	4.33	0.02	37	676
5700	3.47	3.75	4.81	0.02	33	692
5750	3.91	4.22	5.37	0.02	30	707
5800	4.39	4.72	5.93	+0.02	27	721
5850	4.89	5.24	6.52	0.02	24	735
5900	5.42	5.80	7.13	0.02	22	748
5950	5.98	6.38	7.76	0.02	19	760
6000	6.56	6.98	8.41	0.03	17	772
6050	7.16	7.60	9.07	+0.03	14	783
6100	7.78	8.24	9.71	0.03	12	793
6150	8.42	8.90	10.43	0.03	10	803
6200	9.09	9.59	11.14	0.03	9	811
6250	9.77	10.29	11.86	0.03	7	819
6300	10.47	11.01	12.59	+0.03	6	826
6350	11.18	11.73	13.32	0.03	4	832
6400	11.91	12.47	14.07	0.03	3	838
6450	12.65	13.23	14.82	0.03	2	842
6500	13.40	13.99	15.57	0.03	2	846
6550	14.16	14.76	16.33	+0.03	1	848
6600	14.92	15.53	17.08	0.03	1	850
6650	15.69	16.31	17.83	0.03	0	851
6700	16.47	17.09	18.58	0.03	0	852
6750	17.25	17.88	19.33	0.03	1	851
6800	18.03	18.66	20.08	+0.03	1	849
6850	18.81	19.45	20.82	0.03	1	847
6900	19.59	20.23	21.55	0.03	2	844
6950	20.37	21.01	22.27	0.03	3	840
7000	21.14	21.78	22.98	0.03	4	835
7050	21.90	22.51	23.68	+0.02	5	829
7100	22.66	23.29	24.36	0.02	7	822
7150	23.41	24.03	25.03	0.02	8	814
7200	24.14	24.76	25.68	+0.02	10	806

TABLE XLI.

Corrections of K_x, K_y, &c., due to Solar Nutation, for 1850.

Period of Argument XVI., 365d.24.

Arg. XVI.	△ K_x.	△ K_y.	△ K_z.	Var. in 100 yrs.	△ log k_y.	△ log k_z.	Solar Nutat'n.
d 0	″ 2.36	″ 2.33	″ 3.17	″ 0.00	6	105	″ +0.36
5	2.57	2.51	3.36	0.00	6	105	0.57
10	2.76	2.74	3.53	0.00	6	106	0.76
15	2.92	2.91	3.68	0.00	6	107	0.92
20	3.06	3.05	3.81	0.00	5	109	1.06
25	3.16	3.16	3.91	0.00	5	111	+1.16
30	3.22	3.23	3.98	0.00	4	114	1.22
35	3.25	3.26	4.01	0.00	4	117	1.25
40	3.25	3.26	4.01	+0.01	3	120	1.24
45	3.20	3.22	3.97	0.01	2	123	1.19
50	3.11	3.14	3.89	+0.01	2	126	+1.10
55	2.99	3.02	3.77	0.01	1	128	0.98
60	2.84	2.88	3.63	0.01	1	131	0.83
65	2.66	2.71	3.46	0.01	1	132	0.65
70	2.47	2.52	3.26	0.01	0	133	0.46
75	2.26	2.31	3.01	+0.01	0	133	+0.25
80	2.05	2.10	2.82	0.01	0	133	+0.04
85	1.83	1.88	2.59	0.01	1	132	−0.18
90	1.62	1.67	2.35	0.01	1	130	0.39
95	1.42	1.47	2.12	0.01	2	127	0.59
100	1.24	1.29	1.91	+0.01	2	124	−0.77
105	1.09	1.13	1.72	0.01	3	120	0.92
110	0.97	1.00	1.55	0.01	4	115	1.05
115	0.87	0.90	1.40	0.02	5	110	1.15
120	0.81	0.83	1.29	0.02	6	105	1.21
125	0.78	0.80	1.20	+0.02	8	99	−1.24
130	0.78	0.80	1.15	0.02	9	94	1.24
135	0.82	0.83	1.13	0.02	10	88	1.20
140	0.89	0.90	1.14	0.02	11	83	1.13
145	1.00	1.00	1.19	0.02	12	77	1.02
150	1.13	1.13	1.27	+0.02	13	72	−0.89
155	1.29	1.29	1.38	0.02	14	68	0.73
160	1.47	1.47	1.51	0.02	15	64	0.55
165	1.67	1.67	1.66	0.02	16	60	0.35
170	1.87	1.87	1.82	0.02	16	58	−0.15
175	2.08	2.08	1.99	+0.02	17	56	+0.06
180	2.28	2.28	2.16	0.02	17	54	0.26
185	2.48	2.49	2.33	0.03	17	54	0.46
190	2.67	2.68	2.49	0.03	17	54	0.64
195	2.84	2.85	2.64	0.03	16	55	0.81
200	2.99	3.01	2.78	+0.03	16	56	+0.96
205	3.11	3.14	2.89	0.03	16	57	1.08
210	3.19	3.23	2.97	0.03	16	60	1.16
215	3.25	3.29	3.03	0.03	15	62	1.22
220	3.27	3.32	3.06	0.03	15	65	1.24
225	3.26	3.32	3.05	+0.03	14	68	+1.23
230	3.22	3.29	3.02	0.03	14	71	1.19
235	3.14	3.22	2.95	0.03	13	73	1.11
240	3.03	3.11	2.84	+0.03	13	76	+1.00

△ log k_y and △ log k_z are in units of the seventh decimal.

TABLE XLI.—Constants added are, 2″.04 to △ K_x, 2″.00 to △ K_y, 3″.03 to △ K_z, 1 to △ log k_y, and 130 to △ log k_z.

TABLE XLI.

Corrections of K_x, K_y, &c., due to Solar Nutation, for 1850.

Period of Argument XVI., 365d.24.

Arg. XVI.	ΔK_x.	ΔK_y.	ΔK_z.	Var. in 100 yrs.	$\Delta \log k_y$.	$\Delta \log k_z$.	Solar Nutat'n
d 240	″ 3.03	″ 3.11	″ 2.84	″ +0.03	13	76	″ +1.00
245	2.89	2.97	2.71	0.03	12	78	0.86
250	2.72	2.81	2.54	0.03	12	79	0.69
255	2.54	2.63	2.36	0.03	12	80	0.51
260	2.35	2.44	2.16	0.04	12	81	0.31
265	2.14	2.23	1.93	+0.04	12	81	+0.10
270	1.92	2.01	1.70	0.04	12	80	−0.12
275	1.71	1.80	1.47	0.04	12	78	0.33
280	1.51	1.60	1.24	0.04	13	76	0.53
285	1.32	1.41	1.02	0.04	13	72	0.72
290	1.15	1.23	0.81	+0.04	14	69	−0.89
295	1.00	1.08	0.62	0.04	15	64	1.04
300	0.89	0.96	0.46	0.04	16	59	1.15
305	0.82	0.88	0.34	0.04	17	54	1.22
310	0.78	0.84	0.25	0.04	19	48	1.26
315	0.79	0.84	0.20	+0.04	20	42	−1.25
320	0.83	0.88	0.18	0.04	21	36	1.21
325	0.91	0.96	0.20	0.04	22	31	1.13
330	1.02	1.07	0.25	0.04	23	25	1.02
335	1.17	1.20	0.33	0.05	24	20	0.88
340	1.33	1.36	0.44	+0.05	25	15	−0.72
345	1.51	1.54	0.57	0.05	26	11	0.54
350	1.72	1.75	0.73	0.05	27	8	0.33
355	1.95	1.98	0.92	0.05	27	5	−0.10
360	2.18	2.22	1.11	0.05	28	3	+0.13
365	2.40	2.44	1.30	+0.05	28	2	+0.35
370	2.61	2.65	1.49	+0.05	28	2	+0.56

$\Delta \log k_y$ and $\Delta \log k_z$ are in units of the seventh decimal. Constants added are, 2″.00 to ΔK_x, 2″.00 to ΔK_y, 3″.00 to ΔK_z, 1 to $\Delta \log k_y$, and 130 to $\Delta \log k_z$.

TABLE XLII.

Factors for obtaining Δx, Δy, Δz from $\Delta \beta$.

Orbit. Long.		For Δx.	For Δy.	For Δz.
° 0	° 180	+ 0.020	− 0.145	+ 0.322
10	190	0.018	0.148	0.323
20	200	0.016	0.150	0.324
30	210	0.013	0.152	0.325
40	220	0.009	0.152	0.325
50	230	+ 0.006	− 0.151	+ 0.325
60	240	0.003	0.149	0.324
70	250	0.001	0.146	0.323
80	260	0.000	0.143	0.321
90	270	0.000	0.139	0.320
100	280	+ 0.002	− 0.136	+ 0.319
110	290	0.004	0.134	0.318
120	300	0.007	0.132	0.317
130	310	0.011	0.132	0.317
140	320	0.014	0.133	0.317
150	330	+ 0.017	− 0.135	+ 0.318
160	340	0.019	0.138	0.319
170	350	0.020	0.141	0.321
180	360	+ 0.020	− 0.145	+ 0.322

TABLE XLIII.

Parallax and Semi-diameter.

Log. dist. from Earth.	Parallax.	Semi-diam.	Log. dist. from Earth.	Parallax.	Semi-diam.
9.40	″ 35.22	″ 34.02	9.85	″ 12.50	″ 12.07
9.41	34.42	33.25	9.86	12.21	11.80
9.42	33.61	32.49	9.87	11.94	11.53
9.43	32.87	31.75	9.88	11.66	11.27
9.44	32.13	31.03	9.89	11.40	11.01
9.45	31.39	30.32	9.90	11.14	10.76
9.46	30.68	29.63	9.91	10.89	10.51
9.47	29.98	28.96	9.92	10.64	10.27
9.48	29.30	28.30	9.93	10.40	10.04
9.49	28.63	27.65	9.94	10.16	9.81
9.50	27.98	27.02	9.95	9.93	9.59
9.51	27.34	26.40	9.96	9.70	9.37
9.52	26.72	25.81	9.97	9.48	9.16
9.53	26.11	25.22	9.98	9.26	8.95
9.54	25.52	24.65	9.99	9.05	8.74
9.55	24.94	24.09	0.00	8.85	8.55
9.56	24.37	23.54	0.01	8.65	8.35
9.57	23.81	23.00	0.02	8.45	8.16
9.58	23.27	22.48	0.03	8.26	7.98
9.59	22.74	21.97	0.04	8.07	7.79
9.60	22.23	21.47	0.05	7.89	7.62
9.61	21.72	20.98	0.06	7.71	7.44
9.62	21.22	20.50	0.07	7.53	7.27
9.63	20.74	20.03	0.08	7.36	7.11
9.64	20.27	19.58	0.09	7.19	6.95
9.65	19.81	19.13	0.10	7.03	6.79
9.66	19.36	18.70	0.11	6.87	6.63
9.67	18.92	18.27	0.12	6.71	6.48
9.68	18.49	17.85	0.13	6.56	6.34
9.69	18.07	17.45	0.14	6.41	6.19
9.70	17.65	17.05	0.15	6.26	6.05
9.71	17.25	16.66	0.16	6.12	5.91
9.72	16.86	16.28	0.17	5.98	5.78
9.73	16.48	15.91	0.18	5.85	5.65
9.74	16.10	15.55	0.19	5.71	5.52
9.75	15.73	15.20	0.20	5.58	5.39
9.76	15.38	14.85	0.21	5.46	5.27
9.77	15.03	14.51	0.22	5.33	5.15
9.78	14.68	14.18	0.23	5.21	5.03
9.79	14.35	13.86	0.24	5.09	4.92
9.80	14.02	13.54	0.25	4.98	4.81
9.81	13.70	13.24	0.26	4.86	4.70
9.82	13.39	12.93	0.27	4.75	4.59
9.83	13.09	12.64	0.28	4.64	4.48
9.84	12.79	12.35	0.29	4.54	4.38
9.85	12.50	12.07	0.30	4.43	4.28

Motion of the Arguments for Centuries.

Calendar	Century.	L.	t' − 50.	m.	I.	t' − 50.	II.	III.	IV.	V.	VI.	VII.	VIII.
		° ′ ″	″		d	d	y	d	d	d	d	d	d
Julian Calendar.	−300	153 55 8.00	−0.4763	−3414	115.9951	−0.000514	50.3	171	2381	1193.1	239.68	172.2	116.5
	−200	355 7 3.49	0.4536	3251	14.7184	0.000490	150.3	731	437	1344.7	581.56	222.4	27.5
	−100	194 19 1.61	0.4309	3089	138.1417	0.000465	11.4	1297	1451	41.4	319.51	29.5	159.1
	0	33 31 1.86	0.4082	2926	36.8726	0.000441	111.4	1861	2466	193.0	57.46	79.8	70.1
	100	232 43 4.35	0.3856	2764	160.3098	0.000416	211.4	2424	521	344.6	379.34	130.1	201.6
	200	71 55 9.11	−0.3629	−2601	59.0366	−0.000392	72.4	2987	1535	496.2	117.29	180.3	112.6
	300	271 7 16.14	0.3402	2439	182.4726	0.000367	172.4	3550	2550	647.8	439.17	230.6	24.6
	400	110 19 25.43	0.3175	2276	81.2103	0.000343	33.5	4114	605	799.4	177.12	37.7	155.2
	500	309 31 36.89	0.2948	2114	204.6518	0.000318	133.5	4677	1620	951.0	499.00	88.0	66.2
	600	148 43 50.82	0.2722	1951	103.3939	0.000294	233.5	5240	2634	1102.6	236.95	138.3	197.8
	700	347 56 6.92	−0.2495	−1788	2.1380	−0.000269	94.6	5803	689	1254.2	558.82	188.5	108.8
	800	187 8 25.29	0.2268	1626	125.5872	0.000245	194.6	6367	1704	1405.8	296.78	238.8	19.8
	900	26 20 45.92	0.2041	1463	24.3372	0.000220	55.7	6930	2718	102.5	34.73	45.9	150.9
	1000	225 33 8.82	0.1814	1301	147.7903	0.000196	155.7	7493	774	254.1	356.61	96.2	62.3
	1100	64 45 33.00	0.1588	1138	46.5152	0.000171	16.8	8056	1788	405.7	94.56	146.4	193.4
	1200	263 58 1.43	−0.1361	−976	170.0033	−0.000147	116.8	8620	2803	557.3	416.44	196.7	104.9
	1300	103 10 31.14	0.1134	813	68.7530	0.000122	216.8	9183	858	708.9	154.39	3.8	15.9
	1400	302 23 3.11	0.0907	651	192.2260	0.000098	77.8	9746	1872	860.5	476.26	54.1	147.4
	1500	141 35 37.35	0.0680	488	90.9906	0.000073	177.8	10309	2887	1012.1	214.22	104.4	58.4
Gregorian Calendar.	1500	125 34 19.28	−0.0680	−488	80.9006	−0.000073	177.8	10299	2877	1002.1	201.22	94.4	48.4
	1600	324 46 55.79	0.0454	326	204.4585	0.000049	38.9	10863	932	1153.7	523.09	144.6	180.0
	1700	162 23 26.76	−0.0227	−163	102.2280	−0.000024	138.9	11425	1946	1304.3	263.05	193.9	90.0
	1800	0 0 0	0.0000	0	0.0000	0.000000	0.0	0	0	0.0	0.00	0.0	0.0
	1900	197 36 35.51	+0.0227	+163	122.4752	+0.000024	100.0	562	1013	150.6	320.88	49.3	130.6
	2000	36 49 21.09	0.0454	325	21.2521	0.000049	200.0	1125	2028	302.2	58.83	99.5	41.6
	2100	234 26 1.13	+0.0680	+487	143.7322	+0.000073	61.1	1688	82	452.8	379.70	148.8	172.1
	2200	72 2 43.44	+0.0907	+650	41.5140	+0.000098	161.1	2250	1096	603.4	116.66	198.1	82.1

Calendar	Century	IX.	X.	XI.	XII.	XIII.	XIV.	log sin i.	t' − 50.	360° − ☊.	t' − 50.	XV.	XVI.
		d								° ′ ″	″	d	d
Julian Calendar.	−300	129.81	35.04	180.76	19.9	56.38	25.2	−0.0031028	+24.61	+18 46 55.6	+0.631	1190.6	−4.4
	−200	158.06	56.19	6.85	38.8	23.00	3.8	0.0029433	23.44	17 53 46.0	0.601	3724.3	3.6
	−100	186.30	44.09	105.31	38.1	47.71	17.6	0.0027850	22.27	17 0 33.4	0.574	6258.0	2.8
	0	214.55	5.25	231.40	57.0	14.33	32.1	0.0026279	21.10	16 7 17.8	0.544	1993.4	2.1
	100	5.80	53.15	149.86	56.3	39.04	9.9	0.0024719	19.92	15 13 59.1	0.513	4527.1	1.3
	200	34.05	14.30	215.95	15.1	6.26	24.5	−0.0023171	+18.75	+14 20 37.4	+0.483	262.5	−0.5
	300	62.30	2.20	134.41	14.4	30.37	2.3	0.0021635	17.58	13 27 12.7	0.453	2796.2	+0.3
	400	90.54	23.36	200.50	33.3	57.59	16.8	0.0020111	16.41	12 33 45.0	0.423	5329.9	1.1
	500	118.79	11.26	118.96	32.6	21.70	30.6	0.0018598	15.24	11 40 14.3	0.393	1065.3	1.8
	600	147.03	32.41	185.05	51.4	48.92	9.2	0.0017097	14.06	10 46 40.6	0.362	3599.0	2.6
	700	175.28	53.57	11.15	10.3	16.14	23.7	−0.0015608	+12.89	+ 9 53 3.8	+0.332	6132.7	+3.4
	800	203.53	41.47	109.60	9.6	40.25	1.5	0.0014130	11.72	8 59 24.0	0.302	1868.1	4.2
	900	231.77	2.62	235.70	28.5	7.47	16.1	0.0012665	10.55	8 5 41.2	0.272	4401.8	5.0
	1000	23.03	50.52	154.15	27.8	31.57	20.9	0.0011211	9.38	7 11 55.4	0.242	137.3	5.8
	1100	51.27	11.68	220.25	46.6	58.79	8.4	0.0009764	8.20	6 18 6.5	0.211	2671.0	6.5
	1200	79.52	50.58	138.70	45.9	22.00	22.2	−0.0008338	+ 7.03	+ 5 24 14.6	+0.181	5204.6	+7.3
	1300	107.76	20.73	204.80	4.8	50.12	0.8	0.0006919	5.86	4 30 19.7	0.151	940.1	8.1
	1400	136.01	8.63	123.25	4.1	14.23	14.6	0.0005512	4.69	3 36 21.8	0.121	3473.8	8.9
	1500	164.25	29.79	189.35	23.0	41.45	29.1	0.0004116	3.52	2 42 20.9	0.091	6007.5	+9.7
Gregorian Calendar.	1500	154.25	29.79	189.35	23.0	41.45	29.1	−0.0004116	+ 3.52	+ 2 42 20.9	+0.091	5997.5	−0.3
	1600	182.50	17.69	107.80	22.2	5.56	6.9	0.0002732	2.34	1 48 17.0	0.060	1732.9	+0.4
	1700	209.75	38.84	173.90	41.1	32.78	21.4	−0.0001360	+ 1.17	+ 0 51 10.0	+0.030	4265.6	+0.2
	1800	0.00	0.00	0.00	0.0	0.00	0.0	0.0000000	0.00	0 0 0.0	0.000	0.0	0.0
	1900	27.25	47.90	138.45	59.3	24.11	13.8	+0.0001349	− 1.17	− 0 54 13.0	−0.030	2532.7	−0.2
	2000	55.49	9.05	224.55	18.2	51.33	28.3	0.0002685	2.34	1 48 20.0	0.060	5066.4	+0.6
	2100	82.74	56.95	143.00	17.4	15.14	6.1	0.0004011	3.52	2 42 48.1	0.091	800.8	0.3
	2200	109.98	18.11	209.10	36.3	42.06	20.7	+0.0005324	− 4.69	− 3 37 10.2	−0.121	3333.5	+0.1

TABLE XLVI.

TABLE XLV.

Values of the Equation 0″.282 sin (4 *l*‴ + 3 *l*′ − 7 *l*″ + 147°.1.)

Year.	Equa.	Diff. for 10 yrs.
1800	+0.281″	− 3
1810	0.272	15
1820	0.251	27
1830	0.218	37
1840	0.176	45
1850	+0.128	−51
1860	0.073	56
1870	+0.016	58
1880	−0.043	58
1890	0.100	54
1900	−0.152	−49
1910	0.199	42
1920	0.236	31
1930	0.261	20
1940	0.277	−10
1950	−0.282	+ 2
1960	0.273	14
1970	0.254	25
1980	0.223	36
1990	0.182	44
2000	−0.131	+51
2010	0.080	56
2020	−0.023	58
2030	+0.036	58
2040	0.093	55
2050	+0.146	50
2060	0.193	42
2070	0.231	33
2080	0.259	21
2090	0.277	+12
2100	+0.282	− 1
2110	+0.275	−13

Multiples of the Period of this Equation.

	y
1	302.4
2	604.8
3	907.2
4	1209.6
5	1512.0
6	1814.4
7	2116.8
8	2419.2
9	2721.6

Reduction to the Ecliptic for 1850.

Argument = Orbit Longitude + (360° − ☊), or this angle diminished by 180°.

Arg.	0′	10′	20′	30′	40′	50′	Diff. for 10′	Var. in 100 yrs.	
0°	−0′ 0.00″	1.05″	2.10″	3.15″	4.21″	5.26″	1.05″	0.00″	179°
1	0 6.31	7.36	8.41	9.46	10.51	11.56	1.05	0.00	178
2	0 12.61	13.66	14.71	15.76	16.80	17.85	1.05	−0.01	177
3	0 18.90	19.94	20.99	22.04	23.08	24.12	1.05	0.01	176
4	0 25.16	26.20	27.24	28.28	29.31	30.35	1.04	0.02	175
5	−0 31.39	32.43	33.46	34.50	35.53	36.56	1.03	−0.02	174
6	0 37.59	38.61	39.64	40.66	41.69	42.71	1.02	0.02	173
7	0 43.74	44.76	45.77	46.79	47.80	48.82	1.01	0.03	172
8	0 49.83	50.84	51.85	52.85	53.86	54.87	1.01	0.03	171
9	0 55.87	56.87	57.86	58.86	59.85	60.85	1.00	0.03	170
10	−1 1.84	2.83	3.82	4.80	5.78	6.76	0.98	−0.04	169
11	1 7.73	8.71	9.68	10.65	11.62	12.58	0.97	0.04	168
12	1 13.54	14.50	15.46	16.41	17.36	18.31	0.95	0.05	167
13	1 19.26	20.20	21.14	22.08	23.01	23.95	0.94	0.05	166
14	1 24.88	25.81	26.74	27.66	28.58	29.50	0.92	0.05	165
15	−1 30.41	31.32	32.23	33.13	34.03	34.93	0.90	−0.06	164
16	1 35.82	36.71	37.60	38.48	39.36	40.24	0.88	0.06	163
17	1 41.11	41.98	42.85	43.71	44.57	45.43	0.86	0.06	162
18	1 46.28	47.13	47.98	48.82	49.66	50.50	0.84	0.07	161
19	1 51.33	52.16	52.98	53.80	54.61	55.42	0.82	0.07	160
20	−1 56.23	57.04	57.84	58.64	59.43	60.22	0.80	−0.07	159
21	2 1.00	1.78	2.56	3.33	4.10	4.86	0.77	0.08	158
22	2 5.62	6.37	7.12	7.86	8.60	9.34	0.74	0.08	157
23	2 10.08	10.81	11.54	12.26	12.98	13.69	0.72	0.08	156
24	2 14.39	15.09	15.79	16.48	17.17	17.86	0.69	0.09	155
25	−2 18.54	19.22	19.89	20.56	21.22	21.87	0.66	−0.09	154
26	2 22.51	23.16	23.80	24.44	25.07	25.70	0.63	0.09	153
27	2 26.32	26.94	27.55	28.16	28.76	29.35	0.60	0.09	152
28	2 29.94	30.52	31.10	31.67	32.24	32.81	0.57	0.10	151
29	2 33.38	33.94	34.49	35.04	35.58	36.11	0.54	0.10	150
30	−2 36.64	37.16	37.68	38.19	38.70	39.20	0.51	−0.10	149
31	2 39.70	40.19	40.68	41.16	41.64	42.11	0.48	0.10	148
32	2 42.57	43.03	43.48	43.93	44.38	44.82	0.45	0.10	147
33	2 45.25	45.68	46.10	46.52	46.93	47.33	0.41	0.10	146
34	2 47.72	48.11	48.49	48.87	49.25	49.62	0.38	0.11	145
35	−2 49.99	50.35	50.70	51.05	51.39	51.72	0.34	−0.11	144
36	2 52.04	52.36	52.68	52.99	53.30	53.60	0.31	0.11	143
37	2 53.90	54.19	54.47	54.75	55.02	55.28	0.27	0.11	142
38	2 55.54	55.79	56.04	56.28	56.52	56.75	0.24	0.11	141
39	2 56.96	57.18	57.39	57.60	57.80	57.99	0.20	0.11	140
40	−2 58.17	58.35	58.52	58.69	58.85	59.01	0.17	−0.11	139
41	2 59.17	59.32	59.46	59.59	59.72	59.84	0.13	0.11	138
42	2 59.94	60.05	60.15	60.25	60.34	60.42	0.09	0.11	137
43	3 0.50	0.57	0.64	0.70	0.75	0.79	0.05	0.11	136
44	−3 0.83	0.86	0.89	0.91	0.93	0.94	0.02	−0.11	135
	60′	50′	40′	30′	20′	10′			Arg.

Note.—When the degrees of the Argument are read from the right hand side of the Table, the tens of minutes must be read from the bottom; and the Reduction and its Secular Variation are affected with the sign + instead of −.

TABLE XLVI.

Reduction to the Ecliptic for 1850.

Argument = Orbit Longitude + (360° − ☊), or this angle diminished by 180°.

Arg.	0′	10′	20′	30′	40′	50′	Diff. for 10′.	Var. in 100 yrs.	
°	′ ″	″	″	″	″	″	″	″	°
45	−3 0.95	0.95	0.94	0.93	0.91	0.88	0.02	−0.11	134
46	3 0.85	0.81	0.77	0.72	0.66	0.59	0.05	0.11	133
47	3 0.52	0.44	0.36	0.27	0.18	0.08	0.09	0.11	132
48	2 59.98	59.87	59.75	59.63	59.50	59.36	0.13	0.11	131
49	2 59.21	59.06	58.90	58.74	58.57	58.40	0.16	0.11	130
50	−2 58.23	58.05	57.86	57.66	57.46	57.25	0.20	−0.11	129
51	2 57.03	56.80	56.57	56.34	56.10	55.86	0.24	0.11	128
52	2 55.61	55.35	55.09	54.82	54.54	54.26	0.27	0.11	127
53	2 53.98	53.69	53.39	53.09	52.78	52.46	0.31	0.11	126
54	2 52.14	51.81	51.48	51.14	50.80	50.45	0.34	0.11	125
55	−2 50.09	49.73	49.36	48.99	48.61	48.22	0.38	−0.10	124
56	2 47.83	47.43	47.03	46.62	46.21	45.79	0.41	0.10	123
57	2 45.37	44.94	44.51	44.07	43.62	43.16	0.44	0.10	122
58	2 42.70	42.23	41.76	41.28	40.80	40.32	0.48	0.10	121
59	2 39.84	39.35	38.85	38.35	37.84	37.32	0.51	0.10	120
60	−2 36.78	36.25	35.72	35.18	34.64	34.09	0.54	−0.10	119
61	2 33.53	32.97	32.41	31.84	31.27	30.69	0.57	0.09	118
62	2 30.09	29.50	28.91	28.31	27.71	27.10	0.60	0.09	117
63	2 26.47	25.85	25.22	24.59	23.95	23.31	0.63	0.09	116
64	2 22.67	22.02	21.37	20.71	20.05	19.38	0.66	0.09	115
65	−2 18.69	18.01	17.33	16.64	15.95	15.25	0.69	−0.08	114
66	2 14.55	13.84	13.13	12.41	11.69	10.97	0.72	0.08	113
67	2 10.24	9.51	8.77	8.03	7.29	6.54	0.74	0.08	112
68	2 5.78	5.02	4.26	3.49	2.72	1.94	0.77	0.07	111
69	1 61.16	60.38	59.59	58.80	58.01	57.21	0.79	0.07	110
70	−1 56.39	55.58	54.77	53.95	53.13	52.30	0.82	−0.07	109
71	1 51.48	50.65	49.82	48.98	48.14	47.29	0.84	0.07	108
72	1 46.44	45.59	44.74	43.88	43.01	42.14	0.86	0.07	107
73	1 41.26	40.39	39.51	38.63	37.74	36.85	0.88	0.06	106
74	1 35.96	35.07	34.17	33.27	32.36	31.45	0.90	0.06	105
75	−1 30.54	29.63	28.71	27.79	26.87	25.95	0.92	−0.06	104
76	1 25.02	24.09	23.16	22.22	21.28	20.34	0.94	0.05	103
77	1 19.39	18.44	17.49	16.54	15.58	14.62	0.96	0.05	102
78	1 13.66	12.70	11.73	10.76	9.79	8.82	0.97	0.05	101
79	1 7.84	6.86	5.88	4.90	3.92	2.93	0.98	0.04	100
80	−0 61.94	60.95	59.96	58.96	57.96	56.96	1.00	−0.04	99
81	0 55.96	54.96	53.95	52.94	51.94	50.93	1.01	0.03	98
82	0 49.92	48.91	47.90	46.88	45.86	44.84	1.02	0.03	97
83	0 43.81	42.79	41.76	40.74	40.71	39.68	1.03	0.03	96
84	0 37.65	36.62	35.58	34.55	33.52	32.48	1.03	0.02	95
85	−0 31.45	30.42	29.38	28.34	27.30	26.26	1.04	−0.02	94
86	0 25.21	24.17	23.13	22.08	21.03	19.98	1.05	0.02	93
87	0 18.93	17.88	16.83	15.78	14.73	13.68	1.05	0.01	92
88	0 12.63	11.58	10.53	9.48	8.42	7.37	1.05	−0.01	91
89	−0 6.32	5.27	4.21	3.16	2.11	1.05	1.05	0.00	90
	60′	50′	40′	30′	20′	10′			Arg.

Note.—When the degrees of the Argument are read from the right hand side of the Table, the tens of minutes must be read from the bottom; and the Reduction and its Secular Variation are affected with the sign + instead of −.

www.ingramcontent.com/pod-product-compliance
Lightning Source LLC
Chambersburg PA
CBHW032013010726
47493CB00007B/2384
* 9 7 8 3 3 3 7 3 3 2 4 2 6 *